CW01597704

202363186

THE NEIGHBOUR'S SECRET

Also by Sharon Bolton

Sacrifice
Awakening
Blood Harvest
Little Black Lies
Daisy in Chains
Dead Woman Walking
The Split
The Night Train
The Pact
The Fake Wife

The Craftsmen series
The Craftsman
The Buried

The Lacey Flint series
Now You See Me
If Snow Hadn't Fallen
Dead Scared
Like This, For Ever
A Dark and Twisted Tide
Here Be Dragons
The Dark

THE NEIGHBOUR'S SECRET

SHARON BOLTON

ORION

First published in Great Britain in 2024 by Orion Fiction
an imprint of The Orion Publishing Group Ltd
Carmelite House, 50 Victoria Embankment
London EC4Y 0DZ

An Hachette UK Company

1 3 5 7 9 10 8 6 4 2

Copyright © Sharon Bolton 2024

The moral right of Sharon Bolton to be identified as the author of this work has been asserted in accordance with the Copyright, Designs and Patents Act of 1988.

All rights reserved. No part of this publication may be reproduced, stored in a retrieval system, or transmitted in any form or by any means, electronic, mechanical, photocopying, recording, or otherwise, without the prior permission of both the copyright owner and the above publisher of this book.

All the characters in this book are fictitious, and any resemblance to actual persons, living or dead, is purely coincidental.

A CIP catalogue record for this book is available from the British Library.

ISBN (Hardback) 978 1 3987 0986 7
ISBN (Trade Paperback) 978 1 3987 0987 4
ISBN (eBook) 978 1 3987 0989 8
ISBN (Audio) 978 1 3987 0990 4

Typeset by Input Data Services Ltd, Bridgwater, Somerset

Printed in Great Britain by Clays Ltd, Elcograf, S.p.A.

MIX
Paper from responsible sources
FSC® C104740
FSC www.fsc.org

www.orionbooks.co.uk

For Lupe, best dog in the world.

1

Had Anna Brown been a more convincing liar, I might have lost interest in her immediately. But lies are so intriguing, aren't they? Why people tell them, how little they think through the consequences, how desperate they become when in danger of being found out. To my mind, lies are second only to secrets, and those I find deeply exciting. A short while after learning that Anna Brown was a liar, I discovered she was hiding a secret. After that, there was no way I was going to leave her alone.

You might say secrets are my thing.

I first came across her in mid-October, on a day that was crisp and bright, with a downy layer of mist over much of the ground as the sun came up. The trees were still full, and not all of the leaves had turned, but they'd become brittle and when the wind blew, they made the sound that always reminds me of a damp fire crackling.

I'd arrived home the night before in the dark, and was keen to see how the garden had coped during my ten-day absence. What should have been a minor operation had turned complicated with an ensuing infection and I came home from hospital weaker than I'd gone in. I'd still woken early though; I like to think of myself as being the first person in the village to rise. It feels a little like stealing a march on the enemy.

Most of the late roses had faded. I deadheaded where I could reach and rewound a loose strand of honeysuckle. I pulled up the odd weed and was grinding my foot on a snail when I heard voices in the lane outside.

'I must have missed the rain.'

It was Gardner, my next-door neighbour. He is a big, loud-voiced man in his early forties with an estranged wife and a couple of ill-mannered sons with whom he is fortunate not to live. They visit occasionally – the children, not the wife – and the noise becomes unbearable. I have seven confiscated footballs that have landed on my side of the fence. I deny all knowledge of them, of course; Gardner would insist on having them returned, in spite of the damage they've done to my plants.

Gardner is the sort of man who doesn't read a book from one year to the next but has an opinion on everything. I've never seen him take a walk, but he rises early for the gym most mornings. He receives regular deliveries of protein formula, a substance I associate with sickly children and the elderly rather than a man in his prime. I know this because I often take delivery of his parcels when he is out at work.

So, it was definitely Gardner in the lane outside. Needless to say, I had no idea what he was talking about; it hadn't rained in days. A quick glance at the ground could have told him that.

'Excuse me?' The woman replying was as mystified as I, albeit politer than I might have been.

'Your hair's wet. Has it been raining?'

'I swim.'

I've witnessed Gardner's interactions with women many times and they never seem to improve. I was on the verge of returning indoors when the woman spoke again.

'The lake,' she said. 'Top of the lane and through the woods.'

Gardner had obviously asked her where she swam; a smarter man would have worked it out for himself. There is a lane that runs from the back of our small terrace of houses for a quarter mile, ending at a stile. From there a fifteen-minute walk along a public footpath leads to the lake. I say lake, but compared to the splendours of Bassenthwaite, Derwent Water and Thirlmere, our nearest sizeable bodies of water, it's little more than a large pond. I'd never known anyone swim in it before, but each to their own.

'Is that safe?' Gardner was asking.

'Safe in what way?'

I was warming to the woman. She wasn't simpering the way so many women did when talking to Gardner. Her voice was factual, challenging.

'Well, you know. It's deep.'

'You can drown in two feet of water. Depth is irrelevant.'

'It's not exactly clean.'

'It's a lake. It won't be chlorinated.'

I found myself smiling.

'I bet it's cold.'

'Well, there I can't argue. Excuse me, I must—'

'I'm Hugh. Hugh Gardner.'

A short pause. Then, 'Anna Brown,' she said, and that's when I changed my mind and walked right up to the back gate. Some time ago I'd replaced the gravel with flagged stones and so made no sound as I approached to within a couple of feet of where the couple was standing. There is a crack in the wooden panelling and through it I had a rear view of Gardner. He was wearing jeans and a dark jacket, the clothes he always wears to work. He changes into his uniform when he gets there.

I couldn't see the woman but something about the way she'd given her name had intrigued me. She'd called it out like a declaration, a challenge, almost as though she wasn't expecting to be believed. Her accent too was a surprise, although obviously I'd noticed this at the start. She was from the south, home counties at a guess.

'The new baker?' Gardner isn't a man to take a hint. 'I've been meaning to pop in but I've been on nights. Settling in alright? We're neighbours, by the way. Next door but one. I'm on the other side of—'

'Nice to meet you, Mr Gardner. Have a good day.'

I caught a glimpse of a slight figure with damp dark hair moving quickly out of sight. Gardner watched her go, only getting into his vehicle, a ridiculously over-powered American-style truck, when she'd turned the corner. He drove off and I went back indoors.

I had no idea how I'd missed all the signs of occupancy in the house to my left. It had been late when I'd got home and I'd been tired after hours of waiting for prescriptions to be ready and doctors to sign release papers. Even so. Our small terrace of three cottages was once one much bigger house and the dividing walls are plasterboard. Gardner could knock them down with one swing of his fireman's axe were he so minded. The result is that I can hear almost everything that goes on in both houses. I know what TV programmes Gardner watches, the video games he plays and the music he listens to. I know that he breaks wind several times before he gets out of bed in the morning and that he sings in the shower but never out of it. During sexual intercourse he can maintain an erection for between fifteen and twenty-seven minutes, and while he claims to his mates to be a Labour supporter, he isn't.

The house on my other side, though, the bakery, had been empty for a year. I'd grown used to the silence, had noticed nothing unusual last night, but now, knowing it was occupied again, it seemed bursting with sound. I heard clattering in the kitchen and an oven being turned on. A tap ran. She dropped something and muttered 'damn it'. She was working in a hurry. Then light footsteps ran upstairs and the shower sounded. Knowing she was out of the way I went out of the front door and, in the early morning light, took in the transformation next door.

The dull brown panelling, the fake mullioned windows, the dusty plastic loaves and cakes and the red gingham cloths had vanished and in their place was a huge but simple dove-grey fascia reading 'The Bread Basket'. The new glass in the window was festooned with white bunting and an almost invisible plastic shelving system stood ready for the day's produce. I squeezed past a cast-iron table and chairs and through the window saw oak shelves and drawers stretching to the ceiling, Perspex display counters, more tables and chairs, dressers, a flagged stone floor. There was a coffee machine, stacks of bottle-green crockery and gleaming silverware.

What I could see, though, was nothing compared to what I could smell. An absolute symphony of scents. The base notes were yeasty from the loaves still proving, but swaying above them, like instruments rising and falling as the music unfolded, were the richness of warm pain aux raisins, a bittersweet whiff of melting chocolate and the caraway seed scent of rye bread. There was sugar in the air too, fine as talcum powder, floating like the hint of a snowstorm and making my nostrils itch.

So many different scents, making me feel warm and cosy, as though I were a child again, but living in the sort of Enid Blyton-infused world I read about, rather than the Mother's Pride reality. At the same time, an inexplicable sadness was washing over me, as though the smell of The Bread Basket was there to torment, hint at pleasures that could never be mine.

'Good morning.'

I started. She'd taken me by surprise. I, who pride myself on knowing when my neighbours use the lavatory in the night, simply hadn't heard Anna Brown open the front door to the bakery and join me on the pavement. I realised I'd closed my eyes.

'Not open yet, I'm afraid,' she went on. 'Not till seven thirty.'

'No matter.' I couldn't meet her eyes. I felt almost as though she'd caught me helping myself to the croissants she'd placed in the window. She'd arranged them perfectly on the rectangular plate and they lay with military precision, golden as the sunrise, curling in on themselves like peeled prawns.

'I'm Anna,' she said. 'I expect you're my next-door neighbour.'

I dragged my eyes away from the croissants and looked at her carefully. Her hands were covered in flour, so she didn't hold one out to me and I certainly didn't offer one either. I don't like touching people's hands even when they seem clean. Her apron was dirty too, smeared in flour and grease and what looked like apricot jam. Her eyes were a tiny bit bloodshot and I wondered if it was caused by immersion in lake water.

This time, I admit, I wouldn't have caught the lie. This time, she'd prepared herself. Her voice was low and steady, and she had no problem making eye contact. I'd have put her age at late thirties. Her shoulder-length hair was the darkest that brown can be before it becomes black. Her skin was clear but starting to line around her eyes and along her brow. She was less attractive than I was expecting, given Gardner's simpering; in fact, I thought her rather plain, her eyes a little too small and dark, her face rather long. But then I remembered the stream of female visitors I've had to suffer over the years and that Gardner is easily pleased.

I introduced myself and made some comment about the changes she'd made to the bakery. It was politely enough meant, but she seemed a little put out.

'People seem to like the pavement tables,' she said.

'We'll see how popular they are next month,' I said. 'When the winds get up.'

I was trying to be helpful; being from the south, she wouldn't know quite how vicious our Cumbrian winters can be. There are days in January when snow seems to pour down from nearby Tamland Fell like an avalanche, smothering the village in hours, keeping all but the hardiest indoors. November gales could knock the frail from their feet. The idea of creating a café society here was almost funny.

'There are some tables inside as well,' she said. 'And in the courtyard at the back. It's more sheltered there.'

Courtyard? I didn't mean to scoff, but really? She had a backyard, all three of us did. I'd transformed mine, through hard work and a not inconsiderable investment, into a modest but thriving garden. Last time I'd looked into the bakery's backyard, it had been a mess of bins and rubbish left over by the last occupant. I remembered then that I hadn't looked out of the rear window that morning. The hospital stay had affected me more than I'd realised.

'I open at half seven,' she was saying, although she'd told me that already. 'Come and have breakfast. On me.'

'I'm diabetic,' I told her, and after wishing her a good morning – I'm never rude – I went inside.

I couldn't settle though. The milk I'd bought on my way home last night seemed to cling to my tongue and the Weetabix lay heavy in my stomach, as though I'd forced it down dry. It could have been my imagination – I'd closed all the windows – but the baking smells were stealing into my house. The *Today* programme – I listen through headphones out of consideration to my neighbours – was dull and uninteresting. I don't really care whether police in inner cities carry Tasers, and the rising and falling of the pound doesn't affect me.

I was still sure that Anna Brown was hiding something. She'd collected herself by the time she spoke to me, but Gardner had caught her unawares. I wanted to do the same. So, as the seven thirty news came on I switched off the radio and found my jacket. Naturally, I locked my front door. There is a lot of nonsense talked about rural communities being safe but while it's hard to imagine a community more rural, I've seen nothing particularly trustworthy in the people I live among.

Strangers and visitors see the pretty houses, the grandeur of the surrounding hills and assume they've wandered into some sort of bucolic idyll, one with a powerful sense of community in which everyone looks out for each other. They couldn't be more wrong.

I've wondered, sometimes, if it's the combination of isolation, inclement weather and relative poverty that engenders a meanness of spirit among the local population. Petty crime seems to go hand in hand with high levels of unemployment and when everyday life is a struggle, it's hard to show much interest in the well-being of one's neighbours.

Or maybe they just don't like me.

The bakery door still displayed its 'closed' sign. Ms Brown must have seen me through the glass of the front door though because she opened it after only a couple of seconds. She'd changed her apron and washed her hands.

'Hello again,' she said. 'Welcome. Come in.'

I followed her inside, braced against the smell, telling myself it was only chemistry. I would not be so easily seduced a second time.

'I don't recall your name,' I said. I remembered her name perfectly, of course, but I wanted to hear her say it again.

'Anna Brown,' she muttered, and I felt a warm glow of triumph. Her eyes had dropped, her cheeks reddened. She didn't like having to repeat her falsehood but falsehood it was. Anna Brown was not her real name.

'Where are you from, Anna?' I used her Christian name deliberately, to make clear our differing social status. Earlier, I'd only told her my family name, implying that she should address me formally.

'South.' She retreated behind the counter where I noticed loaves were already lined up neatly, each labelled with a little black card with gold lettering: Sourdough, Wholemeal, Farmhouse, Spinach & Cheese Ciabatta, Sweet Potato & Beetroot Focaccia. I'd never heard of most of the bread I could see in front of me.

'Have a seat,' she said. 'It's a bit chilly in the courtyard still. The sun doesn't reach it till mid-morning.'

There were two tables tucked away in a corner of the shop. I had to hand it to her – she'd managed the space very well.

'Where in the south?' I pulled out a chair – wood, painted turquoise, with a padded cushion on the seat – and sat.

Her head twitched to the right. 'Excuse me,' she said. 'Oven timer. With you in a sec.' She vanished.

I'd heard no timer and I have ears like a bat. I made a mental note to check her left hand when she returned. The indentation of a recently removed wedding ring might suggest she was fleeing from a relationship gone wrong.

She returned a few seconds later, bringing nothing with her.

'Did you leave a similar business behind?' I paused for effect. 'In the south?'

'No.' She faked industry by rearranging an already perfectly stacked row of loaves. 'This is a new venture.'

'What brought you to St Abel's Chapel?'

She looked up, a fraction too quickly. 'A vacant shop. Now, what can I get you? Tea, coffee, hot chocolate? Maybe not chocolate, if you're diabetic. How about coffee and a buttered teacake? There's a sprinkling of sugar on those, that's all, and a tablespoon of raisins. That should be OK, shouldn't it?'

'I've had breakfast. Just tea, please. Indian. Loose. And I like to add my own milk.'

Her smile froze for a split second. 'Coming up.'

She turned her back on me as she worked, giving me time to take in the Welsh dresser with its row of homemade jams, chutneys and pickles, and its huge plates of scones: one sweet, one savoury. There was a chilled cabinet selling smoked salmon, cured ham and clotted cream. Directly in front of me on the counter, almost like a challenge, was a plate of pork pies, their crenelated crusts gleaming with animal fat.

I was beginning to feel uncomfortable again. Something about the sheer bounty of the shop seemed to be making me feel smaller. It was as though the loaves of sourdough, the croissants, the pork pies and the teacakes were in league with their baker against me. Everything about the bakery yelled professionalism, competence, and yet there was a flaw here. An illusion. All was not as it seemed.

'You must buy a lot of stock in,' I said. 'You can't produce all of this yourself.' I nearly added, 'Especially when you've been swimming,' but stopped myself. Gardner had accused me of spying on him more than once. It was only a matter of time before he bad-mouthed me to our new neighbour and I'd be an idiot to play into his hands.

'I get up at four,' she replied, without turning around. 'I leave everything ready to start proving or baking the night before. And some things, the pies and the heavier cakes, will last a few days.'

I'd already seen a large decorated cake on the counter, protected by a huge Perspex dome. It was a garish affair, covered in black icing, featuring orange pumpkins and cartoon ghosts. 'Happy Halloween' read the legend around the base, and a small handwritten note to one side informed customers that Halloween orders were being taken.

'Is it me, or does the village seem busy today?' she said, as she poured boiling water. 'I must have counted twenty vehicles going through already.'

I checked the date on my wristwatch. 'Sounds about right,' I replied. 'By midday you'll struggle to cross the high street.'

She turned around then, her dark eyebrows almost meeting. 'Where are they going? There's nothing up that road. Well, not that I know of.'

'But then you haven't lived here long.'

She said nothing else, but her mouth had tightened when she approached again, this time carrying a tray that seemed ridiculously overladen given that I was only expecting tea. She put it down, a little more firmly that she needed to, but then curiosity got the better of her.

'Is there a hotel up there? A conference centre? A lot of the traffic seemed to be delivery vans.'

She removed a teapot, teacup and saucer, spoon, milk jug, sugar basin and a small side plate. I looked up sharply, saw the challenge in her eyes.

'It's a sausage roll.' She gave me a tight-lipped smile. 'My own recipe. Just a taste.'

It was small and perfectly formed, golden as a honeycomb, pastry flakes looking ready to fly away like thistledown at any moment. The sausage gleamed at me from both ends, pink and slightly obscene. I felt my stomach turn over.

'Don't mind my curiosity,' she said. 'I'm a businesswoman. If there's a big hotel up there, it could be very good for me.'

'It's a church,' I told her. 'Perhaps they'll need communion bread.'

I was teasing. I knew she'd be overrun with church-related orders before the day was out. The people who would arrive in the village over the next couple of weeks weren't known for self-denial. Practically on cue, the doorbell sounded, and Anna didn't manage to hide her look of relief. I took advantage of her back being turned to bite into the sausage roll, taking around half of it into my mouth. The pastry burst apart on my tongue. The sausage was warm, peppery, with a hint of something I couldn't quite place, herbal, but with a heat in it. It was gone before I knew it and I found myself trembling. The slick, salty grease of sausage still coated the inside of my mouth and I drank down scalding tea to get rid of it.

The newcomers were church people. They are easy to distinguish from the random tourists who wander through the village from time to time. The church people dress for an outing, for one thing.

Their annual gathering is a big deal for them. Tourists are usually in hiking or cycling clothes.

These three, all women, were no exception. Two were in very smart clothes, given how early in the day it was. High heels, sheer tights, fitted jackets and understated make-up. Perfect hair. They were the sort of women who followed Coco Chanel's fashion trick of putting on their jewellery and then taking one piece off. The younger of the three wore oversized jeans and a college sweatshirt. She had her hands thrust deep into her jeans pockets.

'Oh my,' the oldest said. 'Isn't this heaven?'

'Very nice,' replied the next in line, age wise. The youngest, I'd noticed, was little more than a child. 'A big improvement. Oh, look, Mum. Gluten-free. What a relief. Good morning, you must be Anna.'

'Oh, that smell,' the older one said before Anna could speak.

'I love what you've done to the place,' said the younger, although she'd said much the same thing already.

They carried on like this for a while, ignoring me, so I got up and put the plate with the half-eaten sausage roll on the counter. I didn't trust myself not to finish it if it remained on the table. Momentarily distracted from the group fawning over her interior decor, Anna raised her eyebrows.

'Too rich,' I said.

Her face twitched, then she turned her back on me.

'We hear you're the woman for us,' the younger one said. 'We need a cake.'

'I'm the woman for you,' Anna agreed, and I could see in a mirror on the wall opposite the counter that she was smiling, a much wider, brighter smile than any she'd bestowed on me. It quite transformed her face. 'What sort of cake?' she added.

'A cake among other things,' the older one interrupted. 'But we'll start with the cake. Only, it must be a really beautiful cake.'

This was getting tiresome. I was Anna's first customer of the day and her next-door neighbour to boot, and yet she was practically ignoring me. The newcomers hadn't so much as registered my existence. I might not have been in the shop at all.

'Wedding? Christening?' Anna said.

The child was pushed forward. She seemed incapable of looking at anything but the floor and I'd yet to properly see her face. Also, she appeared to be shaking, as though holding back some powerful emotion.

'A birthday cake, for darling Constance. My goodness, I have no idea where the time goes.'

I'd decided they were three generations of the same family. Daughter, mother, grandmother. Now that I'd reached that conclusion, I could see the family resemblance. All were of a similar height and build, although the girl was slightly taller and quite a bit thinner than the others. All were fair-haired and fair-skinned, the older two with slightly hooked noses, wide mouths and a lot of very white teeth.

I knew, before she opened her mouth, that the girl would be wearing braces. It was the sort of family that set great store by perfect teeth.

'Sixteenth birthday,' the mother clarified. 'We need it in nine days. Does that give you enough time?'

'Of course,' Anna replied. 'Let's look at designs, shall we? Unless you have something specific in mind. Constance, is it? Very nice to meet you.'

I was getting up. I was going to make some remark about the tea being cold, although it wasn't. It was actually very good tea. And then something stopped me in my tracks. The girl, Constance, soon to be sixteen years old, had looked up at last.

She was, quite literally, petrified, frozen on the spot. Her eyes were fixed and unblinking. And blood was dripping onto the floor, on either side of her feet.

The cuffs of the girl's sweatshirt were wet – it was a deep maroon, almost black in colour, or I'd have noticed earlier – and there were damp patches on her jeans, to either side of her hips.

This young girl had slit her wrists and might be about to bleed out in the new bakery.

I settled myself back down and poured another cup.

2

April, the previous year

So, was he mad? Or bad?

Possibly the most frequently asked question of mental health professionals. It was, at the same time, impossible to answer with any degree of integrity. The reasons behind disorders of the mind were as many and varied as their manifestations. Sadly, nuance did not sit well within the criminal justice system.

'We have eight appointments,' she told the boy, after she'd introduced herself. 'Two a week over the next month.'

'I understand.' His polite smile stretched a little wider. 'I'm sorry to be causing so much trouble.'

Jago Moore, seventeen years old, white and very bright, had gone nuts (the headteacher's words) in the cafeteria of his expensive private school six days earlier. He'd broken crockery, hurled chairs at windows, screamed obscenities and run the length of the long communal dining tables, kicking plates, cutlery and food into the laps of the astonished (and, let's be honest, probably a bit gleeful) pupils. As a grand finale, he'd stabbed a physics teacher in the abdomen with a dinner knife and at that point, any glee on the part of the boys had turned to terror and they'd stampeded from the hall like wildebeest at the sight of a scaly tail.

Had the knife been a little longer, a little sharper, the young female teacher might not have lived to hear the end-of-lunch bell. As it was, she'd suffered extensive bruising and a bit of non-serious internal bleeding. She was expected back at school in the foreseeable future. Whether the same could be said of her attacker remained to be seen.

'Could we open the blinds, do you think?' he asked, his eyes narrowing as he looked at the shielded window. His smile, though, didn't falter.

The two of them were sitting at one end of a long, thin room, where she'd placed a sofa for her clients and an armchair for herself. A low coffee table held unthreatening magazines. She'd come across the term *unthreatening magazines* in a manual of best practice and was still trying to figure out what a threatening magazine might be. *Guns and Ammo*? *Black Belt Monthly*?

'I feel claustrophobic with them closed.' Still that unwavering smile.

'The blinds are for your privacy,' she told him. 'There's a street outside and a bus stop. Passers-by might be able to see in.'

'I don't mind. I'd prefer them open.' He looked to be on the verge of getting to his feet. 'I'm going to open them.'

'I'll do it.' She held up a hand to stop him, conscious that already he was setting the terms of their engagement and she was letting him. 'But if it gets too bright, we may have to reconsider.'

'It won't. This room faces west. The sun won't be directly outside until afternoon.'

She pulled up the blind. He was right about the direction, although she hadn't thought about it before. She was right, too, about the bus stop. Three people were less than five metres away and with the office lights on, they'd be able to see inside.

When she turned back, there was a gleam of satisfaction in the boy's eyes.

'I'm sorry to be causing so much trouble,' he said. 'I know how busy you must be. The police too. I'd like that on record, please. That I apologised.'

Still the smile held steady, although the muscles in his jaw must be aching by now. She realised, then, the massive effort he was making to appear normal.

Jago Moore should have been a good-looking boy: tall and slim, with the widening of shoulders and broadening of thighs that happened to boys in late adolescence. His hair was dark brown, on the long side, sweeping down over his forehead to half hide eyes that were a startling pale blue. His face was long and thin, his mouth wide and revealing teeth that were the result of great genes or thousands spent at the orthodontist. He was the sort of boy that hormonal teenagers dreamed about.

She had no idea why his proximity was making her stomach clench. It could only be the disparity between the remarkable self-control she was seeing now, and her expectations following what she'd read about the cafeteria incident.

Witnesses, including the first attending police officers, had reported Jago going into a near-catatonic state following his attack. He'd curled into a foetal position on the floor, jerking and twitching, refusing to respond to questions but repeating, in a manner described as 'dead creepy', most of what was said to him. He'd remained that way for the following four hours.

The next day he'd been suspended from school pending a psychiatric assessment. The police, too, were waiting to hear from her before deciding whether or not to press charges. With only three months to go before A levels, it wasn't a good time for a bright boy to be denied school attendance.

She said, 'I'll be asking lots of questions, Jago, about your life as a whole, not just the incident last week, and I'll be talking to your family too. I want to get to know you well. I'll be taking notes and the report I prepare will enable the police and your school to determine how to proceed.'

Other than his one attempt to get up to open the blind, Jago had been sitting very still. He didn't fidget or let his gaze wander in the way of most of her young clients; he didn't pick at his nails or swing his legs. He seemed entirely at ease and he'd taken the time to dress well, in navy chinos and a cream shirt. His brogues were expensive and polished, and his hair had been washed that morning. He smelled clean. He looked every inch the model seventeen-year-old, apart from that unnatural stillness.

He asked, 'Will I get to see the report?'

Jago's parents were wealthy, professional people, fiercely protective of their son. His father, in particular, had made no secret of being anxious for a mental health diagnosis together with a medicated cure that would enable Jago quickly to resume his A level studies and get his life back on track. The chief investigating officer, on the other hand, a detective sergeant within a year of retirement, had had other thoughts. 'He's a wrong 'un,' he'd confided. 'I wouldn't want him near my kids.'

'I'm afraid not,' she told Jago. 'The report is being commissioned by the police and social services and it will be confidential. They might choose to share it with you at some point but that's up to them. I wouldn't expect it, to be honest.'

Best to set clear parameters at the start. She recognised, though, and didn't like, the tiny feeling of satisfaction she felt at saying no to him.

His brows contracted in a sudden frown. 'But it's my report. It's about me.'

'Let's make a start.' She opened her notepad. 'Tell me about last Tuesday morning. Start from the beginning. When you woke up.'

In response, he flexed the fingers of both hands, a little in the way of a pianist about to play something intense and difficult, before beginning to crack each of his knuckle joints, one at a time, maintaining unblinking eye contact. She tried hard not to wince, although she hated the sound, and idea, of joints being cracked.

The police, in her experience, were often quick to judge but for once, her gut was entirely onside with the detective sergeant. Jago Moore made her flesh crawl.

3

There is no mistaking fear, is there? Constance looked up. I saw her lips part as she prepared to speak – I was right about the braces – and then her face froze. Her mouth was fixed in a tight grimace, and veins leapt out on her temples. I braced myself for the scream, but she held herself together. Barely.

Fascinating.

I waited for one of the others to react, and realised I'd been the only witness to the girl's silent outburst. Anna had turned away to the dresser and was reaching for a white plastic folder. The two older women were watching her. None of them were looking at Constance, and I think she had yet to properly notice me. She thought she was unobserved and had allowed her mask to slip.

Did she know, though, that she was bleeding on the bakery floor? On the floor tiles beside her right foot I could count four spots of blood; a few more on the left side. I really couldn't decide where to fix my attention: on the girl's face, or the gathering specks of scarlet at her feet. As she shrugged her shoulders, I caught a glimpse of a bloodstained bandage, crudely wrapped around her right wrist.

'First decision is fruit cake or sponge,' Anna was saying as she opened the book and the other two moved in closer. 'Fruit is more expensive, but it will last well beyond the birthday week.'

'Sponge,' the mother said. 'We won't need it to keep.'

A startled gasp slipped out of Constance's mouth and she leapt for the door. Wrenching it open, leaving a blood smear behind, she set off running down the street.

For a second, and then another, nobody in the shop spoke and then as the mother moved towards the door, the grandmother's hand shot out like a chameleon's tongue.

'I'll go.' Her knuckles were white on her daughter's shoulder and her voice pitched low in warning. 'You sort out the cake.'

Well, good luck to a high-heeled granny trying to catch a sixteen-year-old wearing trainers.

'Is she hurt?' Finally, someone – Anna – had spotted the blood on the door handle.

The two women exchanged glances. 'Maybe I should,' the mother began.

'Nonsense,' the grandmother replied as she reached for the door, taking care to avoid the blood print. 'She'll have cut a finger making breakfast – I told you that breadknife is too sharp – and didn't bother putting a plaster on it. You know what she's like.'

The bell rang again, and I realised I'd be hearing it throughout the day. As though to labour the point, the grandmother stopped on the doorstep leaving the bell ringing. She looked at me, then at Anna and gave a little shrug of her bony shoulders.

'Teenagers,' she said.

The door closed, the bell fell silent and I watched the older woman totter down the street.

'Would you like to come back later?' Anna asked the mother. 'I'm open till four.'

'No.' The mother gave a long, heavy sigh. 'Let's get it over with. If she can't be bothered to show an interest, she'll have to be happy with what I choose.'

Anna glanced over at me, almost as though I were a friend from whom she could elicit sympathy. I stared back and she looked away.

For the next few minutes the conversation became too boring to recall and I half tuned out. I was watching the street, waiting for Constance or her grandmother to reappear, and only half listening to talk of chocolate, vanilla or elderflower flavouring, traditional design with sugar paste flowers or something more tailored to Constance herself. They came to a decision – I had no interest in the details – and money was handed over.

Throughout, Anna still seemed uncomfortable about finalising arrangements with no input from Constance herself, and more than once repeated her offer of discussing it later, but by the time they'd finished, the shop was filling up and she was anxious to move on to other customers. Not to mention get the blood cleaned up. Blood spatter is hardly what one likes to see in an eating establishment.

I got up and left. I didn't offer to pay. Anna, or whatever her name was, had offered me breakfast on the house and I hadn't asked for the sausage roll. I took out my handkerchief to shield me from any possibility of touching Constance's blood. I would have to throw it away immediately but the alternative – being soiled by another's bodily fluid – was unthinkable.

I turned on the threshold to say goodbye to Anna but she had her back to me and didn't look round. Rude, I thought.

There was no sign of the runaway teenager or granny-in-hot-pursuit on the street, but as I unlocked my own front door, I reflected that the morning had already turned out to be far more interesting than I could have expected.

There were more vehicles arriving as I walked to the post office a short while later. The early delivery vans had been superseded by camper vans and caravans and the place was busy with the annual visitors stocking up on food. It would be easier, of course, for them to call in to one of the giant superstores on the way, but they're all encouraged to shop locally. It's one of the reasons why the annual event is tolerated. There are others, of course.

St Abel's Chapel, the village I'd made my home in recent years, is little more than a long, narrow, rather sombre high street, constructed of slate stone and granite. Lake District planning regulations insist upon a traditional and rather dull uniformity in all the buildings. Houses and shops are tall and thin, their windows designed more to keep out cold than let in light. There are no front gardens, but tenacious ivy and Virginia creeper grow abundantly. When the sun doesn't shine – most of the time in the north-west – it becomes a place of shadows and angular corners.

Dominating the high street, a little like a malevolent power guarding its domain, is Tamland Fell, one of the taller mountains in this stretch of the national park. It lies directly west of the village, stealing light from all but the longest of midsummer evenings.

I had to queue at the post office counter and by the time I'd had my parcels weighed, fixed the required value of stamps on each and posted them through the external postbox (I never give them to the counter attendant), the newspaper section had sold out of copies of the *Telegraph*. No matter. *The Times* would do almost as well. I paid for it, and my usual *Daily Mirror*, collected the parcels that had arrived for me (three of them) and left the shop, almost bumping into Anna Brown on the pavement. She apologised.

I didn't, I'd done nothing wrong. Neither had she, in fairness, we'd simply both been in the same place at the same time. Apologies mean more, I think, if they're not scattered around like confetti.

We set off back, with little choice but to walk together. Normally, I'd find this annoying but I was still intrigued by the so-called Anna Brown.

'I've been at the butcher's,' she told me, although I hadn't asked. 'I've been doing sandwiches at midday. Just cheese, ham and chicken, but they go down well. I've been thinking of trying soup next week. What do you think?'

I pretended to consider it for a few seconds.

'Most people can open a can of Campbell's Tomato,' I replied. 'I wouldn't waste your time.'

She sniffed and fell silent. We stopped to cross the road and had to wait for several seconds.

'Is it some sort of Oktoberfest?' she asked, as a large green van bearing the legend *Pandora Productions* trundled past. 'A lot of the vehicles I saw first thing seemed to be in show business. And there are people in town who look like rock musicians.'

'I think you'll find Oktoberfest takes place in Munich,' I replied. 'And is over with by the first Sunday of October.'

'Similar events have sprung up all over the world,' she snapped back. 'I thought this might be one of them.'

'It's not.'

'Someone in the butcher's just now mentioned the Ingathering. It's called the Ingathering.'

'Yes,' I said.

'Does that sound a bit creepy to you?'

'I never thought of it that way.'

'So, what is it?' We'd reached the other side of the road and she actually stopped walking and blocked my path. 'You're the fifth person I've asked this morning, and no one has given me a straight answer.'

'The locals tell you they know very little about it, that it's a private event, attended by no permanent resident of the village, that it does no harm and brings in a lot of annual business,' I said. 'If you persist in your questions, you'll be told that you'll take more in the next couple of weeks than for the rest of the year, and you'd be well advised to make the most of it and not worry too much about what does and doesn't go on.'

She said nothing but continued to stare at me.

'The visitors, on the other hand, shrug and say, *oh, it's something we do every year. Just a few friends getting together.*'

Her eyes fell.

'Am I right?' I prompted.

'Yes,' she said. 'So, what does go on?'

I smiled. 'I've never been. I know nothing about it, except that people arrive halfway through October, the village gets very busy, but by the first weekend in November, they've all gone away.'

'Something else I've noticed,' she said. 'People are leaving town. Locals, I mean. I must have seen half a dozen people loading cars up this morning alone.'

'I think you'll find it's half-term next week. A lot of the families will be away. Most head out Friday night.'

She nodded. 'I didn't think of that. Seems odd though. New people flood in and those who live here flee before the hordes.'

'You make it sound like an invasion,' I said.

It was meant as a joke, but when I looked at Anna, she didn't so much as crack a smile.

'What did you make of the family this morning?' she asked, changing tack. 'I felt quite bad, to be honest, taking all that money off them. Cakes that size don't come cheap, and she ordered a lot of other party food too.'

'Your new enterprise may not prosper if sales make you uncomfortable.'

Now that wasn't intended to be funny, but she laughed. I was starting to revise my opinion about her being plain.

'Fair point. But it was Constance I was worried about. She didn't seem to be looking forward to her party, did she? She and the grandmother never came back. And she did leave a lot of blood behind for a breadknife cut.'

I thought about telling her what I'd seen but old habits held me back. Knowledge is something to treasure, I always think.

'I hope she's OK,' Anna finished.

'Is there anything you can do about it if she's not?'

She didn't reply, but I felt her stiffen as she walked beside me. Unusually empathetic, I was thinking, and nervous, as evidenced by her rather chattery way of speaking. Uncomfortable in her new name and evasive about her past. I'd already checked for signs of a wedding ring mark on her left hand. Inconclusive, I'd decided.

At that moment a lorry stopped in the middle of the road.

'Excuse me,' the driver, a woman in her fifties with a heavy foreign accent, called. 'Can you tell me where I find Gathering Hall, please?'

'Straight on up the road,' I told her. 'First on the right after you've left the village and carry on to the end. It's a little over two miles. They'll open the gates when you get there.'

The woman nodded her thanks and drove on.

'Theatrical costumiers?' Anna said. 'And that van's got a Dutch number plate. What's going on up there?'

'Are you a curious person, Anna?' I asked as we reached the front door of the bakery.

'Isn't everyone?' she replied, a little defensively.

It was a reasonable challenge. I'm curious myself, and I was becoming very curious about Anna Brown. The difference between us was that I'd grown very practised at concealing it.

But then I had lived here longer.

4

April, the previous year

'I'm going mad, aren't I?' Jago said.

The psychiatrist forced herself to smile. 'I've never used those exact words in a report yet and I don't plan to start with yours.'

Three days after their first encounter, Jago was similarly clean and well dressed. He'd dropped the weird, rictus-like grin, for which she was grateful, but he'd cracked his neck upon sitting down, first to one side, then the other, watching her while he did so. As though he knew she hated it.

She'd opened the blinds before his arrival and was conscious of the hum of traffic outside, the murmur of voices at the bus stop.

'Have you remembered anything more about the incident in the school cafeteria?'

During their first interview, Jago had claimed to remember nothing of his attack, other than a strange, dreamlike scenario of noise, chaos and a deep, internalised rage. *It was like I was burning up*, he'd explained. *And then everything went dark.*

He shook his head. 'It's slipping away. Like dreams do. You remember them when you wake up, but they fade.'

'When the police first spoke to you, you claimed you'd heard voices.'

His face creased in puzzlement. 'Did I? It's all a blur, to be honest.'

'Specifically, voices in your head, urging you on. Do you remember that?'

His lips twitched in the manner of someone mildly amused. 'Do I remember hearing the voices, or telling the police about them?'

No one in the trouble this boy was in could afford to be glib. 'Let's start with the voices. What were they saying to you?'

He shook his head, slowly, thoughtfully. 'There was a lot of noise in the room. Boys were cheering me on. At first, anyway. Maybe that's what I meant.'

He offered the suggestion up like a challenge, as in: *prove to me that's not what happened.*

'And you say nothing like that has ever happened to you before? Have you ever witnessed anything similar? Ever seen someone lose control around you? When you were a child maybe?'

One of her tasks during her time with Jago was to carry out a prescribed risk assessment into the likelihood of him behaving violently again. The protocol she'd be following contained a list of twenty factors, including a consideration of relevant historical events. In simple terms, a patient with a history of violence, even if he'd only been on the receiving end, was more likely to repeat such behaviour. Initial enquiries of his school and parents had thrown up nothing.

Except the report of his form tutor, a dark-haired young woman who'd said she found Jago 'unnerving'. While the boy had never done anything to spark a formal complaint, she'd never liked being alone in the classroom with him.

As Jago responded to her questions, explaining that his parents had never smacked him, that he managed to avoid most playground fights, the psychiatrist made notes. A sudden movement made her look up. Jago had dropped his head so that his temples rested on his fingertips. His eyes were clenched shut.

'Jago, are you alright?'

He glanced up. 'The light's bothering me. It's giving me a headache. Can you close the blind, please?'

'On Monday, you wanted it open. You said it made you claustrophobic.'

'Today, I need it closed. And can I have some water?'

Putting down her notes, she got to her feet, closed the blind and poured water from a jug on the side table.

'You're an angel,' he said, when she handed it to him. His face was clear again and smiling. He didn't look like a boy with a headache. 'Where were we?'

Damn it, this kid was making her dance.

5

I waited until the shop had quietened before popping round again. It was almost four and there'd been a constant stream of visitors. Anna had been quite right when she'd described the pavement tables as popular. They'd been occupied most of the day, as had the matching ones in the backyard.

In fairness, the rear of her property looked a lot better than it had – I had a tolerable view from the window of my office – but I was stopping short of calling it a courtyard for the time being.

Finally, at four o'clock, I heard her pulling the bolts on the front door. I knocked while she was still in the shop. She frowned but came to the door and gave me a tired smile.

'Closed, I'm afraid,' she said, as though the notice on the door wasn't clear for all to see.

'I'm not here for baked goods,' I told her. 'I was wondering if you'd experienced any problems with your telephone today?'

She frowned. 'No, I don't—' and then paused. 'Well, not problems as such, but—'

'The phone ringing but then someone hanging up as soon as you answer?' I hinted.

Looking thoughtful, Anna walked back around the counter to where she'd been transferring plates of unsold goods onto a large tray. 'Yes,' she said. 'How did you – has it happened to you too?'

'Three times.' I followed her in. 'Number withheld so I couldn't return the call.'

She paused, a plate of scones hovering in mid-air. 'I wonder if it was Constance,' she said, almost to herself.

'Who?' I asked, although I knew perfectly well who she meant.

'The girl from this morning. The one about to be sixteen.' Anna looked up at me. 'But how would she have your number? Both of mine are on the business card I gave to her mum, but she wouldn't know yours.'

Well, that was easily explained. 'My landline number is almost identical to yours,' I said. 'The last digit is a two rather than a one. Hugh Gardner's is the same, only his ends in three. All three lines were installed simultaneously with consecutive numbers. Constance could have misdialled.'

Anna nodded her head.

'It still doesn't explain why you think it was she,' I pressed.

'I had a message on my mobile.' She reached into her apron pocket and retrieved a mobile phone. Pressing a few buttons, she held it out for me to read a text message:

Sorry about this morning. You seem really nice. I wish I had someone like you to talk to.

'And you think this was from Constance?' I asked.

'Who else? I'm not sure what to do. Do I reply or not?'

I shook my head. 'I wouldn't get involved. Good to know there isn't a fault on my line, though. Thanks for your time.'

I didn't turn around on my way out of the shop, but I could see in the glass reflection that Anna was watching me, a troubled look on her face.

Mid-October is my favourite time of year, mainly because of the way the night takes everyone by surprise. Late in the afternoon, darkness gathers around us like an ambush, leaping on what's left of the day and gobbling up light. By November, we've grown used to this, but in October we're in denial. We switch on our lights – we have to, or we wouldn't be able to move around safely – but we forget about our blinds and curtains. We cling, foolishly, to the memory of long summer evenings and never dream of how exposed we've become, for an hour or more, at the end of the day. I say 'we'; I don't include myself, of course. My curtains are firmly drawn before five o'clock, my doors locked, and I am out, wrapped up against the cold, walking the darkening streets, learning more about my neighbours than I might do in a whole year of watching them in daylight.

And so I see you, retired navy commander, picking your nose behind the pages of the *Financial Times*. I see you, old lady, polishing the frames on your family photographs daily, making sure they are visible from the street, pretending to the world that your husband didn't leave you for a younger woman, and that your children didn't stop visiting and calling years ago. I see you, the woman who runs the school PTA with such energy and efficiency, I see you slapping your toddler's plump legs when he tosses his loaded spoon to the floor. I see his shocked pain and the gleam of power in your eyes.

And I see you, teenage girl, stealing food from the fridge when your mother is out of the room, and I see the way your father looks at you when he thinks no one is watching. I doubt he will act upon his fantasy, he is a man I've always considered to be cowardly, but he harbours those thoughts all the same and they keep him awake at nights.

That evening, I was to be disappointed. The visitors were still arriving, a regular stream of cars and camper vans up the main road, but again, I thought, fewer than usual. The Chinese restaurant on the high street was not only full but doing a busy takeaway service. The Grey Mare was a pulsating bubble of noise and light; it almost seemed to burst with the combined smells of perfume, hops and sweat. Several of the patrons, all smoking, were standing on the pavement.

The influx, as usual, had made the villagers edgy. Curtains had been drawn early and I missed the rectangles of golden light spilling out onto the pavements. I should have expected this, but I was ten days behind my normal schedule. Life had moved on while I'd been in hospital.

Our village has very few streetlights, and normally around half of them are out of use through vandalism and neglect. That night, though, was clear, even though the moon was on the wane. I did a quick calculation and realised that, in nine days, the night would become very dark indeed as the moon left the sky. The climax of the Ingathering would take place on the darkest of nights.

I gave the pub a wide berth. I've never been inside but even walking past makes me uncomfortable. I was unsettled and edgy; my evening walks are supposed to soothe me, and this one was doing anything but. True, the day had proven more interesting than I'd expected – the mysterious terror and blood loss of young Constance, not to mention the delicious potential of Anna Brown – but if anything, I had a sense of events unfolding around me a little too quickly. I value control and knowledge above all things, and as I walked the dark streets that night, I felt both slipping away.

The Ingathering always unsettles the locals; not usually me, though.

My evening walk takes me to the church and back. It lies at the opposite end of the village to my own house, down a similarly quiet lane which it shares with only one other building: the vicarage. The vicar, a Welshman in his late forties who is surprisingly athletic for a man of the cloth, had just returned home from his evening run and was leaning against the wall that edges his property, stretching something – a hamstring, maybe a quad; physical anatomy isn't really my thing. He likes to think he knows me quite well and so we exchanged a few pleasantries about the weather and my health before he said goodnight. Like most people of intellect, I consider religious faith to be an absurdity, but over the years I've realised that churches are often the centre of a community. One can learn a great deal from regular church attendance.

The vicar, to take the man at the helm as an example, has been a widower these last three years, and has spent two of those conducting an affair with the married headteacher of the local primary school. On Wednesday and Friday evenings, when her husband is playing badminton in nearby Penrith, she slips down the lane wearing dark clothes and enters the vicarage, without knocking, by the back door. A few minutes later, a light goes on in one of the upstairs bedrooms; not, curiously, the one he shared with his late wife. I find that more intriguing than his transgression, although not nearly as useful.

There would be no illicit encounter the following evening, I knew, because the vicar is never in town for the Ingathering. He takes annual leave, walking a pilgrimage somewhere or other, returning only when the newcomers have gone. He insists the timing is coincidence.

As I entered the churchyard, I spotted the burning red dots floating a few feet from the ground and smelled the pungent aroma that told me a group of village lads were gathered, as they often did, smoking the substance they called weed, and drinking Carlsberg beer or cheap vodka. The next day I'd return, gather up the discarded cans and cigarette papers and dispose of them properly. I'd kept the church grounds tidy for most of my five years here and my wombling habit is well known. It takes little time but makes me appear trustworthy.

'Good evening, boys,' I called as I drew close.

A couple grunted. Three of the five kept their eyes on the ground, but I'm used to that response.

I stopped a few feet away and looked at my watch. 'Have you heard anything about the curfew, by any chance?'

'You what?' The de facto leader of the gang screwed up his face at me. He was a fifteen-year-old who was called something like Skin, although I admit that hardly seems likely.

I waved my hand in the air, dismissively. 'I've probably got it wrong, just something I heard in the village. Ignore me.' I turned to walk on.

'What's a curfew?' Skin asked.

I paused. 'Well, it means after a certain time, everyone has to be at home. No one can be out on the streets or – I don't know – in the churchyard, for example. As I say, I've probably misunderstood. And it would only be while the Ingathering's taking place, anyway. Have a nice evening, boys.'

Again, I turned away.

'They can't do that,' Skin challenged.

I pretended to be considering for a moment. 'Well, you wouldn't think so, would you. It's probably not official, just the church – not this church, the one up at Gathering Hall – deciding it would prefer not to have people hanging round after dark. And the local police agreeing to keep the streets clear for the next couple of weeks. Come to think of it, there are laws in place already that would allow the police to do that.'

The boys were all staring at me. Imagine sullen sheep, and you'd have some idea of the expressions I was confronting.

'For example, this could be considered private property, so they'd have a right to ask you to move on. And there's already a law against loitering. At least I think there is.'

'Why?' One of them asked. Not Skin. I'd never managed to learn all their names.

'Good question. Makes you wonder what they're up to, doesn't it? Goodness, is that the time? Nice to see you all.'

I walked away then, conscious of the mutterings I left behind, and couldn't help the smile breaking out.

There was no talk of a curfew, of course. What an absurd idea. But the boys who hang round the village after dark tend to have a lot of empty space in their heads, and nature abhors nothing like a vacuum. Feeble intellects soak up new ideas without challenge, letting them fester and breed, until five young, strong lads become tinder boxes of seething resentment, just waiting for the spark that would ignite the explosion. I had no idea, of course, what form that explosion might take. I was just scattering seeds, seeing what might sprout.

Exhaustion was following close behind me like a needy dog as I neared home. I was fishing in my pocket for keys and so didn't see Hugh Gardner and Anna Brown standing together on the doorstep of the bakery until I was practically upon them.

'Well, if you're sure . . . ' Gardner was saying, as he stood, a little too close in my opinion, to the woman in the doorway.

'Thank you, but I have to be in bed very early,' she replied.

I braced myself for one of Gardner's double entendres but he stepped backwards, giving her some much-needed space.

'Any time,' he said. 'Sleep well.'

My ten days away had made me a little slow, I realised. Anna Brown was a baker, who rose at four o'clock in the morning to start work. Of course she would go to bed early, which was why I'd heard nothing from her house the night before.

Gardner turned on his heel. With narrowed eyes he gave me a curt nod and practically pushed his way past me. By the time I'd recovered from almost being knocked to the ground, Anna Brown was back inside her shop and on the point of closing the door. She looked at me and her eyes opened wide. I felt my face break into a smile a second before realising she wasn't looking at me at all, but over my shoulder. At Gardner?

No, not Gardner. The young girl, Constance, stood beneath a streetlight, not ten metres away. Her eyes flicked nervously to Gardner but he passed her with a simple nod of the head.

Turning back, I saw that Anna was lingering at the shop door. She was watching Constance, and her expression, while not unfriendly exactly, hardly seemed welcoming. Music, a popular ballad I felt I knew but couldn't quite name, was playing rather loudly inside the shop.

As I was pondering the potential nuisance of a neighbour who played music at all hours, Constance approached us like a stray animal, wary of strangers.

'Ah, the birthday girl,' I said as she drew close. 'Come to finalise cake details?'

I thought I heard a sharp intake of breath from Anna.

'I was wondering—' Constance began. She frowned at me but her annoyed look vanished when she turned to Anna. 'Did I leave my phone in your shop this morning?'

She hadn't been in the shop long enough to leave anything behind except bloodstains. I was about to point this out when Anna jumped in.

'I haven't seen it, but why don't we have a look?' She gave me a quick dismissive glance. 'Goodnight. Don't linger in the cold.' Turning her back, she ushered Constance into the shop. I followed suit, quickly entering my own property.

Annoyingly, Anna didn't turn her music down, making it impossible for me to hear what she and Constance were saying to each other. I could hear their voices, could distinguish one from the other, but not make out words. They spoke for about five minutes and when I heard the shop bell again, I stepped to my own front door and pushed it open a fraction.

'I hope it turns up,' Anna was saying.

'Thanks. And thanks for looking. I'll bet my mum's hidden it. She does that sometimes.'

'Constance, I got a text message earlier today. And I missed a few calls. I thought they might have been from you.'

'How could they have been? I don't have my phone.'

'No, of course not. Are you sure I can't give you a lift back?'

Constance declined the offer, jogged to the end of the street and turned the corner.

I made cocoa – without sugar – and took it upstairs. I was ready for bed, was on the point of turning back the covers, when I heard a voice, so loud and clear I thought someone was in the room with me.

'Rachel? It's me.'

It was Anna. Her bedroom lay next to mine, with only a thin wall in between. We were feet apart. I sat down and heard her speak again.

'I know. I know you didn't want to hear from me, and I know it's late, but I need to ask you something.'

Josie Hinton, next door's previous occupant, hadn't kept a telephone upstairs, and certainly never had visitors in that room. I'd never realised before how easy it was to hear through the upstairs dividing wall. I could even hear the mumble of the person on the other end of the line. Whoever it was didn't speak for long, replying to Anna in a short, terse sentence. It seemed fair to say that Rachel, whoever she was, and Anna weren't best friends.

'I understand that,' Anna said. 'But I've been getting odd phone calls.'

A pause.

'I don't know. I've no idea who it was. I wondered if—'

Another terse mumble.

'No, of course I'm not accusing you. Don't be so bloody defensive. I'm just asking, is it possible? That it was him? That somehow—'

Another pause, more muttering down the line.

'OK, I understand.' Anna's tone had changed, become harder, colder. 'Sorry to have bothered you.'

Silence. I waited for the sound of the phone being replaced. It seemed to take longer than it should but finally I heard the click.

Fascinating.

6

April, the previous year

'Only one,' he replied. 'My girlfriend, Lauren.'

The psychiatrist glanced up. She was a good-looking woman, Jago had decided, not too dissimilar to his stepmother. Maybe a year or two older, but with the same dark hair and pale skin. From the way she kept glancing down at her notes, rather than looking him in the eyes, he suspected she was uncomfortable talking about his sexual history.

Or maybe she fancied him.

'You have a girlfriend?' she asked.

'Not anymore,' he answered truthfully, and felt the familiar stab of – what, exactly? Pain, annoyance, anger?

'We broke up three months ago,' he went on. 'But she's the only girl I've had sex with. You have to be careful these days, don't you? I mean, with the whole MeToo business. No one wants to be accused of date rape.'

He saw the psychiatrist's eyes hardening and mentally kicked himself.

'Besides, it's not something I want to do with someone I don't care about,' he went on hurriedly. 'Sex should mean something.'

He watched for her body language to relax and was annoyed to see it didn't happen immediately, or obviously. He'd been a fool to make her wary. He wondered, for a moment, what the chances were of her finding out he was lying. He'd had sex with seven girls (possibly eight, he wasn't entirely sure what happened at last year's Truck festival). Even so, he had the highest body count of the boys in his year. Sometimes, he thought, girls his own age were just too easy.

'Why did you break up?' the psychiatrist asked.

'Lauren's decision,' he said, again truthfully. 'She said it didn't feel right.'

'Did she explain what she meant by that?'

He shook his head. 'Not really. And I didn't want to push her. When a girl says no, she means no.'

He waited for the nod of approval; it didn't come.

'When was the last time you felt guilty about something?' she asked him.

Jago stifled the urge to smirk. Seriously, did people fall for this shit? She was working her way through the Hare Psychopathy Checklist, the standard screening test for potential psychopaths, probably the youth version, aimed at twelve- to eighteen-year-olds. He'd known it was coming and had soaked up as much intel as he could find on the internet.

With the Hare Checklist, clinicians steered their patients – potential psychos – through a series of questions to ascertain how well they fit certain criteria, such as tendency to boredom, to lie, to manipulate others. Each of the twenty factors attracted a score from nought to two, with nought meaning didn't apply, one meaning applied somewhat and two meaning definitely applied. In the UK, a score of 25 was the benchmark for someone with psychopathic tendencies. Frankly, it was crude as dogshit pushed through the letterbox and he didn't imagine he'd have any problem fooling it.

'A week last Tuesday,' he replied quickly. 'I hurt Miss Chang. I know she's OK, but I'm always going to feel bad about that. I wish I could make it up to her somehow.'

If he kept his nerve, he could probably get his score today down into single figures. Much less might rouse her suspicions.

He was actually rather proud of his actual score according to the self-test he'd done the previous night. Thirty-five. Up there with Ted Bundy, Adolf Hitler and Donald Trump.

He realised he was smiling and pulled his face straight; she couldn't suspect that he was on to her.

7

I was up in the dark again next morning, in spite of the tenderness from my recent op making moving around uncomfortable. I heard Anna leave the house and from the window of my office saw her, small torch in hand, jogging up the lane towards the lake.

I waited until she was out of sight before leaving my own house, slipping out of my back gate and into her yard. If she was going swimming, she'd be away for half an hour at least, maybe longer.

Relieved that she hadn't yet got round to installing motion-triggered security lights, I tried Anna's back door. I'm not a sneak, and I certainly wouldn't have touched anything, but I'd have been interested to see the rear and maybe even the upstairs of her house. I don't make a habit of entering other people's properties without their knowledge, but I was more sure than ever that Anna Brown was hiding something.

The door was locked, so the ethics of the question became rather moot.

I was back in my own garden when I noticed a light had appeared in the upstairs of Gardner's house and that his blind was drawn back. This wasn't ideal. Being spied upon by Gardner wasn't something I relished.

While I was still thinking about this, I heard a noise from the lane: a scuffle and then a muffled curse. I recognised Anna's voice immediately. She'd turned back, for some reason, and I'd escaped being caught in her yard by seconds.

I remained still until I could hear her footsteps directly outside. I think I half expected her to bang on my fence and demand to know what I was doing. It was ridiculous, how guilty I felt, and I was grateful I'd kept all the lights in my house switched off. I could pretend to still be in bed.

A scraping sound and then a soft thud. Then, 'Damn it,' she muttered, directly outside my door.

I took courage and stepped back to it.

'Anna?' I risked. 'Anything amiss?'

There was a sharp intake of breath and then she muttered my name. 'Sorry,' she went on. 'I hope I didn't wake you.'

I pulled open the gate. She was still wearing the pale grey tracksuit and carrying the sports bag she'd left with, but I didn't imagine she'd been quite so covered in mud when she set off. Or that there'd been a nasty cut on her left cheek.

'Did you have an accident? Can I do anything?'

'No, I'm fine. I fell over. I'm so angry. I can't find my damn keys either. I swear to God if that lot made me lose them—'

This was most intriguing. I realised she was no longer carrying her torch.

'I'm not sure walking around at night without a light is a good idea,' I said. 'Would you like to come inside and sit down for a while?'

I rather surprised myself at that: I never invite people into my home.

'I had a bloody torch,' she said. 'I dropped the bloody thing.'

Well, really, there was no need to direct profanities at me.

'What's up?' said a new voice, and I saw to my annoyance that Gardner had appeared. 'Blimey, what happened to you?'

Anna looked from Gardner to me. 'Do either of you know anything about the lake?' she demanded.

I was a bit nonplussed by this, and so was Gardner by the look on his face. Mind you, he isn't the sharpest knife in the box.

'I was turned away,' Anna went on. 'There were four men there. At this hour. They wouldn't let me anywhere near it. They actually threatened me when I argued. One grabbed my arm and I dropped the torch. I fell over on the way back.'

'Four men?' Gardner repeated, as though what she'd said hadn't been perfectly clear.

'We have access to the lake and the woods.' Anna, if anything, was growing angrier, as though Gardner and I were responsible for her current state. 'It's in all of our leases. I was clearly told that by my solicitor when I bought the place.'

'You're not wrong,' Gardner said. 'I take the boys up there sometimes. Who were these blokes?'

She made an exasperated gesture. 'They didn't give me visiting cards. Four thugs. Acting like they owned the place. They've no right to turn me away.'

I was enjoying this immensely, especially as I was now reasonably confident that neither of them had witnessed my early morning trespassing. 'I think you need to calm down,' I said to Anna, because I've noticed nothing incenses a certain type of young woman like being told to calm down. Sure enough, she turned on me, her dark eyes flashing. Gardner put a restraining hand out.

'This isn't something you're going to sort out now,' he said. 'And I have to get to work. Why don't you pop down to the police station when you've got a moment? It's probably something to do with that lot from the church. A misunderstanding. It can soon be sorted out.'

Interesting. Gardner had basically said the same thing that I had: he'd told her to calm down, only using more words, but instead of looking as though she wanted to bite his head off, Anna seemed on the verge of grateful tears.

'I've lost my keys,' she said. 'I must have dropped them when I fell.'

Gardner gave a small laugh. 'Well, that problem I can fix. I've got a spare key for your place. Mrs Hinton gave me one years ago. I've been meaning to mention it, but I've barely seen you since you moved in. You haven't had the locks changed, have you?'

She sniffed. 'No, oh thank heavens. I'm so grateful.'

'Come inside for a sec.' He put an arm around her shoulders and steered her towards his back gate.

'I'll make you late for work.'

'Won't take a moment.'

They disappeared into his yard, neither of them giving me a second glance. I walked back indoors, deeply annoyed. Surely I was the obvious person to keep spare keys for neighbours? I was home all day, and a far more responsible person. I simply couldn't understand why that old bitch Josie Hinton had given her key to Gardner.

I wasn't particularly interested in Anna's story about being turned away from the lake, nor was I surprised by it. The church employs a number of security personnel every year. For the most part, they don't bother us, but from time to time they've been known to throw their weight around in the village. Most locals grin and bear it.

Anna Brown's failed swim, and her prompt reporting of it to the local police, was the talk of the post office when I went in.

'She's right, though, isn't she?' said the old man with the Jack Russell. 'We can all go up there if we fancy it.'

'She might be right, but would you take that lot on?'

'And what's she want to be swimming in the lake for, anyway? What's she going to catch in that water?'

'She's swimming, not fishing.' The old man with the Jack Russell considered himself a bit of a wag.

'I mean germs and such. There's a perfectly good pool in Penrith.'

'She makes lovely barm cakes, I'll say that for the lass. My Stan got through three yesterday.'

They carried on in this vein for some time. I didn't try to interrupt, though I was kept waiting for nearly eight minutes, but I didn't hear anything else of interest. Anna Brown was making waves. If she was trying to keep a low profile, that didn't seem entirely wise.

I had my parcel weighed – only one today – fixed the stamps and took it outside to post.

It was still early, but the bakery, on my return, was already busy. A line of four people waited at the counter and both tables were occupied. Anna herself was nowhere to be seen. She would need staff if this kept up. Ordinarily I'd have been annoyed by the potential for increased noise and disturbance but that day I knew the distractions would serve rather well. I dropped off my newspapers, picked up the post and put my bottle of milk in the fridge. One of the local farms delivers milk to people's doorsteps every day but I've always found that intrusive; I prefer to collect milk on my own terms. That done, I slipped out through the back gate, noticing as I did so that there were people in the so-called courtyard next door.

The lane at the back of our houses narrows quickly. A few yards past Gardner's property and it's barely a metre wide. The hedges have thrived and thickened over the years and trees have formed a canopy overhead. The result is a path that exists in a sort of shadowy twilight, even at midday, one that's frequently damp because the sun can't reach the ground to dry it out. Mud has been pushed to the path's edges by successive footfall, allowing undergrowth to spring up, adding to the illusion of entering a long, dark tunnel. There are dog walkers in the village who say their animals won't willingly enter the lake path, but dog owners are idiots in my experience.

The path winds its way up a gentle incline for a little over a quarter of a mile to where a stile leads into an area of woodland. From there it's possible to smell the lake, especially in summer when the water is low and the mud beaches are exposed. In October, the smell of fungus and rotting wood takes over. Another fifteen minutes or so brings the lake itself into view.

I may have given the impression, earlier in my narrative, of our lake being a somewhat poor relation of the great lakes of our national park; in doing so, I've probably done it a disservice. Because when the wind has been absent for several hours and the sky is clear, the lake takes on an almost unnatural stillness, becoming the perfect reflective surface. Surrounding the water are great structural canopies of larch, lime and spruce that reach skyward above the rounded, almost plump forms of the hornbeam and the holly. Cones of juniper, poplar and red spruce stand out like exclamation marks, while foreign species, such as maple and rowan, noted for their autumn colour, create a palate that ranges from deepest bronze, through bright copper, to pale apricot. Ancient yew trees give the planting a solidity while a monkey puzzle appears nothing more than a whimsy.

And all of this we see twice when conditions are right: first, in the real world, and then again in the mirror-image of the water.

Great boulders edge the lake, no doubt carried here by the huge glaciers of the ice age. They are as smooth and perfectly formed as soap bubbles, covered in glistening emerald-green moss. On that morning, bright orange leaves lay like scattered petals across the ground.

I am not a fanciful person by any means, but even I found an element akin to enchantment about the lake at Gathering. At the same time, it spoke to something inside me that I didn't recognise. I felt a pull from the depths of the water, almost a siren call to become one with it, while at the back of my brain, a warning bell sounded.

I drew close to the lake edge to see the water a little troubled by the morning's breeze, and as dull as the overcast sky. At this point, I had to take care; it was unlikely the thugs Anna encountered earlier had left. Keeping close to the shore, but still among the trees, I moved slowly, mainly to be quiet, but also because my eyes were fixed on the ground. After around a dozen steps I heard voices and stopped moving. A second later and I heard them again, some distance away, possibly on the other side of the lake. Emboldened, I moved forward, disturbing some resting geese. They scurried away, making that hideous squawking sound, and launched themselves like a fleet of grubby boats onto the water. Unsurprisingly they attracted the attention of the four men on the opposite bank. I could see them quite well by this time; unlike me, they hadn't bothered dressing in clothes that would blend in with their surroundings. I stayed very still again. After a minute or two they carried on walking and I figured they were far enough away that I needn't worry about them. I emerged from my hiding place and walked down to the beach.

I say 'beach'; it's actually a flat area of ground, damp from the water and covered in avian faeces. I'd cut off my own foot rather than walk barefoot over it, but Anna had obviously been less squeamish. I could see the imprint of both her trainers and her bare feet. Larger prints spoke of the arrival of the men and for a moment I almost felt sorry for her. A young woman, alone, possibly in a swimsuit, in the half-light, surrounded by four strange men. It can't have been an easy experience. I saw the mud squashed where she'd fallen and – there they were – her keys, caught on a bramble. I grabbed them, feeling a measure of triumph I hadn't experienced in years. Josie Hinton's petty-mindedness was foiled at last; now I had a key to the house next door.

A cry from across the water startled me; I'd almost forgotten the four men on the opposite shore. They were looking directly at me, one of them gesticulating. The message was perfectly clear, I was intended to leave, but while my main purpose in coming here had been served, I wasn't quite done yet.

I left the path, tracking left, avoiding the mud where I could, keeping close to the shore, knowing I'd reach a point where, on the opposite bank, the line of trees broke and the vista opened up. It took me several minutes, and the men kept pace.

At last, clambering over some tree roots, I reached the point I'd been aiming for, the place from where I could see Gathering Hall. People in the village talk about the 'Church', as do all of our seasonal visitors, I even do it myself, and yet there is no church building to speak of. Gathering Hall is an old stately home, owned, I imagine – we've never been entirely clear – by the evangelical church that organises the Ingathering.

An old house, possibly Victorian – I have little interest in architecture – the hall stands on a promontory a little way inland of the opposite lake shore. The trees on that side have been cleared, or never allowed to grow, to allow the house an uninterrupted view of the water.

More deliveries had arrived than I'd been aware of and the flat area of land around the front and sides of the house already resembled the sort of massive music festival that one sees occasionally on the news. A small city of marquees had been erected and more were in the process of going up. One in particular, centrally placed, was enormous.

Cargo was being unloaded from lorries and huge temporary lights had already been erected. A thunderclap of noise from industrial-sized speakers rang out, making even me jump, and I was on the other side of the lake.

A field to one side of the house was already filling with caravans and camper vans, some of them enormous affairs. I imagine many of the visitors stayed in the house but even Gathering Hall wouldn't accommodate the hundreds that would arrive over the coming days.

I noticed something else then. A huge horse chestnut tree that once stood proudly on the far bank of the lake had fallen, possibly in the autumn storms that had swept through the county while I'd been in hospital. The roots now formed a massive vertical circle protruding some twelve metres or more into the air; most of the trunk and branches had landed in the water.

'Oy, private land! Clear off!'

To be fair, I couldn't hear exactly what was being shouted at me across the lake, but this was probably close. The four men – I guessed them to be in their late twenties, early thirties, but they were some way off – had walked to the very edge of their own shore as though they were about to wade into the water. Perhaps they thought they could walk on it. I'd certainly enjoy seeing them try, but I was confident enough in the distance – it takes a good forty minutes to walk the circumference of the lake – to risk a little playfulness. I cupped my right hand around my ear and leaned towards them.

They consulted each other, then tried some more gesticulating. One of them raised a pair of binoculars to his face and trained them on me. I considered a smile, even a wave, but settled for raised eyebrows. Knowing it was their only option, two of them set off at a brisk walk around the lake telling me two things: the first, that they didn't know the area as well as I did, because they were going the longest way around and secondly, that they were very serious about maintaining the privacy of the Ingathering. I waited long enough for them to be out of sight of the other two, and of earshot, before turning to leave.

*

Had I been a few seconds sooner, I'd have been able to confront the person hanging around at the back of our small terrace. As it was, I only caught a glimpse of long fair hair as she vanished around the corner, but I was in no doubt about who it was. Constance again.

I should have been resting; I was hot after the walk to the lake and a little shaky, as though the infection I'd caught due to lax hospital practices hadn't entirely gone away. I remembered I hadn't taken either antibiotics or painkillers that morning. Even so, the odd appearance, again, of Constance wasn't something I could ignore. Taking a deep breath, because I was in quite a lot of pain by this time, I walked straight through my house, out of the front door and into the bakery.

Anna was behind the counter, her back to me, transferring some cakes onto plates. They were enormous affairs, bulging like mushrooms from their paper cases, sprinkled with crushed sugar and stained purple from whatever fruit had been baked inside. Each looked large enough to give four people a decent portion and yet they seemed to be single servings.

She glanced around and her eyes widened. Her smile was polite, but nothing more.

'What can I get you,' she said, after she'd carried the plates over to where a trio of visitors were sipping enormous mugs of what looked like frothed milk. 'Takeaway or eat in? I have a table in the courtyard.'

The skin around her eyes seemed redder than it should, given the pallor of her complexion; it almost looked as though she'd been crying an hour or so earlier.

'The bakery seems to be attracting undesirables,' I told her. 'I caught a person loitering in the lane a minute ago. They won't get into my garden, I keep the gate locked, but if you have anything valuable out there I advise you to take care.'

The lines of Anna's face stiffened for a second before curiosity got the better of her. 'Someone wearing a blue sweatshirt?' She lowered her voice. 'With red lettering?'

So, she too had noticed Constance hanging around.

'Possibly,' I replied, like Anna keeping my voice low. 'A young woman, I thought. I could call the police station and report it, if that would help. I can see you're busy again.'

'No, no, don't do that. I'm almost certain it was Constance. You know, the girl from yesterday morning.'

I faked a moment of sudden understanding. 'Ah, the young lady with issues.'

Anna's face hardened.

'But why focus on you?' I went on. 'I mean, the phone calls, the text message, hanging around the shop, coming up with flimsy excuses to speak to you. That's a lot of activity aimed at someone she's barely met.'

Anna didn't reply, but I could tell she was troubled.

'Suggests a certain desperation, don't you think? A clutching at straws.'

The shop bell rang out at that moment and Anna's eyes left mine.

'Good morning!'

I think everyone in the shop jumped at the volume used; this was someone who expected immediate attention.

'Good morning,' Anna replied, as I turned to see a tall man, on the thin side, with silver hair and bright blue eyes, who could have been any age between forty-five and sixty-five. His skin had a tan that suggested he spent much of the year in a warmer climate than Cumbria and his clothes were the sort that country people wear in Hollywood films: corduroy trousers, a checked flannel shirt with discreet cravat tie, a tweed jacket. Everyone in the village knew who he was.

He didn't offer to shake her hand. 'I'm Aran North,' he told Anna as his eyes drifted to the table by the dresser. 'Ladies.' He inclined his head at them. 'Beautiful day.'

The women had been caught unawares; one of them had a mouthful of cake and couldn't speak, the other dabbed a napkin to her lips. 'Minister,' she replied.

'I hear you had an encounter up at the lake yesterday morning,'

North said to Anna. As usual, he'd completely ignored me. 'I thought I'd better clear the matter up.' He looked around, as though only at that moment noticing he'd entered a shop. 'Charming place. What an asset to the village. Is there somewhere we can talk, Miss Brown?'

'Have this table, Minister,' one of the other women said. 'We were just leaving.'

They'd barely touched their food or their hot drinks.

'There's a table outside,' Anna said. 'Will you excuse me a moment, ladies? I'll be right back.'

Without waiting for a reply, she led the way out through her kitchen towards the back door. A gust of cool air hit my face as they went outside. I took a step after them, and another. The outer door was still open.

'Can we help you with something?' said the woman who'd had her mouth stuffed with cake a moment ago, and I realised all three women were watching me, almost as though they expected me to leap over the counter and help myself to the contents of the till. One of them, the largest of the three, got to her feet.

'Bit chilly in here.' She strode past me, practically pushing me out of the way, before taking hold of the outer door and pulling it closed.

8

April, the previous year

The Moore family home lay at the end of a quiet lane, a mile outside the small Dorset market town. It had been a modest Victorian farmhouse and the red-brick façade remained, looking out over miles of swollen green hills. The house, though, had trebled in size, thanks to a massive cedar-clad extension, and enormous floor-to-ceiling windows made the most of the panoramic views. Inside, a vast open-plan space held a kitchen, dining area, work desks and sitting areas; closed doors hinted at more intimate spaces beyond. The surrounding gardens were landscaped and she could see the plastic covering of a swimming pool. It represented a comfortable, almost opulent, lifestyle. Whatever Jago Moore's problems might be, they didn't, on the surface, stem from his home life.

Scratch the surface, though . . .

Morgan Moore was a management consultant who worked long hours in the City, leaving his second, considerably younger, wife to juggle the home and a nursing career. Bella Moore, Jacob's stepmother, was in her mid-thirties, slender and pale-skinned, with glossy dark hair and hazel eyes. She was also around five months pregnant.

The first home visit took place in the early evening, after Morgan had explained he absolutely couldn't get away from work earlier. Something was cooking when she arrived. Something that smelled great.

'So, where are we at?' Morgan asked, as though expecting a progress report there and then.

She hadn't seen Jago on arrival, but somewhere not too far away the sound of a bouncing ball could be heard.

'I want to ask about Jago's mother,' she replied. 'He told me she died when he was very young. I haven't challenged him yet, but I know that isn't true.'

Morgan's first wife had left the family home when Jago was three years old. He'd had no contact with her since.

'He's told people that for years,' Morgan replied. 'When he was younger, it was his way of coping. Death seemed preferable to abandonment for a very young child. To be honest, I could see his point.'

'We think he might believe it himself by now,' the stepmother, Bella, added. She'd been whisking a sauce in a small saucepan but, as she spoke, she glanced around at the rear door to the house.

'Do you mind my asking why she left?'

Morgan frowned. 'Is it relevant? It was years ago.'

Outside, the sound of the bouncing ball stopped. Jago's stepmother looked around again.

'Yes, I think it might be. It's uncommon for children to remain with the father after a marital break-up, even less so for the mother to have no ongoing contact at all.'

Morgan seemed to brace for a blow. 'I caught Sophie abusing Jago,' he said through tight lips. 'I told her I wouldn't expose her if she left and never tried to contact either of us again.' He too glanced around. 'And this is no place to be having this conversation.'

'And she agreed?'

He lowered his voice and leaned a little closer. 'She decided it was better than prison.'

The stepmother switched off the hob and stepped away from the cooker.

'What sort of abuse are we talking about?'

Morgan stepped back, holding both hands in the air. 'No, I'm not going into all that again. Sophie was mentally ill. I had to choose. Help her or protect my son.'

Without another word, he left the room.

Bella's face had paled. 'It was sexual abuse,' she said to the kitchen counter. 'Morgan cried when he finally told me. He said he felt sick for a full year afterwards.'

The psychiatrist gave herself a moment to absorb that. Then, 'I'm sorry to press, but what exactly happened?'

The stepmother shook her head. 'I don't know any details. And I wouldn't advise you mention it to Morgan. I doubt he'll ever willingly talk about it.'

'Do you think Jago remembers?'

For a second, the woman looked frightened. 'How could he? He was a baby.'

Three years old was hardly a baby but she didn't press the point. Inwardly, she sighed. This was not going to be something she could deal with in eight sessions.

'How do you get on with Jago?' she asked.

Bella thought for a few seconds. 'Hard to say. I thought, for a long time, that we were close. We're thrown together a lot when his dad's away. He's a difficult person to read though. I'm not sure I ever really know what's going on with him.'

Deliberately, the psychiatrist let her eyes fall to the other woman's stomach. 'How does he feel about a new brother or sister?'

The stepmother turned away, rinsing cups in the sink. 'He says he's looking forward to it.'

'Do you believe him? Lots of stepchildren would feel threatened by a new arrival in the family.'

Bella kept her back turned. 'Oh, I'd say very little threatens Jago.'

This didn't feel right; this woman, too, was holding back. 'Has he ever given you any reason to be frightened of him?'

The stepmother shook her head. 'No, he's far too clever for that.'

9

I was out of breath by the time I reached my own garden and my scar was throbbing. I had no choice but to sit down. For a moment, I heard nothing other than the cooing of pigeons and traffic in the distance and felt sure I must have missed the encounter next door. Then I heard North's voice.

'I see,' he said. 'Well, I must apologise. Our staff were wrong to frighten you.'

'They angered me.'

It was clear from Anna's tone that North's apology hadn't had its desired effect.

'But they were acting on specific instructions. Our church is here for a very short time and we value our privacy.'

'They were acting unlawfully. Everyone in the village has right of access to the land on this side of the lake.'

I was warming to Anna Brown, I don't mind admitting. I'd heard so few people stand up to Aran North over the years.

He said, 'And yet no one else in the village chooses to abuse that right during the church's stay here.'

'How can exercising a right be abusing it?'

It occurred to me, then, to wonder what Anna's real profession was. I'd already decided she wasn't a baker. Oh, she could bake, of course, the smell that hovered over our terrace like a summer cloud was testament to that. But she was using her skill as a glamour, a sort of cloak, to hide the woman beneath. I was getting more and more curious to see that woman. I was thinking, maybe a lawyer?

North didn't reply immediately, but then he wouldn't; being challenged was something of a novelty for him.

'There's also the matter of the fallen tree. A very old, large horse chestnut has fallen into the water recently. It makes swimming there really quite dangerous until we can get it removed. Which we will, before the end of the year.'

'Open-water swimmers learn to look out for natural hazards,' Anna replied. 'Besides, the lake is enormous. I can easily stay away from the tree.'

Again, a silence of several seconds.

'Your patience would be very much appreciated,' North said, eventually. 'We hold baptisms at the lake. It's a vulnerable time for those who are called, and privacy is important.'

Baptisms? I'd not heard that one before; I wondered if it was even true.

'There was something else I wanted to discuss,' North went on, as though the matter of access to the lake had been settled. 'I'm holding a reception tomorrow evening for fifty people and my caterers have let me down at the last minute. I'd be very grateful if you could step in and supply the buffet. Shall we say £20 a head?'

Silence.

'It's always so difficult to find caterers here, when we have so many mouths to feed over the next two weeks,' North said. 'And people speak very highly of your shop.'

And that was how it was done. He'd offered her a thousand pounds, less the cost of materials, and more business to come. All Anna had to do in return was forego her morning swim for a couple of weeks.

I heard the scraping back of a chair.

'Would you like to see some menus?' Anna offered. She'd given in, of course; there had never really been any doubt.

North's voice, when he spoke again, came from above my head. He'd stood up. 'No, no. I'm sure I can leave it in your capable hands. I'll give you my card. You can ring when you want to deliver, and we'll make sure the gate's open.'

They moved back into the shop, out of earshot. I wasn't sorry. My need for pain relief had become rather pressing.

I remembered, when I got upstairs, that the prescription I'd brought home with me from the hospital only covered three days, and that I'd need a top-up supply from the chemist in the village. After resting for some time, I got up and left the house. I was anxious to get back quickly, not feeling well at all, but was intrigued to see Constance, alone again, slipping into the chemist before me. Not only that, but she was looking up and down the street, as though scared of being seen.

I was in luck. Someone was leaving as I reached the door, and the bell rang only once, allowing me to slip in unnoticed. I crept my way around the units and was rewarded by the sight of Constance staring down at one particular section of merchandise. She saw me and coloured. I tutted and made an exasperated gesture, giving the impression I'd come to the wrong part of the shop, before walking away. In the next aisle, I looked down at some throat lozenges, as though unable to choose between Honey & Lemon and Blackcurrant, and kept my eye on the mirror above the counter that lets the pharmacist spot any pilfering. It also allowed me to see what Constance was buying.

The purchase took place in silence. Constance kept her eyes on the counter, the pharmacist – a discreet man – didn't comment, and she left the shop with no knowledge that she'd been rumbled by someone with no duty of confidence.

Soon to be sixteen-year-old Constance from a devout, church-going family had been buying a pregnancy test. I couldn't wait to tell Anna Brown.

10

April, the previous year

Upstairs, in Jago's room, the psychiatrist took a moment to look around.

'I think this is the tidiest teenage boy's bedroom I've ever been in,' she said.

Whoever had designed the space, the stepmother she guessed, had gone for industrial chic, with lots of galvanised metal and wire framing. Neutrals dominated the colour scheme. One wall carried the solar system, each star represented by a tiny light. On the opposite wall was a collage of old bicycle wheels. It was an interesting room, full of stuff, a cool room. On the other hand, the waste bin was empty, the bed neatly made, the desk clear of clutter. No discarded crisp packets, Coke cans or sweet wrappers. No dirty clothes on the floor.

'How many have you been in?' Jago leaned against the door. She'd deliberately left it open when she'd followed him inside but he doubled around behind her and closed it. She didn't like the slightly insolent gleam in his eyes.

'I work with children and young people,' she told him. 'I try to visit all of them at home.'

'So, what are you learning about me?'

And there was that odd, fixed smile again. All the same, he was different, more assured in his home environment. She, on the other hand, was standing awkwardly in the centre of the room, not knowing whether to remain standing, to sit down, or suggest they move to a different part of the house.

She forced a smile, one that probably looked as weird as his. 'Apart from how tidy you are? You'll have to give me some time.'

'We have a cleaner twice a week and Bella comes in here every day when I'm at school. There's no privacy in this house.'

'Do you mind that? No privacy, I mean?'

He shrugged. 'I've nothing to hide.' Then he smiled again. 'I watch porn on my phone, sometimes my laptop. They're both password protected.'

He was trying to shock her. She parked the porn conversation for another session and walked to a bookcase where she'd spotted a framed picture of a young woman holding a toddler on her lap.

'You and your mum?' she asked.

Jago took a step forward, as though the picture of his mother was drawing him in. 'Not long before I lost her,' he replied, and she noted the careful choice of words.

'How much do you remember about her?'

He shook his head. 'Nothing. I dream about her sometimes, but it's always Bella's face I see. Funny that.'

Jago's mother and stepmother, she reflected, looked a lot alike, but that wasn't so surprising. Men tended to stick to type. It might have been an issue for Jago, though.

'You call her Bella? Not Mum?'

'She's not my mum. She's not old enough. How old are you?'

She ignored that and stepped away from him, letting her eyes fall to the collection of books. She recognised the A level texts on the top shelf – Jago was taking English literature – and the classics on the next shelf down: *Dracula*, *Lord of the Flies*, *The War of the Worlds*, *Treasure Island*, *The Adventures of Tom Sawyer*. All hardbacks; someone had worked hard on developing Jago's love of literature. On the bottom shelf were what looked like the complete works of Thomas Hardy.

'I've always found Hardy a little gloomy,' she said. 'Doomed love affairs, couples drawn to each other only to prove, one way or another, to be each other's downfall.'

Behind her, she could hear Jago breathing. He'd moved closer.

'Do you know he was buried without his heart?' he asked.

11

I've been called proud, but it's a description I reject. I'm more than prepared to compromise my principles when something bigger is at stake. I disapproved, heartily, of the bakery; I disliked the noise, the crowds, the people who stared in through my window as they hung around outside the shop and, more than anything, I disliked the produce sold from it. I am a firm believer in plain, healthy food, and I'd seen nothing in the bakery that could come close to qualifying. Nevertheless, if my plan were to work, I had to become, for a short time at least, an appreciative customer. And so, at a quarter past one o'clock, on my way back from the community library, I called in.

'Soup, please,' I said, when it was finally my turn. 'And a bread roll. Wholemeal. To take away.'

Taking my food away was the only viable option. The place was packed, and judging by the noise I could hear, the outside area was similarly busy.

'Enjoy,' Anna said to me as she gave me my change. 'Nice to see you.'

'Actually.' I let my voice drop. 'Could I come round later? There's something you might want to know.'

She looked uncertain and I saw it would take more than a purchased cup of soup to get her onside.

'About a certain . . . ' I glanced around – the customers were mainly strangers, that is, church people. 'A certain young lady,' I finished.

Anna held eye contact for a second. Her eyes, I noticed then, weren't dark, but a rather pale hazel green; her pupils were unusually dilated, giving the impression of dark eyes.

'Of course,' she said. 'Come at four. I'll have closed by then.'

I was smiling as I left the shop; I'd known she wouldn't be able to resist.

'How was the soup?' she asked me, a little after four o'clock. She'd led me through to the kitchen and I could see how much she still had to do before she finished for the day. A pile of dirty crockery and cutlery was waiting to go in the dishwasher, which was currently mid-cycle, and I'd noticed as I'd walked through the shop that she had very little stock left. Industrial-sized bags of flour and sugar sat on the central kitchen table, alongside trays of eggs, several pints of milk, a bag of lemons and a huge bar of dark chocolate.

The soup had been delicious: a medley of mushrooms, many of them wild, cooked with cream, fresh parsley and a dash of sherry. It had been the best mushroom soup I'd ever tasted.

'A little salty,' I said, before I could stop myself. 'But very nice. And the roll was excellent.'

She gave me a half-smile, in return, I suppose, for my half-compliment, and I sat on one of the tall kitchen stools. I expected her to join me but instead she began breaking eggs into a large mixing bowl.

'Have you always been a baker?' I asked.

'You said you wanted to talk to me,' she replied. 'I assumed it was about Constance, the girl from the church.'

'Yes, I know you've been concerned about her, and I know she's been hanging around here the last couple of days.'

Anna stopped working, her hand hovering over the bowl.

'Almost as though she wanted to talk to you,' I said.

She gave an almost imperceptible nod.

'Well, I may have found out why she's looking so troubled.'

As I told Anna about the pregnancy test, she carried on with her work. I counted a dozen eggs going into the bowl before she turned and poured sugar onto some scales.

'Why are you telling me?' she asked, her back to me.

'Because I don't think you've always been a baker. I think you used to help people.'

It had been a shot in the dark, an articulation of the vaguest of feelings, but it hit home. Anna Brown carried around her an aura of self-esteem and respect. Her treatment at the hands of the church thugs had been an entirely new experience and she'd resisted it. To me, that suggested someone in a senior profession, and I'd already considered a lawyer. At the same time, she'd spotted the potential problem with Constance and seen a responsibility there. That implied doctor. Her masquerade as a baker, miles from home, suggested something had gone very badly wrong in her past.

She turned to face me. 'Why would you say that?' Her face had become rigid, even paler than normal.

I got to my feet. 'Merely a feeling I had about you. I meant no offence.' I set off for the doorway. 'I thought you'd want to know about Constance.'

'But as you said yourself, there's nothing I can do about it.'

I glanced back, twisting rather more sharply than was wise and felt a pang from my scar.

'Maybe I was wrong,' I said. 'What soup are you planning tomorrow?'

She looked puzzled. 'Roast tomato.'

'I look forward to it.'

A couple of mornings a week, and one evening, I volunteer at our local community library. It's something I've been doing for a while. I'm not the most popular amateur librarian; in fact there have been more complaints about me than any other volunteer, but I'm the only one who fully understands the Dewey classification and without me they wouldn't have a clue how to manage the stock control system, or the antiquated computers. The committee who've been running the library since the local authority abandoned it know they can't manage without me, and so we've reached an uneasy compromise. I keep my interaction with the public to a minimum, and I can run the back office how I please.

For the first two hours, the evening went pretty much as normal. The headteacher of the nearby secondary school arrived for her reference books; I'm the only person who knows how to order directly from the British Library, so she only ever comes in when I'm on duty. A few people who work full-time arrived for their usual order of light reading. Mrs Watkins came in for her two historical romances and her work of serious literary fiction, usually a Booker Prize nominee. She never reads the latter, merely orders it in the vain hope of impressing me and anyone else who might be around. I know this because I once slipped a typewritten note between pages 100 and 101 – *Brenda Watkins is a shoplifter* – and wasn't so much as challenged when she brought it back. I checked after she'd left and the note was still there, untouched and unread. For what it's worth, Brenda Watkins *is* a shoplifter, I've seen her slip small items into her bag in the post office more than once. I never say anything. It's no skin off my nose, and the information might come in useful one day.

Other than that, a few young mothers wheeled in their offspring, already in pyjamas, and spent the next half hour listlessly combing through the grubby children's shelves for something they hadn't read a dozen times over. Their children ran around screaming. So far, entirely normal.

At seven o'clock, though, only a half hour before we were due to close, something very not normal happened. Anna Brown arrived.

'Oh,' she said, surprised to see me. I don't know why – I'd never told her I don't volunteer for the library.

'Anything I can help you with?' I asked. 'The new Richard and Judy picks have just come in. And Elly Griffiths' latest has some nice reviews.' I was mimicking her own way of dealing with customers, but I don't think she noticed.

'I was wondering if you kept newspaper archives,' she asked.

'Back to the year 1856,' I told her. 'But only for the *North Lakes Chronicle*. And most of them are in the loft and we need two weeks' notice to find them. National papers we keep for a week, and the *Chronicle* for the last ten years in here.'

'The *Chronicle*,' she said. 'The last ten years should do.'

The place was emptying by this time, and so I could easily leave the counter. I led the way to where we keep back copies of our weekly paper in a series of wide, shallow drawers and showed her how she could find them by date.

'Thanks,' she said, obviously waiting for me to go.

'Anything in particular you're looking for?' I asked.

She shrugged. 'Just getting to know the place.'

I left her to it, only returning when we were five minutes from closing.

'Found what you were looking for?' Over her shoulder I saw that she was reading the issue for late October, three years ago. I'd been watching her surreptitiously from the counter, seeing her disregard most of the issues, but combing carefully through certain ones.

She looked at her watch. 'I should have come sooner,' she said. 'I didn't realise how long it would take.'

As she folded away the newspaper and closed the drawer, I saw that she'd been making notes on a small notepad.

'Do you think it's odd that there's been no mention in the local papers at all of the annual church festival?' she asked me. 'I've gone back ten years. Nothing. I can't believe such a massive annual event hasn't produced some stories over the years.'

'They like their privacy,' I said.

'This is a local newspaper, not a church magazine. They should be driven by the stories, not by what the church wants.'

'Maybe, but this is St Abel's Chapel, not Fleet Street.'

She got to her feet. 'I shouldn't keep you,' she said, a second before her frown vanished again. 'I'll tell you what I did find, though – Mrs Hinton, the lady who ran the bakery before me – she died in the house.'

'Yes, very sad,' I replied. 'Weren't you told?'

'I knew she'd died, obviously, because I bought the place from her estate. I didn't realise she'd died in the property, from carbon monoxide poisoning.'

'Probably worth getting your installations checked,' I said. 'Especially if you're using any of her old equipment.'

'It all has been,' she replied. 'I'm not worried about me. But I found the report of the coroner's inquest and they never managed to pin down what had caused the problem. Everything seemed to be working fine when it was tested.'

I indicated she should precede me to the door; we like to close on time. 'Our best guess was a blocked flue,' I said. 'Causing the gas to back up in the property.'

'Did they find one?'

'No, I don't believe they did. A sad business. Now, if you'll give me a minute to lock up, I'll walk back with you. It's getting quite dark.'

'I think I owe you an apology,' Anna said, as we stepped out into the night.

'How so?' I replied, genuinely surprised. She'd done nothing that I would consider merited an apology.

'For not asking how you are. People say you've been quite unwell, only just out of hospital. I'm sorry, but with everything going on . . . '

'Perfectly understandable,' I replied. 'And I'm on the mend, thank you.'

'I hear you work from home,' she went on after a moment. 'That you're something in publishing. Sounds quite exciting.'

'I didn't realise I was the subject of so much conversation,' I told her. 'And it's really not. I'm a proofreader. Semi-retired a few years now. On health grounds.'

'Ah,' she said. 'So that explains all the parcels you get. I offered to take some of them while you were away but was told you have an arrangement with the post office.'

'I do. But it was kind of you to offer.'

'I would have thought that's all done online now,' she went on. 'Can't they email proofs to you?'

'I refuse to be online. I really don't trust the internet and won't have it in my home. If I need to send an email, which is rare, I use the library.'

Out of the corner of my eye I saw her give me an odd, sideways glance.

'You disapprove?' I challenged. 'You think I'm a dinosaur?' It certainly wouldn't be the first time I'd been called such.

'I think you're rather quaint,' she said.

I wasn't entirely sure what to make of that, and so we walked on in silence for a minute or two. Only when our houses were in sight did she speak again, and this time rather hesitantly, as though broaching a subject that was somewhat sensitive.

She said, 'It said in the paper that you found Mrs Hinton.'

I'd been more than annoyed that my name had appeared in the local rag. It seems absurd to me that we can't control where and when our name appears in the public domain.

'I alerted the authorities,' I replied. 'It was obvious something had happened when she didn't open her shop on Monday morning.'

It had been the noisy crowd of people outside my house that had drawn my attention, but I didn't tell Anna that.

'And it was Hugh Gardner who found the body,' I went on. 'He was obviously the right person to enter a hazardous building.'

'Do you know Hugh well?' she asked, after a few more seconds.

'Oh, he's far too busy with his various girlfriends to socialise with me.'

She was silent for a while. Then, 'You're probably not on X, are you?'

'I have no idea what you just asked me.'

She gave a half-smile. 'Thought not. It's a social media platform. Used to be called Twitter. A lot of people still do call it that. You can search for specific terms.'

I watched her pull her phone from her pocket and tap the home button to awaken it. 'I looked for the hashtag *Ingathering*,' she told me. 'I googled it, actually. Nothing on the main sites, but I found an X account.'

She saw my face and her smile widened. 'Am I speaking a different language? This account is called Sweet Sixteen.'

She held the phone up for me to see. In the poor light I took in a photograph that appeared to have been taken locally – mountains, forests, the gleam of one of the great lakes, a smaller, circular picture of party balloons – all black – with '16' printed in silver lettering, and the bold heading 'Sweet Sixteen'. The screen faded a second before I could read the full text beneath, but I caught a few words: *annual, festival, sinister*.

'One post, so it's a new account,' Anna said, '"Tents going up in St Abel's Chapel. Is that a bell I hear tolling? Hashtag Ingathering. Hashtag Sweet Sixteen."'

I blinked a few times. 'And what do you make of that?' I asked her.

'I wonder if it's a bit like one of those weird American cult churches.'

'Interesting,' I said. 'I suspect a lot of people in the village might agree with you.'

She thought about that for a moment then, 'How about you?'

'Oh, I don't get involved,' I lied.

The next day, at lunchtime, I was rewarded by the sight of Constance sitting alone at one of the tables in the bakery. Anna and I shared a look, a raising of the eyebrows, a silent question. She shook her head, to indicate she'd had no opportunity to speak to her and also, that she was at a loss as to what to do.

'I'll eat in today,' I announced. 'If this young lady doesn't mind my joining her?'

It took Constance a moment to realise I meant her; she shrugged.

'I'll bring it over.' Anna and I shared another look. We were co-conspirators.

I sat down beside Constance, who was intent on her mobile phone – it had obviously turned up – and didn't acknowledge me again. She was wearing yet another sweatshirt with very long sleeves, but I was able to spot that the bandages had been replaced on each wrist by large plasters. They were much more discreet, and probably suggested the wounds had been minor. A real suicide attempt then, or a cry for help?

'You're the young lady with a birthday coming up, aren't you?' I said, pleasantly.

'Next week.' She gave a sideways glance at Anna, who was ladling my soup into a bowl.

After that, I was at a loss myself; I'm not used to talking to young people, but Anna approached our table with a tray.

'I was wondering if you might be looking for work, Constance,' she said as she put my lunch on the table. 'I've got a lot of food to organise and deliver to your campsite this evening. I'll struggle to do it by myself. Might you be around for the next few hours?'

Constance looked up in surprise. 'I have to get back,' she said. 'They'll be wondering where I am.'

'Even so, I'm glad you're here,' Anna said. 'Bear with me a sec.'

She vanished into the kitchen, reappearing a few seconds later with a cardboard box and a sketchbook.

'Your mum and grandma made all the decisions,' she said, as she put the box on the table and pulled out the spare chair. 'But I want you to be fine with it all.' She opened the sketchbook to an inner page and showed us both a coloured drawing of a cake. Even I had to admit it looked nice. Two tiers and multiple layers held together with butter frosting. A simple cake, but a beautiful one, because of the brilliant cascade of sugar flowers.

'I'm using marigolds – your birth flower – as the main theme,' Anna said. 'The cake is carrot cake, and the butter cream is orange-flavoured, but I've made it pale in colour so the flowers stand out.' She opened the box and – I couldn't help it – I peered inside. Constance couldn't resist either and our heads almost met.

'They're not quite dry yet,' Anna said. 'I only made them last night.'

The sugar flowers inside – mainly yellow, orange and crimson – were exquisite and so lifelike I had to stop myself stroking a petal to check that it was rigid and not soft.

'These will ripple down the side of the cake,' Anna said. 'They'll last for years if you want to keep them, but most people don't. The white freesias are for contrast, but a good trick is to have some real ones on display nearby, so everyone thinks the scent is coming from the cake.'

Constance sniffed and I looked up; there were tears in her eyes.

'It's going to be beautiful,' I said. 'What a lucky girl you are. Except, you don't think so, do you?'

Anna gave a quick glance around, as though to check the shop was still empty. 'Constance, you're with friends,' she said.

Well, I wouldn't have gone that far, but I had a feeling it was going to work. Constance sniffed again and looked up – at Anna, not me – and opened her mouth to speak. And then the bell rang out.

'Oh, for heaven's sake, Constance.'

A woman I recognised as Constance's mother stood in the doorway and behind her a man of a similar age who bore a slight resemblance to Constance herself.

'We've been looking for you everywhere.'

'We've been discussing Constance's cake,' I said, for all the world as though I too worked in the shop. 'Do come and see the flowers. I think they've turned out rather well.'

Both parents ignored me.

'Constance,' the father said, stepping back to indicate she should precede him out of the shop.

Constance got to her feet. 'Thank you,' she said to Anna and then the three of them left. The bell fell silent.

'You're right,' I said. 'Something wrong there.'

'Apart from a teenage pregnancy and a suicide attempt,' she snapped.

I waited.

'You're right too,' she went on. 'There's nothing we can do about it.'

I said, 'It wouldn't hurt to have a look around up at that campsite of theirs though, would it?'

'How do we do that? Their security's tight as a drum, they wouldn't even let me near the lake.'

'But you have to go up there tonight to deliver some party food,' I reminded her. 'And you'll need some help. So why don't I come with you?'

'I'm not sure,' she said. 'If she doesn't want to talk to us . . . '

I leaned over the table. From where I was sitting, I could see what Anna couldn't. Constance had left her phone behind on the seat.

'I've heard sixteen-year-old girls are never without their phones,' I said, as I picked it up. 'Looks to me like she left it behind to give you an excuse to find her.'

Anna looked doubtful for a moment; then she smiled at me.

And, just like that, we became a team, Anna and I: Sherlock Holmes and Watson. Or so she thought.

12

April, the previous year

'Hardy's ashes are at Poets' Corner in Westminster Abbey, because he was the foremost novelist and poet of his day,' Jago said to her as, unasked, he walked her to her car. 'But his heart is in his parents' grave at the family church not far from here. I find that beautiful, don't you?'

Behind them, Morgan Moore was watching from one of the downstairs windows.

There'd been something a little intense about Jago's mood since leaving the house. He remained close, holding eye contact. She wanted to beep open her car door but at the same time, didn't want to give the impression of being anxious to get away; especially if he was on the point of opening up. She hoped he wouldn't turn around and see his father's scrutiny.

'It's very nice that he loved his parents so much.' She wondered if Jago was thinking about his mother and whether she could ask him where he'd like his own heart to be buried. It would be a very unusual question, possibly not ethical.

But Jago was an unusual client. One who was still standing too close. She couldn't back away though. The car was immediately behind her.

'Happiness is but the occasional episode in a general drama of pain,' he announced.

'Hardy again?'

'*The Mayor of Casterbridge.*'

At the window, Morgan hadn't moved; almost as though she were an unwelcome visitor he was anxious to see off the premises.

'Is that how you feel? That life is predominantly pain?'

'Of course.' He looked surprised she'd asked. 'You'd be a fool not to. Hardy got that. People call him gloomy, depressing, even morbid. He was simply a realist.'

This really was a conversation for another day; possibly an important one.

She said, 'Not everyone would agree with that. Lots of people live mainly happy lives.'

'You could say that about sheep. They're happy. Or what passes for happy in their tiny little minds.'

'Happy people are like sheep?'

'Men like Hardy are the ones with vision, with clarity. They're the ones who can look into the human soul and see the darkness. They get it.'

She had the feeling she was tantalisingly close to something.

'Do you?' she asked.

'Oh God, yes. I see it all around me.'

'See what?'

'Despair.'

13

I was healing well, and I was glad of it when the time came to load up Anna's car, because we carried box after box from the shop. None of them were massively heavy, apart from the boxes of plates, and those she insisted on carrying herself, but by the time we were finished I was aching again, and a little out of breath.

'I can manage now,' she said, as she stood by the driver's door. 'You don't look too good.'

Well, I hadn't gone to all that trouble to fall at the last hurdle.

'Oh, I'm fine.' I walked round to the passenger side. 'You'll need help at the other end.'

'You've got Constance's phone, haven't you?' she checked as we set off.

'I have.' It was a different model to the one Anna used and she hadn't had a suitable charger. Suggesting the importance of keeping it charged – it might be the only way Constance had of contacting us – I'd volunteered to search among some boxes of old leads I had in the house to see if I could find something suitable. 'Hundred per cent battery,' I added. 'I knew that old junk would come in handy one day.'

'This is very good of you,' she said, as we set off. I couldn't help thinking it was, a little, and that it really wasn't like me to get involved with other people.

The main road north out of the village leads to Wigton and eventually the Solway coast, but we weren't going anything like that far. A little over two miles after we left the last house behind, we turned off along the single track road that leads only to Gathering Hall.

I'd been watching Anna closely as we drove – without appearing to do so, obviously, I'm not a complete amateur – but I could see her eyes in the reflection of the windscreen, a little wider than seemed entirely natural and a crease line between her brows, while her hands gripped the wheel.

I hummed a little tune as we went, so as to appear quite at ease, but stopped when I sensed from Anna's tensed shoulders that she was finding it annoying. We were allies tonight, and I'd do well to remember it, but old habits die hard.

'Wow.' She spoke for the first time as we approached Gathering's main entrance. 'Bit over the top.'

She had a point. The front gates are tall and heavy, wooden, but of a very solid construction that is impossible to see through, and electronically controlled. In front of the gatekeeper's hut – yes, there is one of those – stood a well-built young man with a military air. I don't mean that he was dressed in fatigues, of course, that would be absurd, even by the church's standards, but his trousers and sweater were khaki in colour and he practically stood to attention as we pulled up.

'Catering tent's by the lake,' he told Anna, after she'd explained the reason for our visit. 'Turn right at the first road fork and carry on for a hundred yards. You'll see the blue and yellow bunting.'

The gates slid open and we drove inside along a makeshift road, its surface lined with matting to combat the mud.

The park still looked like a festival, although one tends to associate them with summer and long evenings, whereas the sky was already darkening around us. The site had huge floodlights, the sort you might see at an athletics track or football stadium, but none were alight as yet. Ahead of us stood a large central marquee. Closer to it now than when I'd been by the lake, I could see that several other marquees adjoined it, creating a sort of pavilioned city. A few delivery vans remained, and there hovered over the ground a sense of urgency, as though the people around us were running out of time.

We approached a fork in the road.

'There's the catering tent.' Anna was looking downhill towards another marquee, separate from the main structure and more colourful, being festooned with bunting and balloons.

'If that's the way you want to play it,' I said.

Her foot eased back on the accelerator. 'What do you mean?'

'We're here to look around,' I replied. 'We could, perhaps, mistake our way?'

A tiny smile broke the serious expression on Anna's face and she veered left, heading for the entrance to the main marquee. Without another word we pulled up and got out of the car.

Men were working around us, erecting some sort of structure above the entrance that I guessed would eventually hold a fascia board. An electrician and his mate were trying to control a mass of cable that we had to step over. The way into this tented city would be huge eventually, impactful and imposing, but for now, the plastic flaps hung limply.

'Help you, love?' someone called down at us.

'Caterers,' I replied, before Anna could speak. 'The chap at the gate sent us.' Without waiting for a response, I lifted one flap and gestured that Anna should enter. She stepped ahead and stopped dead. A man, slim, dark-haired, dressed in black jeans and sweatshirt, blocked her way.

'Authorised personnel only.' His eyes narrowed as he looked from Anna to me. 'Are you even supposed to be on site?'

I let Anna answer. I couldn't see much over the man's shoulder – the interior was dimly lit – but he seemed to be guarding the entrance to an English pub. I caught sight of classic pub furniture: a bar with optics, stacks of glasses and bottles on shelves, a jukebox, even signs directing us to the toilets, the smoking area and the beer garden.

The bouncer on the door pointed silently towards the catering tent and we had no choice but to step back. Only when we were several paces away did he retreat back inside.

'Worth a try,' I said to Anna, whose face had tightened.

To my surprise, she said, 'Let's have a walk around.'

I didn't have a problem with that, and so we set off around the marquee's perimeter. We soon passed another possible way in, flaps of plastic tied up loosely to create a doorway, but neither of us could muster the courage to try again.

As we turned the first corner we were startled by a sudden burst of rock music. I didn't recognise it – well, I wouldn't, I never listen to popular music – but from the volume, the incoherent lyrics and the heavy bass beat of the drums, I imagined it to be the sort of music played at what young people call raves.

Between the side of the marquee and the lake was a narrow stretch of unlit land; clearly no one was expected to come down here after dark. We walked on hesitantly, as the ground beneath our feet grew indistinct and ahead of us loomed an annexe, a compact box standing at a right angle to the main structure. A white van was parked directly outside it and several power leads stretched from van to marquee. As we drew closer, we could hear voices and the low hum of an electricity generator.

I led Anna around the van, taking care on the damp ground as we were close to the lake by this stage. As we rounded its bonnet, we caught a glimpse inside the annexe. Desks ringed the small space, each holding computer monitors. More men in black sat in front of them, most wearing headphones.

'Tech centre,' I whispered to Anna, beckoning her on. The marquee ended a few metres further.

'What on earth is going on in there?' Anna whispered back.

I held up a finger to my lips. I'd heard something on the other side of the wall. Beckoning Anna closer, I pressed my ear against it.

'What do you want?' It was a woman's voice. A very young woman. Maybe just a girl.

'Just some company, Hayley,' a boy replied, but the arrogance of his tone belied the humility of his words. 'Shouldn't be a problem for you.'

'I have to get home. Let me get past, please.'

'Don't be like that, Hayley.' A different male voice.

'It's not like we want anything you haven't done before.' A third boy.

'Don't touch me!'

'What the hell?' Anna said to me, no longer bothering to keep her voice low.

'Thinks she gets to pick and choose.' I thought that was the first boy again, but it was hard to be sure. All three voices had taken on a hungry, menacing tone.

'We're not going to hurt you, Hayley.'

'Unless you want us to.'

'Stop it. Get off me.'

'Whoa! She's feisty.'

A scuffle. Then a scream.

Anna slapped hard on the tent wall. 'What's going on in there? I'm calling the police.'

'This way.' I grabbed her hand and pulled her towards where I'd spotted another way in. As I struggled to unlace the opening, Anna continued shouting. 'Hayley, we're coming. Don't you dare hurt her.'

'Can I help you both?'

Recognising the voice, I felt like a child again, caught by the headmaster in an act of wrongdoing. As Anna and I turned in its direction, we saw Aran North coming towards us.

'Anna,' he said. 'How nice. I'm afraid you were misdirected. The catering tent is by the lake.'

'We heard screaming,' Anna pointed out. 'It sounded like a girl was being attacked in there.'

'You heard actors,' North replied. 'Final rehearsal. Absolutely nothing to worry about.'

'This is a production?' Anna looked incredulous.

'Opening night, no less,' North went on, gesturing that we should turn back the way we'd come. 'Which is why things are a bit hectic and you weren't looked after properly. I'll have someone escort you to the right tent.'

'What sort of production?' Anna asked, as we made our way back along the lake edge.

'Church event,' he said, vaguely. 'Hurry up, Paige, you should be in make-up.'

A young girl came rushing towards us. Her clothes had been torn, revealing much of her bra and upper body. Other than a little flustered, presumably at her lateness, she didn't seem at all concerned by her state of apparel.

'Perhaps we can buy tickets?' I said, although I knew perfectly well no one from outside the church had ever been to a performance of the Ingathering.

'Sold out months ago, I'm afraid,' North replied, without looking at me. He called a passing girl. 'Sandy, please take Miss Brown and her assistant to the catering tent. Stay with them until they leave.'

Having dispensed with us, he stepped away, moving backwards. 'Excuse me, I'm wanted at the house. Thank you so much, Anna. Please leave your bill before you go. We like to settle promptly.'

'This way,' said our new minder, Sandy, as North walked away.

'Theatrical production?' Anna muttered to me, as we followed Sandy back to the car. 'Bit dark, wouldn't you say? And why would they need so much space?'

'I believe the audience move from one scene to the next,' I replied. 'Or so village gossip has it. But I agree. It hardly seems a Christmas pantomime.'

When we got back to the car, Sandy reached for the rear door handle, obviously intending to travel down with us.

'Actually, there's stuff on the back seat,' I lied. 'Can we follow you down there? It's not far.'

Sandy shrugged and set off down the path, looking back after several paces to make sure we were following.

'Sorry about the assistant thing,' Anna said, when we were both in the car again. 'He knows you're not my assistant.'

'Oh, I'm having a thoroughly good time,' I replied, and surprised myself a little to realise it was true. 'Don't worry on my account.'

'No sign of Constance.' Anna glanced down at the girl's phone and, right on cue, it began to ring. I reached for it and stopped.

'She won't want to talk to me,' I said.

Sandy had arrived at the catering tent and was indicating that we should pull up to one side of the entrance. Anna did so and turned off the engine; I made sure the car doors were locked. Sure enough, Sandy walked around to the tailgate and tried to open it.

'Hello?' Anna said into the phone. 'Constance?'

She held the phone at an angle, so that I too could hear what was being said.

Sandy rapped on the tailgate; we ignored her.

'I'm using my mum's phone,' Constance said. 'I haven't got long. Where are you?'

'On site. By the catering tent.'

A pause, during which Sandy rapped again. Then, 'Too many people,' Constance said. 'Can I come and find you tomorrow?'

Anna and I shared a look. I gave her a nod.

'Of course,' Anna said, 'I should be free by four if you want to talk properly.'

The line went dead. Constance was gone.

It took an hour to set up the buffet table, and my first lesson as a caterer's assistant was that I should not, under any circumstances, call it a buffet table. Naively, I'd imagined trays of sandwiches and sausage rolls, maybe a few vol-au-vents for the more sophisticated and crisps for the children, but the table we created in that large, chilly tent was nothing short of a work of art.

The first thing Anna did was to throw away the shiny paper the church had used to cover the line of trestle tables and replace it with red gingham cotton cloths of her own. And then she began sculpting.

A great round of parmesan cheese formed the centrepiece, surrounded by towers of artisan breads, cheese straws and savoury biscuits, all of which Anna had made herself. After that, the table was scattered with miniature rosemary plants in earthenware pots. A whole brie was covered in a runny, golden honeycomb, another in a compote of fruits of the forest, and in total I counted over a dozen different kinds of cheese, some of them brittle and veined like marble, others so soft they pooled over the wooden boards. Miniature pork pies and Anna's signature sausage rolls lay like wonderful surprises among stacks of gleaming, sliced vegetables. Tiny terracotta pots held savoury butters, oils and dips, while clusters of grapes, so full and plump they looked ready to burst out of their skins, lolled over platters of cured meats, sausage and smoked fish. Olives of every description gleamed like jewels in crystal dishes while dried fruits and nuts lay scattered like pebbles on a beach. By the time we'd finished, the red gingham was invisible beneath a mass of delicious things to eat, and the entire tent smelled of herb gardens, of summertime, of old wine and new bread. The whole affair looked a little like an explosion in a delicatessen and a lot like an old master's painting. I was informed by a smiling Anna, when an admiring crowd had gathered around us, that it was known as a grazing table.

'More sociable than a buffet,' she said, as we found a moment to catch our breath. 'With buffets people load up their plates and disperse. With this, they have to keep coming back and chatting.'

There were no plates or forks. It was finger food only, primitive and completely unhygienic. I hadn't the remotest desire to take part in something so unhealthy, and yet I didn't ever want to take my eyes off it.

'Did you clear it with Aran North?' I suspected Anna might find herself in a whole load of trouble for her unorthodox approach to catering and wasn't really sure how I felt about it. I enjoy trouble, as a rule, especially if I'm not directly involved, but Anna had worked hard. And it really was so very, very fine.

She didn't seem concerned. 'I did. He agreed it might be fun.'

Someone from the church was approaching us: an older woman we hadn't seen before, who informed us that she was the church treasurer.

'Your money.' She handed over a fat envelope to Anna. 'Would you like to count it?'

Anna took it. 'No, I'm sure it's OK.'

'It looks wonderful,' the treasurer said, without so much as glancing at the food. 'We need to clear the site now. Can I walk you to your car?'

We'd been given our marching orders. We let her lead us out of the tent, only to be waylaid at its entrance by Hugh Gardner, of all people, in full fireman's uniform. It always looked to me like fancy dress, but it gave him a superficial authority that I imagine came in useful at times.

'They told me I'd find you here.' He gave me a quick nod and smiled at Anna. Then he looked over her head – he was a tall man – at the food.

'Bloody hell,' he said. 'Looks amazing.'

'You know your way out?' The church treasurer was at Anna's car by this time, practically clutching the door handle.

'Official business,' Anna said to Gardner. It wasn't really a question; why else would he be here in full uniform?

He nodded over at the big marquee and I noticed a queue had formed. 'Even this lot can't open without a fire safety certificate. They only finished set-up a few minutes ago. Pretty elaborate this year.'

'We need to clear the site now,' the treasurer called. She wasn't much more than three yards away but still felt the need to raise her voice. 'Even you, Mr Gardner.'

'I'm not leaving till I've checked the bonfires,' Gardner told her. 'They're a bit close to the trees for my liking, and I'm not happy with the direction of the wind.'

As Madam Treasurer pulled a radio out of her pocket I turned towards the lake. Against a paler background – the lake was west of us and there was still a smear of light in the sky – I could see a line of bonfires, standing like beacons, around the water's edge.

'Is the wind direction in your power to change?' I asked Gardner.

'The lighting – or not – of the bonfires is,' he replied as he set off towards them. 'Good seeing you both.'

'Why don't we keep Mr Gardner company?' I said to Anna, setting off after him without waiting for an answer.

The fallen horse chestnut tree was very visible from the angle at which we were approaching. A stretch of illuminated tape made an irregular circle around it and a tractor had been abandoned nearby, as though someone had tried to drag the tree from the lake and given up.

'The Minister's on his way,' the treasurer called after us.

'We're going to be quite the party,' I quipped. Anna, with a packet of money in her hand, was less inclined to annoy the church. She looked troubled.

'Maybe we should—' she began.

'How are the boys?' I asked Gardner. 'I haven't seen them for a while.'

'But then you've been laid up,' he replied, striding ahead. 'They're fine. Thanks for asking.'

'Sons?' Anna on his other side was struggling to keep up, and I wondered if she'd noticed that Gardner, up at Gathering Hall, was far from his usual ebullient self.

'Two,' I replied for him. 'Keen footballers. Aged about six and—'

'Seven and twelve,' Gardner interrupted. 'Tom and Jerry. And yes, that was deliberate, my ex-wife thought it'd be sweet. They're good kids.'

'Are you bracing yourself for the dreaded teenage years?' I asked.

Gardner stopped short, bringing me to a halt too. 'What's that supposed—?'

He was interrupted by his mobile phone ringing. He pulled it from his breast pocket and turned away.

'Yeah, I'm down there now,' he said into the phone. 'Well, it will take as long as it takes.'

Anna nudged my arm and nodded back towards the car. 'Maybe we should . . . '

I agreed that we should, and so we left Gardner, staring out across the water, arguing with someone on the telephone. He didn't seem to notice us leaving.

'Nice to be paid so quickly,' Anna said as we drove away from the catering tent. 'You must let me give you something for your trouble.'

She was offering to pay me.

'Goodness no.' I had no objection to money, I rather liked it in fact, but this had been about getting Anna in my debt. 'It was my pleasure.'

We reached the fork in the road from where we could see the main entrance to the big marquee. An elaborate fascia had been erected around it but, frustratingly, the lights above it hadn't yet been turned on and I couldn't read what the massive sign said.

'They're batshit, aren't they?' Anna said.

'Not an expression with which I'm overly familiar but on balance, I'd endorse the sentiment.'

She gave a soft laugh and muttered my name. 'You're a scream,' she added.

All in all, it had been a surprising, and not unfruitful evening, and as it turned out, it wasn't over; as we got out of the car to unload the trays and boxes, Anna turned to me.

'I've left a chilli in the oven,' she said. 'I knew we'd be back late. Please come and join me.'

It took me a moment to process what she'd said.

'It's the least I can do,' she went on. 'And we can talk about the Constance thing. About what our options might be.'

She was inviting me to dinner. Me, not Gardner. And I still couldn't get the sight of that abundance of food out of my head. Eating something that Anna had cooked rather than my planned poached egg on toast might go some way to satisfying the weird hunger that had been churning inside me all the way home.

'Well, if you're sure,' I said. She told me that she was, and so, arms laden again, I followed her inside.

The shop was largely empty; most of the cakes and pastries had been cleared away and the shelves and plates wiped clean. As we walked through to the kitchen, dishwashers were beeping. Anna opened them, filling the room with a light mist of warm steam.

'Working on anything interesting?' she asked me, as we unloaded boxes, and I was struck again by her empathetic approach. She genuinely seemed to care about people.

'Military history,' I replied. 'Japan and Burma in the Second World

War. A bit dry, but I prefer it that way. No danger of being distracted by the narrative.'

'Do you ever do fiction?'

I held a box for her to unload directly into the fridge. 'I prefer not. Fiction editors tend to send a lot of crime and that makes me queasy.'

She looked thoughtful for a moment, then, 'On that subject,' she said. 'Some more stuff has appeared on X.'

'The social media site formerly known as Twitter?' I queried. 'You've been, what do you say, googling again?'

'Here you go.' She handed her phone to me. I held it at arm's length – my near vision isn't too strong. Under the same account she'd shown me in the library, the one named Sweet Sixteen, more posts had appeared.

> *Are the #Sweet16s being groomed? Time to shut the Ingathering down, once and for all. Terrorising teens is child abuse.*

'Who's writing this stuff?' I asked. 'Who's behind this, what do you call it, an account?'

'No way for us to know. If you want me to guess, I'd say someone up at the hall, someone who's less than enthusiastic about being there.'

'But afraid to speak out publicly,' I said, my attention moving down to the next post. 'One of the youngsters maybe. Even Constance herself.'

> *How to avoid the Ingathering. A survival guide in ten posts. Follow the hashtag #DontLetItBeYou*

I put my finger on the hashtag and it took me to a stream of related posts.

1 *Contract Covid. Still a sure-fire way of avoiding undesirable social occasions. Positive tests available from the website. #DontLetItBeYou*

2 *Broken limb. Bit more extreme, and probably needs to be a leg. That said, there is talk of wheelchair accessibility this year. Last resort? #DontLetItBeYou*

3 *Run away. Hell to pay when you get back, but you know what they say – lesser of two evils. #DontLetItBeYou*

4 *Buddy up. Never be alone. Unless the buddy is the one out to get you. #DontLetItBeYou*

5 *Family death. OK, getting extreme now, but when it comes to it, it's Granny or you. #DontLetItBeYou*

I'd got the idea. I gave the phone back to Anna.

'There's a website too,' she said. 'Not that I could exactly access it. Look.'

This time the phone screen displayed the home page of a website with the heading 'St Abel's Chapel', only the word 'Chapel' had been crossed out and replaced with 'Hell'. An image taking up the top third of the screen was unmistakably a photograph of the village. The church, the last few shops of the high street, the library were all visible, along with a distant line of forested hills. In the bottom corner of the image a devil's mask had been superimposed. Below the image a single line of text read: *This site has been moved to the dark web for security reasons*.

'Dark web?' I asked Anna.

'A sort of underground internet. Some very dodgy stuff on it. I've no idea how to access it.' She smiled. 'No point asking you, I suppose.'

It was surprisingly easy to smile back. 'None at all.'

Anna served the chilli with brown rice, a green salad and a mixture of onion, tomato and avocado that she called a salsa. I tried it, gingerly; I'm not good with exotic food and nearly gasped as the flavours of lime, pepper and chilli hit the inside of my mouth. I turned down her offer of wine and was curious to notice that she drank her own glass rather quickly. While we ate, Constance's phone sat on the table between us.

'A teenage girl, pregnant and terrified of telling her family,' Anna said after a few moments.

'Seems the logical conclusion,' I replied. 'But they may already know. They can't have missed those bandages on her wrists.'

'Children of that age often can't see beyond the immediate problem,' Anna went on. 'They've no real concept of the rest of their lives, how much time they have, the extent to which things can change. They see a problem – that might be sizeable – and assume that because they can't see a way around it, there isn't one.'

'In theory, a teenage pregnancy is a problem that can be solved quite easily,' I said.

'Not if you're from a very religious family,' Anna replied.

'Fair point. Of course, she may not be pregnant. Buying a test indicates a suspicion, not confirmation.'

'I guess we'll find out tomorrow. She seemed determined to speak to us.'

'To you,' I reminded her. 'I doubt she'll want to talk to me.'

'Maybe not.'

'And you'll have to respect her confidence,' I said. 'Client confidentiality and all that.'

Anna's face, that had been so open and pleasant the whole evening, seemed to close at that. 'She's not a client. Why would you say that?'

I feigned a shrug. 'No reason. Figure of speech. I don't expect you to share with me anything Constance tells you. Unless there's anything I can do to help her, of course.'

I was getting rather good at this. And I had no fear of missing out on whatever Constance was going to tell Anna. There wasn't a room in Anna's house, never mind what I supposed I was going to have to start calling the courtyard, where a conversation wouldn't be perfectly audible in my house. And even if they did lower their voices, or play loud music, I had a few tricks up my sleeve.

Four o'clock in the afternoon, they'd agreed upon. I'd be ready well before then.

'Was it my imagination or did Hugh seem uneasy up at the hall?' she asked.

'Uneasy in what way?'

'As though he wasn't entirely comfortable with what was going on. He looked tense. As though expecting someone to jump out at him any moment.'

'It would be a brave person, not to mention a large one, who jumped out at Hugh Gardner.'

She laughed. 'You're right. He just seemed on edge, somehow.'

'He certainly didn't like my mentioning his children,' I agreed. 'Which is odd, because in my experience people normally like nothing more than talking at length about their offspring.'

'I take it you don't have any?' she asked.

'Goodness no. I'd make a terrible parent. Far too selfish and set in my own ways.'

'Not sure I believe that. Not the first part, anyway.'

At that moment, something crashed outside Anna's back door. She and I turned to each other.

'Wind?' she suggested. I noticed she didn't move.

I got up and walked to the back door. The light switch was adjacent to the door frame and without asking permission I switched off the kitchen light. Anna's courtyard was in darkness but the moon had risen and the night was unusually clear for October. As my eyes adjusted, I found I could see tolerably well.

The wrought-iron chairs had been stacked so that Anna could sweep the area, the sunshades folded and fastened down. Several large pots with assorted plants stood around, but none appeared to have been knocked over. Everything looked exactly as it should. Except for—

'How likely is it that the wind opened the door of your summer house?' I asked Anna.

'Not very. I bolt it at night.'

'In that case, there's someone in there.'

14

April, the previous year

'Jago, you've mentioned hearing voices three times that I'm aware of. To the police, following the incident in the cafeteria, to your stepmother, and to some of the boys in your house room at school.'

She waited for a reaction. Nothing. He was looking down at the unthreatening magazines on the coffee table but had resumed the unnatural stillness he sometimes adopted. Without eye contact, it was even more unnerving; almost as though he was slipping into the catatonic state the police had reported.

'Three occasions,' she went on. 'And yet, whenever I ask, you claim to remember nothing about it.'

He looked up then, but past her, out of the window. They'd already established that the blinds would be open that day.

'You're a very intelligent young man,' she said. 'And from things you've said to me already, I'm pretty sure you've been googling the psychiatric process.'

His mouth tightened. It was a small response, but she registered the flash of acknowledgement.

'So, I'm sure you know that hearing voices is a sign of certain mental disorders. Are you frightened of me diagnosing you with a condition?'

He pulled a *whatever* face. 'It's what my dad wants. You tick a box, stuff me up with pills and problem solved. I go back to school and he can forget about me again.'

Oh, so much to unpack.

'Your dad wants you to be well again. So do I. And conditions can be treated. Even if you are diagnosed, and we're a long way from that, there's help available.'

'Zombie drugs, you mean? Medicate me till there's nothing left of me inside.'

'That's the last thing anyone wants. Frankly, at this stage, I'm some way from any sort of diagnosis, let alone a treatment plan. And that's how we'll stay, until you decide to open up.'

He leaned forward, forearms on his thighs. He always sat close to her armchair and as he approached her personal space, she had to force herself not to inch backwards.

'What if there's nothing you can medicate?' he asked, with a sly smile. 'What if I'm – you know – evil?'

She swallowed and he saw her do it. His smile widened. Then he seemed to spasm, his shoulders jerking up, his head dropping, hands coming to his face.

'Shit, shit.'

'Jago, what's wrong?'

He stood up. 'Something in my eye. Jesus, it's really stabbing.'

'OK, you need to rinse it. Let's get you to the toilets.' She reached out and touched his arm, relief flooding through her. For a moment there . . . but dust in the eye she could deal with. With luck, there'd be a male member of staff outside who could accompany him into the toilets.

'Can you look, please? It feels like glass.'

There was no way he could have glass in his eye. As he made agitated noises, she half ran to the jug of water and poured a glass, grabbing tissues on her way back.

'Rinse,' she instructed, as she pressed the glass into his hands. Rinsing his eye here would make a mess but he really did seem in a lot of pain. She was on the point of calling for her PA to come in when a red light on the phone system flashed on, telling her that the woman was engaged.

Tipping back his head, Jago poured water into his eye. It ran down his face, dampening the collar of his shirt.

'Shit, it's worse. It feels like my eye's bleeding. I can't see out of it.'

Reminding herself that some people were very sensitive about their eyes, she put the jug down, took hold of both his upper arms and twisted him towards the light. He allowed her to manoeuvre him.

'Hold still. Let me see.' Taking his face in her hands, she stood on tiptoe and angled his head downwards. The eye in question, his left, was damp and slightly red, but there was nothing in it that she could see.

Jago gave a soft moan and his arms clutched hers as he pressed closer. She tried to step back, but her armchair was in the way.

'No, I don't want to,' he yelled, and pulled away from her, at the same time kicking out, upturning the coffee table and sending the water jug flying.

Before it hit the carpet, he made for the door. He'd reached it as it opened from the outside.

'Annaliese, are you—' Her PA stepped back as Jago shot from the room, heading, she assumed, into the men's toilets. The PA took in the broken jug, the water damage, and then her eyes went to the window. Several people at the bus stop outside were staring in.

'What happened?' the PA said.

'I'm not quite sure,' she replied, and felt a cold sense of dread creeping over her.

15

'Don't go out.'

I'd turned the key, was on the point of pushing Anna's back door open when her cry stopped me. She was sitting bolt upright on her chair, her hands clutching the tabletop. Her face, always pale, had blanched.

'There's someone in your back garden, probably helping themselves to the contents of your summer house,' I reasoned. 'Are you happy to let them get away with that?'

'I probably did leave it open. Come to think of it, I did. I was in a rush, getting all the stuff for the church together. Leave it. Your food's getting cold.'

Well, either I was reading too much into the situation, or Anna was decidedly uneasy about someone being in her courtyard. I say 'uneasy', but that look on her face wasn't one I'd describe as unease; no, it was something altogether more interesting.

I peered out through the glass pane. The wind that had caused Gardner so much concern earlier was still very much in evidence; I could see the trees at the back of us bending and swaying and now that Anna had fallen quiet, I could hear it too, the peculiar moan of the Cumbrian autumn. The summer house door banged once, then a second time.

'Well, we can't leave it like that,' I said. 'It'll be blown off its hinges before morning. Not to mention keeping me awake half the night.'

Anna called my name as I opened the door; she really didn't want me to go outside.

'Won't be a moment,' I said cheerily, rather enjoying my masquerade as a person of courage.

I closed the back door behind me, no point in coming back to a cold kitchen, and hurried down the gravel path towards the summer house. The door slammed closed as I reached it. There were two bolts, top and bottom, and I bent to secure the first. It was only as I stood to reach for the upper bolt that I looked in. A summer house, of course, has large panels of glass and with my eyes used to the darkness, I could see inside quite easily.

The interior only had room for two small tables, and I could see both, each with its customary two chairs, but I was more interested in the pair of eyes, roughly two feet from the floor, in the far corner of the space. Before their crouched and frightened owner could move, I pulled the top bolt.

'Anna,' I called. 'Better call the police. I've trapped an intruder.'

The intruder, at that, jumped to her feet.

'Don't, please,' a voice called out, triggering an internal double-take on my part; so much so that my heart started hammering in my chest. The voice calling out to me was male. I'd trapped a man. I took a step back. I'd been positive the intruder – I never for a moment put the open summer house door down to the wind – had been young Constance who'd followed us from Gathering Hall and sneaked into Anna's yard. Had I known I was potentially confronting a man, I might have thought twice about leaving the house.

The male intruder – it was obvious now that he was on his feet – stepped towards the door. He moved slowly, as though determined not to appear threatening, but I took a step back all the same.

'What's going on?' Anna called from the doorway. 'Is there someone in there? I mean, for real?'

'He looks real to me.' I didn't take my eyes off the young man on the other side of the glass panel who, for his part, seemed equally fascinated with me. He looked to be in his late teens, and tall, maybe around six foot; but with that lanky thinness common to teenage boys. He'd be strong, post-pubescent boys usually are. I tried to remember, without looking around, how far it was to Anna's back door.

'He?' Anna said.

'A young man,' I called. 'Were you expecting one?'

If Anna replied I didn't catch it because our visitor had reached the summer house door. It bounced as he tried to open it and then he banged on the inside. I say 'banged', it was more of a tap. He gesticulated, his face contorted as he mouthed something and then realised he could use his voice.

'Open the door, please,' he said. 'I'm sorry. I didn't mean any harm.'

Fair play, as burglars go, this one was polite.

'He says he doesn't mean any harm,' I called back to Anna. 'I wonder what he was planning.'

Such a range of emotions flooding through me. I was still sweating at how close I'd come to a hostile encounter with a large, strong male and all my self-protective instincts were telling me to run. On the other hand, there was something about having another human trapped and at my mercy that was unnervingly satisfying. On a third hand – the unprecedented situation was making me entirely illogical – I wasn't sure how long Anna's summer house door would hold if the boy tried kicking it down. I took another step away and turned back to Anna.

'I think the police—' I stopped. Anna's face had changed. If I hadn't known it to be impossible, I'd have thought she'd died on her feet and that I was looking at her corpse. All colour had drained from her face, even allowing for the lack of light in the courtyard, and her cheekbones seemed on the point of bursting out through her skin. Her eyes were wide and unblinking.

'Is it someone you know?' I asked, knowing it had to be. A stranger, even one acting very eccentrically, wouldn't have caused this reaction.

She didn't reply and I realised she probably couldn't see the face in the window of the summer house, because it was some distance from where she stood, the courtyard was dark and, significantly, I was in the way. I stepped to one side, up against the fence, and watched her. By this time, I was more interested in Anna, I admit, than the boy in the summer house.

'Who is it?'

An odd question, I thought, given that I was pretty sure she already knew. On the other hand, it wasn't an unreasonable one in the circumstances and might actually move the rather interesting situation on.

'Who are you?' I called, before regretting moving so far away. I glanced up at Gardner's upper floor. The last thing I wanted was for him to come outside and take over. His lights were out, though, and there was a chance he was still checking bonfires up at Gathering Hall.

'I'm a friend of Connie's,' the boy in the summer house said. 'Constance. I'm looking for her.'

From behind me came the sound of someone letting out a breath and then that of footsteps on the gravel. I turned back to see Anna had relaxed, her face losing some of that horrible tightness. She came up close and peered around my shoulder.

'I can't make him out.' She almost seemed to be hiding behind me. 'What does he look like?'

Well, I could hardly ask him that, and in the dim light of the summer house it was impossible to make out any detail.

'What's your name?' I moved a little closer so I wouldn't have to shout. 'And why are you here?'

'My name's Connor Graham. Please let me out.'

Anna reached me. 'It's OK,' she said. 'I've no idea who he is. You can let him out.'

Well, the logic of that rather escaped me but I, too, was coming around to the idea that this boy was no threat. I unbolted the door.

'I'm really sorry,' he said, when he stood in the open doorway facing us. 'I didn't mean to frighten you.'

'I wonder what you did mean?' I said.

He looked puzzled. I forget, sometimes, that I supposedly have rather an old-fashioned way of speaking.

'Why are you in my summer house?' Anna said. Unsurprisingly, it was her question that got answered.

'Someone in the pub told me Connie's been seen in your shop a lot.' The boy rubbed his eyes and I noticed that his face looked both shadowed and gaunt, as though he'd been ill. His clothes seemed damp. 'I thought she might be here,' he went on.

At that, he reached into his jacket and pulled out a wallet, fiddling with it for a second before holding it out, open. Anna leaned forward, and then I did too, and we both saw a picture of two young people, heads close together, pouting at the camera. They were both very obviously Constance and the boy in front of us.

'You thought you'd find her in a dark garden?' I asked.

Anna put a hand on my arm. 'How do you know Constance?' she said.

'She's my girlfriend.'

In the nick of time, I stopped myself making eye contact with Anna.

'Except, her parents don't like me,' the boy went on. 'She doesn't know I'm here, but I'm worried about her. I'm really sorry I frightened you, but do you know where I'll find her?'

'I think you'd better come in,' Anna replied.

Back in the kitchen Anna reheated both our plates and served a third to Connor whom she insisted join us at the table. He didn't smell too good and I managed to resist moving my chair away from him. Curious to see how this would unfold, I wasn't about to do anything that would put his back up.

'When did you last eat?' Anna asked, when he'd polished off most of his plate.

'Sorry,' he said. 'I was starving.'

'I think you need to tell us your story,' I said, and Anna touched my hand. She was a very tactile person, I'd decided, and I still wasn't sure whether I minded. I wasn't used to being touched.

'Finish your food first,' she corrected. 'And take your jacket off. It looks soaked.'

We were treated to another whiff of Connor's body odour as he pulled off his wet jacket, but Anna didn't seem to notice. Maybe she was better at hiding it.

'Where have you come from?' I asked, while Anna was serving him another helping.

He named a town in Sussex. 'Connie and her family live there too,' he added. 'We're at school together.'

'Connor and Constance,' I remarked. 'Do friends call you The Two Connies?'

He gave me a blank look.

'Tough crowd,' Anna said. 'I got it.'

My making jokes, albeit not terribly well received, was not the least surprising element of the evening.

'Did you travel alone?' I asked. In the better light of the kitchen, the boy was even younger than I'd thought and Sussex to Cumbria is a long way.

'I hitched.' He looked down at the table as he admitted it, a child waiting for two adults to tell him off. 'I had to walk the last few miles.'

'And when was this?' I asked. 'It hasn't rained today, so I can't imagine how your jacket came to be so damp if you travelled today.'

'I came yesterday,' he admitted. 'My phone's out of charge so I couldn't contact Connie.'

'Hand it over,' I said, getting to my feet. 'It's the same model as Connie's, isn't it?' I added when he looked affronted. 'I have a charger that works. I'll plug it in. Shouldn't take too long.'

'Do your parents know where you are?' Anna was asking when I returned, a short while later.

Connor shook his head. 'There's only Mum. She's used to me staying over with friends.'

Anna met my eyes and I knew what she was thinking: so now we had another child to be concerned about. I hoped she didn't know what I was thinking: that this had started out as an interesting diversion but was close to getting out of hand. I mean, this boy, Connor, would need somewhere to sleep tonight.

'Why are you worried about Constance?' Anna asked, with a sideways glance at me.

The boy's eyes fell. 'Did I say that? I meant, I don't know where she is.'

'She's at the church camp up at Gathering Hall. A couple of miles outside the village,' Anna said.

Connor stopped eating. 'Have they started that weird thing they do?'

'Do you mean the Ingathering?' I asked.

'Why do you say it's weird?' Anna asked.

Connor's eyes dropped again.

'Can you tell us anything about it?' I asked.

He shook his head. 'I'm not part of the church. I only know Connie was worried about it. She said it's some weird shit. Sorry to swear.'

'I can drive you up there,' Anna offered. 'Are you planning to stay with Constance's family?'

Reluctantly, it seemed, Connor put his fork down. He hadn't quite finished his meal. 'No worries,' he said. 'I can find it.'

'You won't be allowed in,' I said. 'Their security is very tight.'

'Connor, do you have anywhere to stay tonight?' Anna asked.

He reached for his jacket. 'Thanks for the meal,' he said. 'I'm sorry to have bothered you.'

His hand was on the door when Anna stopped him. 'You can sleep in the summer house,' she said. 'I'll find a sleeping bag for you. And you can turn on the heater. It won't be comfortable but better than the alternative.'

Connor looked from Anna to me.

'We know you've been sleeping rough,' Anna said. 'And it really isn't the weather for it. I'll drive you to the station tomorrow after you've seen Constance.'

'I'm going to see her now,' he said. 'But thanks. I appreciate it.' He nodded at both of us and went out into the night.

'That was rash,' I said to Anna. 'Inviting him to stay here.'

'He's a child,' she said. 'I feel bad making him sleep outside. And we should have told him we have Constance's phone. He won't be able to call her.'

I took a moment to ask myself if I too felt bad. I certainly felt uncomfortable at the thought of Connor in Anna's shed but wasn't sure whether it was down to concern over him, or unease at having a strange male hanging around.

'He definitely won't be able to call her,' I reminded Anna. 'His phone's charging up in my house.'

Silence for a moment.

'I'll bet he doesn't know about the shortcut either,' I said.

She looked at me, puzzled.

'It will take thirty minutes to get to Gathering Hall the back way, via the lake,' I explained, although I was a little surprised she hadn't realised this herself. 'Over an hour on the roads if he's walking.'

'I should go after him.' She started looking around, as though to find her keys.

'And be on your own in a car with a man you don't know?' I replied. 'Is that wise? And we don't even know if his story's true. Constance may not want him to find her.'

She looked chastened. 'You're right, I shouldn't go after him by myself. And I'm not taking you, before you offer. You've done enough tonight. You need to rest.'

I hadn't been about to offer, but I didn't contradict her. 'Do you think he'll come back?' I asked.

'Well, I hope not, because if he doesn't, it probably means Constance's family have taken him in, but from what I've seen of them, that doesn't feel very likely. So yes, I think he'll come back. I'll dig out some warm stuff and put some more food out there.'

'You can't invite him into your house,' I said. 'You don't know anything about him.'

She shuddered as she began to clear the remnants of the meal away. 'I know,' she said. 'You don't have to do that,' she added, when I opened one of the dishwashers and began to unload the clean crockery from inside.

'You have to be up in the small hours,' I said. 'Even without unexpected guests, you've a lot on at the moment.'

'The church has asked me to cater another function at the weekend,' she said. 'A private dinner party up at the house.'

'I'm at your service, if you need assistance.'

'I'm sorry,' she said. She was smiling at me.

'What for?' I asked.

'For not realising at first how kind you are.'

Interesting. I should have felt gratified at that. It was proof of how well my plan to inveigle my way into Anna's trust was working, but my actual physical response was quite different. To be honest, and I usually am with myself, I felt something akin to guilt.

'So, the father of Constance's baby,' I said, to move the conversation on. 'I wonder if he knows she's pregnant.'

'If Constance has only just found out herself, he may not.'

'Except he said he was worried about her,' I replied. 'And judging by his manner, I'd say his fear was genuine. So, if he doesn't know about the pregnancy, what else would he be concerned about?'

16

April, the previous year

Annaliese looked up to see her PA in the doorway, raincoat around her shoulders. It was a few minutes after five; she'd be on her way home for the evening.

'Got a minute?' the PA asked.

She pressed save on the document she'd been working on and said, 'Sure.'

The PA sidled her way around the half-open door. 'Do you mind me asking what happened here today?'

For a moment, she was puzzled, then, 'You mean with Jago Moore?'

A troubled nod.

'He got something in his eye. No idea what. To be honest, it looked like a serious overreaction but people can be sensitive about eyes.'

Jago hadn't returned to resume their session after the eye incident. A male member of staff had followed him into the toilets, ascertained that whatever had caused the eye irritation had gone and that Jago, physically, appeared fine. The boy had declined to return, though, saying he wasn't feeling well and he'd left without speaking to her again. She'd scheduled a phone call to his home to double-check everything was OK and would be making it in the next hour.

The PA said, 'It's just, I asked him, when he was on his way out, how his eye was and he told me there was nothing wrong with his eye.'

Something told Annaliese to tread carefully. 'He went from being perfectly OK to apparently in a lot of pain very quickly. He was screaming about a piece of glass. I'm surprised you didn't hear him.'

'I heard him yelling that he didn't want to, and then the jug breaking. What was it he didn't want to do?'

'I imagine he didn't want me poking around in his eye, even though he'd asked me to look, and I had no intention of touching it. What's this about, Lou?'

The PA seemed to think for a moment, and then dug into her raincoat pocket. 'He dropped this,' she said. 'On his way out. I called after him but he didn't hear me and I couldn't leave the desk. So, I picked it up, in case it was important.'

She took what her PA was offering. A Post-it note, square and yellow, the same size and colour she kept on her desk. On it was written her home address.

She looked up. 'Jago dropped this?'

'It fell out of his pocket. Annaliese, why would he have your home address?'

'Very good question. There's no way he should have it.'

'And yet he did.'

The PA waited for her to say something else, but there was nothing to say. She had no idea, at all, how – or why – Jago would have her home address.

17

I didn't leave Anna's house until the kitchen had been made ready for the following morning, the summer house converted into a den for Connor – with snacks, a warm drink and a fully charged mobile phone – and I'd been confirmed as Anna's new best friend. It wasn't easy, but I'd made a point of not asking questions, either about herself or what she thought of The Two Connies. I had a feeling Anna would be more likely to confide in someone she believed wasn't overeager for gossip.

I was tired by the time I got in, and more than a little feverish, but even then I was distracted by the orange glow in the night sky above Gathering Hall. The autumnal smell of bonfires, not uncommon to late October nights, was very much in evidence too. In spite of Gardner's concerns, it seemed, the fires would be burning long into the night.

As I lay in bed, waiting for sleep to take me, I could hear Anna moving around beyond the dividing wall. More than once she walked along the short landing to the smaller bedroom, from the window of which she could see into the rear gardens. She was checking to see if Connor had returned. The dilemma the two young people had found themselves in was luring her like a magnet, one she might find impossible to resist.

For my part, the internal agonies of two careless youngsters weren't of particular concern, and I would only feign interest as long as it served my purpose. Far more intriguing was what I'd noticed of Anna's behaviour a couple of hours earlier. The facts, as I saw them, were these:

1. Anna greeted the news of a young male intruder with what I could only describe as terror.
2. Upon learning the identity of said intruder, Anna relaxed to the point of inviting him into her home for food and letting him sleep in her outbuilding.

Which rather begged the question: whom had she initially believed the young man to be?

I was on a last visit to the bathroom when I heard the sound of Anna leaving her house. My first thought was that Connor must have returned. I rushed to the window of my office but as I keep the door locked unless I'm in it, I was only just in time to see a small light making its way up the lane. My first thought, an unwelcome one, was that she was sneaking into Gardner's house under cover of night; she certainly wouldn't be the first female to do so. But the small light, a torch of course, continued its way up the lane past Gardner's house and on towards the lake.

A late swim? Another communication from Constance, with a request to meet by the lake? Neither seemed likely and it was well past ten o'clock. I told myself it was none of my business and went back to bed.

It was no use, though; all thought of sleep had gone. I'd made Anna Brown my business and it seemed she'd made the Church of the Ingathering hers. As I dressed and slipped out of my own back door, I remembered my advice to Anna earlier, about curiosity killing the cat. I was no longer sure, to be honest, whether she was the cat, or whether I was.

Stealing up the lane in her wake, I thought of a third possible reason why she'd left her house, drawn by the glow in the night sky and the occasional laugh or shout drifting on the wind. When you live alone, when your life is essentially shaped by solitude, you are drawn to the life of others in the way night insects are to bright lights. It's hopeless, of course. Peering through the window of a crowded pub doesn't make you part of the group laughing and joking inside; passing close to a couple laden with flowers and wine doesn't secure you an invitation to the dinner party they're heading for. We know all this, and yet there are times when the sense of life hovering out of reach is close to unbearable.

I believed, as I followed Anna up the lane that night, that it was an indefinable feeling in her own breast rather than anything external that was pushing her on towards the bonfires. I had the same urge myself. We were two children, drawn by the bright lights of the fairground.

Except, as I drew closer to the lake, I caught more snatches of sound: voices, calling out at volume, but whether in fear, anger or jubilation it was impossible to tell.

Reaching the woods, I looked in vain for Anna's torch. I pushed on until I reached the lake; I know the way and even among the trees there was enough moonlight. The shouting continued and by this time I could tell that it was coming from across the water.

I moved left, heading west around the lake. From this point on, I had to take care. The ground is uneven, covered with undergrowth, and at times the bank slopes steeply and can crumble. I'm not a great swimmer, was far from my fittest, and the last thing I needed was to find myself in deep water in the dark.

When Gathering Hall came into view, I could see the fires still burning, their flames reflected in the lake, and people on the bank. A lot of people. It was hard to make out what they were doing, but they didn't seem to be simply enjoying the bonfires. Even across the water I could sense an energy, an urgency. There was something of a palaver going on at Gathering. I wondered if perhaps it was Gardner's doing, that maybe he was trying to force the extinguishing of the fires.

I left the water's edge to circumnavigate a blackthorn tree and, seconds after getting back on track, spotted Anna. She was sitting on a flat bank, close to the lake but with a semi-surround of bushes and undergrowth that would effectively make her invisible from the opposite shore. She was watching the activity, not more than thirty metres from us, where people seemed about to take to the water.

Three men were climbing into a motorboat. One of them bent over the engine, another released a rope. At the same time the van we'd seen parked outside the tech tent reversed down to the water's edge. No sooner had it parked than figures pulled open the rear doors and began, rather frantically, to unload equipment.

'Anna,' I said, in a loud whisper. I didn't want to startle her, and I certainly didn't want the people on the opposite shore to hear me. I scared her all the same; she almost leapt to her feet.

'It's only me.' I joined her, crouched low. 'Don't get up, they'll see us.'

She moved aside to let me sit next to her.

'I think someone's in trouble in the water,' she whispered. 'I heard screams when I was putting the rubbish out, and people shouting, like they were panicking. That's why I came up.'

Anna's ears were sharper than mine; I'd heard no screams.

'Me too,' I said.

'There's a lot of kids on that site,' she said. 'I'm amazed emergency services haven't been called.'

I wasn't. The church had a habit of dealing with its own problems.

The boat had left the jetty by this time but seemed to be hovering by the fallen tree. People onshore called directions, but in a confused manner that must have been difficult to follow. I wasn't surprised when the boat stopped moving, the helmsman held up his hand for silence and then all three men on board shone torches around. Anna and I watched thin beams of yellow light dance around the surface of the lake, then up into the branches of the dead tree. The tree appeared to shiver, its branches rustling, as though struck by a sudden gust, although the night was still.

At that moment, the whole area was flooded with light. Outshining the torches by a thousandfold, a great spotlight lit up a huge swathe of the water and the fallen tree, to reveal . . .

Connor.

The foolish boy was in the tree. He was standing on one horizontal branch some ten metres from the bank and maybe three from the surface of the water. His arms were raised above his head, clutching another branch for balance. As we watched, he edged further out over the lake. The branch dipped, dangerously low, on the point of breaking.

'Connie!' he yelled. 'Connie, where are you?'

'What is he doing?' Anna half moaned beside me. 'What possessed him to climb that tree?'

'If you want me to guess, I'll go with trying to get away from someone.'

It was the only possible explanation. Connor must have clambered onto the trunk, possibly fleeing church security, and made his way out over the water. As an escape route it was deeply flawed, but people don't always think logically when they're panicking.

'What on earth did they do to frighten him that much?' Anna asked.

Ridiculous though it was, others seemed about to replicate what Connor had done. The spotlight showed two more figures on the tree, one crawling along the trunk towards the boy, the other some way further, upright, edging along a branch.

A branch that might hold one person's weight for a short while longer; it certainly wouldn't hold three.

'Get back!' Connor yelled at his pursuers. 'I'm not getting off here till I see Connie.'

Someone on the bank called for silence.

'I know you've got Connie!' the boy yelled. 'If you've hurt her I'll fucking kill the lot of you. Connie!'

He was almost hoarse with the effort of screaming, and every time he yelled, the branch supporting him bounced.

A collective gasp went up from the bank as Connor slipped and lost his balance. For a split second he looked certain to fall.

'We have to do something.' In the sudden silence Anna's voice sounded worryingly loud.

The boat, which had been still in the water for the last few minutes, changed direction and started to come our way. Anna twitched beside me, on the point of jumping to her feet.

'I'm letting Connor know we're here,' she said.

'You're that certain he'll trust us?' I whispered back. 'He's known us a matter of hours. Our getting involved might only add to the confusion.'

The boat, meanwhile, was definitely coming towards us. I put a hand on Anna's arm to steady her and she didn't object. The boat got closer, but luckily the torches remained fixed on the water's surface.

'Let's see how it plays out,' I urged. 'The important thing is for everyone to stay calm and get him down from there.'

I was pretending altruism; the truth was I had no desire for the church's attention to be refocused on me.

At that moment, a bird, startled from sleep, went scurrying off across the water. The boat slowed as the man on the helm put the engine into neutral.

'Keep still,' I whispered from the corner of my mouth, even as I wondered how fast I could run. 'The trees will hide us.'

They would unless someone shone a torch directly at us, but I didn't say that. Anna did what she was told, but I could feel her agitation. She wasn't naturally brave, I'd already decided, or maybe something in her past had frightened her badly.

The mob on the bank had grown tired of being quiet. They'd resumed talking, even shouting instructions at each other.

One torch beam shifted and missed us by feet. Had it been better aimed we'd have been caught, frozen like rabbits in a headlight, but instead it lit up a hazel tree a little to our left.

'I heard something,' one of the men in the boat said.

I had no idea why I was feeling so tense, why Anna was a quivering mass of nerves beside me; we hadn't done anything wrong. But there was something so underhand about the way the church people were behaving. Something secretive. And they were doing it, quite literally, under cover of darkness. They wouldn't take kindly to uninvited witnesses.

Hardly breathing, we watched the torch beams dance around, coming close enough at one point to land within inches of Anna's shoulder.

'Good!' yelled Connor, possibly in response to something called at him. 'Get the police. You lot are out of order, not me.'

'Hold it,' called the man in the bow. He stood up, rocking the boat dangerously. 'Anyone there?' he called, and yet again the torch beam came worryingly close to Anna and me. 'This is private property.'

I was half expecting Anna to argue with that, but she held her silence.

'Phil, what the hell are you doing?' called a voice from the shore. 'You need to get that lad out of the tree.'

Several seconds went by and then, finally, when I knew I had to release the breath I hadn't known I'd been holding, the torch beam fell. The man in the boat took his seat again and the engine sounded. It turned and moved back towards the tree. And Connor.

'Why aren't the police here?' Anna whispered. 'I'm calling them.'

'I want to see Connie.' Connor was still yelling, but his voice didn't sound as strong or as sure as it had. He was getting tired, or maybe running out of bravado.

'No signal,' Anna said in frustration. 'There must be up at the hall though. Why haven't they called for help?'

'The church like to handle things themselves. I agree, though. This isn't good.'

We watched the boat draw close to the point where the tree's uppermost branches touched the water and then, once more, the engine was switched off.

'Come on, lad,' one of the men in the boat called up. 'Let's get you down. No one's going to hurt you.'

'Liar! What have you done to Connie?'

The boat moved again, this time one of the men using an oar as a paddle. When they reached one of the wider branches, he grabbed it to steady the craft. Another began, slowly, to climb out.

'There's nowhere to go, lad.' He hauled himself upright and his weight seemed to pull the whole tree further into the lake. 'Either you get off here now or I come to get you. And then we both go in the water.'

He began to move towards Connor.

'And I'm wearing a life jacket. You're not.'

Connor backed away, further over the lake, along a branch that didn't look strong enough to hold him.

'I can't believe I'm seeing this,' Anna said.

At that moment, a second bird scuttled from its sleeping place at the water's edge and sped out of sight across the lake. I felt Anna start beside me. At the same time, the man in the tree strode forward.

And Connor went into the water.

18

April, the previous year

Jago's dad was waiting when he walked through the door. He was sitting in one of the easy chairs in the open-plan area, empty glass in hand. Bella was hovering nervously by the kitchen counter although it was clear from the order around her that nothing needed doing. As usual when there was something going down, she kept her eyes on the floor. She was a coward when it came to confrontation.

'Good evening.' Morgan got to his feet.

Twat.

Jago dropped his bag by the row of coat hooks. 'Alright,' he said.

'Been somewhere nice?'

He shrugged as he straightened up. 'Just hanging out.'

Morgan sighed. 'You know you can't be in touch with school friends. Not till things are sorted out.'

Jago crossed to the fridge and pulled open the door. He wasn't hungry, but it gave him something to do other than stand in front of his dad like a pet dog about to get a whipping. As usual it was full of all sorts of stuff they'd never get round to eating. 'I wasn't with people from school.'

'Who then?'

None of your bloody business.

'Just someone I know.'

'Who, Jago? You can't blame us for being concerned. You're in a lot of trouble.'

He gave up on the pretence of looking for something to eat and closed the fridge door, turning back to face his dad. 'It was Anna-liese, if you must know.'

For a moment, Morgan was lost, then, 'The psychiatrist?'

'Yeah, I bumped into her. We went for a walk. Lost track of time.'

Lying never normally bothered Jago – like most things, he was good at it – but he got an extra buzz from weaving a deceit without, technically, lying at all. He had bumped into Annaliese – had literally, physically and deliberately bumped into her – after he'd followed her from her office to the gym she visited several times a week.

She hadn't exactly been pleased to see him, but he wasn't about to tell his dad that. And he had gone for a walk. Behind her, out of sight. He'd followed her all the way home. After that, he'd hung around outside her house, waiting for a glimpse at a window. Only when the sky had started to grow dim had he given up and made for home.

'You bumped into her?' his dad said.

'She was coming out of her gym, on the Christchurch Road.'

An alarmed glance between Morgan and Bella. 'What were you doing down there? You're not even supposed to go out right now.'

He knew that. He was confined to home, other than essential trips. Of course, no one had actually defined an essential trip and as far as he was concerned, it was open to interpretation.

'Jeez, why don't you just put an ankle tag on me?' Leaving the room, he climbed the stairs, surprised at how weary he felt. He could hear his dad and Bella talking downstairs.

'Does that sound odd to you?' his stepmother was saying. 'Going for a walk with the psychiatrist?'

'Yes, it bloody well does. They shouldn't be meeting up outside scheduled sessions.'

'Do you think we should say something? There must be a professional body we can complain to. Well, not complain, exactly, just say we're concerned.'

'And start the whole process again. If we're lucky. If we're unlucky, the police lose patience and decide to charge him.'

He hadn't thought of that. *Shit.* Fortunately, Bella seemed to be onside. She said, 'We can't risk that.'

'It would help if I could see progress, but all they do is chat and fill out endless questionnaires. In the meantime, we have no clarity about his future.'

Bella said, 'They've got a couple more weeks.'

'And what's going to change in two weeks? Getting information out of that woman is like pulling blood from a stone.'

From the landing, Jago could hear movement, the clatter of glasses or crockery being moved around. Then his dad spoke again.

'When I pinned her down last week she said he's showing no real signs of psychosis.'

A second of silence.

'But that has to be a good thing, doesn't it?'

His dad's sigh was audible, even from the top of the stairs. 'Use your brain. If he gets expelled with a record of violence against a teacher no decent school will have him and believe me, that boy will not cope well with the local comprehensive. We can probably wave goodbye to Cambridge. To any half-decent university.'

As Jago listened to his father talk, his insides were turning cold. Barley Mead School in the next town was a joke, full of thickos, slags and losers. No way was he going there. Jeez, one moment when his self-control slipped, when he'd let his temper get the better of him. One mistake and his life was unravelling.

Bella said, 'You really think a mental health diagnosis and medication will make all the difference?'

The sound of liquid being poured. 'I'd say it's his only chance right now of getting his life back on track.'

19

As the sound of the tremendous splash died away, chaos erupted on the far bank and Anna jumped to her feet. I stayed where I was, transfixed by the scene in front of me.

With considerable presence of mind, the person operating the floodlight re-angled it so that the beam hit the surface of the water where Connor had fallen. It was still rippling out in concentric circles, but there was no sign of the boy himself. No movement beneath the surface, no hand reaching for a lifeline, no gasping face.

The three men in the boat – I'd have a moment to be amused by that when this was over – were all on their feet now, rocking the small craft dangerously, their torches darting about the lake surface.

'Lad!' one yelled. 'Where are you, lad?'

'Come on.' Anna jumped up and set off. She glanced back once to make sure I was following, but I had the feeling that whatever she was planning now, she'd be doing it with or without me. We were heading away from Gathering, towards . . . Oh heavens, towards the beach she used when swimming.

'Anna!' I struggled to catch up. 'I hope you're not thinking of going into the water yourself. It's far too dark, and we have no idea—'

'Of course I'm not,' she snapped. 'I'm calling the police. As soon as I get a signal. And an ambulance. If Connor makes it out of that lake – and it's a big if – he could be on the verge of hypothermia. He'll need medical treatment urgently.'

She was right, certainly about the chances of Connor getting out of the lake. He'd fallen, not into open water where he might have stood a chance, but among the numerous branches and leaves of the fallen tree's crown. It had been massive, at least thirty metres high, and with a crown of a similar width. It would only take one piece of clothing to catch on a branch and Connor could find himself unable to move. He'd plunged into a giant, underwater trap.

'Emergency services could already be on their way,' I said, as we reached the path. 'The church could have called them.' I'd no desire to see the boy drown, of course not, but I really didn't want to get involved with a police report.

'Do you hear any sirens?'

I didn't.

Anna looked at her phone again. 'Still nothing.'

I gave a soft yelp and clutched my side.

'Sorry.' Anna turned back. 'I forgot. You'll be OK, won't you? If I run ahead?'

She noticed, then, that my eyes had left hers and were looking over her shoulder. She turned, and the two of us confronted the huge male figure blocking our escape.

'Everything OK?' A light shone first into Anna's face and then mine, making the lane seem even darker. I recognised the voice though. It was Gardner, introducing me to an entirely new experience: that of being pleased to see him. Calming Anna's nerves over the past half hour had taken a lot of energy and I hadn't realised how much my own had been shredded. My first thought, I admit, as the dark figure came into view, was that we'd been spotted after all, and that the church had sent someone round for us. To do quite what, I had no idea.

It was only Gardner, though, back from work.

'No,' Anna said, before I could speak. 'Everything's not OK. I need to call the police.'

She filled him in quickly. He listened, looking occasionally at me to corroborate the story. I nodded and murmured when it seemed appropriate.

'And you didn't see the lad climb out?' he said, when she'd finished. 'Are you sure? It was dark. He could have made it to the bank.'

'Even if he did, he was terrified of those people,' Anna replied.

'That's why he was in the tree in the first place. He was trying to get away from them.'

'We don't know that for certain,' I said, earning a glare from Anna.

As we reached the houses, Anna made for her own back gate. Gardner stopped her, putting both hands on her shoulders in a way I wouldn't have dared.

'Hold on. Why don't I drive you into Penrith, you can make a report in person.' He glanced at me. 'You as well.'

'No,' Anna argued, turning my way. 'You're exhausted. You need to rest.'

I nodded my head. I was breathing heavily, as though the half-run back from the lake had exhausted me, and I put one hand to my side for good measure. I felt perfectly OK, but I didn't want to spend the next several hours in the police station.

'I can drive myself,' Anna said. 'Or phone.'

'They'll want you to come in at some point,' Gardner argued. 'Might as well get it over with. And no offence, but you look a bit shaky to be driving. You can phone from the car to save time.'

She nodded her consent and the two of them climbed into his truck and drove away, leaving me alone in the dark lane.

I slept late the next day, Sunday, and was woken by the sound of Gardner in the shower. I got up, feeling sore in lots of places, but otherwise in very good spirits. It had been a long time since I'd had quite so much to occupy my thoughts.

As I opened the bathroom window to let the damp air out, I heard the sound of singing. Sound never travelled from our church, so I knew it had to be coming from Gathering Hall. They were known to hold outdoor services when the weather was fine, but given everything that had happened the previous evening it seemed odd, to say the least, if not downright disrespectful.

I was making coffee when there was a knock on my front door. I knew it couldn't be Anna because I could hear the sound of her electric mixer coming from the kitchen, and I really couldn't think who else would be wanting my attention.

Gardner was on my doorstep, casually dressed in jeans and a sweater, his hair still damp from the shower, clutching a mug of what smelled like hot coffee.

'Brought my own,' he told me. 'I know you only have instant.'

I didn't comment on his impertinence, assuming I'd have offered him coffee – I wouldn't have – and instead asked how I could help.

He pulled a face, as though I amused him. 'Thought I'd give you the low-down on our trip to the boys in blue last night.'

It was on the tip of my tongue to tell him I'd find out from Anna, but I had no idea how busy she'd be that morning and, in all honesty, I didn't want to wait.

Gardner gave an exaggerated shiver. 'Bit nippy out here.'

The man was annoying, but he had something I wanted. I invited him in.

'Not much to tell, I'm afraid,' he said, when he'd dropped into one of my armchairs and slung a leg over the arm, giving me a clear view of his crotch. 'Anna made her statement, desk sergeant took notes, said he'd send a car up there. Nothing more for us to do so we left.'

He could have told me this on the doorstep.

'Do they need to speak to me?' I asked.

His head rose, like an animal that had caught a scent. 'Looks like it,' he replied.

I turned to see what had caught his attention. Through the window we could see a police car in the lane outside.

The police had come to see Anna, but they wanted to talk to me, too. Gardner followed us through to the bakery kitchen, although he'd only played the role of chauffeur after the event.

We sat, and Anna, who seemed programmed to be hospitable, offered coffee. We all declined. The constable asked me to confirm my name.

'And you were with Miss Brown last night when she witnessed some unusual activity at the lake,' he went on, when I'd done so.

'A young boy falling into the water and not appearing to come out of it, yes,' I said.

'We attended Gathering Hall at twenty-three hundred hours last night,' the constable said. 'Following the incident witnessed by yourselves and reported to us at Penrith station at twenty-two thirty hours.'

'I met them on their way back.' Gardner can't resist making any incident about himself. 'Both looked pretty shook up.' He shot a sympathetic look at Anna, ignored me completely.

'We spoke to Mr North at the hall and were informed that several youngsters from the church congregation became a little merry last night, having persuaded the local newsagent to sell them some cheap cider.' The constable looked a tiny bit pleased with himself. 'We'll be having words with the shop, naturally. A couple of the young people went into the water but were quickly recovered and sent to bed. I imagine they're nursing hangovers and feeling pretty sheepish this morning.'

Anna looked at me, her eyes wide with confusion. I didn't blame her.

'That's complete rubbish,' she stated. 'One boy went in the water, and he was not a member of the church. He hitchhiked up here looking for his girlfriend. We saw him. He was badly frightened by something to do with the church.'

I held up a finger to catch her attention. 'The important thing seems to be that Connor is alright,' I said. 'Are you sure? Everyone who went in the water came out of it again?'

'That's what I've been told,' the constable replied. 'Every member of the church present and accounted for. No harm done.'

'Well, that's a relief.' Gardner got to his feet.

'No, it's not.' Anna's eyes were fixed on the policeman. 'Connor is not a member of the church. He only arrived yesterday. Have you actually seen him? Spoken to him? Or did you just take their word for it?'

The constable's face became guarded. 'I didn't attend myself,' he said. 'I wasn't on duty.'

'Even so, Miss Brown is quite right,' I said. 'Whoever attended must have asked to see the boy. No police officer worth his salt would simply take people's word for it. Not when we're talking about a possible death.'

'Who attended the scene?' Anna asked. 'Can we speak to that officer?'

The constable resumed his hat and made for the door. 'I don't have that information, I'm afraid. You need to refer any further queries to the desk sergeant at the station. Oh, and the superintendent asked me to remind you both that for the duration of the church's visit, the land around the lake is to be considered out of bounds.'

Anna seemed to grow a couple of inches. 'Oh no, it's not,' she said. 'You can't suspend a public right of way like that. Something about this stinks.'

I reached out to Anna, but Gardner got there first. He put a hand on her arm and shook his head at her.

'Queries to the station please, miss.' The officer left the room and we heard his footsteps striding across the shop before the doorbell rang out.

'It's not impossible, Anna,' I said. 'They'd have to be morally delinquent not to take care of Connor once he'd been recovered from the water.'

'Assuming he was recovered. We've no proof of that.'

'Concealing a death would be a major crime,' I said. 'I can't believe the church, however odd they are, would conspire to that level of criminality.'

'I've probably seen a lot more of what goes on up there than you two,' Gardner added. 'Weird shit, no doubt about it, but not illegal.'

Anna wasn't having it. 'We have a possibly pregnant teenage girl attempting suicide, her boyfriend so desperate to be in touch with her he's sleeping rough, and so frightened of the church thugs that he's prepared to risk drowning. May actually have drowned for all we know. I don't think "weird shit" covers it.'

'Hang on.' Gardner looked mystified. 'What am I missing?' He's not the sharpest knife in the box but, in all fairness, Anna had thrown a lot of new information at him.

Anna shook her head. 'I have to get on.' She got to her feet and made for the shop. 'I've too much to do before tomorrow. You're going to have to excuse me.'

Gardner looked at me. 'Anything to add?' he asked.

'Not my secret to share,' I said, and let myself out the back way. I had work to be getting on with too.

At four o'clock, after a reasonably productive day, I took up position at my front window. I'd had doubts about whether Constance would actually show, given everything that had happened. A few minutes later, though, she appeared at the top of the lane, all bundled up in a coat that was too big and a knitted cap that concealed most of her hair. She made a point of looking up and down the high street before hurrying towards the shop.

Anna must have been listening out. I heard footsteps and then the two of them exchanging a subdued greeting. The bell rang out as the door was closed and locked again.

I'd hoped they'd sit in the courtyard. I had my coat and a blanket ready and would be close enough, albeit on the other side of the wall, to join in the conversation. Not that I would, of course. I wasn't entirely surprised, though, when they seemed to be settling in the kitchen; it was simply too cold to be comfortable outside.

Not too much of a setback though. Our terrace of cottages, once a single house, is very old and was built around a timber frame. Not all of the joists fit snugly and there are several places in my house where it was once possible to see through into the next property. Gardner, shortly after moving in, discovered all of those on his side and stuffed them with wood filler, but Josie Hinton, with poorer eyesight, never had. I'd placed patches of a wood-effect wallpaper over the cracks on my side, so they wouldn't be too obvious on the other, but these could be easily and silently removed.

As I heard the kettle boiling and the clatter of cups and plates, I gently peeled back one of those slips of paper to reveal a slender gap, half a centimetre in width, between an upright and a horizontal joist. About four feet off the floor, it looked out on to a narrow space between Anna's tall, free-standing fridge and a wall cupboard.

To see it on her side, the two occupants of the room would have to be staring straight at it. Even then, given that I'd turned out all the lights in my kitchen and drawn the blinds, the chances of them seeing anything other than darkness were slim.

I wouldn't see much either, to be fair, but I would hear most of what was being said next door.

'Thanks,' Constance said. 'Stupid of me.'

I assumed she was referring to her phone.

'Constance, how's Connor?' Anna asked. 'Have you seen him?'

Silence. Then, 'What do you mean?' the girl asked.

Anna moved around the room as she spoke, and sounds she made drowned out the odd word, but I caught most of it. 'A boy came here last night, looking for you. He said his name was Connor and that he's a friend of yours. He left around nine to look for you. Was he not telling the truth?'

'He can't be here.'

Something I didn't quite catch and then, 'Nevertheless, he was. He said he'd hitchhiked from Sussex.'

'You're kidding me. So, where is he now?'

Oh my! So, Constance knew nothing about Connor's adventure up at the lake last night. How on earth had they kept that from her? There must have been fifty people on the bank. And how was Anna going to break the news that the girl's boyfriend nearly drowned? Could have properly drowned for all she knew.

'He definitely went up to the hall,' Anna replied. 'I saw him there myself. There was something of a fuss, a confrontation. I'm not entirely sure what happened, though. It was very dark and quite confused.'

Silence in the house next door, as I tried to decide whether Anna was being cowardly or wise by skirting around the facts.

'If he's your age, Constance, he really shouldn't be hitching around the country and sleeping rough,' Anna said. 'He's too young.'

'I'd no idea he'd followed me.' The girl sounded on the brink of tears, which would make it harder for me to make out what she was saying.

'He was worried about you. Do you want to tell me why?'

Oh, come on, out with it. I wouldn't have been able to resist, had I been on the other side of the wall. *Constance, are you pregnant or aren't you?*

Anna couldn't ask, I realised. She wasn't supposed to know about the pregnancy test.

'I look at you, Constance, and I see a young girl who's deeply troubled, and who, for some reason, doesn't think her family can help,' Anna said. 'You mustn't tell me anything you don't feel comfortable sharing, but if there's anything I can do to help you, I will.'

Irritatingly, but not surprisingly, Constance began to cry at that point, and for the next few minutes, all conversation ceased.

'Is this something you can talk to your mother about?' Anna tried at last.

'She's the last person I can talk to. She hates Connor.'

'Anyone else then? Whatever your problem is, you need someone.'

'Can I talk to you?'

'Of course,' Anna said.

More sobbing. I was beginning to wonder if all this was worth the effort.

'Constance, are you pregnant?' Anna asked and I gave a silent cheer on my side of the wall.

'How did you know?' Constance replied, which I took as a yes.

'You're not even sixteen,' Anna replied. 'There's a limit to the ways a fifteen-year-old girl with a boyfriend can get herself into trouble. It was a lucky guess.'

Silence.

'Are you sure?' Anna said.

Silence.

'What stage are you at? When was your last period?'

'Does it matter?' Constance sounded close to despair.

'Yes. It will make a difference to the options available to you. You're very slim, so I wouldn't have thought you were much beyond the first trimester, but it's often hard to tell with very young girls.'

'I'm not sure,' Constance said. 'I'm not very regular.'

'Have you seen a doctor?'

Silence.

'Whatever you decide, you're going to need medical help.'

'I can't. My mum will find out and then everyone will know.'

'Constance, a doctor would have to respect your confidence. He or she wouldn't be allowed to share personal information about you with anyone else, not even your parents.'

'He would though. I know he would. He's part of the church too.'

I heard Anna push her chair back and take a few steps around the room. 'I can make an emergency appointment for you with a local doctor,' she said. 'Or there are a number of charities that can help you, put you in touch with the right clinics.'

'I can't.' Constance was on the verge of sobbing again.

'Constance, I know you're scared, and you might think you've nowhere to turn, but that really isn't the case. And a pregnancy is very unlikely to go away.'

'Are you a doctor?' Constance asked, to my surprise. I'd have thought her far too self-absorbed to come to such a conclusion.

'Why would you say that?' I recognised the tightness in Anna's voice when she replied. I'd heard it myself when I'd strayed too far into the personal.

'You seem to know what you're talking about. It's like, I'm not the first young person in trouble you've come across.'

'I'm not a doctor, Constance.' Anna left a long pause after she'd spoken and I could practically hear the unspoken word: *anymore*. Anna wasn't a doctor anymore. 'I'm a baker.'

Yes, now she was a baker, but she hadn't always been. She'd been a doctor. I really couldn't help the surge of excitement. Armed with that knowledge, who knew what I could find out next?

'Is Connor the father?' Anna asked. 'Does he know?'

At that moment, a loud banging sounded. I nearly jumped out of my skin, but the knocking was on Anna's front door, not mine.

'They've found me!'

Constance sounded terrified. I heard a clattering sound as a chair fell to the ground. 'Did you tell them? Did you tell them I was here?'

'Of course not. Constance, what on earth are you so afraid of?'

More banging. And then a male voice yelled, 'Constance!'

'It's Dad. He'll kill me.'

Anna's chair slid along the floor as she too got to her feet. 'He won't kill you, Constance, don't be silly. I'll stay with you while you talk to him.'

'No, you've got no idea what they'll do. They've probably got Connor.'

The banging sounded again. I got up, left the kitchen and strode quickly down the length of my garden. I paused for a second before opening the back gate, in case the church had the property surrounded, but the alley was empty and I let myself into Anna's courtyard. The two of them were still in the kitchen, staring at each other across the table, when I knocked lightly on Anna's back door. They both started, and Constance put her hand to her mouth to hold back a scream. Anna, at least, relaxed when she saw it was me.

'Just a thought,' I said. 'But if Constance would prefer not to be escorted home right now, she could spend the next few minutes in my house.'

'How did you even—' Anna began.

'I saw you arrive,' I said to Constance. 'And then your family a minute ago. It's up to you. If you want to talk to Anna some more, it's a way of avoiding a confrontation.'

'Constance, we know you're in there!' A woman's voice this time. I thought I recognised Constance's mother.

'What good would it do?' Constance said to me. 'They'll find me sooner or later. They always find me.'

Well, that was a thought that sparked a dozen questions.

'I don't see what the problem is,' I said, trying to sound upbeat. 'You came to collect the phone you left behind the other day and had a cup of tea with Anna. No one's done anything to apologise for.' I turned to Anna. 'Shall I let them in? I'll take my time.'

I was offering to give her a few more moments to speak to Constance alone. She realised and nodded.

I walked slowly through to the shop and made a point of looking around for the light switch, even though I knew perfectly well where it was. Before I 'found' it, though, I ascertained that there were three people standing on the threshold of Anna's shop. Two men and a woman. Seemed like overkill to me, for one errant teenager.

I walked, still slowly, to the front door. Goodness me, those were three very cross faces on the other side of the glass. And both men were sizeable. I found myself wondering if Gardner was home. Muscle has its advantages.

'I'm afraid we're closed,' I announced, with a tight smile.

Constance's mother – I recognised her from her first visit to the shop – rapped on the glass. 'I've come for my daughter. Open this door.'

I looked up, down, to both sides.

'Not sure where the key is,' I called to them. 'Bear with.' I patted my pockets and pretended to reach up to the top of the door frame. Then I turned around and feigned examining the shelves closest to the door.

My fun was curtailed, though, by the appearance of Constance and Anna from the kitchen. I stepped back and Anna turned the key – it was in the lock after all, silly me – and the family burst into the shop.

'What are you playing at?' The mother strode up to Constance and grabbed her by the arm.

'Not here,' one of the men warned. 'Take her to the car.'

The other man held the door as Constance was frogmarched through it by her mother. He left with them and the door closed.

'Why was my daughter here?' asked the remaining man, who stood in the doorway as though trying to block our exit.

'She came to collect her phone,' I said before Anna could speak. 'You know what teenagers are like.'

He gave me a brief but filthy look. 'What did she tell you?' he demanded of Anna.

'She told me she'd mislaid her phone,' Anna replied. 'And I told her I'd kept it safe for her.'

'I don't want her coming here again, do you hear me? I'll be speaking to the Minister about this.'

With that, he turned and banged his way out of the shop. I mean that literally; he collided with the door frame and almost fell over. The door closed and the shop seemed unusually silent.

'I suppose that was a threat.' Anna sounded unhappy and it was a salutary reminder that not everyone enjoys conflict. 'I'm going to lose the church business now.'

I wasn't so sure about that; Aran North knew he had to keep the village onside. 'You'll be able to swim again,' I said. 'Every cloud.'

She grimaced. 'After last night, I'm not sure I could. We have to find out if that boy's OK.'

'If he is, he'll be in touch very soon,' I said. 'We still have his phone.'

That got a hint of a smile. 'What on earth is going on up there?' she said.

'Pregnant fifteen-year-old, ultra-strict, churchgoing family – is it really so hard to understand?'

Anna turned and walked back through to her kitchen. I followed.

'It's more than that,' she said. 'You didn't see her when they started banging on the door – thanks for coming round, by the way – she was terrified. White as a sheet and shaking.'

We sat at the kitchen table and looked at each other.

'This is a safeguarding issue if ever I saw one,' Anna said.

I didn't ask how often a baker would encounter safeguarding issues.

'What if Connor isn't the father of that child's baby,' Anna went on. 'What if this evangelical church is a front for something else?'

'Massive paedophile ring?' I suggested, not entirely seriously, but Anna nodded, unhappily.

'It happens,' she said.

'I believe it does. So, what are our options?'

I meant Anna's options, of course; I wasn't getting involved any more than I had to.

'I can contact the police, let them know I'm concerned about a vulnerable minor, but their powers are limited at this stage. Social services might have more success but either course would involve betraying Constance's trust.'

'Do you think she's in real danger?' I asked. 'Imminent danger?'

'Who knows.' She gave a sort of helpless gesture, throwing both hands into the air. 'And what on earth has happened to Connor?'

It was a good question. A second later, we found out.

20

April, the previous year

This was the perfect time of year for open-water swimming. The water was still fresh enough to produce that wonderful post-swim euphoria, but not so cold that spending more than twenty minutes in it would risk severe hypothermia.

Annaliese slipped into the water, letting the cool silkiness wash over her and startling a train of newly hatched ducklings that paddled quickly after their mother. Taking a deep breath, she set off in a fast, graceful breaststroke, face down, gliding through the water, barely causing a ripple on its surface.

She'd had a breakthrough. Maybe. Jago had admitted to the voices that, he claimed, had driven him to attack the physics teacher. He'd been surprisingly forthcoming, given his previous reticence.

'Tell me how they started,' she'd said, wondering why she wasn't feeling the usual surge of excitement when a patient started to open up.

'It was a year ago, maybe longer. Whenever I was feeling under pressure, like for exams or tests, or a big sports event, I'd hear voices.'

'Can you tell me about them? Were they male? Female? Voices you recognised?'

'Sometimes my dad's voice, or one of my teachers. Crystal clear in my head, as though they were with me in the room. Telling me I wasn't working hard enough, that I wasn't clever enough, that I was having weird thoughts about girls.'

An iron footbridge crossed the lake at the midpoint and the swimmers were used to passers-by stopping to wave down at them. This evening it was empty, apart from a solitary figure in black at the far side, largely hidden behind a buddleia bush. Annaliese blinked and lifted her goggles. The figure was gone, but for a moment there, it had looked a lot like Jago. She pulled the goggles off and rinsed them before setting off again.

Had the 'voices' been Jago's own internalised thoughts, they would have been entirely normal for a teenage boy in a high-pressure environment. The fact that they assumed personalities distinct from Jago himself made it a different issue.

'Auditory hallucinations aren't completely uncommon,' she'd told him. 'It's thought up to ten per cent of people experience them at some point in their lives.'

It was the standard response, designed to reassure. She'd given him a second, to let the information sink in.

'They can have several causes and aren't necessarily indicative of a psychotic disorder,' she'd continued, when he'd shown no signs of being even slightly reassured.

'My dad thinks I'm schizophrenic.' He'd looked so miserable at that point that she was on the verge of feeling sorry for him. 'I heard him talking last night. He thinks I need antipsychotics.'

'You would need to be displaying other symptoms before I could even think about diagnosing you with schizophrenia,' she said. 'I haven't noticed any so far. Quite the opposite, if anything.'

If she'd expected him to look relieved, she was disappointed.

'Maybe I'm not telling you everything.'

Something beneath the water's surface brushed her leg, startling her, breaking her rhythm, and she slowed her pace. Realising she was out of breath, she grasped her tow float and turned onto her back.

So, Jago Moore still wasn't telling her everything. She'd gone on to prompt him, listing some typical symptoms of schizophrenia – disorganised thinking, neglect of personal hygiene, loss of interest – ones she already knew didn't apply, and she'd been sure there was something he'd wanted to say. He hadn't.

She was getting cold.

She swam to the edge and climbed out.

This stretch of the bank was secluded. A footpath ran close but most walkers were sensitive about swimmers getting changed. Wrapping a large towel around her, she pulled off her wetsuit and let it drop into her bag, followed by her swimsuit. She glanced around. No one in sight. She let the towel drop and quickly pulled on pants, T-shirt and shorts. Only when she was decent again did she properly stand up and look back over the lake. Something glinted in the early evening sunshine.

Annaliese stepped back to the water's edge.

The person she'd noticed earlier was still there, had moved towards the centre of the bridge, and was actually holding binoculars to his eyes. Binoculars that were trained in her direction.

Her heart started to hammer. It was definitely a young man or a boy. He was tall, slim, dressed in black jeans and T-shirt. He had dark hair. He looked like Jago.

Jago, who two nights earlier had been walking past her gym as she'd left it. Who'd walked straight into her, grasping both her arms to stop her from tumbling over. Had that really, as he'd claimed, been coincidence?

And why would Jago be watching her swim? Watching her get dressed? How did he even know she swam here? Where her gym was?

How did he know so much about her life?

21

Anna and I were already on edge, shaken by the confrontation with Constance's family. We probably shouldn't have jumped out of our skins when something sizeable slumped against her back door, but we did, of course. I have little physical courage, but Anna was the most alarmed. Uttering a muffled scream, she jumped up, a hand clutching her throat.

I was startled too, I don't mind admitting; some very odd things were happening. I think I held it together a bit better though. After the initial start I got to my feet and approached the door.

The sun was very low by this time and Anna's courtyard in shadow. Her kitchen on the other hand was brightly lit, effectively blinding us. We could make out a large figure beyond the glass but its features were indistinct. Whoever it was, though, was pressed very close to the door, as though leaning on it. Something was smeared on the outside of the glass and, to be honest, it rather reminded me of a scene in a low-budget horror film. We watched a hand rise and then a fist rap on the glass.

'It's me,' called a voice we knew.

'Connor,' I said. 'Shall I let him in?'

Once again, Anna was struggling to get a hold of herself; once again, badly frightened by the sight of a young man trying to gain entry to her house.

'Of course,' she said. 'Thank God he's OK.'

Connor was a very long way from OK. He might have escaped drowning but his face was bruised, badly swollen in places. There was a nasty gash in his lower lip and the hollow around his right eye was a livid red; it would be a purplish black in a day or so. He limped into the kitchen, eyes down, one arm around his lower torso as though supporting an injury. His clothes looked and smelled damp.

For several moments, neither Anna nor I spoke, but then, simultaneously, we got to work. I carried a chair over and we both helped him sit. Anna crossed to the sink to bring him a glass of water.

'An ambulance, I think,' I said.

'No.' Connor's hand was shaking; it was an effort for him to lift the glass to his lips. 'I don't want an ambulance. I have to find Connie.'

Anna and I were becoming quite in tune by this time, and I was pretty certain I knew what she was thinking: that Constance's family had done this, that they'd found out about her pregnancy, assumed – probably correctly – that Connor was the father, and dealt with it in the time-honoured way of beating the young man to a pulp.

'Stay with him,' Anna told me, as if I might cut and run. 'Don't let him move.'

I heard her footsteps running upstairs. Connor dropped his head into his hands and stared down at the table. His breathing was audible and stilted.

I said, 'The last time I saw you, young man, you were plummeting towards a watery grave.'

He glanced up. 'You were there?'

'On the other side of the lake. Did the church people pull you out?'

He opened his mouth to speak but Anna arrived back with a brown leather bag. I said nothing as she began to unpack it, but I couldn't help a tight smile of triumph. Anna had produced what appeared to be a professional doctor's case. Keeping my eyes on Connor I let my peripheral vision take in its contents: stationery and prescriptive forms, stethoscope, thermometer, pulse oximeter, alcohol wipes, lubricating jelly, specimen bottles, reflex hammer, syringes, drugs of various kinds, antiseptics, tapes, plasters and bandages.

Telling me to run water as hot as I could get it and fill a bowl, she carried on proving that, at one time at least, she'd been a medical practitioner. I did what I was told, even hurrying upstairs to a linen cupboard and bringing down several small white towels.

'Don't talk,' Anna told Connor as she gently pushed hair from his eyes to examine his face. She found a wound on his scalp and winced. 'This needs stitches.'

Fixing up Connor took the best part of an hour because Anna was nothing if not thorough. Having satisfied herself that he'd taken no drugs or alcohol within hours, she gave him painkillers that made him more comfortable. She cleaned and covered a number of minor cuts and did the best she could with the scalp wound and the cut in his lip. She concluded that he had bruised ribs but didn't think anything was broken. He would live, she told him, but would be pretty uncomfortable for several days.

All the time Anna was working, she asked him nothing that wasn't strictly relevant to his physical condition: did this hurt, how about that, did he feel any pain when he took a breath? When she was finished, she sank back into her own chair, pale, a little shaky, and I could see that the effort of being a doctor again had exhausted her. For the time being, I was in charge. I'd already poured Connor some warm milk and I brought through a pastry from the shop that I cut into small pieces and put on a plate in front of him.

'Eat,' I said. 'And tell us what happened.'

He obeyed one of my instructions at least and the pastry was soon gone. He drank too and put the mug down empty.

'Feel better?' I asked.

He gave me a nod. For a rather uncommunicative teenage boy, I decided, he had a remarkably expressive face. I could read exhaustion, embarrassment and worry in his eyes.

'We know you didn't find Constance,' I said. 'Because she was here a short while ago. So, what happened last night at the lake? Where have you been since then, and who did this to you?'

He looked from Anna to me. 'They're nutters. Out of control. They need to be stopped.'

'We're not arguing,' I told him. 'But you should start at the beginning.'

*

As the day darkened and vanished completely, Connor told us that after he'd left us the night before he'd made his way up to Gathering Hall. He'd been stopped at the gates.

'There was no way they were letting me through,' he said. 'They wouldn't even tell me if Connie was there. Wouldn't get a message to her or anything.'

Pretending to leave, he'd walked a few yards down the road and then, out of sight of the gatehouse, climbed the perimeter fence. Keeping to the edge of the field he'd made his way towards the campsite.

'You were lucky not to be seen,' I said. 'That site's swarming with people.'

'I was seen,' Connor replied. 'I was looking for her dad's car when I nearly bumped into some sort of patrol. Four blokes. They were wearing high-vis jackets and head torches. I ran off but they chased me.'

'Pretty scary,' Anna said.

'I wasn't bothered at first. I'm fast and I'd spotted a back way to the village. But they must have been talking to each other on radios because suddenly there were more of them. They cut me off when I got down to the lake. I panicked.'

'What possessed you to climb that tree?' I asked. 'You must have known how dangerous it would be.'

Connor looked as though he didn't know. 'I didn't think. There were a dozen blokes, maybe more. All after me.'

'What did you think they'd do to you?' I asked.

Anna put a hand on my arm. 'Look what they did do,' she said.

It was a fair point.

'What happened after you fell? How did you get out of the water?'

His head lifted a fraction. 'I didn't fall, I jumped. I figured it was my only chance.'

'Oh, Connor,' Anna sighed.

'It was stupid,' Connor went on. 'I nearly got stuck in those branches. But I managed to swim away. I made it to the other bank and climbed out. They were still looking for me though. They sent people all round the lake. I had to hide in some bushes.'

'You're lucky you didn't catch your death of cold,' I said.

'I think I fell asleep,' Connor said. 'Maybe I passed out, I don't know. Something woke me up and everyone had gone.'

'Why didn't you come here?' Anna said.

He sniffed, then swallowed. 'I was going to. I found a lane that I figured would bring me back this way. Then they jumped me.'

'Who did?' I asked.

'One of them security guards. He was a fucking nutter. Sorry to swear, but he was. He had some sort of bat. A cricket bat I think, and he was laying into me with it. I thought he was going to kill me.'

'Can you describe him?' I asked. 'If you saw him again, could you identify him?'

'Big bloke,' Connor began, and I took that with a pinch of salt. Of course he would describe his assailant as a big bloke. 'Wearing black, but with one of those high-vis jackets. That's how I knew he was one of the guards. He had a balaclava over his face though.'

'How tall?' I asked.

'About my height. Sorry, it was dark. And he hit my head first. I was woozy, just trying to shield myself.'

There were tears in Connor's eyes by this time; he was a tough kid, but a kid for all that.

'Did he speak to you?' I asked.

A head shake.

'He didn't threaten you in any way? Tell you to stay away from the hall?'

Anna put a hand gently on my own. 'Let him finish his story,' she said.

It didn't take long. Connor had lost consciousness. When he came round sometime later he'd been in a small, windowless room on the ground floor of the house. He'd been let out only an hour before he'd arrived, exhausted and in pain, on Anna's doorstep. He'd seen nothing of Constance, or her family.

When he'd finished, Anna and I looked at each other across the table.

'Police?' she said.

'They'll hurt Connie,' the boy protested as she got to her feet. 'If you call the police they'll hurt Connie too.'

'All the more reason,' she argued. 'If the church condone beating up and imprisoning someone who is technically still a child, we need to worry about all the young people in their care.'

'I'm not staying.' He pushed himself out of the chair. 'If you're calling the police, I'm not staying. You can't stop me.'

Anna, showing remarkable presence of mind, I thought, walked quickly to the back door and locked it. She slipped the key into her pocket.

'You're going nowhere in that state,' she told him. 'Now sit down and give us a minute. We're trying to help you.' She turned to me. 'Can I talk to you in the other room?'

I allowed myself to be ushered through to the shop.

'We have to report this,' she said. 'We're talking actual bodily harm, grievous bodily harm, whatever. And unlawful imprisonment. Not to mention lying to the police.'

'He and Connie have been having underage sex,' I reminded her. 'He could be liable for prosecution, possibly her too. I'm not sure this is our decision to make.'

Anna exhaled loudly. 'I didn't think of that. You're right though. If we get the church in trouble with the police, the first thing they'll do is accuse Connor of whatever they can throw at him.'

'Statutory rape is an ugly charge,' I added. 'And no young person would want to find themselves on the sex offenders' register.'

'If we do nothing, we could be leaving Constance in danger,' she countered.

'Let's see what we can find out first,' I suggested.

Frankly, I didn't care one way or the other whether the church was prosecuted, so long as I kept a low profile myself as far as the police were concerned. I didn't even care what happened to Connor or Constance. It was the intrigue that kept me in the game. I hadn't had so much fun in years.

'Good cop, bad cop?' I suggested as we turned back to the kitchen.

'Not too bad,' she warned, assuming – not without reason I suppose – that I would be bad cop. 'We don't want to scare him off.'

I began, once we were all settled around the kitchen table again. 'Yesterday, you said you were worried about Constance. Can you tell us why?'

He gave a half-shrug. 'Isn't it obvious?'

'This time yesterday they hadn't imprisoned and beaten you up,' I retorted. 'So unless the church has a history of violence that you know about . . . ' I waited for him to fill in the gap.

'Have they hurt Constance?' Anna asked. 'Or anyone that you know of?'

Connor's eyes dropped. 'Connie was worried she might be pregnant,' he said to the table. 'She was a bit late – with her, you know, her period.'

'We knew that,' Anna replied. 'She told me yesterday. And she was seen in the chemist, buying a test.'

'She's done a test?' His eyes widened. 'It's definite then?'

'Do you believe the baby to be yours?' I asked.

'Do they know? Is that why they beat me up?'

'Possibly,' I replied. 'Although I'd be a little surprised at Constance coming clean quite so quickly. Maybe she left her test lying around and one of her parents had found it.'

'Why is she so frightened of being pregnant?' Anna said. 'Why are you? I know it's a problem, and I'm not trying to downplay it, but it can be dealt with.'

'You don't know what these people are like. She's not sixteen yet. I'll go to prison.'

'Is this what it's all about then?' Anna asked. 'Connie's pregnancy?'

He shook his head. 'No, it's a lot more than that. She's not safe.'

Anna and I shared another look and, again, I thought I knew what she was thinking. Unsafe seemed a bit extreme, until one remembered the look of terror on Constance's face. And Connor's appalling injuries.

Come to think of it, maybe 'unsafe' didn't seem extreme at all.

'Tell us what's going on up there,' Anna said. 'What's the Ingathering?'

Connor looked from Anna to me. 'Don't you know?' he said. 'You live here. It happens every year. You must know.'

'Anna moved here recently,' I explained. 'I've been here longer, a little under five years, but even people born in the village don't know much about it. Or they say they don't, which comes to the same thing.'

'Tell us what you know,' Anna said.

Connor frowned. 'They call it a rite of passage,' he said after a moment. 'Something all church members have to do the year they reach sixteen.'

Anna shot me a look. 'When we were up there the other night, delivering food, we saw a massive marquee. And we heard something very disturbing going on inside. We were told it was a performance, but . . . '

'That's the Hell House,' Connor said.

We took a second, Anna and I, to register that.

'The Hell House?' I double-checked I'd heard right.

'Connie says they're common in some American states. That church of hers is American in origin, did I mention that?' Connor said. 'This is the only one in the UK that we know of, but it's a big deal. Families from all over the country bring their kids here the year they turn sixteen, because they have to go through the Hell House.'

'And what happens in the Hell House?' Anna asked.

Connor shook his head. 'They're not supposed to talk about it,' he said. 'So that each age group experiences it fresh. Some of the older ones do, though, so the younger ones know a bit about what to expect. It gives some of them nightmares. Connie says a lot of the kids have mental health problems for years because they know they have to face the Hell House.'

Anna turned to me. 'I'm not liking the sound of this,' she said.

'It's supposed to be about teaching kids the consequences of sin,' Connor said. 'So, typically, you might start off in a pub.'

'I caught a glimpse of what looked like a pub,' I said, remembering the little I'd seen of the inside of the marquee.

Connor went on, 'So, they make the kids walk through the pub and they'll see other kids like them – the older brothers and sisters are the actors – getting drunk, taking drugs, and they show them everything that goes wrong. You'll see fights breaking out, people vomiting, being taken away in an ambulance.'

'Doesn't sound too bad,' I said, earning a frown of disapproval from Anna.

'No, it starts pretty mild,' Connor agreed, 'but after the pub, you might see an ambulance pulling up at the hospital and the kid in the back dead on arrival. You'll see his parents freaking out, getting hysterical. You'll go past drug addicts injecting themselves, young girls being trafficked. I think they even act out the rapes. Then you might see a couple getting a bit romantic, and then in the next room the girl will be having an abortion, only it'll have gone badly wrong, and there'll be blood everywhere, and a dead fetus on the floor and—'

'Whoa!' Anna held a hand up to stop him.

'Can you imagine Connie having to look at that?' Connor asked. 'And they usually do a high school shooting as well. There'll be kids in a classroom and then someone breaks in and starts shooting everyone.'

'I think we get the picture,' I said. 'And this is supposed to discourage sin?'

'The last thing they see is hell,' Connor said. 'Half of them are dressed up as devils and they're acting out all sorts of torture. When they make it through hell they have a party. They're full members of the church then.'

'Wow,' Anna said. 'That sounds seriously messed up.'

Seemingly exhausted by the story he'd just told us, Connor closed his eyes and let his head drop into his hands. I'd been on the point of pressing him further, but Anna shook her head at me and got to her feet, muttering something about how we all needed some food inside us. I went along with the reprieve. For now.

Because I'd been watching Connor's face carefully while he'd been talking. He hadn't told us everything. Not by a long shot.

22

May, the previous year

'Have you read any Thomas Hardy?'

It was a sudden change of subject and Annaliese gave herself time before replying. 'I think everyone does at school,' she said. '*Tess of the D'Urbervilles*, in my case. Why do you ask?'

'I think you can tell a lot about a person by what they think of Hardy. Did you like it?'

All too often, she'd realised, Jago tried to drive the conversation himself. It was an obvious, and not too subtle, way of avoiding her questions. This was their sixth session, out of a scheduled eight, and she had a sense of time running out.

On the other hand, he'd brought up Thomas Hardy before; had had some interesting things to say about the nineteenth-century author.

'I wouldn't say he's my favourite,' she replied. 'When we spoke about Hardy previously, you mentioned his view that life was predominantly about pain. Is that how it seems to you?'

He feigned surprise. She knew it was feigned, because his sudden start, his widened eyes were clearly an overreaction. 'Of course,' he said. 'Wouldn't you agree?'

'Not at all. On balance, I find life a positive experience. And preferable to the alternative.'

Jago leaned towards her. Once again, he'd chosen to sit uncomfortably close and she had to steel herself not to flinch. He smiled, knowingly, as he said, 'Maybe you need to read more Hardy.'

'Maybe you should read less.' She smiled too, to indicate a joke. 'Jago, what I'd really like to talk about today is—'

'Do you believe in ghosts, Annaliese?'

She felt the smile on her face freeze.

Jago looked uneasy. 'You said it was OK for me to call you that?'

'Of course.' She gave all her patients permission to call her by her given name and had never had reason to regret doing so before. 'And no, to answer your question, I don't believe in ghosts. Can we talk about—'

He leaned back against the sofa and gave a heavy sigh. 'I knew you wouldn't believe me.'

'Believe you about what? Do you think you've seen a ghost?'

Suddenly, she was on edge. This was new. The trouble was, she had no idea whether it was real or whether Jago was playing with her again. Visual hallucinations were rare, even among patients with extreme psychosis.

'Not seen.' He held her gaze unashamedly. 'Heard. Do you remember I told you I heard voices, that sometimes it was my dad, and sometimes my sports coach, sometimes a next-door neighbour?'

She remembered no mention of a sports coach or a neighbour, but let her head nod in agreement.

'I wasn't telling the truth. It's his voice I hear, always his.'

'Whose?'

'Tom's. Thomas Hardy. I think he's haunting me.'

Annaliese gave herself some time. She didn't believe him; it was as simple as that. Yet doctors in her position did not accuse patients of lying; not without a whole lot more evidence than she had, than she was ever likely to have. The boy was too smart.

'I think he wants me to suffer, like the characters in his books suffer,' Jago went on, when she didn't react. 'That's why I read him so much. I don't enjoy the stories, not really. I'm just trying to find some message that will let me be free of him.'

She found herself wishing, for a moment, that he was telling the truth. This would be a case like no other she'd dealt with. But no, she simply didn't believe him.

'Can you help me, Anna?' His face was screwed up now, as though he was on the verge of tears, but his eyes remained dry. 'Can you give me something that will make him go away?'

'Annaliese,' she corrected him. 'Let's go back to the beginning. Tell me when these voices started.'

He began to talk about the increasingly disturbing things the ghost of Hardy was supposedly saying to him and she felt anxiety growing. This was no breakthrough. This was something else entirely.

23

Connor had told us all he could – or was prepared to – and we decided there wasn't much more we could do that evening, other than get his head wound seen to. We ate first, Anna arguing that it could take several hours for us to be seen in A&E, even on a Sunday evening, and then she drove him to hospital. I stayed behind to wash up and get the summer house ready for Connor to spend another night, assuming A&E discharged him.

I took the opportunity, naturally, to have a good look around Anna's house. Needing the downstairs space to service the shop, she'd created a small but cosy sitting room out of the spare bedroom upstairs. A couple of photographs on a side table could have been of her parents on their wedding day, and there was a similar picture of a family of four. She had very few books, but there was an e-reader on her bedside cabinet, passcode protected, as was her laptop.

I found a nice collection of jewellery in a leather-covered case inside her bedside cabinet, and her clothes in the built-in wardrobe were plentiful and of a good quality. She dressed plainly now but had once had a more affluent lifestyle.

I was a little startled, about forty-five minutes after she and Connor left, to hear a loud rap on the front door. I was in her bedroom at the time, so gently closed the top drawer on her dressing table, making sure everything I'd disturbed had been returned to its proper place, and crept to the window. I pulled back the curtain to see Gardner on the doorstep of the shop.

For a moment I was tempted to ignore him, and then had a much better idea. I made my way down.

'Can I help you?' I asked, as I pulled open the door.

Gardner visibly started when he saw me.

'What are you doing here?' he said, before he could get a hold of his manners. I didn't bother to respond.

His aftershave, cloying and a bit sickly, came drifting in towards me; as did the scent of woodsmoke, altogether more pleasant.

'I was looking for Anna,' he tried again, after a few seconds.

'She's not here.' I stepped back into the shop, my hand on the door. 'Can I take a message?'

'When will she be back?' His eyes flicked up to the bedroom window and down again. I'd deliberately left the light on.

'I couldn't say, I'm afraid,' I told him as I closed the door. 'I'll tell her you called by.'

I glanced back before I went into the kitchen. Gardner was still outside the shop, staring stupidly in at the dark interior.

All things considered, it had been my most enjoyable evening in a very long time.

'I have to go to the police,' Anna announced the next morning, Monday, when I called round for an update. I'd heard her come back late the previous evening – alone – but hadn't wanted to appear too eager for news. She'd already told me that Connor had been kept in overnight at the hospital for observation.

I waited.

'I feel bad about betraying The Two Connies,' she went on. 'But while we were waiting to be seen last night I had time to check the law on underage sex.'

I'd done the same thing but I let Anna go on.

'Sex between a fifteen-year-old and a seventeen-year-old is definitely illegal in the UK, but given that Connor is still under eighteen, and the relationship was consensual, it's likely he'll be dealt with more leniently than if he were an adult. He may get away with a caution, or not even that.'

I'd learned the same thing myself; I'd also surmised that if Constance's family or the church, or both, decided to throw some legal muscle at Connor, his punishment could be a whole lot worse.

'And what they did to him was shocking. They can't get away with that,' she went on.

'Don't the hospital have a duty to inform the police if they suspect someone's injuries are the result of a crime?' I asked, relying on information from TV shows.

'It's complicated,' she told me. 'Easier if there's obvious evidence of a knife or gun attack, but that doesn't apply in Connor's case. My guess is they won't do anything without his consent, and he wasn't giving it last night. He claimed he'd fallen off a bike. They'll keep asking him, but unless he comes clean I don't think they'll act.'

'But you're going to?'

'He confided in me,' she said. 'So did Constance. They both want help, even if they're too afraid to ask outright.'

I nodded.

'I'm going now,' she went on. 'I'll open the shop late. Do you want to come?'

'I might be more use here,' I suggested. 'Minding the shop for you? I'd go to the police myself, but I don't drive, as you know. And a phone call never has the same impact, does it?'

Her eyes opened wide in surprise. 'You'd mind the shop?'

I smiled. 'Of course. How hard can it be?'

Not very, was the answer; in fact, I was surprisingly good at it. I've always been good with numbers, so reckoning up customers' bills was easy, and my memory is quite sharp. I didn't need anyone to repeat their order. I didn't waste time smiling or chatting, as I'd seen Anna do, but no one could fault my efficiency. I even did some baking, popping loaves into the oven and being careful about temperature and timing; they came out perfect.

By the time Anna returned, two hours after she'd left, I'd sold all the fresh morning pastries and taken over a dozen orders for lunchtime soup and sandwiches.

'How did you get on?' I asked, as she started chopping vegetables for the soup.

'Not great,' she admitted. 'They kept me waiting a long time and there was a photograph on the wall of the police superintendent at a black-tie function with Aran North that I had to stare at while we were talking.'

The shop bell rang at that moment. 'I'll get it,' I said, leaving the room before she had chance to object.

'Coffee for two and two toasted currant teacakes,' I said when I returned.

Anna sliced two teacakes and put them under the grill while I found cups, saucers, milk jug and sugar bowl. The coffee was in a heatproof jug behind the counter in the shop.

'They weren't taking you seriously?' I said, as I loaded up a tray. I'd suspected they wouldn't.

'They certainly tried not to, but I kept talking about children at risk, safeguarding issues, and long-term repercussions should anything happen to them, so in the end they agreed to talk to Connor at the hospital and to Constance up at the site.'

I carried the tray through to the shop and poured coffee for the two village ladies who'd stopped by on their way home from shopping.

'I don't imagine either Connie will be pleased,' I said to Anna, when I was back in the kitchen.

'You think I shouldn't have done it, don't you?' she said, as she buttered the grilled teacakes and filled a bowl with her homemade marmalade.

'I think you're between a rock and a hard place,' I said.

Anna's time away had left her with a lot of catching up to do, so I worked with her for another hour and left only at her insistence.

'Oh, I nearly forgot,' I said, as I washed my hands. 'The library called to let you know they do have a copy of *Jude the Obscure* in stock. You can collect it anytime. They've also got *The Woodlanders* and *A Pair of Blue Eyes*.'

I was drying my hands as I gave the message, but when I looked up, Anna's face was as white and pallid as uncooked dough.

'I can pick it up, if you like,' I offered. 'I have to pop in tomorrow afternoon.'

'I didn't order anything,' she said.

I knew that, of course; I'd ordered *Jude the Obscure* on her behalf. We keep order cards on the counter for customers to fill in, but they're all destroyed once the order has been entered on the system. There was no danger of my little experiment being found out.

I shrugged. 'Probably an error. Some of the volunteers aren't too confident around the system. I'll let them know.

'I'm not a fan of Thomas Hardy myself,' I added, as I left the shop. Anna was still looking shaken. 'Bit dark for my taste.'

24

May, the previous year

Jago heard the back door open and close, followed by the usual silence as his stepmother took stock of her surroundings. She always did this. He'd watched her once, hiding just out of sight behind a door at the top of the stairs. She'd stood, a few feet inside the kitchen, still and silent, only her eyes moving, this way and that. She was listening for him, he knew, on the alert for any sounds he might be making: music playing in the bedroom, the battle sounds of the PlayStation, his voice on the phone, although he wasn't supposed to be in touch with his school friends, even the cistern refilling. She was trying to decide whether he was in the house or not.

He thought about calling out to her, a cheery greeting. She'd come and find him then, still in her uniform, ask him how he was, what he'd had for lunch, whether he was keeping up with the work schedule the school sent.

He'd wondered before now what she'd do differently if he wasn't in the house. Whip off all her clothes and run around naked? Put on rock music and karaoke along? Sneak in a lover? Phone his dad and talk dirty? Or just breathe a deep, long sigh of relief and smile to herself in the knowledge that she was alone in the house for once.

He could find out. Without making a sound, he crept from his room and slipped along the corridor to one of the spare bedrooms. Not the one she and his dad had picked out for the nursery; she often came to stand in that and stare around at the increasingly elaborate baby preparations. Instead, he went into the other room and moved beyond the bedroom into the en suite. It contained the house's airing cupboard, one he could climb into. He stepped inside and closed the door behind him.

In the darkness that smelled of lavender and freshly washed laundry, he smiled to himself. How long before she realised she wasn't on her own after all? How long before some primitive instinct warned her of another's presence. How long before she came looking for him?

It was like hide-and-seek. For grown-ups.

25

Anna and I went to the hospital together that evening. I noticed she moved very confidently around the building, but her familiarity with all things medical was no longer a surprise to me.

'Oh.'

She'd been walking a little ahead and was the first to step around a screen between two beds. I joined her. The middle-aged man in the bed, eating yoghurt from a carton, was not Connor.

'Sorry.' Anna apologised as we backed away. 'They've moved him,' she said, unnecessarily.

'Nurses' station.' I led the way back to the desk. Two nurses were chatting over a computer screen and we had to wait some time for them to give us any attention. I cleared my throat twice, but I imagine they have a lot of practice ignoring that kind of thing.

'Can you tell us where Connor Graham is?' Anna lost patience first. 'Seventeen-year-old white male, admitted yesterday via the accident and emergency department with multiple injuries. He was in bay four, bed three last night when I left.'

The nurse looked us up and down. 'And you are?'

'Visitors,' I snapped back, before Anna had chance to respond; these people had no right to demand our identity.

'If you're not family, I can't give out any information,' the nurse replied, and I mentally kicked myself for not thinking of that. 'If you are, I'll need some ID. We're talking about a minor, here.'

'I have reason to believe Connor Graham is at risk,' Anna said. 'If you can't help us, we'll have to go to the police.'

'He left with the police,' chipped in the other nurse, earning herself a glare from the first. 'He was discharged at lunchtime.'

'On whose authority?' Anna asked. 'He wasn't fit to be discharged and a minor can't discharge themselves.'

'I'm afraid that's all I can tell you,' the first nurse said. 'Why don't you call tomorrow and ask to speak to his doctor. She's usually on the ward by ten.'

Not surprisingly, we drove straight to the police station. I wasn't even asked if I minded; Anna simply assumed I'd feel as strongly about it as she did. Using Anna's phone, I called both Constance and Connor on the way, more than once. Neither answered. Expecting to be kept waiting at the station, we were immediately shown into an interview room.

A detective in a cheap suit arrived a few seconds after us. He smelled of the outdoors and gave the impression of being a little rushed. I wondered if he'd been summoned specifically to deal with us, which could only mean someone at the hospital had phoned ahead to warn of our arrival. But then again, maybe I was becoming as paranoid as Anna.

He sat down and spread his hands at us. 'Shoot,' he said.

I wasn't sure that was ever a wise remark to make in a police station.

'Teenage lad has a bit too much to drink, falls over, spends the night in hospital, gets a train home the next day. Don't see the problem myself,' he replied, when Anna had explained her – I mean, our – concern.

'He hadn't been drinking and he didn't fall over. He was beaten up,' Anna objected.

The detective scratched at his head and then examined the underside of his fingernails. 'Did you see that happen?' he asked.

'He told us about it himself,' I added, to show willing.

'By a security guard up at Gathering Hall,' Anna went on. 'Possibly one of the same security guards who chased him on Saturday night, causing him to fall into the lake and nearly drown. And obviously the church lied to you about that.'

The detective glanced down at a notebook. 'When our officers spoke to him earlier today, following a report made by yourself I believe, he told us he'd fallen over after having too much to drink. Illegally, I should add, if he's only seventeen.'

'He's saying that because he's frightened,' Anna said.

'He was very agitated,' I added, because Anna kept shooting me looks, the message perfectly clear: *help me out here!*

'The hospital told us that Connor left with the police,' I said to the detective. 'Is that the case?'

The detective yawned. 'I believe it is. I understand he was driven to the station at Penrith and caught a train south.'

'I examined that head wound,' Anna snapped, as I yawned too and tried, unsuccessfully, to hide it. 'It was possible he had concussion, not to mention a badly cut lip and some possible broken ribs. There's no way he should have been allowed to go home.'

'Are you a medical practitioner?' the detective asked.

'I'm a baker,' Anna replied. Her voice remained steady but her cheeks flushed pink.

'Then I suggest we leave the diagnoses to the experts,' the detective said. 'I did want to pick up on something you said last night. How did you come to meet Mr Graham in the first place?'

Something in the room had changed. It was subtle and I was far from sure Anna had noticed, but the laid-back, head-scratching, bored detective had gone on the attack.

'He came to my house looking for his girlfriend, Constance,' Anna replied. 'Have you spoken to her today? I was told you would.'

'All in good time. Why would he come to your house? Were you and this young woman – Constance? – were you close?'

'We've only known Constance a few days,' I chipped in when Anna seemed at a loss. 'But she and Anna have a rapport – I'm sorry, that means a harmonious relationship. They seem to understand each other.'

'Yes, I know what it means.' The detective gave me a dark look. 'And you're worried about both Constance and Connor, two young people you've known a matter of days?'

'Anna's very empathetic,' I said. 'Young people warm to her.'

Well, that earned me a glare from Anna I didn't feel I deserved. I was only trying to help. Well, not really, but I couldn't see what I'd said that was objectionable.

'I understand Connor spent Saturday night at your house?' the detective added. 'Might I ask what the sleeping arrangements were?'

Beside me, Anna gasped. I, on the other hand, had been expecting a question very like that one.

'Connor was supposed to sleep in the shed on Saturday night,' I said, watching Anna out of the corner of my eye. 'Anna's idea. We put blankets and a sleeping bag in there, made it perfectly comfortable. Anna gave him food too, very generously I thought.'

The detective's eyes slid from Anna to me and back again.

'Do you make a habit of entertaining young boys who show up on your doorstep?' he said.

Anna bristled. 'What's that supposed to mean?'

'In the event, though, he didn't return that night,' I hurried on. 'We'd no idea what happened to him until he knocked on Anna's door some twenty-four hours later.' I turned to Anna. 'Isn't that right?'

She looked as though she were about to be sick.

'Connor Graham definitely told us he spent Saturday night at your house, Miss Brown,' the detective continued. 'He didn't mention the shed.'

'He's lying,' she replied. 'Because he's frightened. He spent Saturday night a prisoner up at Gathering Hall.'

'Are you sure he didn't come back late Saturday night, early Sunday morning?' the detective asked. 'He didn't – I don't know – claim he was cold in the shed and ask if he could come inside and get warm?'

'No.' Anna replied.

The detective leaned back in his chair. 'Well, now you see my problem,' he said. 'I'm getting a lot of conflicting information here. Someone is lying. I just don't know who.'

Anna was unusually silent on the way home.

'What now?' I said, when we turned into the high street and were only minutes from home.

'We've done all we can.' She wouldn't look at me as she pulled up. 'Not our problem anymore.'

'Famous last words,' I said, at the sight of the fancy white Range Rover parked outside my own house.

'What do you mean?'

I nodded to the white car. 'That's Aran North's vehicle.'

26

May, the previous year

'I want this to be over. I want to be back at school, studying for my exams, seeing my friends again. I want to go back to normal.'

Annaliese made a note on her pad. *Wants to be well again.*

'We've only got one more session after this,' he went on. 'Can you give me something? Something to make me better?'

She added a question mark to her previous note. It wasn't the first time he'd asked for medication, and his father had made no secret about that being his preferred solution. Prescribe the right pills and the problem disappears. If only it worked that way.

When she didn't immediately reply he dropped his head into his hands. 'I want these voices out of my head. I want these bad thoughts out of my head.'

During their previous session and at the start of this one, Jago had seemed unusually emotional. Still no tears though.

'What bad thoughts?' she asked. 'Do you think you're going to do something you shouldn't?'

He gave her a long, slow, sly look. 'What if I already have?'

For a moment, she wondered if he was going to mention the lake, following her, watching her. She still hadn't found the right moment to bring that up. If he denied it, and he probably would, it could turn their relationship confrontational. Especially as she still wasn't sure it had been him.

'Hurting Miss Chang, you mean?' she said.

He looked surprised. 'No, I'd forgotten about her.'

She felt her eyes widen before she could stop herself. He noticed. He noticed everything.

'No, I don't mean that,' he hurried on. 'I only mean we've talked about her already. I'm talking about something I haven't told you about.'

'Are you ready to tell me now?'

He considered her again and she made a conscious effort not to fidget under his gaze.

'Are these sessions confidential?' he asked. 'They can't be, can they? If you have to make a police report.'

She felt the familiar prick of interest, her pulse rate picking up as it always did on the brink of a big step forward; she told herself to be cautious.

'My report will make a general recommendation based on how I perceive the state of your mental health,' she explained. 'Both now and at the time of the incident with Miss Chang. In particular, I'll be considering how likely you are to harm someone in the future. But the specifics of what you tell me will remain between us.'

He looked unsure.

'The only time I'm permitted to break patient confidentiality is if I think you might hurt yourself, or someone else,' she added.

He looked shocked. 'I don't want to hurt anyone else. I never wanted to hurt Miss Chang. I couldn't stop myself.'

'I believe you,' she said, although she wasn't sure she did.

Jago brushed a hand through his hair and frowned. 'I think talking about it will help,' he said. 'I think it was the, you know, the pent-up feelings that made me lose it in school.'

He looked anxious; his breathing escalated. Pink blotches had appeared on his normally perfect skin. Were they finally getting somewhere? Or was this another one of Jago's games?

'Talking about what?' she asked.

His eyes were as cold and flat as ever.

'I've done something really bad,' he said. 'It wasn't all my fault, I was only a kid when it started, but I shouldn't have done it.'

'Do you feel able to tell me what it was?'

He jumped to his feet then, so quickly it startled her. 'What if it's like me?' he said, as he stepped away from the sofa. 'I don't mean what if it looks like me, because it would, wouldn't it? I mean, what if it's bad like me? What if, between us, we've made a monster?'

He stood in the middle of her room, staring up at the ceiling, breathing heavily, almost panting.

'Jago, what are you talking about?'

'Bella's baby.'

It took her a moment. Of course, the unassuming stepmother. The pregnant stepmother.

He was watching her now. His breathing, she saw, was back to normal.

'Your new brother or sister? What has—'

'No, not a brother or sister. A son or daughter. I'm its father.'

27

Anna insisted I join her and North. We sat in the shop and were offered nothing, not even a glass of water.

North was wearing a dinner jacket, very well cut, and a black silk bow tie. His dress shirt had studs rather than buttons and his black leather shoes gleamed like dark mirrors. He glanced at his watch before speaking, as though sending us a subtle message: I am important, my time is precious, you are right to feel intimidated by me.

'The food was a triumph on Saturday night,' he began. 'Everyone said so.'

'I'm glad,' Anna replied, looking anything but.

'We're very much looking forward to seeing what you have for us tomorrow,' North went on, as I realised that in spite of his sartorial efforts, he was actually discomfited. She might not realise it yet but Anna, for the moment, had the upper hand. She let her lips stretch into a tight, cold smile. Maybe she did realise.

He turned to me. 'And, if I may, it's nice to be seeing more of you these days. Anna rather seems to have brought you out of your shell.'

I thought him a patronising twat but I gave him a smile that mimicked Anna's.

'Working on anything interesting?' he went on.

'Can we help you with something, Mr North?' I said. 'Did you want to discuss menus for tomorrow?'

He didn't, of course, and it was hardly my business to ask, but Anna gave no sign that she minded.

He said, 'I wanted to talk about Constance.'

'Is she alright?' Anna said.

'Yes, of course.' North frowned for a moment. 'That is, physically she's perfectly well. But we are concerned.'

'How so?' Anna asked.

'How much has Constance told you about herself?' he replied.

'Practically nothing,' Anna said. 'But I've been able to surmise a great deal. She's unhappy, her parents seem unusually controlling, and the ordeal that she and the other young people face at this festival of yours is causing her a lot of anxiety.'

'And a close friend is so concerned about her that he hitchhiked all the way from Sussex,' I added. 'He almost drowned in the lake before being beaten up by your security guards for his trouble.'

North took a moment before answering. 'Connor Graham was set upon by some village lads. Very regrettable, but we do have something of a drug problem on the social housing estate. I believe staff from the church might even have broken up the fight.'

'Staff from the church kept him imprisoned for most of the day,' I insisted. 'Which sounds like a somewhat serious offence to me. Have the police spoken to you about it yet?'

'He was taken to the hall so that we could apply first aid,' North argued. 'He refused all our offers of help. In the end we had no choice but to let him go, as he was insisting upon.'

Anna and I shared a look. I didn't think she was buying it. I know I wasn't.

'And he wasn't badly hurt,' North went on. 'The hospital only kept him in overnight because the lady with him – I imagine that was you, my dear – made a bit of a fuss. The next day his parents phoned Constance's family and arranged for him to be sent home. They'll meet the train at King's Cross.'

The man was lying; I knew it and Anna knew it. For one thing, he couldn't hold eye contact with either of us. His glance kept darting down, to his cuffs, his watch, even his shoes. For another, Constance had told us that Connor only had a mother, who had no idea where he was half the time.

'As to Constance, she's really quite fragile,' North pressed on, as though not considering for a moment that we might not be going along with his nonsense. 'Her parents have given me permission to share something with you, so you'll understand her better.'

'We're listening,' Anna said.

North took a phone out of his breast pocket, glanced at the screen and put it away again. He said, 'Has Constance ever mentioned an older sister?'

After a brief glance at each other, Anna and I shook our heads.

'Her name was Emily, and she turned sixteen two years ago, a few weeks before the Ingathering.'

North's use of the past tense suggested the story wouldn't have a happy ending.

'She vanished,' he went on. 'Ran away one night and was never seen again.'

'She ran from here?' Anna asked.

North inclined his head. 'She'd been unhappy with the church for a long time. It happens, of course, young people are programmed to rebel against authority, and Emily was always strong-minded. She slipped out of the caravan one night and wasn't missed until the next morning, by which time she was long gone.'

'You must have looked for her,' I said. 'The police must have looked. A sixteen-year-old runaway would have been treated as high priority.'

I was relying on TV shows again.

'Of course. The family are still looking. I believe they will always be looking. But can you understand why they're anxious when Constance is exhibiting many of the same behaviours that Emily did before she vanished? Why they get nervous when she slips out of the campsite?'

'What behaviours are we talking about?' Anna said.

North gestured with his hands, shook his head slightly; we were meant to assume he felt a little out of his depth. 'Anxiety, depression,' he said. 'Possible autism, although that's never been diagnosed. She's suffered from eating disorders in the past, even dabbled with self-harm. A young lady with problems, like her sister.'

Anna's eyes narrowed. 'Well then, instead of keeping her under lock and key, why don't they fix the problem at source? Not coming here might be a good start; not making her face that hideous ordeal that you call the Hell House.'

North's eyebrows rose. 'I can assure you, of all the things troubling Emily, of everything bothering Constance, the Hell House is the very least of it.'

'Not the impression we've been given,' I said.

North turned to me, and the look in his eyes hardened. 'What do you know about the Hell House?'

'Connor told us about it,' I said. 'He made it sound seriously disturbed.'

'It sounds like child abuse,' Anna added.

'Do you know how many young people abuse recreational drugs or alcohol, Miss Brown?' North asked. 'How many indulge in underage sex, or casual sex once they've turned sixteen, how many have abortions every year, or get trapped in teenage pregnancies, with a lifetime of dependency on the state?'

'Actually, yes,' Anna snapped back. 'Recent figures indicate around twenty-five pregnancies per year for every thousand women aged between sixteen and nineteen. That's a fifty per cent drop on the peak in the early 1970s but still higher than ideal.'

Anna had to be careful. This was not information the average baker would have. I'm smarter than most people, but everyone would guess her secret if she carried on like this.

'All we're trying to do is get them thinking a little more about the consequences of their actions,' North said. 'To help them learn impulse control.'

Anna scoffed. 'By frightening them out of their wits?'

He gave a soft laugh. 'I think you underestimate how resilient young people are. Have you seen some of the films they watch? Some of the attractions they pay good money for at the theme parks? I think they call them the horror mazes. I promise you our little effort is quite tame in comparison.

'And then there are any number of road safety videos,' North went on. 'The police deliberately make them graphic, to show young drivers the consequences of driving recklessly, or under the influence. I believe schools use similar videos to dissuade children from experimenting with drugs. Encouraging good behaviour through fear is hardly something our church invented.'

I was thinking the man had a point, but Constance's fear, and Connor's on her behalf, had been real.

'Nevertheless, if Constance is emotionally fragile, why on earth would you put her through it?' Anna said.

'The Hell House is entirely optional,' North replied. 'If Constance chooses not to take part, no one will pressure her into it.'

I said, 'That's not the impression Connor gave us.'

North had said all he'd come to say. He put his hands on the table, palms down, on the verge of getting to his feet. 'Ah yes, but Connor is not a member of our church. He was talking on the basis of rumour and supposition.'

I said, 'I'm sure both Anna and I will feel a lot happier if we can see Constance. Satisfy ourselves that she isn't at risk.'

'That will be up to her parents.' North seemed to reconsider. 'I'll tell you what I can do. I'll show you round the Hell House myself. It will have to be in daytime, the evenings are busy, but I'm sure you'll see there's nothing to be afraid of.'

North was on his feet. 'How about it,' he said. 'Shall we make a date?'

I spent a quiet evening working, catching up on reading I'd been putting off, listening to the sounds of Anna getting ready for the next day. She went to bed early, as she usually did, and I thought I wouldn't be far behind. I got caught up in something though, and it was coming up for midnight before I locked my office for the night. I was on the verge of leaving the room when a sound from outside caught my attention.

There are no lights at the back of our small terrace and the night was a dark one. Thick cloud cover blocked all light from the moon and stars. The wind was light. Branches swayed gently, leaves rustled, and from somewhere close by came the call of a fox.

And then a human figure, indistinguishable in the darkness, slipped in through Anna's back gate and made its way across the courtyard.

28

May, the previous year

'Got a minute?' Annaliese's supervisor poked his head round her door as the clerical and admin staff were all leaving for the day.

'Definitely,' she replied. 'Actually, do you have several? I'm out of my depth on this one.'

She felt a sliver of relief at finally being able to admit it. Yesterday, along with some dry-eyed sobs, Jago Moore had told her, in sickeningly graphic terms, that his stepmother had seduced him at the age of thirteen, that the two of them had been having regular sex for the past four years, his father's frequent absences from home making it easy.

His feelings of guilt, his fears for what would happen when the baby arrived, and his terror of his father finding out, had led, he claimed, to his outburst at school.

'You can't tell anyone,' he'd insisted. 'If you tell anyone I'll deny it. I'll claim you made it up. I can't let him find out. He'll kill me.'

Her supervisor came into the room and closed the door. 'Jago Moore,' he said.

Why wasn't she surprised? 'I have one more session with him,' she said. 'Tell me—'

'No, you don't.' Her supervisor pulled up a chair and sat.

She said, 'Sorry?'

His face was unusually stern. 'Not alone, you don't. Louise came to see me earlier.'

Louise was her PA. 'What's this about, Peter?'

'The cleaner, one of the agency staff, had had a word with her.'

'And what?' she said, unable to keep the edge from her voice. 'I'm not keeping my room tidy enough?'

Fair play to him, he wasted no time. 'She found condoms in your waste bin.'

It took her a moment.

'She found what?' She pushed back her chair so that she could see the bin beneath the desk.

'Not that one.' He twisted round in his chair. 'The one by the sofa. The one the clients use.'

The tiny ornamental bin by the sofa was there to catch the used tissues that were an occupational hazard. She always made sure she had tissues, a bin, and water to drink on hand.

'Condoms?' It wasn't possible.

'Used condoms. Two to be precise, on two separate occasions. The most recent being yesterday.'

She swallowed.

'On both occasions, Jago Moore was on your appointments list. Louise tells me you didn't leave the room at any time while he was with you.'

The room seemed smaller somehow, the air thicker. 'I'm struggling to know what to say.'

He sighed. 'Well, let me save you some time. I don't believe for a moment that anything untoward has been going on between you and that boy.'

She would feel relieved about that when she had time. For now, she was struggling not to be sick. He'd put used condoms in her waste bin? How? More to the point, why?

Her supervisor said, 'If you didn't leave him alone in here, how did he do it?'

So many thoughts tumbling round in her head, most of them panic-stricken. 'He was here for the first appointment after lunch yesterday. He emptied his pockets before he left. I wasn't paying much attention, but I thought I saw a used tissue and maybe a bus ticket. Nothing else. The time before that, I can't remember, I'm afraid.'

'Has he given you any reason to feel uncomfortable before this?'

She told her supervisor about the 'chance' meeting outside her gym, and about the watcher by the lake who had looked a lot like Jago.

'There was no point reporting it,' she said. 'I had nothing concrete to go on.'

A thought struck her. 'He dropped a Post-it note in front of Louise one time. It had my home address on it. I had no idea how he knew it.'

Her supervisor showed no surprise; he'd already known that.

So, Jago was trying to set her up.

'I guess the condom could have been concealed by the tissue,' her supervisor said. 'The point is, we have to assume he wanted it to be found. We have to ask ourselves what he's up to.'

29

The curtain had risen on the evening's performance when we arrived at Gathering Hall on Tuesday night.

Anna drove us in through security and we were directed up to the house. Taking no chances, the church had a member of staff follow us up on a quad bike, and we could see a further two people waiting by the kitchen door to help us unload.

They couldn't stop us looking, though, at the line of youngsters waiting to enter the main marquee, or their parents hanging around, chatting a little, trying to disguise their nerves. With the lights on around the entrance, the fascia we'd been unable to make out on our last visit stood out clearly against the night sky.

The Hell House.

'I really don't have a good feeling about that,' Anna said as we drove past.

While the biggest house in the area, Gathering Hall certainly wasn't as grand as its name suggested. A solid, square, stone building, it stood two storeys high, its only ornamentation a large, recessed, arched window above the front door. There was no garden to speak of. Instead, the parkland came right up to the front door.

The wind felt stronger up at Gathering, singing around the hall's chimneys and the ropes of the marquees. Flaps of unsecured canvas banged out discordant rhythms and the amplified sounds of screams, shouts and even gunshot coming from the main marquee were disquieting to say the least.

It didn't take long to unload as we were only catering for twenty-five of the church elders, not much more than a big dinner party, according to Anna. The church had sent down heat-retaining containers from the hall's kitchen; the food had already been cooked and simply needed to be plated and served.

More church people were waiting for us inside, I counted eight at one point, most young, but one or two older, possibly there to supervise. Some were dressed in black trousers and white shirts, the waiters, I presumed; others wore aprons, determined to help us in the kitchen.

Very determined. They hovered like wasps around a forgotten jam tart, demanding to know what we needed and what they could do, before we even had chance to look around the kitchen.

'Can someone show me the lavatory?' I said, not because I needed it, but because it might get at least one of them out of Anna's face. She needed a few minutes alone, to look around, take stock, plan, and she wasn't being allowed it. 'And we came without barbecue tongs. Can someone find us a pair? Oh, and some tweezers, and small scissors, the smallest pair you can find.'

We had no need of barbecue tongs, tweezers or scissors, and I thought for a moment Anna would give the game away, but she caught my eye and answered with a gleam of hers. Two minions vanished in search of sundry implements and one came with me, leaving five for Anna to cope with.

The interior of Gathering Hall that I got to see was plain and functional. The walls of the back corridor were painted a pale yellow and strip lighting ran the length of the ceiling. Opposite the back door a narrow staircase ran up to an upper floor. The place smelled of school dinners and disinfectant.

'So, have you been through the Hell House yet?' I asked my minder, a young woman of around twenty. 'Mr North's offered to show Anna and me around. I'm wondering what to expect.'

'I did it four years ago.' Her voice was tight, as though I'd insulted her by assuming her to be sixteen. The young are so easily offended.

'Ah, then you might have known Emily,' I said. 'The girl who ran away two years previously. Is there any news?'

My mistake, her previous look hadn't been offended. This new one: the pursed lips and glacial stare, this was offended.

'Here you are,' she said, indicating a door directly ahead. 'I'll wait outside.'

I went in, took in the 1930s plumbing and coal tar soap, and stepped to the good-sized window. Locked, with no key in sight. I filed the information away and flushed the lavatory for good measure.

'Still here?' I said cheerily when I opened the door. 'I'm sure I could have found my way back. It's this way, isn't it?'

I set off towards the back staircase I'd spotted earlier.

'Not that way. That's the wrong way. You can't go up there.'

Reaching the stairs, I looked up: narrow enough to make crossing someone coming the other way an intimate experience but otherwise unremarkable. A length of fancy red rope strung from one stair wall to the other suggested access was restricted and sure enough, I saw a small square notice that read *Staff Only*.

My minder put a hand on my arm. 'You need to come back to the kitchen,' she said.

I didn't move. 'Madwoman in the attic?' I suggested. 'Let's go and see.'

Alarm flashed in the poor girl's eyes. 'I'll have to call someone.' She didn't move, though. She'd been told not to leave me alone and that seemed to outweigh all other considerations.

I put my head onto one side, as though thinking hard about something. 'This is ringing a bell. Servants' staircase, leading only to a few attic rooms and the roof.'

My minder looked close to panic. 'We're not allowed up there,' she said.

'No,' I replied, unhooking the rope. 'You never have been, have you? Only staff have rooms up here. Oh, it's all coming back to me.' I started up the stairs. Giving a barely audible squeak, my companion followed. 'Children broke the rules, didn't they – what was it, three, maybe five years ago – with terrible consequences.'

We'd reached the halfway point. 'It was the talk of the village,' I said. 'Albeit in very hushed voices. No one wanted to make a fuss.' I carried on up. 'No one ever makes a fuss over church business.'

The young woman hesitated only a few seconds before following me up.

'This is the only point in the house where the roof can be accessed, isn't that right?' I was at the top by this time, gently twisting the doorknob, holding my breath in case one of the staff members who slept up here would be hanging around. I'd gambled on them being busy at the Hell House.

The short corridor was empty. Four internal doors – to bedrooms, I assumed – were closed. The six metal steps that led to the roof were a pace or two to my left.

'And youngsters had got into the habit of sneaking up here.' I'd reached the steps. 'To sit on the roof and watch the festivities below, having a cheeky drink, smoking some cannabis.'

'I never smoked weed. And it was only cider. We were only messing about. You really can't go up there.'

Well, what a stroke of luck. This girl had been one of the sixteen-year-olds involved in the incident four years ago. Just kids, messing about, watching their peers go in and out of the Hell House from their vantage point on the roof and, yes, maybe they were indulging in some illegal substances, but no harm was meant. Or so they repeatedly insisted. No harm at all.

Until one of them died.

The door at the top of the metal steps was locked but the key hung from a hook directly above it. I unlocked the door, pulled back bolts from its top and bottom and ducked to make my way outside. The wind hit me full in the face and the smell of bonfire smoke rushed into my nostrils. From the Hell House marquee I could hear the thud of rock music and the screeching of banshees. (At least, that's what it sounded like; I had no idea if actual banshees were involved.)

I turned to the young woman, half in, half out of the doorway, torn between frightened and furious. She was going to be in trouble for allowing me to come up here. She followed me, though, when I moved away from the door.

'This is where it happened, isn't it?'

I saw her nod, miserably, out of the corner of my eye.

We were in a narrow space between two of the roof apexes, invisible from the ground. I walked towards the side of the house, watching where I stepped, and reached a flat area that held a large chimney stack. Being careful – I think I've already made clear I'm not a brave person – I stepped to the edge.

I had a perfect view of the Hell House. I could see the queue of youngsters waiting to go in, could almost sense the mixture of excitement and apprehension they'd be feeling. With the wind bringing tears to my eyes the multitude of lights strung around the tents cast long, shaky rainbow streaks into the darkness and the music had a demonic sound. There was a sense of immense privilege being up here, looking down on mortals.

'This is the first time I've been up here since,' the girl at my side said, and I realised then that it had been the place and her own memories drawing her up here, not me.

'What was her name?' I asked. 'Polly? Penny?'

'Phoebe,' she said. 'Phoebe Page. She was my best friend.'

'Did you push her?' I asked, more to get a rise than anything else. I knew this girl hadn't pushed Phoebe.

'No!' She was as horrified as I'd expected. 'No one pushed her. She fell. There was an inquest. We all had to go. It was an accident.'

'Of course,' I said. 'Silly of me.'

The inquest had indeed concluded that Phoebe Page's death had been a tragic accident; I'd read about it in the local paper shortly afterwards.

'You left her alone, though,' I said. 'Knowing she'd had a lot to drink, and probably high as a kite on cannabis, you left her alone on the roof.'

Tears filled the girl's eyes. 'We didn't mean to. We thought she was right behind us.'

'And yet one of you locked the door,' I said. 'So she couldn't get down.'

'Not me.' The girl looked horrified. 'I didn't do it. I'd remember something like that, wouldn't I?'

'Of course you would,' I replied, in what I hoped was a gentler voice. I'd no wish for this girl to slip into hysterics. 'Not your fault at all.'

I'd had my fun and it was time to get back. 'Look at the time,' I said as I set off towards the roof door. 'I've let you distract me when I've heaps to do.'

The two of us returned, in silence, to find the kitchen empty.

'You couldn't find out where Anna is?' I asked my minder. With an undisguised look of relief, she said she'd investigate and committed the cardinal sin of leaving me alone.

Not that there was much I could get up to. The room around me – a large Victorian kitchen that had been modernised periodically – looked well prepared for the evening's festivities. Two range ovens on opposite walls were lit, throwing out a lot of heat and making the windows opaque with condensation; a dresser, stripped of its crockery, held around a dozen wine bottles and several large water jugs; a large oak table in the centre of the room held boxes from Anna's car; piles of various-sized plates stood ready beside the warming ovens. The blackberry sauce for the main course had already been transferred into saucepans on the hotplates and the sauceboats stood nearby. There was no sign of cutlery but I imagined that was already on the dining table.

Two doors led out of the kitchen into the interior of the house. The one I'd already half explored on my trip to the facilities had taken me past a series of smaller, cloakroom-type spaces and the aforementioned back staircase. The other, I judged from the voices I could hear, led to the dining room and the various reception rooms of the house. There was a single external door. I was on the point of wandering over to see if it was locked when a white face appeared at the window above the sink.

I jumped, I don't mind admitting, but my alarm lasted only a second. It was Constance. I pointed to the door and moved towards it. She did the same, like my reflection in a mirror.

'Can I help you with anything?' My minder was back, hovering in the doorway, as though not liking to come too close to me.

'Fresh air,' I told her, praying Constance had ducked out of sight. She had. 'I need the door open for a second.'

I reached it and tugged on the handle; the door was locked.

'Can you find me a key?' I asked.

She looked uncertain. 'Try a window? Anna's in the dining room, by the way. She said she won't be a minute.'

I looked back at the windows and fanned myself for good measure. 'They're locked too.'

'There should be a key. Hanging up between the sink and the draining board.'

There had been a key, in exactly that spot, but there wasn't anymore. In the few moments I'd been alone, I'd found it and slipped it into my pocket, figuring it might come in handy before the evening was out.

'It's not that hot, is it?' The minder said, when we'd ascertained that the window key had indeed vanished.

'It will be later. You don't want your caterers fainting on you, do you? Be a love and find it.'

With ill-concealed annoyance, she left the room again.

I turned back to the window and rapped lightly on it to attract the attention of the girl I was pretty sure was still out there. Then, keeping a close eye on the reflection of the room behind me, particularly the two doors, I wrote a message, backwards, on the glass.

Lavatory window. 30 mins.

The first course, at Aran North's request, was a miniature version of the grazing table we'd provided for the opening night. Everything had been prepared in advance, so Anna and I had only to unpack the breads and biscuits, the flavoured butters, the cured salmon, marinated prawns and grilled vegetables, arrange everything beautifully on six wooden boards and hand them to the minions to carry through. In the kitchen, though, we deliberately avoided giving our helpers anything to do, in the hope some would get bored and wander away. For a while it seemed to be working and two of them did. Others remained in the dining room to serve drinks. Not for a moment, though, were we left entirely alone.

The barbecue tongs arrived and I used them as a back-scratcher, making Anna giggle. The plates and dishes for the main course went into the warming ovens and Anna checked the temperature on all the heat-retaining containers. I started to warm through the blackberry sauce that would go over the pre-cooked duck breasts.

All the time we were working I kept a close eye on the clock and when thirty minutes were up, I excused myself again. By this time, the grazing platters were coming back from the dining room and there was enough bustle for me to slip away unseen.

In the lavatory, I used the key to open the window.

'I'm here,' Constance whispered from a short distance away.

I beckoned her over.

'We've been phoning you,' I said. 'Anna's very worried.'

She had to stand on tiptoe to talk to me, her hands clutching the bottom of the window frame. 'They took my phone away,' she replied. 'Do you know where Connor is? I think they beat him up. One of the other kids saw him being carried away bleeding.'

I kept my voice low; we had no idea who might be hovering nearby. 'Anna drove him to hospital. We're not sure where he is now though.'

She glanced around. 'That means they've got him again. This is really messed up. I can't get out. None of us can. They won't let us past security.'

Behind me, someone knocked on the door. 'Everything OK in there?'

'It's occupied,' I snapped back, signalling to Constance to hang on for a second.

On the other side of the door, my name was called. 'Anna sent us to check on you,' they said, which I knew was a lie.

'Two minutes,' I called back. 'Must have eaten something that disagreed with me.'

'Can you get to the lake,' I whispered to Constance. 'Stay away from the bonfires and they won't see you. Come to the dark side of the jetty and look across the water. Ten, fifteen. Anna and I will meet you there.'

30

May, the previous year

'Why is he here?'

Jago had visibly started when he'd spotted Annaliese's supervisor in the room. She felt a mean rush of satisfaction at his discomfort and acknowledged that Jago Moore really did bring out the worst in her.

The window blinds were down. She and Peter had already agreed that, come what may, they weren't being moved.

'Dr Atkinson is my supervisor,' Annaliese explained. 'It's his job to monitor how I manage my client relationships, and to offer advice when I feel I need it. As this is our last scheduled session, I thought it would be helpful. Why don't you sit down, Jago?'

The boy didn't move.

Her supervisor gave Jago a broad smile. 'You might find a male perspective useful.'

'Of course, if you prefer, we can arrange to video the session.' Annaliese watched Jago's gaze move to the video camera set up on a tripod directly facing where the boy normally sat. 'Then Dr Atkinson—'

'Peter,' her supervisor corrected.

'Then Peter and I can review the session later,' she went on. 'Whichever you feel more comfortable with.'

She watched the boy's body tense, a sudden tightening, a flicker in his eyes that spoke of imminent violence, and felt her own body mirroring it. She drew her feet closer to her body, put her hands on the arms of her chair, ready to jump to her feet if necessary. She was glad, and felt guilty at the same time, that Peter sat between her and Jago, and that Peter was a big man.

Reaching a decision, Jago strode to the sofa and collapsed down. He pushed his feet out so that his legs were stretched beneath the coffee table, leaned back and folded his arms. Presenting, at the same time, both aggressive and defensive body language.

Well, they hadn't expected it to be easy.

She began, as she and Peter had agreed, with the usual routine questions about Jago's week, what he'd been up to, how things were at home. His replies were mainly monosyllabic, terse, close to rude. They told her nothing other than the boy's extreme unease with the situation.

When twenty minutes had passed of their scheduled hour, Peter put his fountain pen down on the coffee table. It was their pre-arranged signal.

'Before we go on, Jago,' she said. 'There are a few things we want to talk to you about.'

She went on to detail the discovery of the used condoms in her waste bin, the Post-it note with her home address, the apparent coincidence of his being outside her gym and her suspected sighting of him at the lake.

'You can understand why that sort of behaviour would be of concern to us,' Peter said, when she'd finished.

The boy had become still as a statue. Several seconds passed.

'Jago?' she prompted. 'How do you explain all those things?'

'I knew you'd do this,' he said.

'Do what?'

His eyes fell. 'Make out it's all my fault,' he mumbled.

'I'm not following.' She shared a glance with her supervisor. 'Did you put condoms in my bin?'

He sighed heavily and shook his head, but his eyes were still on the coffee table. He wasn't denying it so much as – she had no idea what he was doing.

'Was that you at the lake?' she asked.

'What lake?' he replied, automatically. 'I don't know what you're talking about.'

She shared another look with her supervisor.

'Let's move this on,' Peter said. 'During your last session with Annaliese, you mentioned a troubling relationship with your stepmother. Would you like to talk about that a little?'

He looked up. 'What do you mean?'

'You said you and she were in a sexual relationship,' Annaliese added, although there was no way he could have forgotten what he'd said.

His face screwed up. 'That's disgusting. Why would you say something like that?'

'You said it, Jago, not me. You told me she seduced you when you were thirteen. That the baby she's carrying is yours.'

He jumped to his feet.

'I'm not listening to any more of this. You're sick.' He turned to Peter. 'She's lying to you. She's evil. You don't know half of the things she's done, made me do.'

He stepped away, walking backwards, holding out his hands as though to ward her off.

'I want my dad,' he said. 'I'm going to talk to my dad. I'm going to tell him everything.'

Giving an audible sob, he turned, pulled open the door and ran from the room.

The door slammed shut behind him.

'Well, that went well,' her supervisor said.

She tried to muster a smile and couldn't. There was only one word for what she was feeling right now. Dread.

31

'I hope we're not putting Constance at risk,' Anna said, as we left her house and set off up the lane. It was a little before ten o'clock. 'I don't like the idea of her creeping about the grounds in the dark, especially making her way to the lake.'

'Neither do I,' I agreed, although frankly I didn't care one way or the other. 'But it seems to me she's at risk whether we act or we don't. And approaching us this evening suggests she wants our help.'

I'd already told Anna about Constance's suspicions that Connor was still being held prisoner at Gathering Hall. We'd agreed it seemed far-fetched, but not entirely beyond belief.

'Why would they do something so stupid?' Anna had said. 'I mean, sooner or later, someone's going to miss him.'

'Why would they beat him up, and construct an elaborate lie to cover their tracks?'

'It does suggest they have something major to hide, doesn't it?'

I agreed that it did.

'At the very least, Constance should be able to give us contact details for Connor's mother,' I said, as the lane narrowed, becoming the tunnel-like track that led up to the lake. The latticework of branches above us whistled as we made our way through. Not the best of nights for nocturnal adventures.

'If Connor hasn't gone home,' I said, stepping around an exposed tree root, 'we can get the Sussex police involved. They should be able to put more pressure on the force up here than we've managed.'

'That's for sure.'

Anna had stopped walking, was looking back the way we'd come. 'Did you hear something?' she asked.

The night was a mass of noise. 'What sort of something?'

'A twig breaking, like there's someone behind us.'

There was no one behind us that I could see. The hedge on either side of the track was in constant motion and shadows darted around like pixies. Nothing human that I could make out.

'The wind's making quite a racket,' I said. 'You go ahead, I'll keep a lookout.'

We swapped places and carried on. Constance, too, all being well, would be making her way to the rendezvous point.

The cacophony overhead continued. Dead leaves rustled, branches scraped against each other, several broke and fell to the ground. Invisible creatures fled at our approach, taking flight above our heads, or scrambling for cover at our feet. Then, from some distance behind, came the slurping sound a foot makes when it's pulled, with some difficulty, from mud.

I turned back, without alerting Anna, who was already on edge, but ten yards back the track became almost completely dark and I could see nothing. The Duke of York and his ten thousand men could be on our trail but as long as they kept quiet and at a fair distance, we wouldn't know.

Saying nothing, I pressed on. We emerged from the narrow track, climbed the stile and moved through the woodland towards the lake. From this point, we had the added risk of falling trees to worry about. The October winds invariably fell at least one tree in this patch of woodland, and it would be just our luck for it to happen tonight. The moon, such as it was, had slipped behind a cloud.

'Where did you say to meet her?' Anna whispered, as we reached the beach.

'I told her to go beyond the jetty and look for our lights,' I replied. 'Keep going.'

Slowly, because even with torches, it was very dark, we followed the shore towards Gathering land. When the house emerged from behind the trees and we could see the bonfires, burning low now, but still with small groups of spectators gathered around them, we turned off our torches.

Stopping from time to time to rescue snagged clothes from brambles, we crept forward. I caught the glow of yellow eyes, but it was only a curious fox that didn't linger.

'There,' I said, at last.

To one side of the jetty was a small figure. I switched on my torch, pointed it at her and circled. I was rewarded by seeing the figure move. At that moment, Anna grasped my shoulder.

'I think someone followed us up.'

I switched my torch off again and we waited for our eyes to adjust to almost complete darkness. The moon, back again after its attack of shyness, was a slim crescent and the stars seemed tiny and very far away. The lake, though, gleamed with a dark luminance and we could make out the shapes of trees and rocks on the bank. Someone in dark clothes, remaining perfectly still, would be hard to spot, but once they moved, especially if they kept close to the shore, we'd see them.

We saw nothing.

'Maybe not,' Anna said after a few minutes.

Constance, meanwhile, was making her way towards us and we had no choice but to press on. She emerged, hair first, out of the darkness, followed by a pale face and hands. She was practically within touching distance before we could see what she was wearing, a dark jacket and jeans, sneakers on her feet. She walked straight into Anna's arms.

'Thank you,' she whispered, when Anna had released her and we'd settled down on the damp ground. I'd pay for such recklessness in the morning, but both Anna and Constance felt the need to be low and out of sight.

Nothing of importance was said for at least five minutes. Constance told us that she was okay and repeated her worries about Connor. She hadn't been able to contact him, though, because her parents had confiscated her phone. In hushed tones, glancing at me, she told Anna that no one else knew what the two of them had discussed previously. Her pregnancy, obviously.

'Can we talk?' she said to Anna, with another glance at me.

OK, enough was enough.

'Constance, I saw you in the pharmacy last week.' I ignored Anna's grimace and her warning frown. 'I'm sorry to be blunt, but Anna thinks, and I agree, that the first priority is to get you medical attention.'

'I can't argue with that,' Anna said. 'We both want to help.'

I gave Constance a smile and an encouraging nod.

Anna said, 'I think the best thing is for me to contact social services on your behalf. They can insist upon seeing you, in confidence, and they can organise a doctor's appointment. If necessary, they can arrange for you to be moved to a place of safety.'

'They can do that?' Constance's eyes opened wide with disbelief.

'Of course. There are laws to protect vulnerable children and until you're eighteen, you're legally a child.'

'What about Connor?'

'Can you give us his mother's contact details?' I said.

'Her number's in my phone,' Constance replied. 'I don't have it anymore.'

Honestly, the way young people depend on their phones. What was wrong with a good old-fashioned address book? Or the memory? 'Her name and address then? If we're worried about him, his mother has to be our first port of call.'

Constance gave me some details, vague, but probably enough.

'Constance, the church are very convincing,' Anna said. 'They've persuaded the police there's nothing to worry about. If we're going to help you, if I'm to have a chance of getting social services involved, you'll have to give us something concrete to go on.'

'Connor said you were worried about the Hell House, but Aran North said you won't be made to go into it,' I added. 'He said it's optional.'

Constance shook her head. 'It isn't. We have to do it. Everyone has to.'

'Mr North told us about your sister,' Anna said.

She started. 'What? What did he tell you about Emily?'

Anna and I shared a look; Constance's agitation had stepped up a level.

'That she ran away two years ago,' Anna said. 'That she's still officially listed as missing.'

'And that you've been suffering similar mental health problems yourself,' I went on, because a bit of frankness and honesty was called for. 'Obliging your parents and the church to keep a watchful eye on you.'

'Constance, we're not accepting what they tell us as fact,' Anna said. 'And we're certainly not judging, because mental health problems are nothing to be ashamed of, but we have to tell you the other side of the argument. You need to know what your parents, and the church, will say, if you seek help.'

Her face twisted. 'They're liars. They're such liars.'

'How are they lying?' I asked, although I had a feeling I already knew what Constance was about to say.

'Emily isn't missing. She's dead.'

32

May, the previous year

'I'm not following. You're saying there's nothing wrong with him? That he's faking it?'

Morgan Moore looked on the verge of getting to his feet. Less than five minutes into the meeting with Jago's parents, Annaliese sensed she was losing control of it. At least she didn't have to handle it alone; Peter had insisted on being present.

The stepmother, whom she was seeing for the first time in weeks, seemed to be trying to shrink into the sofa, to make herself invisible. Her pregnancy was more pronounced now and she had the classic pinch-faced look that hinted at morning sickness and extreme tiredness.

Annaliese and Peter had talked at length about whether or not to inform Jago's parents about his claim to be the father of his stepmother's baby. They'd concluded, although she knew neither of them were entirely comfortable with the decision, that while they would have to at some point, now wasn't the time. These two would have a lot to deal with in the coming months. It would be cruel to throw everything at them at once.

Of course, they'd discussed whether it might actually be true. On balance, Annaliese didn't think so; she'd seen too much evidence of Jago's ability to lie and dissimulate. But it couldn't be ruled out.

'No, that is the opposite of what we're saying.' Peter's voice was reassuringly calm. 'Jago is a young man with serious mental health problems. Just not the ones he's been at some pains to present to us.'

Annaliese said, 'I believe, and Dr Atkinson agrees with me, that Jago is showing signs of emerging psychopathic personality disorder.'

Silence, while Morgan tried to process what she'd just said. His wife, who'd been sitting quietly by his side, spoke for the first time.

'What does that mean?'

Annaliese paused for a moment, in case Peter, who'd had more experience with such cases than she, wanted to jump in. When he didn't, she said, 'In simple terms, it's a disorder that presents with deficient emotional responses, a lack of empathy and poor behavioural controls. Commonly it results in persistent antisocial and even criminal behaviour.'

Morgan glared back at her; the stepmother, on the other hand, had a sudden spark of interest in her eyes.

'He demonstrates manipulative behaviour, a strong tendency to be in control at all times, and poor impulse control,' Annaliese added.

Peter stepped in then and she was grateful. The next bit would be hard.

'In such cases we frequently see strong genetic influences,' he said. 'It's quite possible that Jago's mother had similar tendencies. If you were still in touch with her—'

'We're not,' Morgan replied.

Annaliese gave the situation the moment it seemed to need.

'What about these voices?' Morgan demanded. 'He's hearing voices, for God's sake. Voices in his head told him to attack that physics teacher.'

'I don't think so,' Annaliese replied. 'I think, possibly in the face of some – very understandable – pressure at home, Jago has been trying to convince me that he's a schizophrenic, so that I can prescribe medication and he can resume his life. But there simply isn't enough evidence for me to confidently diagnose schizophrenia. At this stage, medication won't help him.'

'You're saying he's lying?' Morgan demanded. 'You're calling my son a liar?'

Jago was a proven liar, but pointing it out probably wasn't the best idea.

'Can you help him?' the stepmother asked.

Honestly? Annaliese didn't know. But saying as much wouldn't take them any further forward. 'Work with younger patients has shown some promising results,' she said. 'I'm going to prescribe cognitive behavioural therapy. That can help with identifying and tackling negative thoughts and behavioural patterns.'

Silence.

'It can be a very effective form of therapy,' she added. 'But I should warn you not to expect immediate results. It takes time. And patience.'

'More of this, you mean?' Morgan snapped. 'You carry on seeing him for months on end, it costs me a fortune and he stays in limbo.'

'We would refer Jago to another practice,' Peter said. 'His relationship with Dr Clayton Brown has become problematic. It wouldn't be ethical for her to continue. Or for him to continue coming into this practice.'

Annaliese waited for that to sink in, for them to demand details of how a relationship between doctor and patient could become problematic.

'You're washing your hands of him?' Morgan said, instead.

'No, we'll ensure he gets the best possible care,' Annaliese insisted. 'But that won't be here.'

'Can he go back to school?' the stepmother asked.

'What about criminal charges?' Morgan practically spoke over his wife. 'Will he face those?'

'We're recommending the police drop criminal charges,' Peter explained. 'Being caught up in the criminal justice system is the last thing Jago needs right now. We can't guarantee anything, but they usually follow our recommendations.'

'We don't think it's a good idea for him to return to school,' Annaliese said. 'The pressures of the school environment aren't what he needs right now. With local authority support he should be able to continue his studies and maybe even take his exams at home. We have to focus on his health right now.'

Morgan dropped his head into his hands. 'He won't recover from this. You've taken away my son's future.'

She and Peter shared a look. Shooting the messenger was a common response to being told your child had serious mental health difficulties that almost certainly would impact upon the rest of his life. Jago's parents were in shock right now, and they were frightened. If she had to be a punchbag for the time being, she would be.

Because for these two, the problems had only just begun.

33

The stunned look on Anna's face was hardly surprising; Constance had just told us that her sister was dead.

'Do you mean, you're afraid she's dead?' I asked.

'I know she's dead. They killed her.'

'Constance, I'm not following,' Anna said. 'You're saying that someone connected to the church killed Emily? And what, the others covered it up, to avoid – I don't know – disgrace? Unwanted attention?'

'No, it's worse than that. It wasn't an accident or anything, it's not some lone maniac, it's part of why we're here. It's the main reason we're here.'

Neither Anna nor I had a ready response and I knew exactly what she was thinking: we'd come up here thinking we were dealing with an eccentric, evangelical church and authoritarian parents and now . . .

Constance didn't wait. 'Every year someone dies in the Hell House,' she said. 'They pick someone who deserves it, and they kill them. It's not the various tableaux that are supposed to keep us in line, it's the thought that the worst of us will die. You think we'd be scared of it otherwise? A cheap horror maze? I've seen scarier stuff at Alton Towers. It would be a laugh, if that's all it was, except it isn't. One kid who goes in there doesn't come away alive.'

Still, Anna and I had nothing.

'They picked Emily because she was a troublemaker,' Constance went on. 'She was no angel, I admit that, but nothing really bad. She drank, smoked a bit of weed, had a couple of boyfriends. What was worse though, was that she called their bullshit, told them their church was a sham and they were all hypocrites. She kept threatening to leave, as soon as she was old enough. They knew she could cause trouble for them so they shut her up before she could.'

'And you think this has happened before?' I asked. 'Before Emily, I mean?'

'Yes, every year.'

'Constance, this can't be true,' Anna argued. 'There must be a hundred families at the Ingathering, three or four hundred people. There's no way they'd all conspire to murder a child.'

Constance started to cry. 'You don't believe me. I knew you wouldn't.'

Remarkable though the girl's story might be, she certainly seemed to believe it. At that moment, I heard a scraping sound from somewhere close by. Anna and I made eye contact; she'd heard it too. I switched the torch off, Anna gently shushed Constance and we waited.

A twig cracked. It might be nothing, but my nerve was close to giving out. I counted to sixty in my head and finally, when nothing more was heard, I let myself relax.

'We need to take Constance to the police,' I said to Anna.

'The police won't do anything,' Constance said. 'They came up after you reported seeing Connor fall in the water, but they just spoke to Mr North and went away again. They didn't look round, they didn't talk to anyone else. They're probably in on it too.'

A fresh sound. A man, coughing. Anna and Constance jumped to their feet. I followed a second later, and then the man appeared.

Connor.

Of course, I'd known all along it had been Connor following us up to the lake; I'd spotted him at the back of Anna's house late the previous night and was pretty sure he'd spent it in her summer house again. Where he'd been that day I had no idea, but I'd seen a figure hanging around in the shadows as Anna and I left to meet Constance. It's all very well though, knowing for certain someone is trailing your footsteps; the suspense of waiting for them to make themselves known can still be intense.

Meanwhile, a squealing Constance had flung herself into his arms. He lowered his head so that his chin rested on her hair and for several seconds they clung to each other. Anna and I shared a look.

'At least he's OK,' I said.

She gave me a half-smile.

I cleared my throat. When that didn't work, I leaned over and tapped Connor lightly on the shoulder. Only then did he release Constance.

'We heard you were on a train,' I said to him.

'I got off at Preston. I wasn't leaving Connie here on her own.'

'You don't look well,' Anna said. 'You shouldn't have left hospital, never mind hitching back here again. You did hitch, didn't you?'

'I'm fine,' he insisted, although his rather rapid breathing suggested otherwise. 'And I slept in your shed last night, hope that's OK.' He looked down at the girl still clinging to his arm. 'Are you OK?'

She nodded. 'I had a positive test though. It's— I'm—'

'I know,' he said. 'It's cool.'

'It really isn't,' I said. 'Even if Constance is imagining the danger she's in at the hall—'

'I'm not,' Constance snapped.

'—which I sincerely hope she is, you've still been badly beaten up by person or persons unknown and she's a fifteen-year-old girl with an unwanted pregnancy. The situation is a very long way from cool.'

'I can take care of them,' Connor said. 'Connie and the baby.'

'I want a termination,' Constance interjected, surprising all three of us. Anna and I waited while she spoke to Connor.

'I know you'll look after me, and I know you'll do your best for the baby, but it's just not the right time.'

Connor took a deep breath.

'We're too young,' Constance went on. 'Please say you understand.'

'Whatever you want,' Connor replied, and I don't think I was imagining the look of relief on his face. Determined to do the right thing he might be, but few seventeen-year-old boys relish the idea of becoming father.

'Is this something you can talk to your parents about?' Anna asked Constance.

She pulled a shocked face. 'Are you kidding me? They already think I'm trash. This will only confirm it.'

'Constance!'

We all jumped, but the shout had come from the opposite shore, from near the bonfires.

'They're looking for me.' Constance pressed closer to Connor.

'How about this,' Anna said, lowering her voice, although no one could possibly hear us from across the lake. 'I can drive you both into Carlisle tomorrow. We can go to social services and ask for the two of you to be placed under an emergency protection order. You'll be able to see a doctor, Constance, and get counselling about the termination, to make sure it's really what you want. Your parents won't be able to interfere with that, but you will have to think about what happens to you long term. You might both be placed in care until you're eighteen.'

'Constance!' Another shout from across the lake.

'Why don't you think about it,' I said to the girl. 'Go back to your parents now, get some rest and call us in the morning. I've got something for you.'

From my pocket I pulled a cheap mobile phone I'd bought in Penrith earlier. 'It's so we can contact each other. My home number and both of Anna's are programmed in,' I said, ignoring Anna's look of surprise. 'Can you keep it hidden?'

Constance nodded and tucked the phone away in her jeans pocket. 'Please help me,' she said, her damp eyes going from Anna to me. 'I think they know about the baby. And they definitely know about Connor. I think I'm next.'

'Constance!' The shout was even closer this time; I thought I saw someone at the water's edge staring in our direction.

'You can't let her go back there,' Connor said.

'I've only got four more nights,' Constance pleaded. 'On Saturday

I have to go in the Hell House. I don't think I'm going to come out again.'

'Then you're safe for four more nights,' I told her firmly. 'Keep your head, don't do anything to make your family or the church suspicious, and we'll talk to you tomorrow.'

She seemed to see the sense in that. Giving Connor a last hug, she stepped away and we watched her make her way back around the lake. When she vanished from sight, Anna, Connor and I began our own journey back.

'I'm really not happy about leaving her,' Anna said, after she'd stumbled over a tree root and I'd pulled her back to her feet.

'Me neither,' Connor muttered.

'Well, neither am I,' I added, although I was fine with it. 'But I don't think any of us want to be accused of abducting a child under cover of night. Which is what would happen if we took her now. In daytime, it will be a different matter.'

'It can't be true,' Anna went on, as a cloud passed in front of the moon and we lost what little light we'd been relying upon. All three of us paused to get our bearings. 'What she told us about the Hell House . . . '

'It is true,' Connor insisted. 'Everyone knows it.'

'Families wouldn't bring their children to a place where they knew for a fact one of them would die.' Anna was standing very close, practically hissing in my ear, and I could see that Constance's wild claims had thrown her. 'And children don't just go missing, not in this country. They go on the Missing Persons list, there are police investigations. And sudden deaths are looked into. It can't be true.'

'I agree it sounds far-fetched,' I said, holding up my hand to forestall Connor. 'But it wouldn't be the first time that parents have murdered their children. Or allowed others to do so.'

Anna uttered a sound, half sob, half moan, and I could tell she thought I was heartless because my reaction had been less extreme than her own.

'We can't let her go back there.' She turned to face back the way we'd come. 'We have to get her out.'

Well, Connor looked on the brink of storming Gathering Hall too, and so I took hold of Anna's arm. 'We'd have no chance of getting anywhere near her,' I reasoned. 'We'd probably find ourselves arrested for breach of the peace, or something.' I glanced at Connor. 'Or beaten up again. Come along, we'll talk when we're home.'

I went ahead, pulling Anna behind me, making sure Connor followed. So far from the village, we were vulnerable to anyone who might be hanging around with evil intent. Finally, the three of us reached the narrow lane that would take us home and I gave Anna a minute to get her breath back. Connor still didn't look too good; he probably needed to be back in hospital.

Anna wiped her sleeve across her face and sniffed hard.

'You can't help her if you go to pieces,' I said, glancing from one to the other, so that Connor knew he was included too. They both glared at me, but when I half shrugged and turned away, they followed. We reached the bottom of the lane and I led the way to Anna's property. We'd left it unlocked and a dim light on in the courtyard. I went in ahead of the other two and so was the first to see the man sitting at one of her outdoor tables. Gardner.

He said, 'We have to stop meeting like this.'

To my surprise, he had a laptop open on the table in front of him. I wouldn't have guessed him to be computer-literate, but we live and learn, as they say.

'Came to show you something,' he said to Anna, after we'd introduced him to Connor. 'Or you. I had a feeling you'd both be out together somewhere.' He smiled. 'Up to no good.'

'Let's take this inside,' Anna said.

Her kitchen was comfortingly warm after the chill night, and the usual array of cooking smells danced around us; there was something about being in Anna's home that invariably lifted the spirits. As I was mulling on this, the others gathered around Gardner's laptop.

I joined them, to see that they were looking at the home page of the same website Anna had shown me days earlier. The heading 'St Abel's Hell' remained, as did the message about finding the actual site on the dark web. Only the photograph had changed. The previous picture of the village had been replaced with one taken from the grounds to the east of Gathering Hall. The house itself was visible behind clusters of trees and bushes.

In the foreground were four freshly dug graves.

34

May, the previous year

Annaliese arrived home unusually tired. The meeting with the Moores that afternoon had taken a lot out of her, and she couldn't help a sneaking suspicion that, on the whole, she hadn't dealt with Jago quite as well as she might. It was possible that, albeit subconsciously, she'd given the boy the impression that her interest in him was something more than strictly professional. On the other hand, she might be caught in the age-old trap of a woman's tendency to always believe herself responsible for the bad behaviour of the male.

Workmen were busy outside her building, a pneumatic drill noisily tearing apart the concrete pavement directly below her living room window. Temporary signs and a rogue water stream running down the street implied a burst water main. Knowing the work might continue into the evening, Annaliese felt the headache that had been threatening for the last few hours spring into life.

Trying, and failing, to ignore the insistent thud of the drill, she opened the car boot and pulled out four carrier bags of groceries. Bracing her shoulders against the weight, she hurried indoors. The lift took her up to the first floor and she lowered her bags to find the flat keys. The drilling, thankfully, had stopped.

Inside the flat her landline was ringing. Her mum always phoned at seven, getting fretful if there was no answer. Wedging the door behind one of the carrier bags, leaving the others in the hallway and abandoning her handbag on the hall table, Annaliese strode down the short entrance hall.

The phone stopped ringing a second before she reached it. She lifted the receiver, ready to return her mother's call, when an instinctive sense of danger struck, as though a cold wind had rushed through the flat. She turned to see Jago Moore standing in the doorway. He'd picked up her shopping, was holding the door open with one outstretched foot.

In the time it took her to absorb that yes, he really was there, he stepped inside and let the door slam shut.

'Nice place,' he said, his eyes flitting past her to take in the kitchen, the archway that led to the living area. 'Just how I pictured it.'

'Jago, you can't be here. You need to leave immediately.'

For a second, he stared at her. Something in his eyes had changed, become harder and, at the same time, less intelligent. She'd seen no previous evidence of drug use in his behaviour, but she wouldn't rule it out now.

The pain in her head started to pulse, beating in time with the accelerated rhythm of her heart. She could feel the clamminess of sweat around her neck and her clothes seemed to have become tighter. She was conscious of an entirely new sensation: this wasn't unease, or wariness; this was fear. She was deeply afraid of the boy in her flat.

The drilling outside sounded up again. He flinched at the sudden noise before a sly smile crept across his face. Three, maybe four seconds passed and then Jago broke eye contact to look behind him. For a moment she thought he was doing as she'd instructed, that he would leave, but instead he lowered the shopping before lifting the door chain and slipping it into place.

He leaned back against the door, a pose suggesting arrogance, a sense of control. This was her space, and yet he'd taken it. Raising his voice to be heard above the drill he said, 'I saw the report.'

'The practice is referring you to another psychiatrist.' Annaliese could hear her voice sounding forced, high-pitched and unsteady. 'You should address any questions to them. Now, you need to leave.'

He took a step forward, then another, his eyes moving steadily from left to right, taking everything in. To his right was the bathroom, the only place in the flat with an internal lock, a place she had no chance of reaching; to his left the hall table on which she'd dropped her bag. Her mobile phone was in it.

She was still clutching the landline receiver like a weapon.

He stopped outside her bedroom door, pushing it open so that he could see inside. She'd left in a hurry that morning; there would be clothes strewn on the floor, the bed unmade. Her stomach clenched at the glimpse of intimacy she'd inadvertently given him.

'Cosy,' he said. 'Bit messy for my taste, but I can be flexible.'

Annaliese began tracing the number buttons on the phone receiver that she still held. She could press nine three times without him noticing, as long as she held eye contact. The operator would hear what was said in the room, would pick up on the emergency. They were trained to do that.

He said, 'Don't do that. Put the phone down.'

She couldn't panic; there had to be some way to take back control of the situation.

'I won't tell you again.'

The knife block was to her right, three paces away. The biggest knife was massive, would cut him to ribbons. Did she have the nerve?

He took a step towards her, then another. One hand, his left, went to the waistband of his jeans. He gave it a tug, as though to loosen it, as though his jeans were too tight.

Oh God help her: the arrogant stance, the assumption of control, the out-of-context sexualisation. These were classic rape signals.

'This is my home, Jago. You don't get to tell me what to do.'

He was younger, faster, stronger that she was. If it came to a fight, he'd win.

At that second, the drilling stopped; the silence seemed to have a presence of its own.

He said, 'You called me a liar.'

'You are a liar. You lied about me. You planted false evidence in my place of work. I'm calling the police now, and if you come anywhere near me, you'll definitely be facing criminal charges. Unlike your school I won't give you the benefit of the doubt.'

Light flashed in his eyes and she braced herself to dive for the knives. Then, just as fast, his face changed. His expression crumpled, as though he was on the verge of tears. She told herself to stay on guard. The boy was a consummate actor.

'That's why I need you.' His voice had taken on a whining tone and his arms wrapped themselves around his upper body. 'Don't you see? I'm not lying, I get confused. You have to carry on seeing me.'

Fighting the instinct to step back, to give him any ground, she said, 'You need a new counsellor now. We'll see that you get one, but coming here won't help your case. Why don't I phone your father? You can wait for him outside.'

He put one hand to his forehead. 'I don't feel well. Can I have some water?'

Another game; he'd be complaining about the light next. 'No. You need to leave.'

He edged closer, a tight smile on his lips. 'I know you like me, Anna.'

'I don't like or dislike you,' she lied. 'You're a patient.'

'I see the way you look at me.'

He was almost close enough to touch her; every instinct told her to scream but she knew if she did he'd leap at her.

'Leave,' she repeated.

'That time at the lake, you knew I was watching you. Do you like me watching you?'

'Get away—'

A hammering sounded at the door, startling them both.

'Wessex Water. Anyone home?'

'I'm coming!' she yelled, even as Jago dived towards her.

He grabbed her by the shoulders, pushing her back against the counter, but in that last split second he'd lost his nerve. He knew it was over. She shrugged him off and half ran back along the hallway. The chain was off and the door opened in seconds.

A man in a high-vis jacket held an ID card up. 'Sorry, love, we've got to switch your water off for an hour or two. I'm just warning people to fill their kettles now.'

She wanted to hug him. She wanted to sink to the floor and let the tears come.

'No problem.' She forced a smile, before turning back.

'Thanks, Jago,' she said, indicating that he should make his way out of the flat. 'I'll be in touch.'

35

'This can't be real,' I said. The three of us were still staring (somewhat stupidly, I thought, in the case of the other two) at the laptop screen. 'These computer types can do some very clever stuff now. And those graves appear to be less than two hundred metres from the hall. That wouldn't go unnoticed.'

'You think it's photoshopped?' Connor asked.

Gardner poured himself a second cup of coffee. 'Photoshopped or not, someone's trying to get our attention.'

'Our attention?' I asked.

'Someone's attention,' he clarified.

'That's what I think,' Anna said. 'I think the same person is behind both this and the X account I found. Probably one of the kids up there.' She tried, unsuccessfully, to stifle a yawn.

'You need to get to bed,' Gardner said to her. 'What time do you have to be up?'

She had to be awake at four, fewer than five hours away, and we hadn't even got started on the cleaning up after the church dinner.

Over the last half hour, though, we'd taken Gardner into our confidence; it had been Anna's idea, but even I could see the benefit of having someone else involved. Also, I'd been curious to see how he would react.

'You should probably get some rest too.' He turned to Connor, who was slumped over the table. 'You can sleep in the boys' room,' he added, surprising all of us. 'I keep the beds made up in case they turn up out of the blue. It's too cold to be sleeping rough. Even in Anna's luxurious summer house.'

'You sure?' Connor asked, as the thankful look in his eyes made him seem even younger than he was. 'Thanks.'

Anna smiled gratefully at Gardner, too; he winked back at her. I cleared my throat and said, 'We still haven't decided what we're going to do.'

'Aran North and Superintendent Benson are like this.' Gardner held up his right hand, his index and middle finger crossed, to indicate the two men were close. 'The police won't take on the church until they have to, and it'll need a lot more than the word of a fifteen-year-old with mental health problems to convince them.'

Connor roused himself. 'Connie doesn't have mental health problems.'

'Maybe not,' I said, although I'd come to much the same conclusion myself. 'But if her parents and the church say she has, whom do you think the authorities will believe?'

'What about her claim that one young person dies every year?' Anna asked Gardner. 'Have you heard anything like that before?'

'Well, not as such.' He looked troubled. 'Come to think of it, though, the Ingathering has been a bit accident prone. There was that kid who fell off the roof a few years ago. Young lad, I think.'

Anna and Connor both looked startled.

'Nasty business,' Gardner added. 'I was on site when it happened, so naturally I had to deal with the body until the medical team arrived. That was an accident, mind you. Kids drinking too much, larking around. It happens. Nothing to do with the Hell House.'

At that moment, Anna's phone pinged. 'Constance,' she said. 'She got back to the caravan alright.'

'You've been here the longest,' I said to Gardner. 'Anything else we should be worried about?'

To my surprise, he thought about it for the better part of a minute; I'd expected an immediate denial, an assertion that the whole idea was ridiculous.

Eventually, he said, 'I remember the girl – Emily, was it? – disappearing the year before last. We had volunteers searching the countryside for days. The police decided she'd left the area. There was talk of her being seen at the bus station.'

I said, 'In which case, she'll be on the Missing Persons list. We can check that.'

'I wish you'd told me about the other night,' Gardner said. 'About Connor being bullied into the water.'

'What would you have done?' I asked. 'You're not a police officer.'

Gardner gave me the look that men of a certain type typically resort to when they feel they're being challenged.

'So, two young people have died or disappeared up there in recent years,' Anna said, quickly. 'The one who fell off the roof and Emily. Does that strike either of you as being a bit unlucky for an annual church festival?'

'Four graves,' Connor reminded us. 'Maybe there's another two we don't know about.'

We turned to look at Gardner's laptop. The screen had gone to sleep again, but I was sure we could all remember the stark image of the graves.

Gardner said, 'I've some authority up at that site. They can't refuse me admittance.'

'How will that help?' I asked.

'I suggest we have a look first thing. Meantime, all three of you look knackered. Why don't we reconvene tomorrow? Come on, Connor, I've probably got a spare toothbrush somewhere.'

Connor pushed himself to his feet.

'We?' I queried. 'We look around in the morning?'

He inclined his head. 'You and me. Fire and safety inspection. You game?'

And so, a little before seven o'clock the next morning, Wednesday, while it was still dark, I left my house to find Gardner waiting by his monster truck.

'That kid's gone again.' He greeted me without so much as a good morning.

'Connor?' I said, although he couldn't reasonably have meant anyone else.

'Let himself out in the night,' he went on. 'Didn't hear a thing. Mind you, I sleep like the dead. Think we should tell Anna?'

Anna was up, of course, lights shining out of her kitchen window. 'I think she's stressed enough. Let's hold off for now.'

'Easily bruised flower, that one,' Gardner said, as he climbed into the driver's seat, and it struck me as an accurate, if somewhat patronising, description of Anna. She was a pleasant person to be around, but hardly robust.

'What do you make of it all?' Gardner asked. 'It's obvious Anna's pretty shaken up. You, I'm less sure about.'

'The people at the hall were very edgy last night,' I said, as we set off. 'They barely left Anna or I alone for a second. And we definitely watched Connor being bullied into the water on Saturday night.'

He seemed to be thinking about that for a moment. 'All the same, it's a bit far-fetched. A conspiracy to kill kids, so the rest of them will be terrified into behaving?'

'Certainly seems that way,' I agreed.

'Even if one or two are prepared to go along with it, and that's stretching credibility, there are – how many families up there?'

'About a hundred.'

'And they're not religious nutters. It's not some cult that locks itself away from the world.'

'No, it's not,' I said. 'Sorry, can you pull over for a second? Just here. Right, won't be a moment.'

I opened the door and climbed down. I'd spotted something, or rather a series of somethings: posters tied around the lamp posts on the road out of the village. I pulled the nearest – a flimsy affair on light card – away from the post and carried it back to the car.

'Where the hell did that come from?' Gardner asked, when I'd climbed back into my seat and we'd both examined it by his car's interior light.

That was a homemade missing poster. The predominant photograph was that of a young girl who bore a distinct resemblance to

Constance. The information beneath it told us that Emily Collins, aged sixteen, had last been seen at the Church of the Ingathering in St Abel's Chapel and was believed to have come to harm. There was a phone number to call with any information.

'Your guess is as good as mine,' I replied. 'But it looks like you were correct last night. Someone is trying to draw attention to what's going on up at the hall.'

Gardner released the handbrake and we drove a little further.

'I still can't see it,' he said. 'These are regular folk. This is just something they do once a year, down a few beers, catch up with some mates. It's not likely they're murdering their own kids, is it?'

'No,' I agreed. 'But that's often how the worst crimes happen. When something's beyond the imagination of most normal people, most normal people let it slip by.'

He gave me a sideways glance. 'You sound like you know what you're talking about.'

I shrugged. 'I watch a lot of TV. One picks things up.'

We soon arrived at Gathering Hall. Gardner showed his ID, but we were allowed in without dissent.

'I'll let Mr North know you're here,' the security guard called as we drove onto the site.

The park was still in darkness. The huge floodlights were turned off and to the east of us were mountains that would keep the rising sun at bay for some time yet.

'Where do we start?' I asked. 'We might have taken them by surprise but they'll be marshalling the troops in the next few minutes.'

'Oh, I think we head straight into the lion's den.' Gardner steered the truck towards the main entrance of the huge, tented structure. 'Let's see what they're up to at this hour.'

He parked directly outside and jumped down before I had chance to argue.

Not that I would have, necessarily; Gardner's sheer physical presence was giving me an odd sort of borrowed courage. I left the truck and he handed me a high-vis vest, so that like him, I looked passably official. As I pulled it on, he began unthreading the lacing that held the main entrance together.

'Even I'm never allowed in unescorted,' he said. 'Makes you wonder what they're hiding, doesn't it?'

Looking back, I saw the security guard who'd admitted us; he was watching from his position by the gate, his handheld radio at his mouth.

Ducking beneath the door flap, I joined Gardner in the facsimile of a pub. As the two of us shone our torches around I could make out wall lights, posters promoting alcohol of various kinds and wooden screens to create an illusion of privacy between tables. A long bar had a mirrored fascia, rows of optics, pumps for beer and cider. In the darkness it was all very realistic. Gardner, meanwhile, had wandered some way ahead and was shining his torch on the marquee's floor. Tiny, inset spotlights suggested a pathway.

'Shall we follow the yellow brick road?' he asked.

I couldn't help a stab of nerves, but it was what we'd come for.

'It's like Ikea,' Gardner said as we set off. 'One way only.'

I had to take his word for it; I'd never been in an Ikea.

The space beyond the pub quickly became narrow and claustrophobic. Dirty brick walls pressed in on both sides. There were doorways of rotten wood and rusting refuse bins, even piles of rubbish left to rot. The place stank, telling me that much of the rubbish, at least, was real. Gardner would have seen all this before but, if anything, he appeared even more uneasy than I felt myself. I wondered, as I followed him through the alley, why he'd chosen to come in here first, rather than looking for the site of the graves outside. The path curved to the right, taking us in a new direction. As we left the stench of the alley behind, our torches started to pick out painted trees and road signs.

I heard the rustle of static suggesting someone was using a radio close by and, from outside the marquee, the sound of low-pitched voices. Security, it seemed, were already on our trail.

Gardner paused by a vehicle: a real car, its bonnet crumpled against a very lifelike tree. My heart was beating uncomfortably fast by this time. Maybe it was the knowledge that we weren't supposed to be here and that when we were caught – sooner or later we were bound to be caught, I knew enough about the church to know that – there'd be trouble.

Voices. Very close.

Abruptly, Gardner changed direction. He'd spotted an unobtrusive door in the internal wall, a fold of plastic that simply needed to be unhooked. We moved through and the highway scene gave way to a woodland. Dark tree trunks were painted on the walls around us and it had been so cleverly done that it looked as though the forest went on for miles. Directly ahead was what appeared to be a real tree. I touched the bark as we drew close and the trunk seemed solid. Crinkled leaves lay strewn across the path at our feet and the earthy smell of soil and rotting vegetation filled the space.

We'd moved several paces into the woodland when we heard what sounded like a strangled cry.

Gardner spun around, his torch beam dancing. 'What was that?'

I had no answer to give.

'Did that sound human to you?'

It had.

He led the way into the gloom as fresh sounds sprang from the silence: an odd, animal-like scrabbling and something like human sobbing. The path edged around a clump of bushes, just tall enough for us to be unable to see ahead. Looming above I could see the thick branches and dull, dry leaves of an oak tree. I'd even kicked aside a couple of acorns in the last few seconds. I brushed my hand over the bushes and felt the prickly dampness of real leaves. I was about to make some comment about how cleverly the place had been designed, when Gardner cried out and vanished. I followed quickly.

Before us was a boy, about eighteen years old, hanging by the neck from the thickest branch of the oak tree.

36

Jago had perfected the art of entering the house unheard. He let the back door close gently and stepped inside the cloakroom. Voices were coming from his father's study, and that meant he could get upstairs without being seen. He left the cloakroom, stepping slowly, because slow meant silent. His father was finishing a call.

He was still on edge after talking to Annaliese. He had no idea what had made her overreact like that, but he knew he was done with women and their mixed signals.

'Right,' Morgan was saying, as Jago edged around the kitchen's central island. 'You can expect to hear from my solicitor.'

Bella had been cooking again; the heavy-duty knife she used for chopping root vegetables was in the sink, waiting to be washed. In the study, all was silent.

Jago paused on the first step. The stairs were wooden, uncarpeted, and while he'd tried to memorise the various places where the boards squeaked, sometimes they took him by surprise.

Bella's voice sounded flat when she said, 'They won't take him back?'

'"Better for all concerned if Jago does not return,"' his dad replied. 'Tell me how that's better for Jago, exactly? How is that better for me?'

'It's not my fault, Morgan.'

Jago heard his father sigh.

'You're not really going to get solicitors involved, are you?' Bella said. 'How can that help?'

So, he wasn't going back. It was a stupid school anyway. Full of slags and losers.

His dad said, 'Attack's the best form of defence.'

'Not always. At least there won't be any criminal charges. That has to be a good thing.'

That could change if Annaliese reported his visit that evening; she was more than capable of twisting things to make him look bad.

Bella said, 'It might be time to accept these people have a point. That Jago has serious problems we can't fix by ourselves.'

'He's got a temper, that's all. A few anger issues. He just needs to learn better control.'

What could she say though? That he'd come round to her flat, they'd talked for a few minutes and then he'd left. When she'd asked him to. Even Annaliese couldn't twist that into something he'd done wrong.

Meanwhile, silence in the study.

'What?' his dad demanded.

'Morgan, I think we both know it's more than that.'

Jago forced his attention from what had happened at Annaliese's flat to what was going on now in his dad's study. What was Bella saying about him, exactly?

His dad wanted to know too. 'What are you getting at?'

'It's not your fault, they were quite clear about that. He gets it from his mother.'

'Gets what from his mother?'

Yeah, Bella. What did he get from his mother? And what would you know about it anyway?

She said, 'He can be cruel.'

'Oh, tell me we're not back on the guinea pig?'

Christ, he'd thought that had been forgotten. How old had he been? Twelve? Thirteen? He'd asked for a puppy and she'd given him a dumb rodent, as though it was remotely the same. The stupid squeaking thing had got out after a couple of weeks and been killed by the neighbour's cat. Bella had actually accused him of deliberately leaving the cage open.

'That animal was tortured. Those injuries I kept finding, they weren't self-inflicted. And there was nobody here but the two of us.'

He'd been experimenting, that was all. All kids did it. Wings off insects, frogs put in jars in the hot sun. Every kid did that sort of thing.

She said, 'We can't stay in denial forever.'

His dad sounded cold. 'What do you suggest?'

'Maybe there's somewhere we can send him. A private facility. Somewhere he can get the treatment he needs and still take his exams. When he's better he can get back on track. He might lose a year or two, but lots of kids have gap years.'

A gap year? Was she fucking serious?

'Are there such places?' his dad was asking.

'I found one in North Wales. It's called Ty Newydd. They specialise in young people with emotional problems. It's a secure facility, run in the same way as a psychiatric hospital. He'll be safe there.'

'Do we need a referral?' His dad actually sounded interested. They were going to send him to a nuthouse. Could they even do that?

'I had a quick chat with the administrator. She told me that, on the basis of what's happened and the treatment Jago's had so far, there would be a good chance they'd take him. And as he's not eighteen yet, we wouldn't need his agreement.'

'Actually, that could work. It would give us some thinking time.'

Jago could hear the smile in Bella's voice when she spoke again. 'Exactly. Time to get used to having a new family member around the house.'

37

There was enough light in the marquee to see that the boy dangling from the tree was still alive. His legs were kicking frantically and he was clutching at the rope around his neck.

Gardner had reached the rope that held the boy to the tree and was tugging on it. 'Hold on, lad,' he called up. 'I've got you.'

I almost leapt into the air when a hand landed on my shoulder.

'You're on private property,' a voice said in my ear. I turned to see three men had caught up with us. One was the security guard from the gate; the other two were equally well-built and grim-faced.

'Fuck sake, get the lights up,' called another voice, as I backed away from the security team. 'Who let these clowns in?'

In response, a massive overhead light came on, revealing the internal walls and ceiling of the marquee. A man in his twenties wearing jeans and a black sweater was hurrying towards us.

Gardner, meanwhile, had stepped back from the hanged boy. With the lights up, it was obvious he was fine. He was being lowered to the ground by a harness suspended from a gantry. The rope around his neck was loose. He grinned at us as his feet reached the ground.

'What's going on?' Gardner demanded.

The man in black made straight for the boy. 'You've interrupted an extra rehearsal of the hanging scene,' he snapped at us. 'Obviously, we have to take care with stunts like these. Everything OK, Tom?'

'Fine, yeah, better that time,' the boy replied.

'What can we do for you, Mr Gardner?' One of the security guards stepped forward.

'This marquee is private.' The second was more to the point.

Gardner gave the two of them a dismissive glance. 'Safety inspection,' he said. 'I've had a phone call about flammable material being stored illegally up here. Can you get all the lights up, please?'

'Mr North's on his way,' the guard from the gate said. 'You need to leave now.'

The third man took hold of my arm.

'I think you'll find it's an offence to prevent an officer from the Fire and Rescue Service going about his business,' Gardner responded. 'Take your hands off my associate or we'll be talking about an assault charge on top of that.'

My arm was dropped.

'Thank you. Now step away, sir. All three of you, please.'

'Find what you're looking for?' said a voice behind us that I recognised as Aran North's.

Gardner repeated his story about potential flammable materials.

'Phone call from whom?' North was less easily intimidated than his security staff. 'Received when? And who do I talk to down at the fire station about this?'

'That would be me,' Gardner replied. 'I got a call first thing this morning, so came out straight away. It came into my personal phone, so obviously it was someone who knows I'm the fire officer in charge of the site. To be honest, I suspected it might be a prank, but I needed to be sure.'

'And are you satisfied?' North asked.

'Not yet.'

North shook his head. 'You're welcome at the site anytime, naturally, Hugh,' he said. 'But we'd appreciate being warned in advance.'

'I'd like to have a look around the hall,' Gardner said.

'I'm afraid that's not possible,' North replied. 'Some of our guests haven't left their rooms yet.'

'I think you'll find under section forty-five of the Fire and Rescue Services Act, I'm authorised to enter premises for the purpose of investigation,' Gardner said. 'We'll start on the top floor, make our way down.'

I was starting to feel a grudging admiration for Gardner.

'If you're referring to the 2004 act, then you need to give us twenty-four hours' notice,' North countered.

'That only applies to private dwellings,' Gardner said. 'Gathering Hall isn't a private dwelling.'

'Yes, it is, it's my private dwelling, and I want twenty-four hours' notice before I'm prepared to admit you.'

Stalemate. I had no idea which of the two men, technically, was in the right and I suspected neither of them was entirely sure. Ultimately, Gardner wasn't about to risk his job over it. 'I'm going to have a walk around the grounds,' he said. 'Unless you have a problem with that too?'

'None at all,' North replied. 'Simon and Ray will show you out.'

We left the marquee by a side entrance and found ourselves close to the water's edge. I think Gardner must have become disorientated inside the marquee – I know I had a little – because he started when he saw the lake.

'This way, I think,' I said, indicating that we follow the shoreline east. 'I thought I recognised one of the trees in the picture.'

I wasn't expecting to find four graves, of course, or even signs of disturbed earth. I was more certain than ever that the picture had been photoshopped, but I knew Anna would expect us to make sure.

I arrived at the spot first. The beech tree with the fallen branch that I'd recognised was still there, but there was no sign of disturbed ground. The tangle of grasses, mosses, wildflowers and ferns that made up the undergrowth hadn't been troubled, not even by footsteps.

'No bodies here,' I said.

No reply. When I turned, I found that Gardner hadn't followed me to the site of the non-existent graves. He was by the lake, staring out over the water. Trying to make no sound, I crept back towards him.

'Are you feeling quite well, Hugh?' I asked when I was close.

He started, almost as though surprised to see me.

'You seem distracted,' I went on.

'I'm good,' he said, but I caught him trying to suppress a shiver.

'Not everyone likes the water,' I said. 'And this lake can be gloomy at times.'

'It draws me,' he said. 'I've never liked it, but I can't seem to stay away.'

He shook his head and turned away from the water. 'I should get back. Work.'

The four graves we'd supposedly come looking for had slipped his mind. I said nothing. I knew we wouldn't find any graves here.

'It was good of you to come up,' I said, as we set off back towards his vehicle. 'Anna will feel better knowing something is being done.'

'How about you?' He gave me a long, measured look.

'Sorry?'

'What's your interest in all this? You've been here, what, four years, five at most, you don't say boo to a goose, no one knows the first thing about you and now you're running around the place like Miss Marple on acid.'

I should have known getting chummy with Gardner could be a mistake.

38

Feeling numb, Jago stepped into his bedroom and closed the door. If his parents were to glance up the stairs, he didn't want them to have any hint that he'd heard everything they'd just said.

A burning feeling ran through him, starting in his gut and warming every last particle of his body. He took several deep breaths and told himself to be careful. That was anger building, and he couldn't afford that now.

Send him away? They were going to send him to some private loony bin? *She* was going to send him away?

He needed to be ice. All brain. Feelings put aside till later. He took several deep breaths, willing his body to be calm, to be cold. Back to numb inside. Yes, that was good. He had something to do, something that couldn't wait any longer.

He sat down at his computer and pressed a couple of random keys to wake it up. A search lasting fewer than five seconds found the email address of the family liaison police officer that had been assigned to his case following the incident in the school.

That's how he'd learned to think of it. *The incident*. Something that had happened, not to him exactly, but in which he'd hardly been mainly instrumental.

He composed an email. It didn't take long. He could think on his feet remarkably well.

Dear PS Obicoa

I hope it's OK to be in touch with you like this. I don't know where

else to turn. I need help so badly.
My councillor, Doctor Annaliese Clayton Brown, has been forcing me to have sex with her. I think people in her office, her secretary for example, might know what's been going on but they all cover for each other, don't they?
She has an appendix scar about four inches to the right of her navel. I wouldn't know this unless I was telling the truth, would I? I've been to her flat. I can give you dates and times.
This isn't right, is it? She shouldn't be doing this. I want it to stop. I daren't tell my parents, I know they won't believe me.
Please help me.

Jago.

He thought about adding a sad face emoji and decided against it.

Sitting back in his chair, he realised his hands were sore. He'd been clenching them while he was typing. Anger had crept up on him after all. He checked the email through once more and added a spelling mistake for good measure before pressing send.

He expected to feel better. Surprisingly, he didn't. The anger was creeping up on him again. He restarted his deep breathing routine. He couldn't afford to lose control, not tonight of all nights.

Because this was the night he really fucked his father over. This was the night he told him the truth about that baby he was so proud of.

39

As we reached the village Gardner tried again, 'Are you really concerned about what's going on up at Gathering or just trying to curry favour with Anna?'

'I could ask the same question of you.' I made a mental note that while Gardner and I might be cooperating, we were hardly becoming friends.

Whatever he might have said in reply, I wasn't destined to hear it, because he turned into our street. A second later Anna appeared and beckoned us both inside.

'Gone?' Not surprisingly, Connor's disappearance was uppermost in her concerns. 'What time did he go? Did he leave a note?'

'No note, and I couldn't say.' Gardner took a bite of the bacon sandwich Anna had had waiting. 'I got up for a pee around two and the door to the kids' room was closed then. It was open when I got up at six, so sometime between those times would be my best guess. I didn't hear him go though.'

'He doesn't trust us,' Anna said.

'Let me call his mobile,' I said. 'Anna, can I use your phone?'

She nodded permission and I dialled Connor's number. No reply.

'We could try Constance,' Gardner said. 'He must have tried to reach her last night.'

'Do we really want to worry her?' I argued. 'She's in a fragile enough state as it is. And Anna will be seeing her at four today.'

'I won't,' Anna said. 'She called half an hour ago. There's some seminar thing at the hall this afternoon and she won't be able to get away. She said can we do it tomorrow instead. She asked me to tell Connor, so she can't have heard from him.'

'That's not great,' Gardner said.

'I'll see if I can contact his mother,' I offered.

'There's something else,' Anna said. 'Have you seen this?' From the counter she retrieved one of the posters Gardner and I had spotted on our way out to Gathering. 'This is Constance's number.'

'Goodness, I didn't spot that,' I said.

'Constance put the posters up?' Gardner said.

'That doesn't seem likely,' Anna said. 'Why would she rock the boat when she's relying on us to get her away from there? She should be keeping her head down.'

'She's a very confused young woman,' I chipped in.

'I've also found a Facebook page,' Anna said. 'Emily Collins's page.'

'So, she is alive?' I said.

Anna shook her head. 'No, that's not what I meant. It's about her. About her being missing. You see them a lot on Facebook. They're usually done by a family member, trying to get attention on the case, appealing for information. They can be quite successful.'

'What are you thinking, Anna?' Gardner asked.

She looked directly at him, as though about to issue a challenge. 'Child grooming gang,' she said.

Neither Gardner nor I replied.

'We know it happens,' she went on. 'Why would it not happen in a nice, middle-class community? How do we know Connor really is the father of Constance's baby?'

'Oh my,' I managed.

'I'm going to tell the police,' Gardner announced.

Anna and I both gave him surprised looks; hers seemed genuine.

'Connor is a child at risk, already known to them. He was in my care, technically, when he vanished,' Gardner explained. 'I can't not update them about this.'

'I guess so,' Anna said. 'But they won't do anything.'

'Maybe not. But at least we'll have done the right thing.' Shoving the last of the sandwich into his mouth, he got to his feet. 'I've got to get to work,' he announced. 'Catch up later?'

A little after six that evening, my landline rang.

'Hello?' I wasn't expecting a call, very few people had any of my numbers, and the sound of the house phone, loud and rather shrill, had unnerved me.

'It's Hugh,' the caller said, as I heard the exact same words coming through the wall. He was in his kitchen. I didn't want him to know how easily sound travels from one house to another so I walked towards Anna's side and lowered my voice.

'Have you got a few minutes?' he asked. 'Appreciate your advice on something.'

Well, it's hard to resist a request like that. 'I can put the kettle on,' I offered.

'No, not here. Meet me in the pub in ten minutes? It's important, or I wouldn't ask.'

I thought about it. 'Fifteen,' I said, and put the phone down. I had things to do before I could meet Gardner.

The Fox and Hound was busy, as it usually is early evening. If Gardner had called me here to talk about Gathering Hall, it didn't feel an entirely wise choice of venue. I could see several people from the church, including some I'd helped cook dinner for the previous night. Gardner and I were noticed, as we carried our drinks towards a window table. He seemed conscious of it too. As we sat down, he gave a long, appraising look around.

'The community library is open until seven thirty,' I said. 'We could go there.'

'If I appear in a library, folk really will get suspicious.'

I almost laughed. 'Any repercussions from our visit this morning?' I asked.

He pulled a face, meant to indicate disinterest. 'North phoned the boss. I stuck to my story about an anonymous tip-off. Boss couldn't care less what happens up at the hall. Told me to make sure my paperwork was up to date and that was the end of it.'

'I found Connor's mother,' I volunteered. 'She told me she had no idea where Connor was, she hadn't seen him for days and if I bothered her again, she'd report me.'

'Report you to who?'

'She didn't say. I suspect substances were involved.'

'Poor kid,' Gardner said. 'I reported his brief reappearance here to the police. They took a note.' He shrugged, telling me that the police weren't overly concerned about Connor.

'What did you want to see me about?' I asked.

He pulled a brown envelope from an inside jacket pocket and handed it over. 'This was pushed through my door sometime today,' he said. 'While I was at work. Don't suppose you saw anyone hanging around?'

Without replying, I took hold of the envelope. There was no mark of any kind on the front or rear but Gardner had clumsily torn open the seal. I slid my hand inside and pulled out a single sheet of paper. Dated August last year, from the Mail Online, it showed a story with an accompanying picture.

'Recognise anyone?'

The photograph of the woman outside an official-looking building, being hurried along by a dark-suited man as she kept her head down, was unmistakably Anna. Same build, same height, same hair, albeit shorter than she wore it now. The headline read: *Shamed Psychiatrist Escapes Jail.*

I took my time, pretending to study the story. I didn't need to read it. I knew exactly who Anna Brown really was. I'd known since Sunday evening when I'd found this exact cutting in a small cardboard box in Anna's dressing table. The following day I'd done an extensive online search and had found this same story and several others like it.

'Annaliese Clayton Brown,' Gardner said, in a low voice. 'I remember it on the news, although I'd never have made the connection.'

Neither would I without the visual prompt, but like Gardner I remembered the case. Annaliese Clayton Brown was a child psychiatrist who'd become embroiled in a horrific murder case in Dorset the previous year. A seventeen-year-old boy whom she'd been treating, a boy obsessed with the novels of Thomas Hardy, the darker ones in particular, had killed his father before raping and attempting to murder his pregnant stepmother. The whole nation had been shocked by the crime.

Jago Moore – even the name caused a trickle of ice to run between my shoulder blades – had been a beautiful-looking boy, thin and vampire pale but with a perfectly shaped face and big dark eyes. His hair was dark brown, his smile wide but sad. Half the teenage girls in the country had fallen in love with him, in spite of what he'd done. There had even been fears of copycat killings, such was his impact upon the national consciousness at the time.

At his hearing, because he'd been declared mentally unfit to stand trial, he'd tried to pass the blame onto his assigned clinician – Anna – claiming they'd been in an intimate relationship, and that she'd egged him on to commit the deed so that they could be together. He'd even claimed that the two of them had been together earlier that night, had planned the murder in detail.

Clayton Brown had been investigated, first by the police and then by the General Medical Council. The boy's allegations couldn't be substantiated, his testimony was contradictory and full of holes and she had alibis for many of the times they'd supposedly met. No evidence against the doctor had been unearthed and she'd never been charged. The public backlash, though, had proven too much for her and she'd left her profession behind. The Mail's headline was typical clickbait, and completely inaccurate. There had never been any real question of Anna facing prison.

'Easy to be wise in hindsight,' Gardner said, 'but I had a feeling about that one.'

'Anna?' I queried.

He pulled a face. 'Something didn't quite add up,' he went on. 'Could never put my finger on it, but—'

I thought, but didn't say, that his instinctive distrust of Anna probably stemmed from her refusal of his amorous advances.

'You have no idea who put this through your door?' I said, instead.

'None at all. What do you think I should do?'

'Nothing stays quiet for long in villages like these,' I said, conscious that arguably, something pretty serious was being kept quiet up at Gathering Hall. 'If you and I and the sender know, it's a pretty safe bet that everyone will before long.'

'That's what I think. I need to show it to her.'

I couldn't disagree. 'How will people take it, do you think?' I asked.

'I think they'll be thrilled. Apart from two weeks in the year when the church is here, nothing ever happens in St Abel's Chapel. This'll keep the gossipmongers in business for the rest of the year.'

'Will they be supportive of Anna, or . . . '

Gardner said, 'Are you kidding me? I don't give her till Christmas once this gets out.'

'She's put a lot of work into that bakery,' I said. 'A lot of money too. Feels unfair, when she doesn't seem to have done anything wrong, that someone should be determined to make trouble for her.'

'There is another possibility,' Gardner said.

'What's that?'

'It's a warning,' Gardner went on. 'Anna's been poking her nose in where some might argue it doesn't belong. She shuts up about the church, leaves Constance alone, or everyone finds out about her past.'

'In that case, why involve you? Why not send this to Anna herself?'

'Maybe they did. Maybe it didn't work, so they had to up the ante a bit.'

'You really think the church is behind this?'

'I think you and Anna have got them rattled and they're fighting back.' He paused and drank. 'Can't wait to see what they've got in store for you,' he said.

40

Four hours earlier

'Dr Epstein tells me you've had a good week, Jago,' the visiting psychologist said. 'Why don't you tell me what you've been up to?'

They were in Jago's room at the high-security psychiatric hospital. Several mental health professionals had been employed in the process of sending him here – his was one of the most shocking and high-profile crimes in recent years. Fortunately for him, they weren't all as smart as Annaliese Clayton Brown. Had she had her way, he'd be in juvenile prison right now.

Not that she'd given up. He received regular visits from forensic psychologists determined to catch him out and he knew she was behind them all. When he thought of Annaliese, fury churned inside him. Come what may, he was not going to prison.

Because this place really wasn't too bad. His room was clean and comfortable, the food perfectly decent. He had a video player and, while the films were carefully monitored, there was no shortage of them. The library was well stocked and there were regular classes and activities that kept the boredom at bay. There were days when Jago almost thought he preferred his new life to the one he'd left behind.

Being here, remaining here in the face of pressure to get him transferred to prison, required a delicate balancing act. He had to show enough symptoms of being ill to be allowed to stay, but not so many that he was watched closely. He had to be a model patient, but one who remained well within the treatment parameters.

So far, he thought, he was doing rather well. In the meantime, the idiot in the chair opposite had asked him a question. The usual one.

'Saw a good programme last night,' Jago replied. 'About the Royal Marines. Did you know, in the right circumstances, everything can be a weapon?'

As expected, the man was unable to help a nervous eye-flick around the room. Jago could almost see him making a mental note to tell the staff to be more careful about the TV shows the patients were allowed to watch.

He said, 'I hear you had some success in art class.'

The TV show had taught Jago nothing he didn't already know. He'd been looking for potential weapons for most of the fifteen months he'd been here; almost as long as he'd been planning ways to break out.

It was an OK place, but that didn't mean he was planning to stay forever. He had things to do.

'I won a painting prize.' Jago composed his face into an expression he was pretty sure was modest pleasure. He practised his repertoire in the window reflection when he was alone. He wasn't allowed mirrors, of course, because broken mirrors made excellent weapons; even the staff here had worked that one out. 'I did a copy of Edward Munch's *The Scream*. From memory. I didn't get it quite right.'

He'd had high hopes of the art room at first. There'd be Stanley knives, scissors at a pinch, and even paintbrushes could take someone's eye out. Sadly, metal blades were forbidden and even the brushes were carefully counted away every evening. He'd thought about trying to smuggle out some of the white spirit used for cleaning, but to start a fire, he'd have to get hold of matches, and while a fire might be a useful distraction, it wasn't exactly a weapon.

'Why would you choose that particular painting?'

'It helps me,' Jago said. 'When I want to scream, and I do, all the time, I picture it and it's as though the figure is screaming for me. It helps the urge go away.'

Another tight smile. The bloke really didn't know what to make of him. 'Well done for winning,' he said. 'How did that make you feel?'

Jago suppressed a sigh. 'They let me choose the prize,' he said. 'I had an extra hour in the IT room.'

The IT room was closely monitored and internet access subject to all manner of restrictions, but he'd been surprised how easy it was to get round the various rules. Most inmates were only interested in accessing porn and that held no interest for him. He'd found some useful information thanks to the IT room: where certain people lived now, for example, and how easy it would be for him to get there. It had also given him the opportunity to smuggle out a cable that was currently concealed beneath his bed. A cable, wrapped tightly around the neck – well, that had possibilities.

He noticed, then, that the lace on the psychologist's left shoe was undone and knew, as clearly as though someone had yelled it in his ear, that it was the sort of random occurrence that could prove deeply significant.

'I hear you've asked to be relieved from kitchen duty? Not enjoying it?'

The kitchen had been Jago's best hope, until he'd learned that only the most trusted patients, who'd been in the facility for years and who were medicated up to the eyeballs, were allowed anywhere near the knives. On the few occasions he'd worked in the kitchens Jago had been assigned peeling, with a peeler, not a knife, whipping, and taking out the rubbish. He'd spent the better part of one session trying to work out how an egg whisk might be fashioned into something useful and had been forced to give up. Working in the kitchen couldn't help him. Gardening was next on the list. Gardeners must be able to access all manner of weapons.

'Not really,' he said. 'My stepmother was such a good cook. It makes me feel sad, being in the kitchen. Reminds me of too much.'

The bloke flinched. How he coped with the really dangerous patients Jago had no idea. 'Well, that's understandable,' he said. 'Been in the gym much?'

'A couple of times,' Jago risked, hoping he wouldn't check. 'When I've got the energy. The meds make me tired.'

He'd been in the gym every day. When he was allowed outside, he ran laps of the surrounding grounds. He was fitter and stronger than he'd ever been. From time to time, he was forced to take his meds, and that always slowed him down, but he'd become quite adept at hiding them between his top front teeth and upper lip, and most days he managed to spit them out.

Loose weights would be very effective coshes, but every single piece of gym equipment was checked carefully before patients were allowed to leave.

The bloke got to his feet. 'Well, you seem to be getting on well enough. Same time next week?'

'Thanks, Steve,' Jago said, although he knew the man's name was Stuart. He lay back on his bed, hands behind his head. 'I might have a nap before dinner. Feeling a bit woozy.'

Through half-closed eyelids Jago saw Stuart stop just short of the door and bend to tie his shoelace. Without making a sound, he sat up. It wasn't so much that he had an idea as that the idea had grabbed ahold of him, getting him up and moving before he had time to consider whether it would work or not and whether now was the right time.

He was on his feet, breathing lightly, ready to spring. He felt like an athlete before the race of his life.

As Stuart remained half crouched, eyes on the floor, Jago strode silently up behind him and grabbed the other man by the collar and belt. Then, before the man even knew that something very bad was happening, Jago hurled himself, and the man he now held, forward.

The bones of the man's skull gave a resounding crack as his head made contact with the wall. He let out a sound that was something between a groan and a sigh and slipped to his knees. Jago swung him back and into the wall once more. This time, when he let go, Stuart collapsed. Out cold. Possibly dead.

Either would do.

He couldn't help the surprised giggle slipping out. All these months racking his brains trying to figure out how to get his hands on a weapon and there had been one in his room all this time. Why hadn't he thought about the wall?

41

I left Gardner in the pub. He'd spotted some people he knew and when we'd finished our drinks – he was polite enough to wait for me to finish mine – he went over to join them. I declined his invitation to tag along – his words, not mine – and slipped out into the night.

Anna must have been waiting for me because I'd no sooner put the key in the lock than she appeared on her doorstep.

'I need to talk to you,' she said. 'Have you got a minute?'

I followed her through to the kitchen.

'Constance called,' she began. 'Connor isn't answering her calls. I had to tell her we haven't seen him since last night. I thought she was going to lose it.'

'Not ideal,' I agreed, pulling out a chair.

Anna sat facing the window, as though to keep an eye out for Connor's return. 'She says she's being watched all the time,' she went on. 'She isn't sure she'll be able to slip away tomorrow.'

'If she doesn't, we'll still have two more days. She doesn't go into the Hell House until Saturday.'

As I spoke, I realised I was, inadvertently, giving credence to the notion that harm would come to Constance if she went into that odd marquee on Saturday evening.

Anna said, 'I saw you going out with Hugh. Did he say anything about Connor? Has he told the police he came back and then vanished again? Did they know anything?'

'He has,' I confirmed. 'But don't hold your breath. I don't think they were particularly interested.' I glanced at my watch; I had things to do before the evening was over.

'There's something else.' Anna frowned at my impatience. 'Something bigger. I was in Penrith when Constance called. I went in after I closed the shop.'

Penrith is our nearest sizeable town.

'I went to the coroner's office, to see if I could access public records, but that wasn't possible without knowing who I was looking for, and I don't have any names, only Emily's, and she's not officially dead.'

I followed that. Barely. Anna was looking for suspicious deaths linked to the church; deaths that occurred during the Ingathering.

'They suggested I try the *North Western Telegraph*, archives department. I didn't hold out much hope, because I'd already combed through our local newspaper and found nothing, but the *Telegraph* was a different story.'

'The *Telegraph* isn't subject to the same local influences as the *North Lakes Chronicle*?' I suggested. 'No one trying to suppress bad news?'

'Exactly. The *Telegraph* covers coroners' inquests as a matter of routine. I went back ten years. It took a long time, because deaths in October might not have their inquests until months later. At first nothing, no mention of the church, or the Ingathering, or Gathering Hall. Then, four years ago, a girl called Phoebe Page fell from the roof and broke her neck.'

'Hugh said something about that,' I reminded her. 'Although I thought he said it was a boy. Odd, given he was on the scene at the time. The sex of a dead body isn't the sort of thing you'd overlook. Or forget.'

Anna said, 'The inquest concluded with an open verdict.'

'Meaning the death was suspicious but nothing could be proven one way or another?'

'There was speculation that the girl and some of her friends had been playing on the roof and she'd fallen accidentally. None of the others would admit to having seen that happen, though, so that line of enquiry went nowhere.'

'Suicide?' I suggested.

'Another possibility, but no note, nothing to suggest she was depressed or anxious about anything in particular. She was sixteen.'

She sat, waiting for a reaction.

'I'm guessing you found more,' I prompted.

'The following year, three days before the festival finished, a sixteen-year-old called Lara Clark hanged herself in the woods behind the hall.'

I took a moment to be impressed by Anna's powers of recollection. She wasn't referring to notes. 'Gosh,' I said. 'Odd that Hugh didn't say anything about that, don't you think? He must have been aware, even if the church did try to hush it up.'

'Coroner's verdict was suicide,' Anna said. 'She had a history of anxiety, depression and self-harm, but no one seriously expected her to take her own life.'

'Potential suicides can be clever about covering their tracks,' I said. 'And then two years ago, Emily disappeared?'

'She did. There was no coroner's inquest, obviously, but the *Telegraph* covered the disappearance.'

'Anything last year?' I asked.

'Yes. A girl called Maisie Best, also sixteen, drowned in the lake. She went swimming one night by herself, entirely out of character, and got into trouble.'

'Not impossible,' I said.

'But very unlikely for a half-decent swimmer. Again, an open verdict.'

'Anything else?' I asked.

'Isn't that enough?'

I couldn't argue. Four sixteen-year-old girls were either dead or missing presumed dead in as many years, all linked to the Church of the Ingathering.

'Four graves,' I said, thinking back to the photograph on the mysterious website. 'They wouldn't be at the hall, of course. Their families would have arranged the burials, probably miles from here. Looks like Hugh was right. That photograph was about getting attention.'

'Constance isn't hysterical or attention-seeking, she's genuinely at risk,' Anna said.

'Have you taken this to the police?' I asked.

Her eyes dropped. 'They won't do anything. You've seen how they are with me. And they must already know about all this.'

'How will you feel if you don't try and something happens to Constance?'

She looked up then. 'What about you?'

'Me?'

'Yes, you. Why does it have to be me?'

I was saved from having to respond by the kitchen telephone. It was shrill and jarringly loud, presumably so Anna would hear it above the noise of a busy shop. Shooting me an annoyed look, she got up to answer it.

'Yes, this is she.' She turned away so that I could no longer see her face.

Silence followed for at least a minute, which I admit, doesn't sound very long, but is for a one-sided telephone conversation. I got up and wandered to the window. Anna's courtyard was dark and the kitchen lights made it hard to see anything beyond the glass.

'When did this happen?' Anna said, eventually. I could see, in the glass, that she'd wrapped her free arm tight around her body. 'And what are you doing?' she said next. 'What are you doing to find him?'

Another long silence, during which she seemed to take a deep, shuddering breath. 'Thank you for letting me know.' This time she sounded defeated. 'Will you keep me informed?'

She put the phone down but didn't move for a second or two. Then she reached out to take hold of the counter, as though to steady herself.

'Anna?' I moved towards her.

No response. She started when I touched her shoulder, as though she'd forgotten I was in the room.

'Sit down.' I steered her back to her chair. 'Let me make some tea.'

'I don't need tea,' she replied, in a flat voice.

I caught a look at her face as she sat. She was always pale, but her skin had taken on the look of wax. Had she been lying motionless at that moment I might genuinely have thought her deceased.

'Something stronger,' I suggested. 'You've obviously had bad news.'

'He's out.' She seemed to be speaking to herself rather than to me. 'They've let him escape.'

'Who? Who's out?' I pride myself on being ahead of the curve most of the time, but this was something new.

Still, she spoke to herself, or to thin air, giving no sign of knowing I was still in the room. 'He knows where I live. He ordered that library book. He could be here now.' Her eyes darted to the window. 'I knew this would happen. I knew they'd never be able to keep him locked up. He's too clever.'

Her eyes were bright and glassy, as though she was on the verge of tears; at the same time, her hands were shaking. I realised I was looking at extreme fear, possibly even terror.

'Anna, what's going on?' I pressed. 'You're scaring me. Who's out? Who's escaped?'

She muttered something under her breath. Without my prior research I'd probably have had no idea what she'd said, but forewarned, I caught it. Blimey!

Jago. Jago had escaped.

Well, just when I thought things couldn't get any more exciting.

'Jago Moore,' I said, and it wasn't a question. The time for pretending had gone, it seemed to me.

Her bright, tear-filled eyes fixed on me. 'You know,' she said, and again it wasn't a question. 'How do you know?'

Sitting back down, I told her the real reason I'd met Gardner that evening: that someone had sent him a newspaper cutting revealing her past, and that he'd wanted to ask my advice about how to deal with it. I told her – although this part wasn't strictly true – that I'd advised him to sit tight for the foreseeable future, that Anna needed her friends to stay loyal and watch her back in the coming days. I went on to say that she had to prepare herself for the worst: that sometime in the following weeks, more likely days, her past would become public knowledge and the entire population of St Abel's Chapel would know that their new baker, Anna Brown, was really disgraced psychiatrist Annaliese Clayton Brown.

When I'd finished, a tear escaped her right eye. I watched it slither down her cheek, catching the light like a liquid diamond, and had the oddest impulse to lick it away.

'Who would do such a thing?' she asked. 'This troublemaker? Why would whoever it was not come to me?'

'Cowardice,' I replied. 'Most people steer clear of direct confrontation.' I thought for a moment before going on, then decided to poke a bit further. 'And maybe disapproval,' I added. 'Some commentators, ignorant I'm sure, thought you might have contributed to what happened with that deeply troubled young man.'

I was understating the case. Annaliese Clayton Brown had not come out of it well; there were numerous Jago fans on social media who'd believed his version of events entirely.

'Well, whoever it is got it wrong,' she said, and I wondered, with something akin to disappointment, whether she might be about to deny her involvement in the Jago Moore case, pretend she wasn't whom I now knew her to be. It would hardly be credible, and she'd go down in my estimation if she tried.

'I'm not Jago's psychiatrist,' she said.

To be fair, I was surprised by how resolute she sounded, given she had to be lying.

'Annaliese is still in Dorset as far as I know,' she continued. 'She's going to start practising again now some of the fuss has died down. Whether his getting out will stir it up again, who knows. Probably.'

I was baffled, I don't mind admitting. I'd been so sure when I'd uncovered the story of Jago Moore and his disgraced clinician. I'd never have pushed the cutting through Gardner's letterbox if I hadn't been certain. And I definitely wouldn't have given her that entirely fake message about the Thomas Hardy books at the library. But Anna really didn't look like she was lying.

'But, you seem—' I began, unsure how to proceed without giving myself away. 'I thought you must have been a doctor at one time. Your medical knowledge is, well, it isn't common.'

She gave a heavy sigh. 'I was a nurse,' she said. 'In my old life, I was a nurse. A senior one. A good one.'

Well, talk about the rug being pulled from under me.

'So, how did you know this – Jago, is it? How did you know Jago Moore? Why would the police call you to let you know he'd escaped?'

'Brown is my maiden name,' she replied. 'And until I moved here I was always known as Bella. But legally, I'm Annabel Moore. I'm his stepmother.'

42

'This afternoon? What time exactly?'

It cannot be good news, when you open the front door to find two uniformed police officers on your doorstep, but this was quite the last thing Annaliese had expected. She did a quick calculation when the female officer, the one who'd done most of the talking so far, told her what had happened. Jago Moore had been on the run for five hours.

He could be anywhere.

'How's the man he attacked?' she asked. She'd met Stuart Townsend once, a perfectly nice if entirely unremarkable man.

'Serious but stable, we understand,' the woman told her. 'He's in the Royal Berkshire Hospital, but not in intensive care.'

She could call later; the hospital might give her an update if she explained she was a colleague. If not, someone in her network would know.

She felt and ignored the stab of anger. There was no satisfaction in being proved right. Jago Moore belonged in a category A prison, not a hospital. He was a psychopath, no question, but a very high-functioning one. He knew exactly what he was doing.

At the same time, guilt niggled. Had she reported his visit to her that last evening, called the police immediately instead of deciding to consult Peter the next day first, they might have made a home visit that night. They might have stopped the murder. She'd never entirely dismissed the suspicion that she was partly to blame for what had happened to the Moores.

'How did he get out of the grounds?' she demanded. 'That place is a high-security facility.'

'He stole a key card from Mr Townsend,' the man replied. 'That got him out of the building. He was seen by two patients on gardening duty jogging around the grounds in sports clothes and wearing a backpack, but we understand he'd rather got into the habit of doing that since he was admitted. He's well known for being a bit of a fitness fanatic, so no one thought it was unusual. We suspect he scaled the wall at some point. To be honest, no one really knows yet.'

'He wasn't missed for over an hour,' the female officer added.

Annaliese didn't even try suppressing the sigh of annoyance. Anyone could have predicted this. So how come only she had? 'What are you doing to find him?'

'Our colleagues in Thames Valley are leading the search,' the male officer replied, almost defensively. 'But we understand his description has been circulated in the usual ways and local media informed. He glanced at his watch. There'll be a bulletin on the early evening local news. Any time now.'

'There has been one possible sighting,' the female officer said and went on to name a service station not far from the secure hospital. 'Not confirmed, because there's no CCTV footage that we can find, but a motorist remembers seeing a young man approaching people asking for a lift.'

'Unfortunately, he didn't catch which direction the male in question was intending to travel,' her colleague said. 'But as I'm sure you know, the A34—'

'Leads directly here,' Annaliese said.

'Exactly. And given the nature of the accusations Jago Moore made against you when he was arrested—' the female officer said.

'Unfounded accusations,' Annaliese interrupted. She really didn't like the way these two were speaking to her.

'As you say, madam.' The woman's lips tightened. 'But given the nature of those, unfounded, accusations, we have to consider the possibility that Jago might be making his way here.'

'He won't be,' Annaliese told them.

'Excuse me?'

'He won't come for me. He was never really interested in me. I was a distraction.'

A glance between the two of them. 'I'm not following?'

'You know how a magician uses distraction to pull off his tricks? He makes you look one way, so you don't see what he's really up to.'

The two officers looked puzzled, although she'd hardly asked them to grasp a difficult concept.

'Jago used me, used his accusations against me, to distract attention from the woman he was really obsessed with.'

'And that would be?'

'His stepmother, Annabel. She's the one he'll go after. She's the one you need to warn.'

Annaliese suppressed an urge to cross to the phone, to contact Annabel herself. Four hours missing. Jago could be in the north already.

43

'I still think if Morgan and I had met when Jago was younger things might have been different. He might have accepted me as his new mum.'

I'd made Anna tea, laced with brandy I'd found in her cupboard. I even added some to my own mug although I rarely drink alcohol. I don't mind admitting, you could have knocked me flat with a thistle-down. I'd been so sure. The photograph of Clayton Brown in the paper – yes, her head was down so you couldn't see her face too well – but it could have been Anna. Anyone would have made the same mistake. Gardner did.

I pride myself on being a bit smarter than Gardner.

'But he was too badly damaged,' Anna was saying. 'His mother abused him horribly. She played weird sexual games with him when he was a toddler. I had no idea such things happened until I met Morgan. I think he'd shut his mind to it for a long time, because he couldn't believe a woman would do such a thing to her own baby. And then he had to live with the guilt, because he'd let it go on for longer than he needed to.'

Anna swallowed down tea that was too hot and her eyes began to water again.

'Plenty of men abuse their own children,' I said. 'It can't be too much of a stretch that the odd woman would do it too.'

She kept her hands wrapped around the mug, as though its warmth was comforting. 'Well, Jago's mother did, when he was too young to have any idea what was happening or how wrong it was. But it totally distorted his attitude to sex. And when Morgan met me—'

She broke down at that moment, letting her head fall into her hands, sobbing audibly. When she managed to stop, she ran the back of her hand across her eyes.

'He picked a woman who looked like his ex-wife,' she said, as I spotted kitchen roll on the counter and got up to fetch it. 'Why would he do such a thing?'

'Men have a type,' I handed it to her. 'He probably couldn't help himself.'

She cried for a few more minutes, tearing off segments of kitchen roll to wipe away tears that kept coming, and I told myself to be patient. The Morgan Moore she was telling me about, whom presumably she'd loved, had been murdered by his own son. And she'd been there, had seen it happen.

'When did you know there was something not right about Jago?' I asked, when I judged it was time she pulled herself together.

Sniffing, she crumpled the used tissues into a sodden ball. 'He was twelve when Morgan and I met. The time when hormones are raging and bodies are changing and all sorts of feelings can get very confusing.'

'And a young boy going through puberty, whose view of sex has been hideously distorted by early experiences, is forced to share a home with a woman who reminds him of his mother?'

Her eyes narrowed. 'You sound like you blame me.'

I patted her hand, allowing my own hand to linger. 'Don't be absurd. No one could have predicted how things would turn out. Was he odd from the start?'

She shook her head. 'No, at first he was rather sweet. We talked about books and paintings and we watched TV shows. Morgan worked very long hours so inevitably Jago and I were thrown together a lot. I became fond of him. I only started to be concerned after we'd all been living together for about a year.'

I calculated quickly. If Morgan and Anna had met when Jago had been twelve, then a year after they married, he'd be around fourteen, possibly the worst age for unfulfilled sexual longings. Most fourteen-year-old boys fixated on girls at school; Jago had turned to the young, attractive woman at home.

'He started doing things that made me uncomfortable,' Anna went on. 'I'm talking about small stuff, that I'd struggle to explain to someone else, that might seem entirely harmless, but things that felt wrong.'

'I think I understand,' I said, although I had no clue; I was just trying to sound sympathetic.

'He'd sit too close to me on the sofa when we were watching TV,' she said. 'And he'd make comments about clothes I was wearing or how my hair looked. Nice comments, on the surface, but not the sort you really want to hear from a fourteen-year-old. And he'd bring me tea in bed in the mornings, even get in beside me, on Morgan's side.'

'I can see how that might make you uneasy,' I said, because I was starting to get it.

'And he was always watching me. I couldn't get up to go to the loo without his eyes following me. I think he watched me while I was asleep too.'

Well, that sent a shiver down my spine; sleeping is when we are most vulnerable. The thought of someone watching me while I'm asleep isn't something I want to contemplate. It's one of the reasons, I think, why I've never allowed myself to be in a relationship.

'He did what?' It was the sort of statement that needed a reaction.

'I woke up one night to find him at the foot of the bed, staring at me. It nearly gave me a heart attack. I'd started screaming before I realised it was him. It was lucky, in a way, that the house was so remote, because otherwise we'd have had neighbours calling the police.'

'How did he explain that?'

'He was very apologetic. He said he'd heard noises coming from my room and knowing his dad was away he'd wanted to make sure I was alright. It sounded plausible on the surface, so I even made a joke about it probably being me snoring. But I knew he was lying. I put a lock on the door after that.'

She was silent for a few seconds and I had nothing to say. I was trying to take it all in. I still hadn't got over being wrong about who she was.

'And you have no idea how many times he did it before you woke up and caught him?' I said. 'Did your husband notice any of this? Did you talk to him about it?'

She shook her head. 'Morgan was away a lot,' she said. 'He always worked long hours. And it's a horrible accusation to make about someone's son, isn't it?'

'It is,' I agreed.

'I'll tell you one thing though. No one questioned that lock on the bedroom door. Not Jago or his father. It was like, on some level, they knew what was going on and weren't prepared to bring it into the open. So, I told myself I could deal with it. That sooner or later Jago would find himself a girlfriend and that at eighteen he'd go to university and we'd be free of him. That sounds awful, I know.'

'Understandable.' I was rather proud of how well I was playing the supportive friend. 'And did he? Find a girlfriend?'

Her face screwed up. 'A couple. But it was like he was flaunting them. He'd bring them to the house and fawn all over them in front of me. He even had noisy sex in his bedroom when he knew I could hear them. The girls didn't like it. Well, they wouldn't, would they? No relationship lasted beyond a few weeks. They could sense he wasn't really into them.'

This was interesting stuff, I'm not going to lie, but I needed to move things along. 'I'm guessing things came to a head?'

'I got pregnant.' Tears sprang into Anna's eyes again. 'Two years ago this December. We'd been trying for ages, and I had various medical issues. It hadn't been easy. I was starting to think it would never happen. And then it did. And stupidly, I thought it would sort things out with Jago, too, that once he saw me wobbling around the house like an oversized sow he'd see me as what I was – an older woman, with wrinkles and baby fat and stretch marks. I was so stupid.'

The murder had taken place in May. Anna would have been four or five months pregnant, had probably known the sex of her child.

'Anna,' I said. 'The newspapers, all the coverage at the time, gave the impression that it was his psychiatrist Jago was obsessed with, that she narrowly escaped being struck off. But you're saying it was you?'

Anna gave a dismissive shake of her head. 'Jago had been obsessed with me for years. Since we'd told him I was pregnant he'd been getting increasingly unstable. Moody, aggressive, even violent. The attack on the teacher was the last straw for the school and they insisted we get him professional help. Enter Annaliese. She was nice, actually. She helped me after it happened. It was she who persuaded me to try wild swimming. But he'd only known Annaliese a couple of months. It was me, not her.'

'So, there was never really an issue with the psychiatrist?'

'I don't think so. Oh, I'm sure he played games with her. He couldn't help himself. And he certainly made some vile accusations, which is why she was investigated, but nothing he said stuck. She'd covered herself well, taken all the right precautions. She hadn't done anything wrong.'

'So why accuse her and not you?'

She shrugged. 'Anything to deflect blame. And also, because he still thinks he and I will be together. In his twisted way, he's protecting me.'

So much made sense then. Anna's barely concealed unhappiness, her constant state of nervousness, her fear when Connor had first turned up out of the blue.

She took a deep breath. 'For the first few months he was in the psychiatric hospital he wrote to me every few days. I've no idea how he managed it, he shouldn't have been allowed to be in contact with me at all, but he talked someone into posting the letters. He's very manipulative. That's one of the reasons why I moved away, as far away as I could get. I needed to be somewhere he couldn't find me. When I saw the vacant shop notice, in a place I'd never even heard of, it seemed like the answer to a prayer.'

'And these letters? What did he say?'

'He told me he was sorry about the way things had worked out, that he was sorry I'd lost the baby, but that he and I would have children of our own once he was free. He never said he was sorry for killing his father. I think he saw Morgan as an obstacle to be cleared out of the way. He's a monster.'

She got up then, rinsed her mug at the sink then poured water from the tap. She didn't drink though, and I think it was her internal agitation that was prompting her to move around.

Still facing the sink, she said, 'He made those absurd accusations against Annaliese in the hope the courts would be more lenient with him. In a way it worked, because all the public attention was focused on her. Few people not directly involved in the case were aware of the role I played, because Jago refused to talk about it.'

'He denied being obsessed with you?'

She let her head fall and rise slowly. 'I think some of the police officers thought there'd been something between the two of us. When I told them about Jago claiming to be the father of the baby, they asked me if it was true. One of them even said it was a pity I miscarried, because there was no way to prove it one way or another.'

'Jago claimed to be your baby's father?' I was annoyed at myself for asking unnecessary questions. After all, Anna had been perfectly clear. But really, this was far from a normal situation.

'That was the start of the row that night,' she said. 'We'd had Annaliese's final report following the weeks she'd spent counselling him and it wasn't good news. She thought he was lying, basically, about the voices he supposedly heard. She prescribed cognitive behavioural therapy, which was the worst possible outcome as far as Morgan and Jago were concerned. Without medication, the school weren't going to accept him back, which meant he could probably say goodbye to a good uni place. And he'd told her that he and I were supposedly having an affair, that it had been going on for years. Morgan was furious. There was a blazing row, and Jago kept insisting it was true. And then—'

She stopped.

'Another brandy?' I suggested. To my surprise, she nodded her head.

'Jago said some dreadful things,' she said, when I handed her the glass. 'Monstrous things. Morgan hit him. He shouldn't have done that, but I don't blame him. And then, it all happened so quickly. Jago grabbed one of the kitchen knives and flew at his father.'

I got up then and turned away. Talk of violence has an extreme physical impact upon me. My temperature soars and I start shaking. Sometimes sweat pours off me. I have to work very hard to remain calm.

'He stabbed him over and over again. Blood flew everywhere.'

It was cooler near the sink and the window. I grasped the cold tap, wanting to run it but at the same time, needing not to distract Anna. I had to hear this.

'I couldn't move,' she was saying. 'I wanted to help Morgan, to grab a knife of my own, or something heavy and whack Jago over the head, but I couldn't move. And then I could. I ran.'

'Out of the house?' I sidestepped so that I could see Anna's reflection in the window glass.

She shook her head. 'No, upstairs. I thought if I could get to the bedroom I could lock the door and phone the police. I told myself there might be a chance Morgan was still alive but I knew there wasn't. I'd been a nurse for years. I know what death looks like.'

'Did you make it to the bedroom?' Newspaper reports had been sketchy on the details of what happened at the Moore house that night. Jago had gone on the run but had been apprehended by police very quickly. Emergency services had arrived in time to save the stepmother's life.

'Jago caught me before I got to the top,' she said. 'I lost my grip on the banister and I fell onto him. He overbalanced and both of us went tumbling down the stairs. The floor at the bottom was stone. He lost a tooth.'

She didn't need to complete the sentence. Jago had lost a tooth; she'd lost her baby.

Not to mention her husband.

'Even in pain, even with blood pouring from his mouth, he could still – hurt me.'

Anna was being deliberately obtuse, but I didn't ask her to clarify.

I knew Jago had raped her as his father lay dead beside them.

It seemed the talk of actual violence was over so I risked turning away from the sink. I was still far too hot though. 'Will he come looking for you, do you think?'

'I'm sure he will.'

'Well, then I'd better check the back gate,' I announced, pulling open the door and stepping out. The wind was strong and cold, making its usual clatter and I didn't like the way it could disguise other sounds. The cooler temperature helped a lot though and I could feel my heartbeat settling down.

I checked the bolts on Anna's back gate and made sure the summer house door was firmly latched. A fit young man could easily scale the wall but I saw no need to make it easy for him. Back in the kitchen, I locked and bolted the back door and then went carefully round the ground floor of Anna's house, checking all the window locks. She sat at the kitchen table while I did all this, staring down into her brandy glass; I was fairly certain she'd refilled it.

'He won't get in here,' I announced, when I'd finished. 'Your locks are sound. But it's probably worth being cautious. If anyone knocks tonight, even if you're sure it's one of the Connies, don't let them in. Ring me, or Hugh, first. We'll check out any untoward visitors.'

She gave me an exhausted smile.

'We'll talk tomorrow,' I said. 'About the Connies, about those other young people and about Jago. But you take priority now. Keeping you safe, that's the important thing, until this disturbed young man is back where he belongs.'

'Thank you.' She got to her feet.

'Get some sleep now. Promise me you'll try. And don't worry. These walls between us are paper-thin.' I tried a smile. I didn't like revealing one of my secrets but it seemed the occasion merited it. 'If you scream in the night, I'll hear you. I can be round here before you draw breath.'

To my astonishment, she held out her arms for a hug. 'You've been so good to me,' she mumbled.

I find physical contact abhorrent. I couldn't remember the last time I'd touched someone other than an accidental brushing of shoulders or an unavoidable handshake. And yet I found myself mirroring Anna's gesture, unable to take my eyes from hers, like a mouse hypnotised by a snake. I stepped towards her and then she was in my arms, her body pressed against mine. She was soft and firm at the same time – how is that possible? – some inches below my height, so that the crown of her head slotted below my chin. She smelled of vanilla and lavender, a strange mix of confectionery and cosmetics, and when she leaned the side of her face against my chest her hair tickled the underside of my nose. I thought I might sneeze but instead the worst possible thing happened.

I had an erection.

Oh, I know, you assumed I was a little old lady, a typical village busybody who has no real life of her own to speak of and so spends her days hovering at the edge of other people's. Well, shame on you for not thinking beyond the obvious.

I'm a white male, a fraction short of six feet tall and will be thirty-nine on my next birthday. Don't bother asking me when that is; I haven't celebrated a birthday since I was twelve and don't intend to start again. Normally, when I'm not post-op, I'm quite fit and strong; nothing to compare with Gardner, of course, but one shouldn't bet against me in a fight. My name, if you're interested, is Liam McCabe.

So, why have I been leading you down the garden path?

It's all about secrets, you see. I sometimes think my life revolves around them. Uncovering those of others, peeling back the layers until the raw, vulnerable core is exposed for all to see and judge; I can't describe the rush of sheer joy that gives me. At the same time, I'm fierce in guarding my own treasures. I am an iceberg, less than a tenth visible on the surface, and even that icy tip is far from what it seems.

Ask five people in the village what they make of me and I guarantee you'd receive five different answers. I am a master of deception, a consummate liar, a chameleon, shifting colours to suit my surroundings, giving everyone I encounter the impression that most suits their particular prejudice. No one ever comes close to knowing the real me. I've given you a glimpse, of course, but even you have much to learn.

Stick around.

Anyway, there I was, with a problem.

I honestly thought I had my emotions under better control. It's not as though I find Anna Brown or whatever we were supposed to call her now especially attractive. I don't find any woman attractive, beyond a fairly surface acknowledgement that the one in question is aesthetically pleasing. I'm not attracted to men, either, before you wonder. I've simply never seen the point of sexual relationships. Distracting, complicated, messy.

But there I was with a proud and firm erection and the knowledge that Anna was as aware of it as I was. Needless to say, I pulled back, just as her arms dropped to her sides.

Did I say something? Was an unwanted erection something one apologised for? It had never happened to me before and I was floundering on entirely strange shores.

'Thank you,' she said, stepping away. 'I'll be fine.'

Was she thanking me for being aroused? Was that how it worked? Probably not. More likely expressing gratitude for what she believed to be my kindness. She was also being tactful.

I followed her through the shop and out of the front door. It was a toss-up, frankly, which of us was most relieved to see the back of the other.

I spent the evening acutely conscious of Anna on the other side of the paper-thin walls. While trying to eat my dinner I could hear her moving around in her kitchen, getting things ready for the morning. I thought I could detect the yeast smell of bread proving but that could have been my imagination. I heard her open the back door at around nine o'clock and my heart skipped. Was she coming round? But no, a few seconds later it closed again and she drew both bolts. A trip to the outside bins then. I wondered how much courage it would have taken, to open the door onto the night, convinced as she was that Jago was coming for her.

I heard her switching off the downstairs lights before climbing the stairs. I followed, although it was early for me to retire, and then ran back down again so that I wouldn't have to hear her in the bathroom. The unexpected hug, it seemed, had created an intimacy I was totally unprepared for. When the sound of the lavatory flushing died away, I crept back upstairs and loitered on my own landing like a stalker, alert for the sound of curtains being pulled, for the low hum of an upstairs television. The creaking of her bed springs was almost painful.

I was growing stiff and cold. The heating in my own house had turned itself off and I'd been standing still for some time. I forced myself to move, to prepare for bed, to climb into it, acutely conscious that Anna was lying only feet away.

How would I ever face her in the morning?

As it turned out, I didn't have to worry. Hugh Gardner gave us something entirely new to focus our minds on.

Another corpse.

44

Sandbach service station on the northbound M6 wasn't the first place Jago would have chosen to spend his first night of freedom. Indeed, there were moments during those long, wakeful hours on the edge of the lorry park when he wished he hadn't bothered, that he was still safely tucked up in his room in Broadmeads with the thought of escape nothing more than an exciting plan for an indeterminate future. But the driver who'd picked him up that afternoon was leaving the motorway to head east and Sandbach, he'd informed Jago, was his best chance of getting another lift north.

It hadn't been the case. The car drivers he'd approached as night had fallen either claimed to have full cars or not to be going far enough his way to make it worth his while. He suspected most of them weren't prepared to take a young male into their vehicles after dark. The lorry drivers had largely finished travelling for the night.

After an hour of hanging around in the car parks he knew he'd been noticed by two blokes in high-vis jackets. They were maintenance staff, probably wouldn't care what was happening on the outskirts of the station as long as it didn't cause them any hassle, but it wouldn't do to push his luck. Besides, you should never underestimate what bored manual workers will do to break up the monotony of their daily lives. He'd given up on getting a lift, made himself scarce and resigned himself to spending the night outdoors.

He didn't expect to sleep and mostly didn't try. He was bruised and sore from his exertions earlier in the day and, in spite of his sweatshirt and jacket, his gloves and beanie hat, he could feel the temperature dropping around him. The rain held off but as the night went on, damp seemed to seep up from the ground. At least the small, electrical substation he'd huddled beside kept the worst of the wind off.

It was only one night, he told himself, and no night lasts forever. He was well over a third of the way from the high-security facility in Berkshire to where Bella was living now in the north-west. The next day would take him there.

At one point in the night, he'd pulled a sheet of A4 paper from his jacket pocket. It was a printout of an email, one that had been handed to him by one of the hospital's administrators a couple of days earlier. There wasn't nearly enough light to read it, but he didn't need to. He knew what it said. And who had sent it.

Dear Mr Moore,
I'm a little unsure of the correct way to approach you, but I know email correspondence is usually passed on to patients at your facility, after it's been carefully vetted by those in authority, of course. So, keeping fingers crossed!
I'm in my final year of psychiatry training and researching the impact of cultural themes and movements upon individual behaviour. Your case intrigues me, as do you, and I'd love to establish a correspondence, maybe even meet one day? I live in the north-west of England currently (a charming place called St Abel's Chapel, perhaps you know it? I work part-time in the new bakery to help fund my studies).
A simple return email will suffice in the first instance, if you'd like to take this further.
Also, do you have enough reading material? Your love of the works of Thomas Hardy is well known, something we totally have in common. I have a first edition of The Mayor of Casterbridge I'd like to send you as a gift, if that is possible.
I look forward to hearing from you.
Dr Andrew Brown MD

Clever Bella, to find a way of getting in touch with him, and of proving that it was definitely her. He'd been with his father when Morgan had bought that first edition in a second-hand bookshop in Lyme Regis for his wife's last birthday.

And she'd told him exactly where she was. Even so, he doubted she'd expect to see him quite this soon!

All would be well. He had some food he'd smuggled from the dining room over the past few weeks, and some money – thank you, Stuart. He couldn't wait to see Bella's face when he knocked on her door.

45

I was woken from a very disturbing dream that I really don't want to dwell on by a loud banging on the back door. Heart thudding – well, it wasn't going to be good news, was it? – I pulled on a dressing gown, caught a look at the time – 0553 hours – and hurried into the small spare room I use as an office. It took me a few moments to unlock the door but when I pulled up the window, I saw a torch making its way along Anna's path. Her gate, and mine, were wide open. The knocking sounded again.

'It's me, Hugh,' Gardner – it was he – called out. 'You in there, Anna?'

She was. A low humming sound ceased, and she pulled the bolts on her door.

Gardner glanced up at me. 'Morning.' His grim face belied the greeting and I noticed he hadn't said *good* morning. I also noticed he was carrying what looked like a stack of leaflets or small posters. He raised his right hand to give me a better look at them, but in the dim light it was impossible to see clearly. 'You're going to want to see this,' he finished.

'It couldn't wait till daybreak?' I asked.

Light flooded Anna's courtyard as she stepped outside. I watched her take the top paper from Gardner and hold it up to the light from the kitchen window. 'Oh my God,' she muttered.

Gardner put a hand on her arm. 'Let's go in,' he suggested. As Anna stepped back inside, he glanced up at me. 'You coming?'

I was.

*

Anna and Gardner were both sitting at her kitchen table when I arrived, minutes later. She glanced up at me and I thought her face coloured a little. She pushed a sheet of A4 card towards me.

'I couldn't sleep,' Gardner said, as I looked down. 'The night shift does that to me sometimes. Went out for some fresh air. These were strung around the village. I think I got them all.'

'Thank you,' Anna said in a small voice and at last I glanced back up. She looked deadly pale.

At first, I'd thought it was yet another copy of the missing posters that had been displayed around the village the previous day, and then I saw the obvious and very disturbing differences. The heading at the top said 'Missing', but the photographic image showed the body of a young girl on the bare floorboards of a disorderly room. Random items of clothing lay strewn around her, as did takeaway cartons, cigarette stubs and upturned beer cans. The girl, who had long fair hair, was naked from the waist down. Her face was obscured by the camera angle and by a superimposed black bar across her eyes. Blood and bruising around her genitals suggested a brutal sexual attack and a livid red line around her neck that she'd been strangled. The line of text beneath the image said:

Is This Emily?

'Same thing on that website,' Gardner said. 'I checked before I came round. The picture of the graves has been taken off and replaced with this. Obviously, nothing I could do about that. I'm really sorry, Anna.'

'What does this have to do with Anna?' I asked.

'Look again,' she told me, pushing the poster a little closer to me; I think I'd edged it away somewhat.

Reluctantly, I let my eyes drop back down; the implied violence on the image was already making me feel queasy. Beneath the line querying whether the victim might be Emily were a few more lines of text: the same appeal for information, a telephone number to call, some details about—

I let my eyes open wide. 'Anna,' I said. 'This is your number.'

The telephone number to contact with information was that of

Anna's mobile; and according to Gardner these posters had been put up all around the village.

She dropped her head into her hands. 'Who's doing this? Who could be so cruel?'

We all started at the sound of a car engine outside. Gardner got to his feet.

'It's the police,' he said. 'I called them.'

I felt my heartbeat pick up.

'I couldn't let this go,' Gardner said. 'At best, it's ruddy malicious. And if this really is Constance's sister, well—'

He didn't need to go on.

'We're not actually under arrest, are we?' Anna said, a few minutes later, as the three of us climbed into Gardner's truck and he reversed out of the lane. 'We can't be, or we'd be in one of the police cars.'

'I think you'll find we're helping the police with their enquiries.'

I was easily the least perturbed of the three of us, on the surface at least. Beneath it, my insides were churning. I would never normally have brought myself into direct confrontation with the police. It had to be Anna's influence. Another very disconcerting thought.

Dawn still seemed some time away as we left the village.

'Why my number?' Anna asked, as we joined the road to Penrith. 'Are they suggesting I had something to do with Emily's death? How could I? I was in Dorset when she was last seen.'

'Which can easily be proven,' I replied. 'So, there's really no need for you to worry. It's about attention. What remains unclear is whether it's a misguided attempt to get the authorities focused on what might be going on up at Gathering Hall, or a rather more sinister play by some sort of self-appointed Lord of Misrule to create confusion and distrust among us.'

Gardner raised his eyebrows. 'Bit early in the morning for logic of that level.'

'Well, let me know when you feel up to some reasoned discourse,' I snapped back.

'Imagine if Constance sees one of those posters,' Anna said. 'Or if her parents do.'

Gardner said, 'I won't be surprised if the police try to play this down too. They'll take our statements, open a file and close it again.'

'I think four dead teenagers is getting tricky for any police force to play down,' Anna said.

Gardner gave a sharp glance sideways. 'Four? What have I missed?'

'Maisie Best drowned in the lake last year,' Anna replied. 'Lara Clark, three years ago, who hanged herself. And Phoebe Page, who fell off the roof. Four sixteen-year-olds, with their whole lives ahead of them. It's wicked.'

She'd memorised their names; she really did care what had happened to them. Anna was like no one else I'd met before.

At that moment, the vehicle lurched as the wheels hit the grass verge. Anna let out a squeal. Gardner muttered an apology and steered us back on track.

'Everything alright, Hugh?' I asked. 'Have you thought of something?'

He shook his head. 'That's three,' he said, before swallowing hard. 'Three dead girls.'

'I think we just found the fourth,' Anna replied. 'That poor girl on the posters must be Emily Collins. Constance was right. Her sister was murdered.'

46

Long-distance lorry drivers woke up early, he discovered. Long before it was light, Jago was roused from a cold and uncomfortable slumber by the sound of an engine starting. As the lorry in question pulled away he could hear low-pitched voices and smell cigarette smoke.

He pulled himself upright. His clothes felt sticky and he was so cold it hurt. He badly needed to pee but strode the three hundred metres to the service station toilets rather than relieving himself in the scrubland. To have any hope of a lift north he'd have to clean himself up a bit.

He walked awkwardly. The exertions of yesterday had taken their toll on his body and he hurt more this morning than he had the day before. He hadn't known, until he put it to the test, whether he could leap high enough to grasp the low-hanging branch of a beech tree that grew within ten metres of the perimeter wall. He hadn't known, until he'd done it, whether he'd have sufficient upper body strength to pull himself up until he was sitting astride the branch.

Easing his way towards the trunk and then inching out along a second branch, one that took him over the wall, had been nerve-racking but not difficult. The fifteen-foot drop from branch to ground was where it could so easily have gone wrong. The force of the blow had taken the wind from him, and he'd lain still for several seconds, feeling sure he'd done some dreadful damage. But he was still breathing, still conscious. He'd moved each limb in turn. Nothing broken.

In the men's lavatories, at the line of wash basins, a tall thin man with a Welsh accent asked if he was OK.

'I could do with a lift north,' Jago replied.

'Glasgow any good?'

Jago smiled. The road to Glasgow was perfect.

'Why don't I get you a cup of tea?' the man suggested.

47

We might not have been under arrest, but we were strongly encouraged to remain at the police station for the following two hours. There were moments, as the three of us were interviewed separately, when I wondered if we were being deliberately kept out of the way. Whether something might be happening back at the village the police didn't want us to see. Eventually, we were allowed back together in what I believe is known as a family room. I doubt I'll ever have a family but if I did, this wasn't a place I'd hurry to bring them.

A cardboard box of grubby toys sat in one corner. The chairs had some pretentions towards being easy, in that the backs and seats were plastic-covered foam, but they were cold and sticky, the wooden arms dull from lack of cleaning. Beneath the small window a table held a kettle and mugs but no tea, coffee or milk and not even Anna showed any urge to provide refreshment.

She and I spent the time – some forty minutes in all – filling Gardner in with what we knew, including the truth of Anna's identity. He took it well, and offered, as I'd done the previous evening, to check her locks when we got home. He went further than I'd done, in suggesting she move into his spare room at nights until Jago was apprehended again. All the time, though, he looked preoccupied, as though he knew something we didn't. He was far from his usual ebullient self.

'I'm hoping Connor will turn up.' Anna smiled at Gardner to soften her refusal of his offer. 'He'll need that room more than me. Thank you, though.'

The sky outside had softened to a dull grey when the door was pushed open and a young police constable carried in a tray of what smelled like fresh coffee. He was followed by the police superintendent who dismissed the constable, handed out coffee himself and settled into the last remaining armchair. He fixed us all with a singular look before speaking, as though taking the measure of each of us. I suspected it was a trick to intimidate; it wasn't as though he hadn't met us all several times previously.

'The remains that appeared on the posters found at St Abel's Chapel this morning were those of a young white female from Sacaton, Arizona,' he said at last. 'I got our tech team out of bed early and they did what they call a reverse images search. Nothing on the internet, which I suppose we should be grateful for, but they ran a couple of searches that only law enforcement agencies have access to and found the exact same image in an American manual of homicide investigation. That's a sort of bible for murder enquiries in the US. It contains a lot of quite graphic imagery, including the one used this morning. Significantly, the young woman in question was killed nearly a decade ago.'

Gardner breathed out noisily.

'Not Emily Collins, then,' Anna said.

The superintendent gave a sigh that, I think, was supposed to indicate patience in trying circumstances.

'What we can't explain, Miss Brown, is why your telephone number appeared on the posters. You still maintain that you weren't responsible for printing and displaying them?'

'Yes.' Anna's voice sounded firm, but I could see her hands trembling. 'Why would I do something so vile?'

'You seem to have something of a fixation on the church,' the superintendent said. 'Which they find odd, considering the business they've put your way.'

'Do you have a printer, Anna?' I asked. I knew she did, of course. I'd seen it.

She glared at me. 'Yes, why?'

'Because it should be a very simple matter for the superintendent's tech team to check its memory and satisfy themselves that the posters weren't produced by you.'

Her glare became a grateful smile. 'I thought you knew nothing about technology,' she said.

'Very little. I do know, though, that there are a few CCTV cameras around the village. Not many, but a few. I imagine they might help identify the culprit.'

The superintendent said, 'We've already put feelers out to those cameras we know about. Nothing so far.'

Anna said, 'What these posters suggest to me is that someone other than the three of us is concerned by the high death rate of teenage girls at this annual church festival.'

She turned to the superintendent. 'How many people have you talked to up there? There are hundreds of people at Gathering Hall, dozens who must know something. One of them will crack.'

The superintendent glanced at his notes. 'And these girls are Maisie Best, Emily Collins, Lara Clark and Phoebe Page?'

I'd mentioned none of the girls' names in my interview, but I wasn't surprised that Anna hadn't held back. Meanwhile, Gardner had got to his feet. Crossing to the window, he stood looking out at what I already knew was nothing more engaging than the police station car park.

'None of the dead girls were murdered.' The superintendent gave Gardner a curious look. 'Two accidental deaths and one suicide.'

'Allegedly,' Anna snapped back.

Gardner leaned on the window ledge, dropping his head onto his hands.

'Are you alright, Hugh?' the superintendent said. 'Do you need to take a break?'

Gardner lifted his chin an inch or so. 'I'm fine.' The glass misted over as his breath touched it.

'This can't be easy,' the superintendent said.

Anna and I shared a look. 'What is it, Hugh?' she asked, getting to her feet.

Gardner straightened and turned back to face us. 'My daughter died when she was sixteen,' he replied. 'She'd been depressed for a long time, all sorts of issues, and she took too many pills one day when she should have been at school. She managed to find her way up to the lake. We've no idea if she meant to drown herself or if it was an accident.'

'I'm so sorry,' Anna said, as tears filled her eyes. She really was very easily moved.

'I am too,' I added. 'Do you mind my asking when this was?'

'Five years ago,' Gardner replied. 'Not long after I moved to St Abel's Chapel. And before either of you ask, it happened in February. Absolutely nothing to do with the church.'

'I wish I'd known.' Anna walked over to Gardner and put a hand on his arm. 'I'd never have dragged you into this if I'd known how hard it would be for you to deal with.'

'I wish I'd known too,' I said. 'I'm so sorry, Hugh.'

'No worries.' He gave me an encouraging nod.

The superintendent cleared his throat. 'Miss Brown, there's another matter I need to bring up. We've had some communication with our colleagues in Thames Valley. About a Jago Moore. We've been asked to keep a close eye on your property until he's located.'

Anna nodded, muttering something that sounded like 'thank you'.

'Have you had any communication at all with this individual?' the superintendent asked her. 'Has he tried to contact you since he broke out of the hospital?'

She shook her head.

'Well, be sure to let us know the instant he does.'

'I wonder if he could be behind the posters,' I mused. 'He's certainly had time to get here.'

At that moment, Gardner's phone sounded. 'Are we done here, George?' he asked, when he'd pulled it from his pocket. 'I'm needed.'

'Of course,' the superintendent replied. 'Thank you for your assistance.'

Gardner had almost left the room when he remembered that he was our transport.

'I'll see Miss Brown and Mr McCabe get home,' the superintendent told him. 'I need a few more minutes with them both.'

'Is there any news on Jago?' Anna asked, as the door closed behind Gardner and the sound of his footsteps faded away. 'Has he been seen in the area?'

'Not to my knowledge,' the superintendent replied. 'I'm sure it won't be long before he's apprehended, but in the meantime, I'd encourage some careful behaviour on your part, Miss Brown. Keep a charged mobile phone handy at all times, don't leave your doors and windows unlocked and stay well away from isolated places.' He fixed her with a look. 'That includes the lake and any part of Gathering Hall property.'

'You won't frighten me into keeping quiet,' Anna replied. 'I know there's something going on up there and if you won't take me seriously, I'll take my story to the papers. They'll listen to me. Notoriety has some benefits.'

I wasn't sure about that, but I admired Anna's spirit.

'We are taking you seriously,' the superintendent replied. 'Your statements are on record and we're considering a report to the coroner. Whether he chooses to reopen investigations into the deaths of the young girls, I can't say. But I can tell you confidentially that I've been troubled by events at Gathering Hall for some time.'

Well, that surprised me. I'd assumed the superintendent and Aran North to be thick as thieves.

'One thing I wanted you to know.' He glanced at the door. 'About Hugh Gardner.'

At last.

Anna shot me a puzzled look.

'I'm not sure he's someone you should be involving in these suspicions of yours,' the superintendent said.

'He didn't look comfortable just now,' I said, when the superintendent seemed at a loss as to how to continue. 'I imagine we stirred up some very difficult memories.'

'It's worse than you know,' the superintendent said. 'Hugh regularly takes time off work for mental health reasons. He's a good officer, which is why the service keeps him on, aside from reasons of compassion and all that, but he has his troubles.'

'What sort of troubles?' Anna asked. 'If you can tell us?'

'It's a poorly held secret,' the police officer replied. 'And I don't normally like to gossip, but in this case.'

He took a deep breath. Anna and I waited.

'Hugh was telling the truth when he told you about his daughter,' he went on eventually.

'Hardly the sort of thing he'd lie about,' I interjected, earning myself a disapproving frown from Anna.

'What he didn't tell you was that he had a younger sister growing up,' the superintendent went on. 'She was murdered in a local park aged sixteen. Her killer was never found.'

'Oh, my goodness.' Anna looked shocked and I composed my own face into what I hoped was a similarly surprised expression.

'There was only one suspect,' the policeman went on. 'He was questioned at length, but there was never even remotely enough evidence to charge him.'

Anna's eyes opened wide as she grasped what the superintendent was trying to tell us. A hand flew to her mouth.

'Hugh was the suspect,' I said, because I could tell neither of the other two were going to say the words. 'Hugh was suspected of murdering his sister and then, some years later, his daughter died, at the same age. This is deeply troubling.'

Anna looked on the verge of being sick. Deeply troubling didn't even touch it.

48

St Abel's Chapel. Talk about a one-horse town.

Not even a town, strictly speaking, barely a village, and if it had a horse, the nag would be on its last legs.

He could see most of it as he approached, one central high street with a few stubby roads branching off. Above the whole, as though on the point of swallowing it, reared an ugly mass of rock, more slag heap than a peak you might see in the Alps. Scraggy bits of vegetation clung to its lower slopes, while its upper reaches gleamed damp, as though rain fell constantly.

The buildings were stone, some rendered and white-washed, all with gabled upper windows. The paintwork was garish. None of the few shops he could see looked familiar. He could have stepped back in time a couple of decades.

He had no idea what had possessed Bella to lock herself away here, but they didn't need to stay. She had money. The sale of the house had fetched nearly two million and his dad had had life insurance, pensions and investments coming out of his ears.

By rights, that money was his.

Jago stopped walking on the edge of the village. Partly to get his breath back; he'd been half jogging for some time, having got off the bus a stop early to avoid being set down in the heart of the village. He had to assume the police were looking for him by this time. He'd seen no pictures of himself in the various bus stations and service stations he'd passed through, and half of him was disappointed about that, but he knew all officers on duty would have been told to look out for him. He really had to watch it until he and Bella were safely away.

The effing bus driver hadn't warned him he'd have two miles to walk. His pulse was racing and he didn't think it was just the exercise. A year, five months, four days and the wait was over. He'd see her today.

Already the sun was low on the horizon. It was four o'clock. She'd be closing the bakery about now.

Better leave it another hour, maybe a bit longer. She'd need time to close the shop, clear everything away. She wouldn't thank him for turning up while she was still working, all dusty and sweaty from the shop. Better leave it a bit.

He started to walk up the street towards the village centre, keeping his hat pulled down over his ears in case someone – Bella of course, who else? – happened to drive past. She wouldn't know him from shape alone. He'd bulked up a lot in the time since they'd seen each other. She'd like his new muscular frame. Women always did.

Halfway up the high street he spotted a public library. As he pushed open the heavy double door and stepped inside a librarian glanced up from behind the desk and gave him a small smile. Nodding politely, he crossed to a table that held the daily newspapers. He sat down, hoping she wouldn't notice how damp and grubby he was, and opened *The Times*, knowing it might make a better impression than the *Mirror*.

After only a few minutes, she appeared at his side. 'Can I get you a coffee? Or a tea?'

She was an older woman, in her forties at least, but she looked nice. She kind of reminded him of some of his mates' mums. She saw his look of uncertainty and added, 'It's complimentary.'

'Thanks,' he said. 'Coffee, milk and two sugars, please?'

He wished he'd had the courage to ask for three sugars but that was unusual enough to make her suspicious.

'You from the church?' she asked him when she brought the steaming mug back.

'How did you guess?' he replied, rather proud that he hadn't lied.

'Only visitors we get this time of year. How's it going up there?'

'Oh, you know, usual,' he said. 'Busy. I needed a bit of peace and quiet to be honest.'

She nodded, as though that made perfect sense. 'You're not the first to come in here with that tale. Stay as long as you like. Well, till seven thirty. That's when we close.'

Perfect. 'Do you have any Thomas Hardy?' he asked. 'He's my favourite.'

49

'Will you?' Anna asked that evening, holding up a bottle of white wine, fresh from the fridge and gleaming with condensation.

I smiled. 'I will.' I didn't drink, strictly, but I wanted Anna less on edge and if I drank, she'd be more likely to. 'Thank you.'

Anna had changed out of the cream chinos and long-sleeved T that she invariably wore in the shop and was wearing a green, close-fitting woollen dress and shoes with heels. It was considerably more stylish than anything I'd seen her wear so far and I couldn't help the thought that it might be for my benefit. I could smell meat casseroling in the oven and had a pretty good idea I'd be invited to stay for dinner.

I was nervous, I don't mind admitting, about more than the events of the past few hours. My relationship with Anna had taken a turn I wasn't prepared for, and I wasn't entirely sure which way I should be steering it from here. If indeed I could steer it.

We hadn't seen each other since the police constable had dropped us off that morning. She'd had a lot of work to catch up on, having missed most of her early bake time, and I'd felt the need of some time on my own.

And now the dress, the wine glasses, the meal in the oven: well, they all seemed to be pointing one way.

'I've sent three texts to Constance today,' she said, as we settled ourselves down. 'Nothing back.'

Her phone was on the table by her left hand and that, in itself, was unusual; she didn't normally carry it around like a safety blanket.

'I imagine her parents will be keeping a very close eye on her.'

I put a hand on my glass, felt the dampness of condensation. 'I wouldn't worry too much. Anything from Connor?'

Her face tightened as she shook her head. 'Nothing.'

I let go a heavy sigh, to indicate that I too was worried about Connor.

Anna tipped her own glass towards her mouth, taking considerably more than a sip. 'What do you make of it all?' she asked. 'Come on, you've a brain the size of a planet, or so everyone tells me. You must have some theory.'

'It's difficult to escape the conclusion that all is not as it should be in the Church of the Ingathering,' I said.

'It's the Hugh thing I find chilling.' Anna lowered her voice, even glanced in the direction of Gardner's house. 'I mean, the chief suspect in his sister's murder—'

'Long time ago,' I interrupted, as if that would make any real difference.

'—and then his daughter dies at the same age.'

'Probably by her own hand,' I pointed out.

'Yeah, well, there's a lot of that about. Liam, he lives next door to you. He's our friend.'

Well, I wouldn't go that far.

'He's always seemed a decent man,' I said. 'I mean, he was quick to offer Connor his spare room, wasn't he? Not everyone would do that.'

Anna's face fell, and I knew she'd be remembering that Connor had last been seen heading towards Hugh's house to spend the night. And that we only had Gardner's word for it that the lad had vanished sometime in the early hours.

'Is he home, do you know?' She stretched up in her chair, as though by doing so she could see into the lane outside. She couldn't. She could barely see beyond her courtyard.

'He's not. He went into work at one thirty, which probably means he's doing the two o'clock till ten shift. He often goes to the pub after work, so I guess he'll be home sometime after eleven.'

She glanced at the clock. It was a few minutes short of eight o'clock. We had plenty of time before Gardner came home.

'I'm sure Connor's fine,' I said.

At that moment, a notification sounded on her phone. I recognised it as a news alert, but she grabbed it before shaking her head. 'I'm going to try Constance again,' she announced, and began tapping away on the keypad.

By this time, Anna's glass was already half empty. I'd barely touched mine. I wanted a clear head.

Pressing send on her message she asked, 'Do you think the superintendent suspects him?'

I took a deep breath, as though giving myself time to consider. 'Are you thinking that, if there is something wrong up at Gathering Hall, people are jumping to the obvious but not necessarily correct conclusion that the church itself must be responsible?'

Anna blinked at me, as though not quite following.

'When, in actuality, the church and its unusual habits are merely a convenient cloak for the real perpetrator?'

She continued to stare. Honestly, was I the only person in the world capable of logical thought?

'I can't believe it,' she said after a few seconds, meaning she didn't want to believe it. She'd caught up though: dark deeds up at Gathering might not be down to the church itself.

'Neither can I,' I said. 'It's probably too much of a stretch. But you can understand why Hugh might be a person of interest.'

'You mean because of what happened in his past?'

'Well, that too,' I said. 'But I was really thinking that he has access to the site at all times. He doesn't need to sneak or blag his way in like the rest of us. And someone in the uniform of the emergency services will always be given the benefit of the doubt.'

'People trust firemen,' she agreed.

'He's exceptionally strong,' I added. 'But firemen have to be, so I suppose that proves nothing.'

Her face creased. 'He seems so nice.'

'Serial killers often do,' I said, relying on TV dramas again. 'That's how they get away with it.'

'I can't believe this,' Anna said. 'Why aren't the police doing something?'

'I imagine they'd argue they don't have anything to investigate,' I said. 'Officially, the three dead girls died by accident or suicide. Emily Collins is only missing.'

At that moment, I thought I heard something in the lane outside. Not wanting to alarm Anna, I got to my feet as though doing nothing more than stretching my back and ambled over to the window. On the draining board sat an unwashed mixing bowl. Anna had been making a cake known as red velvet and the bright scarlet colouring made me feel uneasy.

'Are you OK?' Anna asked. 'You've known Hugh longer than I have. It must be even harder for you?'

'It's a worrying prospect,' I admitted.

In the window's reflection I could see Anna's pale face watching me. Were I so inclined, I knew, the scene was perfectly set for seduction: a frightened female, a protective male on hand, an already established sexual attraction. She'd changed her clothes before I came round, was wearing high heels; I found myself wishing I knew more about how women's minds work.

Meanwhile, all seemed quiet outside, and Anna had already told me her back gate was locked and bolted.

'We could still be getting carried away.' I turned round to face her. 'All the deaths up at the hall could be accidental. Hugh might be nothing more than a very unlucky man with a troubled past, and even Constance and Connor could be letting their imaginations get the better of them.'

She took a deep breath and gave me a half-smile. 'You're right, of course. I guess this Jago business has me jumping at shadows.'

'But—'

I saw her smile fade. 'What?'

'Being here reminded me of something I shouldn't have forgotten,' I said. 'The accidental death in this house.'

Anna's eyes widened.

'Josie Hinton died of carbon monoxide poisoning that was never properly explained,' I reminded her. 'I sounded the alarm when she didn't open the shop, but—'

'Hugh found her body.' She gulped. 'A fireman would know how to kill someone with carbon monoxide, wouldn't he?'

'Possibly.'

Anna's hands clutched the tabletop. 'Maybe she saw something she shouldn't have.'

'Anna, we shouldn't frighten ourselves unnecessarily. I mean, what's he going to do? Batter down our doors with his fireman's axe?'

I smiled, as though I'd been joking.

'He wouldn't need to,' she said, as her already pale face drained. 'Not in my case, anyway. He has a key. Mrs Hinton gave him a key.'

'I thought he'd returned that.'

'He did. But he could have made a copy.' She emptied her glass and gave a short, forced laugh. 'So, I have my murderous stepson on the run from a psychiatric hospital, almost certainly heading this way, and one of my new friends, who I thought I could rely on and who probably has a key to my house, is a serial killer.'

I walked back to the table and took hold of the wine bottle, a second before she reached for it herself, and tucked it away in the fridge. Anna drunk, I'd decided, was a complication I really didn't need.

'I doubt both of those things are true,' I said. 'But it won't hurt to keep our wits about us.'

'You're right.' Her phone sounded again. A text. 'Constance. At last.' She opened the message. 'Connor's been in touch,' she told me. 'Thank God, they're both alright. She's meeting him by the lake this evening.'

She glanced up at the clock.

'At nine o'clock. In an hour. What on earth?' She frowned at the phone. 'Oh, predictive text gone wrong, I think. It looks like he's told her to bring an overnight bag. They want to take me up on my offer of driving them to Carlisle tomorrow.'

'She's leaving the hall tonight?' I asked. 'That's not wise. She'll be missed.'

Anna was scrolling through the long message. 'No, she's going to slip away after breakfast and come here. Connor would like to sleep in my summer house if I don't mind.' She looked up. 'I can't let him do that, not with everything going on. Oh, I'm so glad he's OK.'

'Hugh's spare room is probably out too,' I said. 'He can sleep in my house. I'll make him up a bed on the sofa.'

Anna pulled the corners of her mouth down in sympathy. 'You'll hate that. Someone else in your house?'

It seemed she knew me better than I'd thought. 'Needs must,' I told her. 'He can't sleep here.'

She smiled at me. 'Thank God for you.'

I made a point of looking at my watch, although I could see Anna's kitchen clock perfectly well. 'I should get back,' I said. 'Can you reply to Constance and ask Connor to knock on my door when they've met up?'

'Oh, don't go,' she replied quickly. 'I put a tagine in the oven. It'll be ready in ten minutes.'

Perfect.

'What's a tagine?' I asked.

She smiled again. 'If you don't stay you'll never know.'

Hardly logical, but I didn't point it out; Anna was impacting me more than I'd realised.

'I'll stay,' I said. 'Thank you.'

'Good.' She held eye contact. 'Am I allowed another glass of wine if I keep my minder with me?'

Letting a small laugh slip out, I opened the fridge door and retrieved the bottle. Acting the host rather well, I thought, I carried it back to the table and leaned over her shoulder to refill her glass. She cocked her head, as though about to look up at me, and driven by an impulse I couldn't begin to explain, I did something completely unprecedented and very unwise.

I kissed the top of her head.

I knew immediately it was the wrong thing to have done. Anna stiffened. Quickly, I replaced the wine in the fridge and moved away so that my back was against the oven. I could feel the heat of it burning through my clothes but as far from Anna as possible seemed the safest place to be. I could have ruined everything.

When she met my eyes, her own were filled with tears. 'I'm not ready,' she said, her face a picture of unhappiness. 'I'm sorry. I like you, but it's too soon.'

I wasn't following.

'I really value your friendship,' she hurried on. 'Please say you understand.'

'Of course I do,' I said, although I hadn't a clue. 'My fault entirely,' I went on, because one thing I do know about women is that they love to be in the right.

She gave me a brave smile and at that moment I was saved by the sound of another text message. Anna glanced down.

'Constance again,' she said. 'I hope – oh!'

'What now?'

'She can't get away. She wants me to meet Connor and tell him, or he might go looking for her.'

It felt safe, finally, to step away from the oven.

'You can't go to the lake,' I told her. 'We have no idea where Jago is, even before we get on to what might or might not be going on in the house at the end of the street.' I nodded in the direction of Gardner's property.

'If Constance doesn't show, Connor will go to the hall looking for her.' She got to her feet. 'We can't let him get beaten up again.'

I noticed her use of the word *we*.

'So, why doesn't she text him and explain?' I asked. 'Why text you?'

For a second, Anna looked taken aback. 'Maybe she did and couldn't get through,' she said. 'Maybe he's already at the lake and there's no signal there.'

'That could be right,' I said. 'I don't use mobile telephones but it sounds possible.' I sighed. 'OK, I'll go. You stay here. Save me some tagine. I hope you made enough for three. More like four, given Connor's appetite.'

She bent to unfasten the straps of her high-heeled shoes. 'Sweet of you, but I'm coming. We'll be fine if we stay together.' She forced a brave-looking smile. 'I mean, what can possibly go wrong?'

'Hold onto that thought,' I said, as I pulled on my coat.

We left the house two minutes later, both sensibly shod and in warm, dark clothes.

Gardner's truck was parked in the lane outside.

50

Bella looked different. Her hair was shorter and she seemed thinner. Mind you, the last time he'd seen her properly she'd been pregnant, so that shouldn't be surprising. She looked older, though, which he hadn't expected.

The strain of it all, he guessed, of having to uproot herself, make a new life; the stress of missing him.

Such a small house, compared to the one they'd all lived in together in Dorset, practically a cottage, and much of the internal space given up to the shop she was running now. He wondered how she could stand it.

He'd arrived in the lane outside the house at six o'clock, two hours ago, and had scaled the wall to find himself in a sizeable backyard set out with tables and chairs. A small summer house in the back corner was unlocked and he'd let himself inside. It would be a decent enough place to wait until he figured it was time to make himself known. A puzzle he couldn't figure out was that a sleeping mat and bag, a pillow and a couple of bottles of water were stacked neatly in one corner.

He'd had plenty of time, the last two hours, to watch her at work. At first, as he'd guessed, she'd still been in her work clothes, her hair scraped back as she'd carried stuff in from the shop and stacked it away in the fridges. Then she'd started prepping for the next day: measuring out ingredients and assigning them to a row of plastic bowls, frying up savoury flavours, grating citrus fruit and soaking raisins. As time had gone on, he'd grown increasingly impatient, but had made himself stay calm.

He had to give her time: to change into something more flattering, to have a shower, put on make-up, all the things she used to do before his father got home. She didn't like being caught not looking her best. When she finally appeared in that green woollen dress he remembered so well, with her hair loose, he'd known it was a sign.

That dress had always been his favourite. He'd told her many times how much he liked it. Somehow, she knew he was here. He'd been on the point of leaving the summer house, had been rehearsing what he'd say as he opened the back door – would, *Honey, I'm home*, be appropriate? She'd get the joke, wouldn't she? – when he'd heard the gate of the next house along and had quickly dived back into the shadows.

He'd watched the bloke – the old bloke, late thirties at least – unfasten his jacket and run his fingers through hair that was definitely thinning on top, before rapping on Bella's back door and being welcomed inside.

Who the fuck was this?

Knowing he was taking a stupid risk, Jago had slipped out of the summer house and crept towards the kitchen window. He saw her pour the wine, watched the two of them chatting.

He saw the bastard kiss her. He'd been on the point of bursting in then, but Bella's response had calmed him. He'd seen that look before. The bloke was chancing his arm and she'd put him right.

Out in the dark, Jago told himself to take it easy. She, at least, had done nothing wrong; nothing really wrong. She shouldn't be inviting blokes into her house at that hour, let alone pouring them wine, but her intentions, at least, had been fine.

The bloke though? That twat needed to watch himself.

But now something was going on. He could sense a new energy in the room, saw increased agitation on Bella's part. He watched them staring down at a mobile phone before pulling on coats. Making no sound, he slipped back inside the summer house and crouched low. He heard the back gate clang shut and counted to ten before he risked creeping out.

He could hear them talking in the lane. He was on the point of stepping close to the back gate so he could hear what they were saying when something occurred to him.

He hadn't heard a key turn in the lock. Had she actually left the back door unlocked?

51

'He's back,' Anna hissed in my ear. 'You said he was at work.'

'He should be.' I knew Gardner's work schedule better than he did. More than once I'd seen him checking his phone calendar to find out when his next shift started and each time, he could have saved himself the trouble by asking me. I mean, a rotating, eight-hour shift system, it's not hard. 'He could be off sick,' I added. 'Or claiming to be.'

'What do we do?'

'Wait here,' I told her, before squeezing the latch on Gardner's gate. It opened with barely a squeak. No light shone from the kitchen window.

'Be careful,' Anna instructed.

I wasn't unduly worried. If Gardner appeared I would simply claim I was coming for news. He was hardly going to jump me in his own garden.

Our rear gardens, little more than a yard in Gardner's case, aren't large and I reached the back door in fewer than a dozen strides. Like mine and Anna's, his door was mainly reinforced glass and I was able to see through into the kitchen beyond. Unwashed dishes lay on the draining board by the sink; a packet of cereal and a half-empty milk bottle sat on the counter facing me.

I could see light coming from the sitting room at the front and heard the low buzz of the television. A sports match, probably, Gardner rarely watched anything else. I retraced my steps to the gate and slipped back into the lane.

'He's in there,' I said. 'Watching TV. Safe enough.'

Anna looked troubled, but when I suggested again that she wait in her house, she set off up the lane.

'He'd have come to see us, don't you think,' she said, when we'd travelled a few yards. 'If he had nothing to hide. He'd have come to see if anything else had happened, or to fill us in with anything he'd learned.'

'Not everybody reacts the same way,' I replied. 'Let's hold off judgement.'

'You're a better person than I am,' Anna told me.

'Not true,' I replied. 'I just seem to have a steadier nerve right now. And given what you've been through, that's quite understandable.'

She took my arm then, pressing the side of her body close to mine. Talk about mixed signals. Honestly, how did ordinary men deal with these shenanigans?

I switched on my torch when we were out of sight of the houses and Anna did the same with the light on her mobile phone. We kept talk to a minimum so that we could stay alert. I didn't think Gardner would be following but there was still the wild card of Jago Moore to take into consideration. I knew I'd heard something outside while Anna and I had been talking in her kitchen.

I don't think we realise, until we're on full alert, quite how much sound is contained within an ordinary autumn night. The scrambling of small creatures in the undergrowth that normally would go entirely unnoticed takes on an added significance when you're half expecting to be pursued. Was that a startled hare or a human watcher in the shadow of the trees? Was that gleam of eyes really nothing more than a shy fox? And the wind. The wind has a thousand voices, from a soft whispering threat to an angry roar; we heard many of them on the short walk up to the lake that night.

We reached the woodland at the end of the lane without incident. From that point, it was only a short walk to the lake, but we had no real idea where to meet Connor and it seemed our only option was to make our way around the water's edge in the direction of Gathering Hall.

As it came into view, we could see that the evening's performance, if one could call it that, was underway. Lights surrounded the giant marquee and the persistent pulse of bass notes skimmed across the water, punctuated by human screams. The wind had picked up, scooping heaps of fallen leaves and whirling them around like dervishes. It was a disturbing night, even without the threat of a killer close at hand.

We walked further, until we could make out people around the marquee and other tents.

'There's someone by the fallen tree.' Anna was looking at the far bank. 'I definitely saw a pale face. I'll bet that's him.'

'Only one way to find out.' I circled my torch three times. We were rewarded by seeing a human form step out of the shadows.

We watched and waited, occasionally getting glimpses of a slender, dark-clad figure moving towards us around the water's edge. I calculated he had about two hundred metres to go.

'They must have arranged to meet at the tree,' Anna said. 'Not wise. Too close to the hall.'

The figure coming our way slipped out of sight as he passed behind some bushes that grew right down to the water's edge. When he emerged, he risked switching on his own light, keeping it pointed to the ground.

'No signal here.' Anna had been looking at her phone. 'We were right about that. Constance wouldn't have been able to text him. Looks as though he was on the point of going to find her.'

'He's coming up to one of the small feeder streams,' I said. 'If he stumbles in that we could have a sprained ankle to deal with. And then there's that beach area where the waterfowl nest. If he disturbs that lot there'll be the mother of all rackets and the game will be up.'

At that moment an absolute cacophony of noise burst from the main marquee, as though all the demons in hell were welcoming the arrival of a fresh batch of sinners. Which, come to think of it, was probably exactly what was happening.

'You think?' Anna said.

'Maybe not.' My eyes were still fixed on the torchlight making its slow way towards us. 'He needs to watch the bank there. It gets quite steep.'

'I didn't realise you knew the lake so well,' Anna replied. 'Don't tell me you're a wild swimmer too.'

'Give me some credit.' I spoke without thinking but Anna took it for a joke and gave a soft laugh.

'Should we go and meet him?'

'Probably. Before he has a mishap.'

'Mishap? Seriously, who taught you to speak?'

We set off in the direction of the hall. After only a minute or two I stopped. 'Anna, I don't think that's Connor.'

Giving a sharp intake of breath, she pressed close behind me as the small beam of light continued towards us.

'What do we do?' she asked.

'Keep still a minute.'

The beam drew closer. Connor, or the figure we'd mistaken for Connor, had reached the steep climb of the bank now. From that point, he would have around fifty metres of dense woodland to walk through and we'd largely lose sight of him.

'What height is Jago?' I asked.

'Oh God,' she whispered.

'Hold it together, Anna. What height? What sort of build?'

'It can't be him.'

'Anna,' I prompted, letting irritation colour my voice.

'About five eleven, maybe six foot. Similar to Connor. Similar build too, but darker hair. I can't see him anymore, can you?'

I couldn't. Too many trees in the way. Then a quick glimpse.

'Well, it's not Jago,' I said. 'Unless he's wearing a blond wig. I think it could be Constance. Looks like she got away after all.'

Anna breathed a heavy sigh of relief. 'So where's Connor?'

It was a good question. A minute or two later we got the answer. Because Constance started screaming.

I ran towards the sound of her voice, registering that screams had a language of their own. Had Constance been startled, she'd have let out a sharp, short cry, more akin to a yelp than what we were hearing now. This was prolonged screaming: a deep breath in followed by a long, agonising wail. This was the sound of horror.

I saw, without surprise, that people on the opposite bank had heard her too. Lights shone in our direction and black figures were making their way towards the edge of the lake. We'd reach Constance first but we wouldn't be alone with her for long.

We were in the thickest part of the woodland and I couldn't afford to run flat out. The ground was ankle-deep in fallen leaves and could be hiding any number of hazards. Some twenty metres ahead I could see Constance, hands clutched to her face, staring at something directly in front of her. Something we couldn't yet see.

'We're here, Constance!' Anna found the breath to yell. 'We're coming.'

Constance twitched in our direction and must have seen our lights. She stopped screaming and wrapped both arms around her body.

Shouts rang out from church land. A small crowd was heading our way. I estimated it would take them ten minutes, seven or eight if they hurried.

Constance was still staring at the trunk of one of the larger beech trees. From the angle we were approaching we couldn't see exactly what she was looking at – the tree blocked it from view – but it seemed safe to say it wouldn't be something we'd be glad to look upon.

A sudden sharp pain stabbed into me. I gasped, hand clasped against my side as Anna caught up.

'What?'

'Stitch,' I said, hoping it was a stitch. Internal damage following my operation wasn't something I wanted to contemplate. As I set off again, still in pain, Anna followed. I reached the tree that Constance had yet to take her eyes from. Her head began to shake from one side to the other.

'I can't,' she said. 'No. It's not . . . How can . . . ' Her mouth opened wider as though she was on the verge of screaming again.

The people from Gathering Hall were running towards us.

As I joined Constance Anna was close on my heels. I smelled her perfume and felt the warmth of her skin as she pushed past me and wrapped her arms around the girl. The two of them clung together and all three of us stared at the huge beech trunk.

Or, rather, at the body of the young man strapped against it. As Constance approached, in the poor light, it would have looked as though Connor was standing upright, waiting for her. Only when she was practically upon him would she have seen the lifeless stare, the congealed blood running from his gaping mouth, the pale, waxy skin, the massive head wound.

Nylon rope, brown like the trunk, held Connor in place around his chest, waist and head. It had been a cruel joke, designed to inflict maximum distress upon whoever came upon the scene first.

No wonder Constance had screamed. I took a deep breath as, predictably, Anna began to do the same.

52

A short distance behind, concealed in the undergrowth, Jago watched all hell break loose.

Bella and her new friend had found a corpse. An actual stiff. He let the giggle slip out; it wasn't as though anyone would hear it above the racket they were making.

Seriously, this was one fucked-up place. The sooner he got Bella out of here the better.

53

We were escorted to Gathering. When the men who reached us first announced their intention of taking us to the hall, I'd demurred, but quickly realised Anna wasn't about to leave Constance. Not to mention the girl was clinging to her as though she might never let go.

'Do not lay a finger on that body,' I announced in as loud a voice as I could manage without shouting. 'This is a crime scene and interfering with it in any way constitutes a major criminal offence. The police are on their way.'

A matter of minutes before the men from the hall had arrived, I'd assumed possession of Anna's mobile phone and taken several photographs of Connor's body while it was still strapped to the tree. I didn't trust the church people not to move it, even cut it down, to interfere with the course of justice in some way. Having ascertained that, closer to the hall, there was a signal, albeit weak, I'd also sent two of the pictures – I hadn't time for more – to Anna's Gmail account. Even if the church went to the extraordinary lengths of confiscating and destroying Anna's phone, the evidence would be saved. With seconds to spare, I'd called 999 and reported the finding of a dead body.

The church wasn't covering this one up.

Anna even said as much to me, in a sad voice that I could barely hear above Constance's weeping. 'They won't write this one off to natural causes.'

They weren't past flexing their muscles though. One heavy-set fellow took hold of my arm and tried to pull me along before I told him in no uncertain terms to unhand me. And yes, I really did say unhand me: habits of a lifetime. Another two took charge of Anna and Constance. Anna didn't object. Her entire focus was on the weeping girl at her side, until that girl was forcibly pulled from her arms by her parents and dragged from our sight.

Police sirens sounded in the distance as we began the climb up the hill towards Gathering Hall.

54

Only when he heard sirens did Jago decide to make himself scarce. Keeping low and to the shadows he stole away and ran back down the hill to Bella's house.

He let himself in.

Earlier, he'd guessed correctly when he'd thought Bella might not have locked her door and had slipped inside. Only for a few minutes. Much as he wanted to take his time, get to know Bella's new home, he was more concerned to see where she and her friend were going. And then, he'd had a stroke of luck. Bella still kept spare house keys in the cutlery drawer, exactly as she'd done at home, and he'd found three, all of which fit the back door. Counting on her not noticing in the short term, he'd taken one.

The kitchen had cooled in the time he'd been at the lake but still smelled of Bella and of food. His two favourites. From the huge double fridge he took a covered plate of sausage rolls and another of pork pies. He ate standing up, pushing food into his mouth, before tidying the kitchen. By the time he left the room, he would have put money on not even Bella realising someone had been in it. He'd even opened the back door and wafted it a few times to let out any lingering smell of himself.

Upstairs in her tiny bathroom – there wasn't even a proper tub, just a walk-in shower – he stripped off and spent a long time beneath the hot torrent. He dried off, replacing the wet towel with an identical dry one from the airing cupboard before wiping down all the damp surfaces.

He didn't want to spoil the surprise now, did he?

Grateful for all the practice he'd had moving invisibly and soundlessly around a house – some things you never forgot – he slipped into Bella's bed.

He was woken by the sound of a car pulling up outside. Scrambling quickly out of bed to peer from the window, something tight clamped around his heart when he saw a police car in the street. Had he time to get dressed, dash downstairs and slip out the back way? Panic took a hold of his throat and began to squeeze. He watched Bella – and that fucking bloke – climb out and then, thank God, the car pulled away.

Sweat broke out on his temples and the back of his neck.

The bloke stayed on the pavement, watching Bella to her front door. Only once the shop door had clanged shut did he turn and make his way up his own front path and into his house.

Standing in the dark bedroom, Jago heard Bella lock and bolt the shop door before climbing the stairs. This was it. He jumped back into bed, already feeling himself getting hard.

He could hear movement in the house next door, that bloke climbing his own stairs. He hoped Bella wouldn't squeal too loudly when she saw him. The last thing he needed was some twat trying to play knight in shining armour.

She reached the top of the steps. Jago thought his heart might be about to leap out of his chest. She'd know by now, wouldn't she? She'd have sensed his presence. That had to be why she was hesitating on the landing.

He heard a long and heavy sigh – not quite what he'd expected – and then the door to the bathroom opening. After several moments, he heard the shower running again.

Could he join her?

He was on the point of getting out of bed to do exactly that when a thought struck him. Bella would be exhausted. It was coming up for four in the morning, she'd probably been awake for nearly twenty-four hours, and she'd had a hell of a shock that evening already. He already knew she wasn't the most robust of women and that had never bothered him – no one was perfect – but maybe this wasn't the best moment for a big surprise.

He dressed quickly, grateful that his clothes had dried off somewhat, and pulled the covers straight on the bed. While the shower was still running, he slipped out of the house.

55

It was nearly noon the next day – Friday – when I made my way round to the bakery. I'd been surprised earlier to hear the familiar sounds of Anna getting ready for a day in the shop. After being awake most of the night, forced to undergo several hours of questioning, both at Gathering Hall and the police station, I'd been exhausted and assumed she would be too.

I stood outside for a few minutes, watching her through the shop window. Her face was paler than usual and blotched around the eyes where she'd been crying. Her dark hair, usually neatly styled, had been crudely pulled back from her face and was held by an elastic band.

The shop, like its owner, wasn't looking its best. Many of the shelves were empty – she'd had no time for baking – but the smell of fresh coffee, cinnamon and cloves filled the air and the place seemed as busy as usual. She caught sight of me and gave a quick smile, followed by a lift of the eyebrows. Did I have any news?

I did. Minutes earlier I'd taken a phone call from the police superintendent. He'd told me that Connor's post-mortem was due to take place that day, but that the initial examination, carried out at the scene by the police doctor, indicated that cause of death was a sizeable head wound.

He'd also told me that Hugh Gardner was being held for questioning. I'd had no choice but to inform the police that the last time I'd seen or heard from Connor was late on Tuesday evening, when he'd accompanied Gardner home to spend the night in his house.

'Four days, though,' I'd said to the detective sergeant interviewing me. 'Four days from my last seeing Connor to finding his body. He could have been anywhere, met anyone in that time.'

Looking troubled, the detective had been less discreet than was strictly wise.

'The on-duty doctor thought Connor had been dead for several days,' he'd told me. 'He'll know more when the post-mortem is done, but it doesn't look like the lad was killed last night.'

'Well, that does throw a different light on things,' I said.

He hadn't argued.

Nor had he told me that Aran North had also been taken in for questioning, but I'd spotted the church leader as I emerged from one of the interview rooms. Finally, it seemed, the police were getting serious about Gathering Hall.

I'd neglected to ask about Constance during my time at the police station but as Anna and I were driven home in the small hours she told me that the girl was under sedation and in the care of her parents. They knew about her pregnancy and were being supportive.

'This one's different,' Anna muttered, as the police car pulled up outside the bakery at around four o'clock in the morning. 'No attempt to make it look like an accident. It's like he's upping his game.'

I climbed out first and held the car door open. 'He being the killer?' I asked.

'Or he wants something different now,' she added. 'And that obviously wasn't Connor who texted Constance last night. Whoever killed him has his phone.'

'Let's talk about this tomorrow,' I said. 'We both need some rest. Make sure you lock your doors properly.'

Another thing we'd learned at the police station was that there had still been no sightings, anywhere, of Jago Moore.

'It might not even have been Constance who texted me.' Anna had pushed back against my attempts to steer her towards her house. 'Why would she tell me she couldn't get away when she obviously could? Maybe someone else sent me that message. Maybe we were all meant to see Connor trussed up like that.'

'Anna, I don't think . . . '

'Is that even possible? To mimic people's phones like that? He might have stolen Constance's phone too I suppose, but . . . '

'Tomorrow, Anna. It's far too late for this sort of conversation. Don't forget to lock up.'

Finally, she'd given in and gone inside. As I'd walked back to my own property – I wasn't remotely concerned about the potential for Jago Moore to show up, in fact I was rather hoping he would – I'd reflected that Anna was proving rather more insightful, and resilient, than I'd anticipated.

And so, a little before noon on Friday, I pushed open the shop door, nodding a greeting to the two women who were drinking coffee and eating Anna's carrot cake. I'd already learned it was one of the few cakes that could last several days.

'Hungry?' Anna managed a half-smile even as tears filled her eyes. She was no doubt thinking of the other male she'd fed recently, who wouldn't be eating ever again.

'I thought you might need some help,' I replied.

She gave a barely audible sniff. 'You could butter some rolls? Kitchen counter. About twelve for starters. And the dishwasher needs emptying.'

It was a measure, I thought, of how much Anna had been affected by recent events that she accepted my offer of help without protest. She joined me in the kitchen as I was unloading the last of the knives from the dishwasher's cutlery tray.

'Where do you keep this?' I held up the eight-inch blade for her inspection.

'In my handbag,' she quipped. We shared a smile to acknowledge the grim joke before she pointed to a magnetic knife block on the wall by the sink. I put the knife in place along with several similar ones.

'Smells nice,' I said, meaning the large pan of soup on the hob. 'I'm surprised you had time.'

'I didn't go to bed. Most of the baking was beyond me, though. I had to drive to Tesco in Penrith first thing. Please don't tell anyone.'

Back in the shop, the doorbell rang.

'Lips sealed,' I promised, as she turned to leave the kitchen.

'Liam.' She looked back. 'What if it was Jago? What if he's been here for some time and he saw Connor here? What if he jumped to the wrong conclusion and—'

She couldn't finish but she hardly needed to. What if, thanks to her stepson, she had another death on her conscience.

'Even if Jago is here, he couldn't have arrived much before Wednesday night,' I told her. 'And the pathologist thinks Connor has been dead for several days. Honestly, I don't think Connor's death is anything to do with you.'

I saw her eyes move in the direction of Gardner's house.

'I think we should check up on Constance, don't you?' I suggested. 'What do you say we drive up to Gathering after you've closed?'

Anna agreed to that and so, a little after four o'clock that afternoon, when dusk was already falling, we climbed into her car.

'How easy would it be to make murder look like an accident or a suicide?' she asked, as we set off.

'I'm hardly an expert on such matters,' I replied. 'But with a careful plan, a decent knowledge of forensics and a given level of physical strength, I'd say it's more than possible.'

'Someone strong could hold a young girl's head under the water for long enough to drown her,' she said.

'Poor Maisie,' I said. 'Especially if she'd been drinking and if her mind was on something else, say a break-up with a boyfriend.'

Anna gave me a quizzical look.

'Just exploring possibilities,' I said.

She seemed to accept that. 'Hanging wouldn't be so easy, but not impossible,' she said.

'Lara Clark was quite a slight girl,' I replied. 'Far from robust.'

At that moment, one of the delivery trucks from the hall appeared and Anna had to steer onto the verge to let it past. When we set off again, she remained silent and continued so all the way to Gathering. To our surprise, we were waved straight through the gates and told to drive to the main house. Aran North was waiting for us in the entrance hall.

'I thought we'd see you both sometime today.' He led the way into a small office at the side of the house. 'Terrible business. I'm sorry you had to be in the midst of it.'

Neither Anna nor I spoke as he closed the door behind us and gestured us to seats. I had the feeling we had the upper hand and it looked as though she might know it too.

'That poor young man,' North went on. 'I don't think the family welcomed his relationship with Constance and he certainly made a nuisance of himself here, but no one could have foreseen this. Please sit down.'

'Really?' I remained on my feet. 'No one here foresaw another young person dying on church land?'

'Where's Constance?' Anna asked.

'In the family caravan,' North told us. 'She's understandably very distressed. And has some important decisions to make about her future.'

'Can we see her?' Anna asked.

'She's not seeing anyone today,' North replied. 'Maybe tomorrow, I can ask her parents on your behalf. Look, I'm sure we'll all be more at ease if we sit down. I can send for some tea?'

Anna and I both took seats. North did the same.

'Constance is due in the Hell House tomorrow,' Anna said. 'Are you really going to put her through that after what's happened?'

North looked shocked. 'Of course not. The Hell House is entirely optional. I wouldn't be surprised if Constance's family leave early, probably first thing tomorrow. On the other hand, they might decide to remain in the hope her birthday celebrations will prove a helpful distraction. She may even decide to go through the Hell House after all, but that will be up to her.'

'You're actually going ahead with it?' Anna asked in disbelief. 'After what happened to Connor?'

'Twelve months of planning goes into the Ingathering and the Hell House,' North countered. 'Not to mention a great deal of money. It would be a disaster to cancel at this stage, even if we have only two nights left. Not to mention a lot of young people being very disappointed.'

I saw Anna take a deep breath.

'Notwithstanding everything that's happened, I do think the two of you have the wrong impression of the Hell House,' North hurried on. 'I really do think you should come and see for yourselves. What about tonight or tomorrow? I'll make sure both your names are on the list.'

'You were questioned by the police last night, weren't you?' I asked him, while Anna was still processing the invitation. 'I saw you at the station.'

'Naturally. That poor young man was found on church land.'

'Whom do you suspect?' I asked.

'I asked you in here for a reason,' he said, neatly avoiding my question. 'I came clean with the police last night, so I might as well with you too.'

We waited.

North allowed his eyes to roam around the room for several seconds. 'I've believed for a while now that something might be amiss in the church community,' he said eventually. 'Nothing concrete, I've withheld no evidence. I simply had an uneasy feeling.'

Anna and I shared a look.

'Three young people have lost their lives in the past four years,' North went on. 'And a fourth gone missing. We were relieved, of course, when the coroner concluded natural causes in each case, but I wasn't comfortable. It didn't matter how many times I reassured all our families that there was nothing to worry about, I couldn't convince myself.'

I said, 'You think they were murdered? That someone in the church community is a killer?'

North met my eyes with a fixed stare. 'It was something I couldn't rule out.'

'So why didn't you cancel the Ingathering?'

His mouth twisted, as though struggling for the right words.

'It's our main source of income,' he admitted. 'If we cancel it, the church will go bankrupt. You can't blame me for trying to avoid that for as long as possible.'

'Well, I'd say you're there now,' I said. 'There was nothing accidental or suicidal about what happened to Connor.'

'True,' North admitted. 'But I understand a person from the village is helping police with their enquiries.'

He meant Gardner, of course.

'That would be the ideal solution as far as you're concerned, wouldn't it?' I said.

He got to his feet, telling us our meeting was at an end. 'I'm not sure *ideal* is the word I'd use in the circumstances.'

North showed us to the door himself, repeating his invitation that we return that night or the following to experience the Hell House and join him and some of the church elders for dinner afterwards. We parted on cordial terms.

'Do you believe him?' Anna said, as we set off for the car.

'It sounds plausible enough,' I replied, a little hesitantly. I'd just spotted a young woman, my 'minder' from a few nights ago, hanging around, as though waiting for us.

The girl, I never did ask her name, waited until North had gone inside and then strode towards us.

'Why would he do that?' Anna hadn't noticed her. 'Invite us to inspect the Hell House? That's twice now. Why does he care what we think?'

I tugged on the door handle, but Anna hadn't unlocked the car yet and it didn't move.

I said, 'I think we've rocked the boat rather too vigorously. He's trying to get us onside.'

'Or shut us up. I wish we could see Constance.'

'I want to ask you something.' The girl had reached us, was staring up at me with a face I could best describe as scared yet defiant. Her cheeks were pink, her jaw clenched but her wide-eyed stare didn't waver.

I pulled the handle again, but the car was still locked.

'Why did you say kids went up to the roof a lot? Drinking and smoking? Who told you we did that? How could you know that?'

'I've no idea what you're talking about,' I replied. 'And I promise you I'd never use the word *kids*.'

'On Tuesday night, you practically accused me of pushing Phoebe off the roof. You said me and my friends were always up there, getting drunk and stoned, and you said we'd locked the door so she couldn't get back downstairs. There was nothing said about a locked door at the inquest. Who's been telling you this stuff?'

'Liam?' Anna was looking bewildered.

'Young lady, I think you're confused. And if you'll excuse us, we have to get going. Anna?'

Anna unlocked the car and I practically leapt inside.

'What was that about?' she asked, as she drove us towards the gate.

'I was asking questions on Tuesday night. You're not the only one who's been doing a bit of detective work.' I forced a smile. 'And the young woman's wrong. Full details of Phoebe Page's accident came out at the inquest.'

Anna said nothing more. At that moment, her phone began to ring. 'It's Constance,' she said, holding the phone so that I could hear. I took it from her; she was driving after all.

'Hello Anna.' The girl sounded subdued and I wondered if she'd been sedated.

'Constance, how are you feeling today?' Anna asked, as we drove out through the gates.

'I'm OK,' she replied, although she didn't sound it. 'I've told Mum and Dad everything. They're helping me sort it out.'

Anna pulled over, rather abruptly. 'Liam and I are a few minutes away,' she said. 'We can turn back and come and see you?'

A two-second pause and then, 'No, thank you. I'm fine. Mum's with me. And Granny. They're looking after me.'

Anna shot me a look; I shrugged my shoulders.

'Constance, you know where I am.' Anna was reluctant to give up. 'Ring me anytime.'

A new voice sounded. 'Thank you, Miss Brown, but I think Constance is best left to her family now. Good afternoon.'

The line went dead.

56

Jago was crossing the main lawn at Gathering with some of the church youngsters he'd met earlier that day when he spotted Anna's car. He made an excuse about remembering a family thing and left the group. He found a bench some distance away where he was sure he wouldn't be spotted and waited for her to appear.

It had been an interesting day.

He'd slipped onto Gathering land a couple of hours before dawn, shortly after the police left the site. Even at that hour there had been people around, including several of a similar age to himself, and no one took any particular notice of him. Getting cold as the sun had come up, he'd joined a religious service and then a communal breakfast in one of the marquees.

He'd even started chatting to some others his age. He'd gone along to a seminar with them, then had lunch, and they hadn't questioned his story about this being his first time at the Ingathering, that he was the only child of parents who'd recently joined the church, and that they'd arrived late because of a problem with his dad's work.

He'd been nervous, at first, in case someone recognised him. His escape from Broadmeads must have made the news, he was practically a celebrity after all, but to his surprise, and a little to his chagrin, no one so much as mentioned Jago Moore. Instead, the talk was partly about something called the Hell House, some sort of theatrical performance in the huge marquee.

Mainly, though, everyone wanted to talk about the murder in the woods, the boyfriend of one of the girls on the campsite. He'd been killed by someone involved in the church, if rumours had it right, and it wasn't the first such murder. According to them, a sixteen-year-old died every year. The killer stalked the campsite dressed in a fireman's uniform and the church elders knew about it, even knew who the killer was, but they protected him because they knew the fear of knowing one of them could die kept all the kids in line.

To be fair, it all sounded a real blast and part of him was sorry he couldn't stick around. But the clock was ticking; come four o'clock Anna would close the bakery and she'd be waiting for him. He'd been on the point of making his excuses and slipping away when he spotted her car.

He hung around, and after half an hour or so, she came out of the hall, still with that same bloke from next door who, frankly, would be lucky to see the month out with his skin in one piece. They climbed into her car and she drove them away.

Time to get back to the village.

57

Anna was quiet on the short drive home, barely responding to attempts on my part to engage her in conversation. By the time we reached the village I was verging on annoyed. It wasn't as though we had nothing to talk about: Constance, Connor, Jago, Gardner. It didn't matter, nothing could draw her out. Something was bothering her, something she wasn't inclined to share. It was enough of a change from her confiding nature of the past couple of weeks to convince me she was deeply troubled.

I was too.

'Should we take North up on his invitation?' I said, as she pulled up around the back of our terrace. 'Guided tour of the Hell House followed by dinner at the hall? We might see Constance.'

She gave me a wide-eyed stare.

'Might not be a bad idea to be out of the house this evening,' I went on. 'Until we know for certain your former stepson has been apprehended. Not that it's a problem if you prefer to stay home. I'm more than happy to stand guard again.'

I tried a half-smile and got that same rabbit-in-the-headlights stare in return.

'I could pick up some wine from the newsagents?'

Finally, she blinked. 'I don't think so. Thank you, but I need some time.'

And that was that; a barely polite nod of the head, and she was out of the car, closing her garden gate behind her, shutting me out.

*

Darkness fell quickly and I closed my own house up for the night, all the while keeping my ears open for what Anna was up to next door. At first all seemed normal. I heard the sound of chopping, of electric whisks and blenders, of ovens beeping and taps running, chairs being moved around in the shop, a vacuum cleaner.

Then she left. I heard her back door closing and the lock turning. I made it to the upstairs window in time to see her car's rear lights disappearing. For a few seconds, I allowed myself to wonder where she might be going. Then decided to find out.

At my desk I tapped random keys on the keyboard to wake up the desktop computer.

Five days ago, when Anna had driven Connor to hospital and left me alone in her house for several hours, I'd given myself access to all of her devices. It's really very simple when you know how and have the right software.

My occupation as a publisher's proofreader, one who insists on working from old-fashioned hard copies, is entirely fictitious but surprisingly easy to maintain. Twice a week I take parcels, of an appropriate size and weight to be manuscripts, to be weighed at the post office. The address on the envelope is that of a PO Box in nearby Penrith. A few days later, I collect those same parcels and, at a post office in Penrith, send them back to myself. Everyone in the village believes me to be continually working on new books.

When one works in cybersecurity, which is what I actually do for a living, one simply does not advertise the fact; my client list alone would make me of interest to numerous bad actors around the world.

Among other things, most of which I was pretty sure she'd never spot, I'd taken the risk of linking Anna's phone with one of my own, so that via the Find My Friends app, I could track her movements at all times. It hadn't been necessary until now.

And so, in real time, I watched her leave the village and take the road to Penrith. My heart started beating uncomfortably quickly when I realised she was heading for the police station, but she turned off some distance away and pulled up in the car park of the

Holiday Inn. I watched her enter the building and move through it, eventually coming to a stop in what I guessed was her room.

Anna had decided she didn't want to be in the village tonight and she was trusting no one, certainly not me, with her whereabouts.

I was pondering the wisdom of calling her on some pretext to see what she'd say to me, assuming she even answered the call, when I heard the back gate of her property swing open and shut. Interesting. There was no way she could be home, she was demonstrably in Penrith. Had Gardner been released?

I got to the window in time to see a young man of around eighteen approach her back door. He was tall, with dark hair, pale skin and an athletic build; I recognised him immediately as Jago Moore. He glanced round and even looked up in my direction, but I was confident I was hidden behind the half-drawn blind. Certainly, he didn't react in any way that suggested he'd seen me. Instead, he unlocked the door and let himself inside.

Well, I have to admit, I was surprised. When I'd sent Jago the email care of Broadmeads Hospital (still thinking that Anna was the shamed psychiatrist), the most I'd been hoping for was that he'd assume it had come from her, that it was her way of letting him know where she was, and that it would spur him on to get in touch.

I'd hardly expected him to break out of a secure facility and show up here.

On top of that, the enterprising young man had got hold of a key and was now waiting for his erstwhile stepmother to come home. I couldn't imagine his intentions were in any way honourable.

Events seemed to be unfolding rather faster than I'd anticipated.

58

His reunion with Bella was not going as planned.

This was not how Jago had imagined them being together again after more than a year apart. He'd pictured long, dark evenings and late suppers, making plans for the future, closing eyes to put pins in maps – Bali? Why not Bali? It would be a great place to start their new life together. He'd imagined making love well into the night, of sleeping late and waking in a warm tangle of limbs.

None of his daydreams over the last fifteen months had involved sneaking around in the dark, sleeping rough, hanging out with bible-bashing kids and sitting in an empty house, not even daring to put the lights on in case one of her nosy neighbours came to investigate.

Where the fuck was she?

Wandering from room to room, he wondered if she and the bloke next door might be out together somewhere. He sat, in the dark kitchen, feeling his rage grow until he heard movement through the wall. Wherever Bella might be, she wasn't with the neighbour.

He was hungry. He found the remains of a chilli in the fridge and warmed it through in the microwave. There was wine too, but he knew any amount of alcohol would slow him down, so he drank water. He cut himself a slice of carrot cake. He was tempted to leave his dirty dishes on the draining board; he wasn't sure Bella really deserved his consideration, but there was always the possibility someone else might see signs of his presence and he couldn't risk that.

His clothes felt filthy. He wished he could risk putting them through the washing machine but he couldn't be caught with nothing to wear. Bella should not be putting him through this. He would need to make his feelings clear when he finally caught up with her.

In the upstairs sitting room he found her laptop. She hadn't changed her password – he'd have to talk to her about being more careful – and so he opened up Google and searched for his own name. He was a little mollified to see so many stories about himself, several using quite a flattering photograph taken before his arrest.

He'd been spotted at the service station on the A34, which troubled him for a moment, but he could have gone anywhere from there. He was getting to the end of these stories when the sound of a car engine startled him. Bella? But the car was at the front of the house; Bella parked around the back.

Closing the laptop, he moved quickly to the window of Bella's bedroom and looked down.

The police.

There was a patrol car in the street outside. He watched two officers climb out and walk, in that heavy, deliberate way the police have, to the shop door. The window, inches from his face, reverberated with the knocking.

'Miss Brown?' One of them called. 'You at home? It's the police.'

Jago heard the creak of footsteps in the house next door.

A second knock made the house tremble. Jago waited for the twat next door to open his own window and call down; he was the busybody sort who'd always want to be involved when anything was going down. Strangely, he didn't.

Then both police officers turned and walked back to the car. Instead of driving away, they sat, engine running, in the street outside. Jago fought back a wave of nausea. This wasn't about the murder of that lad up at the hall. This was about him. The police outside were here to protect Bella. From him.

59

Saturday was a strange sort of day. Mists from the mountains rolled down in the early hours, bringing rain that continued through much of the morning. Puddles filled to bursting point. From the murky dawn till late afternoon the sky never lightened beyond the colour of a stream-soaked stone and by the time darkness fell again, it came as something of a relief. At least we no longer had to pretend it was still daytime.

Anna arrived home a few minutes after six o'clock in the morning. I'd been sleeping lightly – a little uneasy, I admit, at the thought of Jago Moore on the other side of the partition walls – and was woken by the sound of her car. I made my way downstairs as she opened her back door.

I'd been forced to concede a grudging admiration for Jago Moore. He'd certainly proved himself capable of moving around a house quietly; apart from the ping of the microwave, I'd have known nothing of his presence. On top of that, either he'd stayed put for the thirty minutes the police car had sat outside – which must have taken nerves of steel – or he'd managed to slip silently away again.

Either way, young Mr Moore was not a combatant to be underestimated.

I waited as Anna pulled off her coat and got to work – opening cupboard doors, switching on ovens, filling the coffee machine – and wondered when Jago, if he was still in the house, would make his move. And how I might react. I could hardly listen to her screaming without calling the police. At some point, I'd have to run outside, bang on the door, shout her name. It would be risky. Jago Moore was both capable and ruthless.

That said, so was I.

Nothing happened. The sounds next door continued to be entirely normal and after several hours I could only conclude that Jago had left the house again.

All through that rain-drenched day I was conscious of time running out. Sometime in the next few hours the final performance of the Hell House would take place. No sooner than Satan and his imps had rejoiced over a new batch of sinners, then the dismantling of the huge, tented village would begin. The youngsters would party and the entire church community would heave a collective sigh of relief. They'd be troubled about Connor, of course, but he wasn't exactly one of their own. In their eyes, disaster had been averted.

It wasn't over yet, mind.

As light faded, the wind stepped up. Keeping all the lights in my house turned off, I retired to my office; my command centre, as I fondly think of it. I have solar-powered cameras on several of the trees and outbuildings around Gathering Hall, including one at the main gates, and I can keep a close eye on church proceedings without ever leaving my house.

The heavy rain was keeping most of the church community indoors, but the show had to go on, as the saying goes, and I could make out several umbrellas following torch beams around the grounds. Sometime in the next half hour the queue for the Hell House would start to build.

I never worry about my cameras being found. In the unlikely event that someone connected to the hall spotted a piece of my equipment among so many of their own, they would never be able to trace it back to me. I was concerned, though, about the mobile phone I needed to track that night. For the last thirty-six hours or so its location had been unavailable – probably switched off – but I would need it to move soon.

Anna's call came right on cue and I let the answer machine pick it up.

'Liam, it's me. I guess you're out or . . . ' There was a pause, as Anna tried to imagine what I'd be doing that would prevent my answering her call. At that same moment, the phone I was looking for became active again. Excellent. Gardner was leaving the police station.

'Anyway, hope you're OK,' Anna went on. 'I've just had a text from Constance. She says she's being made to go into the Hell House after all and she's really frightened. I'm going up there. I'll take North up on his invitation. Nothing can happen if I'm in the marquee, surely. And she's probably getting herself worked up over nothing. Except for the Connor thing. Anyway, if you get this – I don't know what I want you to do. Nothing you can do, I suppose. I'd better get going.'

She ended the call and then, after five minutes or so, her rear door opened and closed. I heard the sound of her engine starting and saw the gleam of headlights as she swung the car around in the lane. For a second her lights flooded my darkened room, but I didn't think she could see me, standing motionless well away from the window.

When I was sure she'd driven away, I went back to my computer.

Gardner was on his way home. I'd known he'd be released sometime today; the police didn't have nearly enough evidence to charge him. Yet. I was banking, of course, on him staying at home tonight, keeping his head down, licking his wounds. It was a risk, but what is life without the odd risk?

I got up again and crossed to the room's built-in wardrobe. I keep it locked, naturally, as well as the door to the room itself. One can't be too careful.

The beige salopettes and matching jacket I pulled on over my own clothes were once worn by an officer in Hampshire Fire and Rescue. I bought them several years ago on eBay. They differ in several details from the uniform worn by the Cumbrian service, but in the dark I knew they would pass. They already had on several occasions when I'd been mistaken for Gardner going about his business up at the hall.

The text Anna had referred to in her call did not come from Constance. I knew for a fact that Constance and her family left Gathering Hall at three o'clock that afternoon, towing their caravan behind them. I'd watched them leave, thanks to a fairly basic ANPR system. There are limits to the number of registrations it can search for, but I'd programmed their family car into it when Constance first came to my attention. They'd be well south of the Lake District by now.

I sent the text to Anna.

Two days after she and I first met Constance, I'd had possession of the girl's mobile phone for nearly twenty-four hours. She'd left it – probably deliberately – in Anna's shop. Under cover of finding a charger, I'd had more than enough time to open it up, access her data, switch on a tracker and copy her number. A couple of hours ago, I'd locked Constance out of her own phone so that I could send a message to Anna in her name. I'd release it later that evening and she'd probably never know anything had been amiss.

How soon, I wonder, did you spot that I'd been playing Anna? That I'd if not created, then at least fostered her growing interest in Constance? Did you realise, for instance, that the phantom phone calls to the shop that first morning were made by me? That it had been I, not Constance, who sent Anna the text message?

Sorry about this morning. You seem really nice. I wish I had someone like you to talk to.

Few women in my, admittedly limited, experience can resist such a cry for help.

I built the crude website too, a simple matter of a home page with a photograph and a few lines of text; and I set up the Sweet Sixteen X account. Both were exceptionally simple in their level of technical sophistry – they'd taken me a matter of minutes – but they'd served their purpose of pulling an already concerned Anna into the web I'd been spinning around Gathering Hall. The posters featuring Emily Collins's face and the revolting picture of the anonymous dead girl had likewise been my work, but I had no fear of being found out. I've made a point, since I moved here, of keeping on top of all the

CCTV cameras around the village. Yet another reason for my nightly walks. I'm never spotted where I don't want to be.

Anna Brown had intrigued me from the outset; from her very first lie. I'd been poking the bear, so to speak; pushing at her boundaries, testing how far they'd stretch. The fictional character I most admire is that of Iago in Shakespeare's *Othello* and I've long been entranced by the idea of creating discord and chaos for the sheer joy of it.

I didn't have Connor's phone for nearly as long as I'd had Constance's, but he too had needed a charge when he'd first appeared in Anna's back garden. His data and cyber identity, like Constance's, I'd been able to download onto my own system.

And of course, once I'd killed him, luring him from Gardner's house to the lakeside with a fake text from Constance, I'd taken possession of his actual phone, making further cyber subterfuge unnecessary.

Yesterday, Anna asked me how easy it would be to make a murder look like an accident or suicide. Pretending to be surprised, I'd told her I thought it possible, with a careful plan, a good knowledge of forensics and a certain amount of physical strength. I could have added national security-level cyber skills.

I left my house, tugged my collar up against the rain, collected what I needed from the garden shed and began the short, dark walk up to Gathering Hall.

60

'You won't leave me, will you, Jakey?' The girl pressed even closer to Jago – a moment ago, he wouldn't have thought that possible – and her hand brushed his. The daft cow actually thought they were going to hold hands. At least she had an umbrella.

He was on the brink of losing his temper. Two days now he'd spent at Gathering Hall – hungry half the time, in clothes that weren't warm enough and in the company of immature half-wits who couldn't think beyond who fancied who and how they could get hold of booze to consume in the woods when their parents were busy. The strain of pretending to be like them was wearing him down. Plus, he was starting to notice odd, sideways glances coming his way, whispered conversations just out of earshot. These guys barely had a brain cell between them but, on some level, they were starting to figure out that he wasn't one of them. Sooner or later, someone would mention him to a parent, or one of the church officials, and his time would be up.

The group he'd become friendly with the previous day had dwindled to four, three girls and a boy, and he knew, instinctively, that they were the least cool of all the kids on the site. He'd been consigned to the losers' group, one of whom – a girl – had become annoyingly clingy. He'd made a mistake telling her his allotted time in the Hell House was the same as hers – seven o'clock, Saturday – and she'd come looking for him, finding him when he'd been on the point of slipping back down to the village.

Candy – effing stupid name – wasn't the sort he'd normally look twice at. Too short, thin around the shoulders and no tits to speak of but plenty of meat around her arse and belly. Her eyes were OK but her teeth were crooked and her chin seemed to disappear into her neck.

Purposely, he slowed his breathing. It helped, sometimes.

It was hard to see beneath the river of umbrellas that was the queue, but he thought there might be six or so people ahead and another twenty behind. He turned around, moving out of the shelter of Candy's umbrella, and spotted some people he'd met the previous day. A boy who was tall for his age but whose face was riddled with acne scars spotted him looking and held his stare. Jago turned away.

Lights at the entrance to the marquee came on, illuminating the giant sign: *The Hell House* and a collective shiver of anticipation ran through the line of people.

Entrance would be staggered, he'd been warned, because in smaller groups, the messages about sin and redemption would be more likely to resonate. In some places, each entrant was expected to travel through the various tableaux entirely alone.

Jago realised his hands were shaking, a sure sign that he was on the verge of losing it. He was racking his brains to come up with an excuse to slip away before it became obvious that he wasn't on tonight's list of attendees.

Six fifty-seven. Three minutes to go. It would be punctual, his new, sort-of mates had told him. The Hell House always opened on time.

Apart from the odd nervous giggle, the queue had fallen silent.

He could claim he needed a piss. They'd think he was bottling it but who cared?

Six fifty-eight.

'They say it's worse than ever this year.' He felt Candy's breath against his ear. 'What if it's true, what they say? That someone will die?'

Jago knew who'd be top of his list.

Six fifty-nine.

The canvas drapes concealing the entrance drew apart in the way of stage curtains to reveal a black interior. Then a gust of smoke – dry ice, obviously – billowed out. Two figures stepped from inside the marquee and surveyed the queue. Someone behind Jago gave a low-pitched squeal.

The two newcomers – men, judging by their height and build – stood motionless at the marquee's entrance. They both wore black with long red cloaks. Masks of red, ridged plastic changed and exaggerated the contours of their faces, giving them the sneering, twisted expressions of demons, and black rams' horns curled away from their temples. It was probably a trick of the light, or coloured contact lenses, but both men's eyes looked black as coal.

The queue started to move.

Stepping to one side, he bent to the ground as though to tie a shoelace. 'I'll see you inside,' he said to Candy. Luckily, the press of the queue behind pushed her on.

'Mark Johnson,' he told the demon confronting him when he was upright again. He held his breath, hoping the bloke wouldn't know the real Mark – the tall, spotty guy several places further back. After several seconds, and a scan down a list, he was nodded through. Breathing a sigh of relief – by the time the gatekeepers realised they had an imposter on their hands, he would have slipped out the back way – Jago stepped through the entrance into darkness.

At first, nothing. The marquee doors closed behind him and he was alone in a sea of blackness. He could see nothing, hear nothing other than the drumming of the rain on the marquee roof. Then,

'Hello?' called a nervous voice.

A giggle.

A shushing sound.

His whole body started in alarm as music blared out. He recognised the piece, a house track, but it was painfully loud. And then, around him, spotlights began to flash on and off, grabbing his attention, forcing him to turn and look, this way and that, until he was almost dizzy. Each floodlit reveal showed a fresh horror: a kid passed out in a pool of vomit; a lad who'd been sniffing coke with blood streaming from his nostrils; a girl being gang raped over a table; a boy being kicked in the kidneys by a group of thugs. The actors were real, terrifyingly good and unnervingly close to him.

Sounds of violence, of terror, broke through the deafening music.

Jago could make out enough of the background to see that they were supposedly in an English pub. He caught glimpses of the long, mirrored bar hung with optics, of pub furniture, of signs indicating toilets and the fire exit.

It wasn't like any pub he'd ever been in.

He could feel the thud of the bass reverberating in his chest and wanted to put his hands to his ears to dull the all-encompassing sound. The flashing lights were disorientating; already he couldn't have pointed to the tent's entrance.

To his left, a bloke held a knife against another's throat. A yell behind made him jump round to see a man holding a young woman by the collar of her shirt. His fist was raised, as though about to strike.

Then all the lights went out and the music stopped. As his ears hummed in the aftermath, Jago could hear someone nearby panting; he hadn't realised anyone was close. He found himself turning on the spot, brushing the back of his neck, nervous of someone creeping up on him. He could see nothing.

A small light appeared, close enough for him to see that it was in a lantern held by another man dressed as a demon.

'Come with me,' the demon ordered in a voice that was both distorted and amplified, before turning to lead the way through the darkness. A boy who looked familiar followed and then a girl who, thankfully, wasn't Candy. With no other plan, Jago went along, bringing up the rear of the small group.

They walked into the darkness. After a few seconds, Jago realised they were following pin pricks of light on the ground. As light grew again, they saw dirty brick walls stretching up on either side of them and a stench crept into his nostrils. Piss, vomit, rubbish long since left to rot. Somewhere above his head a cat screamed and then a spotlight appeared to reveal the body of a young male slumped against the alley wall. It must be the effects of clever make-up and low-level lighting, but Jago could have sworn the boy had been dead several hours. A syringe lay in the corpse's outstretched hand and his left sleeve had been rolled up to reveal a bare forearm with multiple puncture scars.

The demon led them around a tight bend into more blackness. Jago hung back. He'd seen a door in the brick wall. A way out?

'Keep up!' the demon ordered, his eyes fixed on Jago.

With no choice, Jago stepped forward, thankful to leave the stench behind. Around him, the darkness seemed to be fading. Shapes emerged ahead and dull colour followed as the light increased. Jago saw trees and road signs. The demon stepped back, allowing the three youngsters to approach the scene of a road traffic accident. A car – real – had hit a tree, one that also looked real. The left side of its bonnet and wheel arch had caved in. As the three of them drew closer, Jago thought he could smell petrol. The spotlight on the car grew brighter to reveal a girl in the passenger seat. She was dressed for a party but waxy pale, with a massive head wound on the left side of her face. Her eyes were wide and staring.

'I think I'm going to be sick,' one of Jago's companions muttered.

'No!'

They all spun in the direction of the horrified cry. Another boy had appeared, an actor in the tableau. His clothes were bloodstained and dishevelled.

'They said it would be OK,' he told them, as he drew closer.

The girl in the group backed into Jago.

'They told me a couple of drinks wouldn't make any difference. They told me I could easily handle a car with only a few pints inside me.' He pointed back towards the car. 'I think she's dead.'

Sirens sounded.

'Oh God, the police. I can't believe this. I've ruined my life.' Sobbing, the boy leaned over the car roof and let his head drop to the metal. Darkness fell.

Another spotlight appeared and one of the demons stepped into the light.

'Come this way,' he encouraged.

Jago and his companions moved through more darkness. He couldn't be certain but had a sense they were zigzagging their way through the giant marquee. When the lights came up they revealed a witness box, judge's chair, complete with bewigged judge, and a rapidly typing clerk. They were in a courtroom. The same boy who'd driven the car was standing in front of the judge.

'Causing death by dangerous driving, I sentence you to life imprisonment.' The judge banged down his gavel and the boy was led away, past a leering group of men in prison uniforms who'd stepped out of the darkness. A second before he disappeared, he turned back to Jago and his companions.

'Don't do it,' he yelled at them. 'Don't drink and drive.'

'Subtle as a brick,' Jago muttered, but his heart wasn't in it. The Hell House was already disturbing and his journey through it had barely begun. He had to find a way out.

As a scream rang out from somewhere in the marquee, their demon guide urged them on again. This time, Jago hung back and, when he didn't think anyone was looking at him, strode away from the group until the darkness enveloped him. He kept going until he backed up against the cold plastic of one of the marquee's internal walls.

He saw the demon and the two other kids turn to the left and vanish. This was his chance. Finding an outside wall was the key. If he followed it he'd find an exit.

He started walking, arms outstretched. After a minute or so, his hands touched another of the marquee's inner walls. Going right would take him back in the direction of the entrance so he went left, following the wall's line until it ran out. He stopped, felt around. Nothing. He stepped forward a pace and found it again. He'd found a doorway.

He inched his way through to the other side and could see a little.

This time, he was in a woodland. One that smelled real. The lights were low and he guessed this wasn't a scene about to be used anytime soon. Instinctively, he knew he needed to keep going, straight ahead.

Then movement caught his eye. A figure was emerging from the darkness. A woman. She didn't look like one of the actors, she was normally dressed for one thing, but she didn't seem a kid either. And she had a mobile phone in her hand, using the torch to see her way. Her height, her shape, the way she moved – he started towards her. While he was still several paces away, she wrapped her arms around her upper body in a gesture he knew well. Suddenly, his heart was racing.

'Bella!' All this time he'd been stressing out about getting back to the village and she'd come to find him. 'I'm here.'

He heard her gasp as she turned to face him. Her face clenched in what, had he not known better, he might have thought was horror. He was an idiot, he'd startled her. He should have known a nervous type like Bella would be on edge in a place like this.

'Bell, it's me.' Arms held wide, a smile breaking out on his face, he strode towards her.

She ran.

61

The Hell House marquee complex had a number of side entrances that the church pretentiously called stage doors, and I made a point of knowing all of them. Each year, once construction was complete, I came up at night to make sure none had been changed from previous years. It happened rarely, and when it did, I made a careful note.

Of course, I'd never managed to take a victim in the marquee before. There were too many people around once the performance was underway, and security was tight at other times. The rumour that a young person died in the Hell House each year was the sort of hysterical exaggeration and distortion of facts that one expected from teenagers. One of them did die – I made sure of it – but I wasn't about to risk everything I'd put in place for the sake of dramatics.

That said, there was something about this particular set of circumstances that was urging me on. What do they say? If you're going to go, do it with a bang.

And I would have to move on after tonight.

I'd be sad. I'd enjoyed my time in St Abel's Chapel, more than most of the places I'd hung my hat over the years, and Anna's arrival had provided an intriguing and distracting frisson. I'd even toyed with the idea that she might be enough to persuade me to stop.

But Anna, you see, was smart enough to become suspicious. She wasn't quite there yet – leaving the message on my answer machine had proven her willingness to trust me a while longer – but her questions and doubts would feed on themselves over time. She wouldn't entirely fall for my carefully constructed narrative that Gardner was the killer.

Anna presented too big a risk. It was a pity, because I genuinely liked her, but it was time for our association to come to an end. And that, unfortunately, meant that she had to come to an end.

Choosing a 'stage door' that was some way from the special effects control room where most of the technical support staff hang out and on the side of the marquee that faces the lake (where I was least likely to be spotted), I left the evacuation chair lying close against the marquee wall. It was an expensive piece of kit but had proven invaluable before now for moving bodies around; a corpse is surprisingly heavy. I left the tent opening unlaced, knowing I might need to leave in a hurry.

As expected, I found myself in the abortion scene, one of the least pleasant in a grim catalogue. A hospital bed took centre stage, its sheets covered in blood. A wax effigy of what was meant to be an aborted fetus lay towards its lower end, gleaming in a pool of gore. The actors, waiting for their audience to arrive, stood by the bed. The young girl who would be playing a recently dead corpse wore a bloodstained hospital gown; the other three were dressed as a nurse and her two parents.

I nodded a greeting when they all looked my way, but they took my arrival in their stride. No one ever questioned the fire officer. The youngsters often assumed I was part of the show; the staff that I was Gardner or one of his colleagues. His insistence on being able to access any part of Gathering land during the festival had more than played into my hands the last few years.

I knew that Anna, who would have arrived some time before me, would have used the main entrance and been attached to a small group before being led around the exhibits. It takes a little under an hour to complete the Hell House, so unless she was pushing ahead – which wasn't entirely impossible knowing Anna – she'd still be making her way through the interior.

With a small, handheld torch to light the way, I left the abortion room. I came across a sharp left turn and found myself in what I like to call the 'corridor of bedroom horrors'.

Were I to approach this long, thin stretch of the marquee from its opposite side, I'd meet first a nice-looking boy of about fifteen playing a harmless, world-construction video game. The next scene I'd encounter features a wholesome young girl lying on her bed, text messaging a friend. The third bedroom shows the same young boy (we know it's him because the clothes are identical), but he's progressed on to a more violent game. He's gained weight, his hair is long and unkempt and his clothes dirty. We see the girl again, to find her scantily clad, wearing far too much make-up, taking photographs of herself in provocative positions.

When we come across both teenagers for the third and final time, the boy's room is covered in dirty plates, empty beer cans and porn magazines. The girl is on the point of being raped by someone whom, we presume, she met through one of those online chat rooms.

I spotted one of the candle lanterns that heralds the imminent approach of a demon and a trio of youngsters. Not wanting to be seen more than necessary, I shone my torch along the wall until I found an opening and stepped through into the woodland scene.

Not empty, as I expected. Instead, Anna was racing towards me. With Jago Moore in hot pursuit.

62

Jago sped after Bella. From somewhere close by came a crash of thunder followed by a demonic voice demanding that those approaching abandon hope.

Not bloody likely. Not when he was this close.

Bella vanished around a bend but he was getting the hang of how the place worked. The official route weaved its way through the giant marquee but the walls held numerous, almost invisible doors to allow staff to move around quickly. Even when the light faded to almost nothing, he could feel his way along the walls.

He reached the point at which she'd disappeared and stopped to take stock. Another clap of thunder rang out, drowning all other sound. Where the hell had she gone?

He turned on the spot to see a figure standing against the wall, some distance away. A helmet and visor concealed the bloke's face and his jacket and trousers were covered in reflective strips. A fireman, here on official business. Except, it kind of rang a bell. A fireman? Some of the kids he'd spoken to had mentioned a fireman, hadn't they? Or someone who posed as a fireman?

As the noise of the thunder died away a clanging sound became apparent. Jago looked up to see Anna fifteen feet above him, climbing steps – metal by the sound of them – and painted black so they were barely visible. Turning his back on the fireman, he ran after her, reaching the bottom of the steps and running up, using the rails to push himself up faster.

He had to catch her. He had to stop her before she reached the bedroom. She'd put a bolt on the bedroom door. She'd lock it and phone for help. He had to stop her, make her understand he'd had no choice, that he'd done it for them.

Halfway up the steps he was struggling to get his breath and his thoughts whirled around his head in a frenzy. He'd gone somewhere else then, to a time he'd left behind. He wasn't at home, his dad wasn't lying dead at the bottom of the stairs, and Bella needed him.

He'd reached the top of the stairs. He was clinging to the rail, out of breath and Bella could only have gone through the door directly ahead. He pulled it open, to see the steps had brought him to a narrow metal gallery, close to the marquee roof, that ran three sides of a rectangle, around a vast open space below.

Jago took a moment, to glance down.

He was staring directly into hell.

63

The hell pit is the grand finale, the climax of the Hell House. It is the largest display in the marquee and the most disturbing. A deafening cacophony of recorded sound provides the backdrop to the howls and screams and roars of several dozen actors playing either the demons in hell or the unfortunate souls doomed to suffer eternal torment. Fires blaze, fake of course but very realistic, and the scenes of torture depicted would turn the strongest stomach.

I have my moments but, really, some very twisted imaginations go into putting this together every year.

Unlike all the other displays, audience members don't mingle with the actors in the hell pit. Instead, they view them from above, passing along a galleried walkway that circumvents the horrors below. By the time the stomachs of the braver have been turned, and the timid scared to death, they are steered like cattle back down the steps and into a soundproofed chamber known as the purgatory room. Once in there, the three audience members are kept in darkness for several minutes before being forced to choose a life of sin, or one of redemption and godliness.

They choose redemption, naturally, whatever course their lives might take in reality, because that's where the party is.

I'd already planned that the purgatory room would give me the ideal chance to approach Anna; in the darkness she wouldn't even see me coming.

And now Jago Moore had stolen a march on me.

64

Jago's legs could no longer hold him upright. This was the real hell. He was staring down at actual hell. It wasn't possible. And yet it was right below him.

It seemed to be a city, far bigger than should be possible in that space, one with skyscrapers, towers and churches, roads, bridges and houses; yet a desolate city, almost destroyed by nuclear war or plague. Semi-naked people sat, crawled and staggered around. With a zombie-like clumsiness, they scrambled over rubble and fought for scraps among rubbish. They were filthy, pale as corpses, their faces distorted with wounds and hideous defects. One creature, impossible to tell whether it was male or female, gazed up at Jago with a face that appeared to be melting onto its chest.

Scenes of torture were everywhere. He saw a man stretched on a rack, another strapped into an ornate chair, with blood pouring from dozens of small wounds. A third hung upside down from a wheel.

Fires blazed. From fifteen feet above he could feel their heat. Smoke stung his eyes and the stench of sulphur had him on the verge of gagging. The demons had gone, as though their cartoon scariness would detract from the horror of what he could see now, and in their place, on a pedestal directly in front of him, stood a black angel.

.Had his heart stopped beating? Was he actually dead?

Thunder shook the marquee. The gallery trembled and the sky around him – where had the sky come from, he was in a tent? – turned crimson. Scarlet bolts of lightning danced around his head.

The angel's wings, impossibly huge, stretched out around its body, and its head and face were concealed by a black cowl. It held a massive black and silver sword upright, its gauntleted hands clasped around the hilt.

Jago knew he would die for sure if that angel were to lift its head and see him.

65

Jago, I could tell, was stunned by his first glimpse into the hell pit. It takes some people like that, the first time they see it. I know I never linger near it. No sooner did I see him falter and clutch the rail than I knew he'd never catch up with Anna. She, wisely, had avoided looking down, and was racing along the gallery's length. If she reached the corner, and I had no doubt she would, the speed she was running, then she'd be along the third side of the rectangle, through the soundproofed door and down the opposite steps before her stepson came anywhere close.

Events were playing out in my favour. Anything happening up on the gallery would be witnessed by several dozen people below, not to mention the dark angel. (He's usually played by a bricklayer from Peterborough. A nice bloke, according to the odd snippet I'd picked up and tall enough to look imposing. His face, though, is cherubic and creased in a permanent smile, not remotely threatening. For that reason, he never lifts his head.)

And so instead of joining Jago on the gallery, I ran around the back of the hell pit and into the purgatory room, arriving as Anna's footsteps sounded on the steps.

I slipped into the darkness behind them.

66

Jago had pulled himself together enough to reach the end of the metal gallery. He just had to hold it together a little while longer.

The door through which Bella had vanished opened to reveal steps leading down into a room that was black as pitch. Someone – it could only be Bella – was at the bottom, shining the light of a mobile phone around as she scanned for an exit.

'Help!' she screamed into the darkness. Yes, definitely Bella. 'Let me out.'

Jago let the door close behind him. Like magic, the din of the hell scene had gone; this new space was soundproofed. And very hard to get out of, if Bella's failed attempts to find a door were anything to judge by. She turned and looked up.

'Don't come near me.'

'Bell, we need to talk. I can explain.' He took a step down towards her.

'No, Jago, I mean it. You shouldn't be here.'

As he reached the halfway point of the stairs, she switched off her phone light, plunging the room into unbroken darkness.

A fresh sound made him jump. A keening wind, interspersed by cackles of laughter. Great. More sound effects.

'I'm sorry I scared you.' He'd made it to the bottom of the steps. 'I'd have let you know I was coming, but I thought the police might be monitoring your phone.'

She didn't reply. If that bloody wind would only pipe down he might be able to hear her breathing. He set off in the direction where he thought he'd seen her last.

'I don't blame you,' he said, as he took one tentative step after another. 'For what we did. I never have.'

Had he heard a whimper?

'I wanted it as much as you.'

He changed direction.

'And I'm so sorry about the baby. You must know I never planned that to happen. But we can try again. As soon as you like.'

His outstretched hands touched the smooth surface of the wall. 'We're together again. That's the only thing that matters.'

Suddenly, there was light again. Her phone torch, aimed directly at him. She was inches away and she didn't look scared anymore. That had to be a good thing. Didn't it?

'No,' she said. 'It's not going to happen.'

Something clenched tight around his insides. 'What are you talking about?'

Her face could have been carved from stone. 'We're never going to be together,' she told him. 'You killed your father.'

'But—' his hands were shaking. 'You know—'

He couldn't go on. It was as though all oxygen had been sucked from the room. What was she saying?

'You have to go back to the hospital, Jago. It's the only place you belong now.'

It was a test. It had to be, because if he couldn't be with Bella, there was nothing in life left for him.

'You don't mean that.'

'I do. I'm calling the police.' She raised her phone and took her eyes off him to glance down.

Taking his chance, Jago dived towards her. She stepped back but he caught hold of her arm and they fell against the wall, their bodies colliding. He felt an erotic stab in his groin at being close to her again. She struggled but he was too strong for her. He only squeezed her wrist for a second, maybe a few, before she squealed in pain and dropped the phone. He put his hands on her throat, only to keep her still, only to make her listen.

She wouldn't listen though. She threw back her head and

screamed. So, of course, he had to hold her tighter. She kicked and squirmed, making odd choking noises in her throat. What the hell was she doing? Was she mad? He squeezed again.

'Stop it, Bella, stop fighting me. Don't make me hurt you.'

The sudden pain took him completely by surprise.

He froze and the pain surged. The keening of the wind seemed to be growing louder. He heard that unearthly cackle again and stared into Bella's eyes. Unflinchingly, she looked back.

His hands had fallen from her throat. In the dim glow of her phone he saw her lean back against the wall, a look of horror stealing over her face. He became very conscious of his heart, beating hard and fast. Somehow, he dragged his eyes from hers to look down.

A knife handle was protruding from his abdomen. His hands, clutched around it, were damp and sticky with blood. His own blood was pouring from him. With every beat of his heart more of it spilled out. Without warning, his legs gave way and the ground hit him hard. Bella's face above him seemed hazier, less real than it had.

The light from her mobile phone was fading. Darkness was coming for him. He thought of the scenes of hell he'd witnessed minutes earlier.

Well, at least he wouldn't have far to go.

He saw Bella open her mouth to speak, but the last words he heard in this world weren't for him.

She said, 'You can come out now, Liam.'

67

'You can come out now, Liam.'

As I stepped out from beneath the steps, Anna picked up her phone and shone the torch down onto her dying stepson. I would have some explaining to do, I knew, about why I was in the Hell House dressed in a fireman's uniform and why I hadn't leapt to her defence, but I figured it was nothing I couldn't handle. Anna, almost certainly, would be in shock and entirely malleable. She might not even remember much of what had just happened.

She'd come here with a knife, though? I'd never had expected her to be quite so – resourceful.

As I stepped towards Jago I said a silent prayer that he'd be dead already; it would make things so much easier. I moved carefully, so that I didn't have to get too close. I knew there'd be a great deal of blood, and I don't think too clearly faced with blood.

I avoid blood during my own – experiments; there are many more imaginative ways, I've found, of bringing life to a sudden end.

'Do you need to sit down?' I asked Anna, holding out my hand for her phone. 'Let me call the police.'

Maybe I could get out of these clothes before the authorities arrived. Once hidden, their existence would be my word against hers.

'Are you sure?' she said, looking the very opposite of shocked and malleable. 'Your fingerprints are on the knife, not mine.'

I noticed then what I should have seen before: Anna was wearing gloves.

And the knife sticking out of Jago looked very like the one I'd unloaded from her dishwasher the previous day. She'd even joked about keeping it handy in case she needed a weapon. I looked up, swallowed and took a deep breath; that was a lot of blood pooling on the floor around the boy.

'Do you have a better plan?' I asked, aware that my voice didn't sound too steady.

'We put him in the lake,' she said. 'That's what you usually do, isn't it?'

I had no ready reply to that.

'It can't be long before the next group get here,' she went on. 'How do we do it, exactly?'

She was right, about the imminent arrival of the next group at least. And if my prints were on that knife, well, along with the fireman's uniform, it wouldn't look good. Not to mention that a forensic search of my house would uncover all sorts of things I really didn't want coming to the light of day.

How could I not have seen this coming? I, who plan everything down to the very last detail.

Enough. I could figure it out when we'd dealt with Jago. I pulled out my own torch and stepped back beneath the steps to find the staff door. The corridor behind was mercifully empty.

'Help me get him over here,' I ordered.

Anna didn't argue and together we dragged the boy's body along the floor. We'd leave blood behind, but I didn't see a way around that; there simply wasn't time for a clean-up. We left the purgatory room to find ourselves only metres from another of the 'stage doors' and within seconds, we'd dragged Jago outside. A minute longer and I'd collected the evacuation chair. By the time Jago was strapped in place, both Anna and I were breathing heavily. We hadn't spoken again.

From there, it was a ten-minute walk to the lake and the rain worked in our favour. Had it been a fine night, there would invariably have been people around the perimeter of the marquee, even down at the water, waiting for the lighting of the bonfires. In the deluge, everyone who wasn't in one of the marquees or the hall was sheltering in their caravan.

Anna watched me weight the body at the point where the lake was deepest. We had to avoid the fallen tree, of course; sometime in the coming months that would be raised and it would be better for both of us if Jago's body was never found.

Without a body, there would be no proof that he'd ever arrived in St Abel's Chapel. Without a body, the search for him would eventually be stepped down and the police would conclude that he'd effected a successful escape.

I won't deny, the thought that Anna should join her stepson in the water did occur to me while we were working, but she was careful to stay several paces away from me, ready to run at the slightest provocation. She didn't trust me, and I could hardly blame her.

'Do you want to check he's dead?' I asked, before I tipped Jago into the water.

'Does it make a difference?' she replied.

It didn't of course. Alive or dead, Jago Moore was going in the lake. A few seconds later he'd vanished from sight.

'If he's ever found, we let the police conclude he fell foul of the same killer who took Connor and the others,' I told her, as we watched the last bubbles rise to the surface.

'And that's supposed to be Gardner?' she asked, surprising me again. 'How can you be sure they'll go for him, not you?'

There seemed nothing to be gained by not telling her.

'If they search his property, which they almost certainly will if another corpse is found, they'll unearth Emily's body in his backyard. Along with a few trophies from the others I kept over the years.'

She took a step away from me and her eyes opened wide. Finally, I'd broken her composure. 'How?' she managed.

Not easily, was the answer. Emily had proven one of the more difficult of my Sweet Sixteens. She'd fought like the blazes when I'd jumped her by the lake and had taken nearly twenty minutes to die. By the time I was sure she'd gone, her neck and shoulders were covered in bright red marks.

On top of that, she came free of her weights and floated to the water's surface overnight. I found her early the next morning and dragged her out before anyone was stirring up at the hall. As luck would have it, Gardner had been away on an all-inclusive holiday with his kids and by the time he got back, a massive leaf fall had covered any signs that the flagstones in his backyard had been disturbed.

'Why Connor?' she asked. 'He wasn't a sixteen-year-old girl.'

'Too good an opportunity to miss.'

It was the honest truth. I'm not fixated on sixteen-year-old girls at all. I've taken victims of all ages and both sexes in the past. But Gardner's history with girls of that age, his long-dead sister and more recently his daughter, had been clear signs pointing the way. As soon as I learned about both, I knew he'd be the perfect fall guy for my northern adventures. I always make sure I have someone in place to take the blame. That, more than anything, is the secret to how I've escaped justice all these years.

'The lady who used to live in my house?' Anna asked.

'Wrong place at the wrong time,' I said. 'She saw something she shouldn't have. Call her collateral damage.'

She was silent for a moment.

'It doesn't feel right,' she said. 'Hugh taking the blame for what you did.'

'What we did,' I corrected her. 'But it may not be necessary. Other than Connor, all the deaths are considered accidental or suicide. And it probably won't be possible to pin Connor's death on Gardner. The evidence against him on that one is all circumstantial.'

'Do you think he killed his sister? Even his daughter?'

'Very unlikely,' I replied. 'I mean, what are the chances of two killers living next door to each other?'

She said nothing.

'Three killers,' I corrected myself. My tentative smile was met with a scowl.

At that moment, we heard a shout from the direction of the hall.

A group of youngsters had braved the rain.

'We should leave,' I said.

Anna didn't disagree and so I folded the evacuation chair and we started making our way through the wood.

'Will you stay?' I asked when we were in the lane leading down to our houses once more. 'In the village?'

She took a while before replying. 'I think so,' she said. 'I've nowhere else. How about you?'

No, I would not be staying. I'd give it a couple of weeks, let the excitement around the Ingathering die down, and then move on. My house was owned by one of several limited companies I've established over the years, all of which are themselves owned by nominated shareholders. I sit behind them, unseen and undiscoverable other than by the most rigorous forensic search. Which, as long as I continued to be careful, would never be required. Naturally, Liam McCabe is not my real name.

'I think I'm done here,' I said. 'I hear the call of pastures new.'

We walked in silence for a while.

'You could come with me,' I suggested, surprising myself.

She gave a soft laugh. 'Oh, I don't think so. You're a bit old for my taste, Liam.'

It took a second or two for what she'd said to register. When it did, I stopped walking. 'Was there something between you and that boy?'

She didn't reply, but she too had stopped moving. She seemed to be waiting for me.

'Was anything you told me true?' I asked.

She turned to face me then. She was beautiful in the darkness, but I no longer thought her vulnerable. Suddenly, I was acutely conscious that she stood between me and the way back to the village. And that a woman who could leave the house with one knife might well have another concealed about her person.

'Was Jago Moore the father of your baby?' I asked.

She smiled. 'I guess that's something we'll never know.'

She gave me a moment, perhaps to absorb the implications of her words. She even seemed on the point of speaking again, but thought better of it and set off back down the lane once more. I followed.

I kept a very safe distance.

Acknowledgements

Thanks to the usual team: Anne Marie, Rosie and Jessica at the Ampersand and Buckman agencies and to Sam, Leodora, Lucy, Ellen, Aoife, Sahil and Paul at Orion. I couldn't do it without you.

Credits

Sharon Bolton and Orion Fiction would like to thank everyone at Orion who worked on the publication of *The Neighbour's Secret* in the UK.

Editorial
Sam Eades
Leodora Darlington
Sahil Javed

Copyeditor
Laura Gerrard

Proofreader
Jenny Page

Audio
Paul Stark
Jake Alderson

Contracts
Dan Herron
Ellie Bowker
Alyx Hurst

Design
Tomás Almeida
Joanna Ridley

Editorial Management
Charlie Panayiotou
Jane Hughes
Bartley Shaw

Finance
Jasdip Nandra
Nick Gibson
Sue Baker

Marketing
Lucy Cameron

Production
Ruth Sharvell

Publicity
Aoife Datta

Sales
Jen Wilson
Esther Waters
Victoria Laws
Toluwalope Ayo-Ajala
Rachael Hum
Ellie Kyrke-Smith
Sinead White
Georgina Cutler

Operations
Jo Jacobs
Dan Stevens

If you enjoyed *The Neighbour's Secret*, don't miss Sharon Bolton's previous gripping and twisty psychological thriller . . .

A new job. A new home. A new start.

It's all Anna wants.

But in a closed rural community, strange traditions and a suspicion of outsiders mean everything is not as it seems.

Three teenage girls have vanished at the annual Gathering as they reach their sixteenth birthday.

No one seems to be investigating.

And a fourth girl begs Anna for help, fearing that she will be next to disappear.

Everyone has secrets.
Anna is watching everyone.
But who is watching Anna?

Don't miss Sharon Bolton's Richard & Judy bestseller *The Split*

SHE'LL NEVER STOP RUNNING.
BUT HE'LL NEVER STOP LOOKING.

A year ago, Felicity Lloyd fled England for South Georgia, one of the most remote islands in the world, escaping her past and the man she once loved. Can she keep running her whole life?

Freddie Lloyd has served time for murder – and now he wants her back. Wherever she is, he won't stop until he finds her. Will he be able to track her to the ends of the earth?

TOGETHER THEY'LL FIND THEMSELVES TRAPPED ON THE ICE AND IN DANGER. WHO WILL SURVIVE?

Don't miss Sharon Bolton's gripping thriller about privilege, power and revenge, *The Pact*

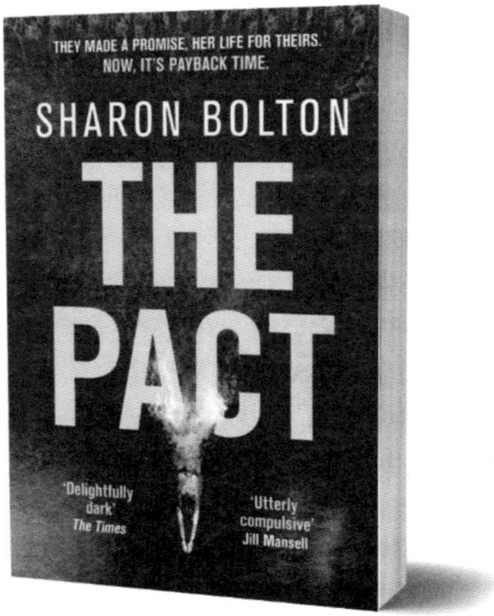

THEY MADE A PROMISE, HER LIFE FOR THEIRS.
NOW IT IS PAYBACK TIME.

A golden summer, and six talented teenagers are looking forward to the brightest of futures – until a daredevil game goes horribly wrong, leaving three strangers dead.

Eighteen-year-old Megan takes the blame for the crime, leaving her friends to get on with their lives. In return, they each agree to a 'favour', payable on her release from prison.

Twenty years later Megan is free.
It is payback time.
And her friends start disappearing, one by one . . .